ALMOST

ALMOST

Stephen Michael Marek

iUniverse, Inc.
Bloomington

Almost

iUniverse books may be ordered through booksellers or by contacting:

iUniverse
1663 Liberty Drive
Bloomington, IN 47403
www.iuniverse.com
1-800-Authors (1-800-288-4677)

ISBN: 978-1-4620-2955-6 (sc)
ISBN: 978-1-4620-2962-4 (hc)
ISBN: 978-1-4620-2961-7 (e)

Printed in the United States of America

iUniverse rev. date: 07/27/2011

CHAPTER 1

I t is 4:45 a.m. on an early spring morning. The alarm clock buzzes. It is twenty-three degrees outside. I haven't slept a wink. I have been up all night, haunted with the thought of leaving my wife of twenty years and my two children. I am repulsed with myself, but oddly excited at what I am about to do.

I slowly slink out of bed and walk toward the bathroom, the hardwood floors creaking with every step. It sounds as if a percussionist is following me around. We live in a one-hundred-year-old house in an upscale neighborhood in Bloomfield Hills, Michigan. I stop and look back at my wife. She doesn't know that when I leave for this very ordinary business trip, as I have done hundreds of times before, it will be the last time we say our good-byes ... forever!

Being the scum of the earth does not come easily for me, but then again, neither does becoming some inmate's love interest at Jackson State Prison. Thinking of what I have done and what we have become makes me physically ill, but I have left myself no other option: I must leave to protect my family from the humiliation they will all have to endure even if my wife and I divorce. How deluded have I become? Am I leaving to protect my family or me?

As I stand looking at the pathetic reflection of myself in the mirror, I cannot believe what has taken place in my life. With my head hanging low and my hands gripping the sides of the sink, I puke until my guts feel as if someone is pulling them through my mouth with a pair of pliers ... my body heaves in agony.

Just then, Samantha, my wife, places her hand between my shoulders and asks, "Are you okay? Maybe you should go back to bed and call this trip off for a few days … sounds like you're catching the flu."

I reply in my weakened state, "Go back to bed—I'll be okay. You know I can't call off this trip. Today we take possession of Dillianquest—I have to go. I will wake you before I leave. Now go back to bed; it's too early to be up."

Samantha and I have been trying to repair our marriage for some time now, but it is hard to mend a broken relationship. She's had more than one marital indiscretion but swears all that is history.

She kisses me on the shoulder and disappears. I make myself sick; we have been trying to make it work … and this is how I repay her for her efforts? God should strike me dead now before I cause her and the kids so much pain. And I will cause them great pain!

Barely able to look at my disgusting reflection in the mirror, I wonder how this could be happening to me. I have always tried to do what was right, not ever intentionally hurting anyone—or so I made myself believe. Always trying to do the right thing … how cliché. I close my eyes and contemplate my past, my head still hanging low with shame.

I am not one for wallowing in past mistakes. For someone in my position, hindsight can bring on paralysis, so I start to think about what lies ahead: an unthinkable adventure that will take me to … where? I am not so sure. But the one thing I am certain about is that my destination will offer warmer weather, firmer bodies, and a ton of cash.

If I stay and end up facing *my* own music, it will certainly mean that I will be sharing a cell with heaven knows who. I envision a mountain of a man with an appetite for boys like me. I hate to think about what kind of terror he and his buddies would rain down on my body. I am six feet tall and in great physical shape. I take pride in my appearance; it helps with sales. Many people, mostly women and a few gays that I met along the way, have said that I have a very attractive build and great ass. It's that great ass I did not want to share with any of the boys in lockup!

Still leaning on the sink with the occasional dry heave, I think about the evening when all this shit started. I was sitting alone at the Ocean

Side Shanty, a small bar and grill off the beaten trail in Beaufort, South Carolina. It had been recommended as a great place to eat. It was located on a dark gravel road on some backwater inlet.

I recall the distinct smell of the evening breeze gently wafting the unique scents of the sea across my face. You could taste the salt in the air. That is something that a kid from Michigan would never forget. The night was pitch-black in the swampy lowland. A single light on the road, barely visible in the dense ocean fog, marked the entrance to the bar. Only a handful of patrons sat inside. I recall sliding onto a stool at the bar and ordering a scotch from a bartender named Levi.

The night started off innocently enough, but somehow I ended up shooting pool with a thirtysomething, drop-dead gorgeous woman who called herself Contessa. She had seemed to appear from thin air. I don't even remember how we got started, but it reminded me of one of those letters I had read in *Playboy* as a young boy, the kind that always began with, "I never thought this could happen to me." To be honest, I never thought my story could have happened to me, either, but it did. It was about to change my life forever—and not for the better!

Contessa was tall, with the silkiest, longest, most flowing jet-black hair I had ever seen. It glistened in the dull bar light. She swirled it about in a most erotic fashion, brushing it back off her forehead with her full open hand. Her hair would tumble back to the same position as before. Her tight, low-cut jeans exposed a firm stomach with just the hint of a tattoo peeking out from the front of her pants. Her snugly fitted T-shirt commanded my attention. Lust was everywhere in my thoughts. She seemed genuinely glad to be there at that moment!

This amazingly beautiful woman was clearly a wonderful blend of exotic South American and Spanish heritage, judging from her richly bronzed, sensually supple skin. She smelled exquisite as she invitingly sauntered back and forth in front of me, taking her turn playing pool. Bent over the pool table, she stroked our shared cue and struck at the white cue ball without success. She did not say a word; she just smiled and tossed her hair back and handed me the cue without acting particularly eager to let it go. Contessa was tempting me.

Her eyes were dark as West Virginia coal and twinkled like diamonds in the low-hanging bar lights. She shot lustful thoughts directly into my soul. She was stunning, amazing—and her attention was fixed solely on me. How could that be? It did not matter, as I was mesmerized and drawn wholly into her spell. I was no match for this creature.

As she purposefully leaned over the table, my eyes were treated to an unbelievable sensual feast. I was transfixed, seemingly helpless, staring at this exceptionally beautiful woman ... so firm, so finely shaped. Dare I fantasize what having sex with her on the pool table would be like? How incredible! I felt like a thirteen-year-old boy seeing his first naked woman ... one who was willing to do anything he asked. I had been reduced to a quivering mass of useless male flesh, unable to even form a coherent sentence.

The back pockets of her jeans bore an embroidered symbol from her heritage, a symbol that meant love ... or so she said. The symbol, a swirl of beads and colors, would not release my gaze. It kept my attention fixed upon her gorgeous, firm ass ... there was no reason to fight it. I couldn't. She was winning this battle. The stilettos firmed her legs. Her perfectly shaped ass swayed from side to side as gracefully as palm fronds in the cool evening breeze. Watching her walk about the place kept me in a trance.

As she passed in front of me, she would ever so slightly brush against my groin, sending waves of chills to every nerve ending in my body. She glanced up at me as she handed me the pool cue we shared. Her scent was intoxicating. I was lost in her. She leaned into me, pressing her breasts into my chest, and whispered in my ear with her hot, moist breath dancing off my neck, her warm hand caressing my side. "It's your shot, big boy."

Suddenly, the memory of Contessa released its spell on me as Sam came into the bathroom with coffee in hand, bringing me crashing back to reality. I took the cup of coffee and placed it on the sink, kissed her on the forehead, and turned on the shower.

"I thought you went back to bed," I told her.

"I tried to, but I couldn't get back to sleep. I had this heavy feeling in my chest ... you know, something does not feel right. I'll go check in on the kids just to make sure everything is okay."

"Good idea," I said. "I'll be down in just a few minutes."

Standing in the shower with the warm water caressing my body, I wondered if she knew. I quickly reviewed the past months in my head. Had I done something, said something, or left something around that would make her suspicious? I didn't think so. I thought I had been acting like myself, whatever that meant.

Sam was an incredibly insightful person. She would dream with such clarity, and the odd thing was that many of those dreams would come to pass—maybe not right away, but most would come to be reality in some shape or form. I have always downplayed her dreams as coincidental, but this time, she was onto something that she just could not fully grasp. She did not know that her intuition was correct. Something heavy was about to happen to her that she did not see coming ... and it was all my fault.

My trip to Beaufort was supposed to be a short one—only a couple of days to wrap up the deal. I jokingly told Sam, "March in South Carolina is going to be so much nicer than any part of March in Michigan. I should take my golf clubs with me and extend my stay."

She replied in a firm, fun voice, "I don't think so, bucko." So I packed accordingly: a couple of suits, a few ties, and some casual clothing, but no golf clubs. I might be scum, but I was not stupid.

I had always packed a little extra, just in case I had to extend my trip. I remember one such time in New York City, when a two-day trip ended up taking over a week. At the time, I had not been prepared; on subsequent trips, I made sure not to get caught off guard. The extra clothes and time that I would need this time wouldn't raise too many flags.

Once packed and ready, I entered the kids' rooms for one last look. I enjoyed being a dad and was actually looking forward to seeing the kids all grown up and off the family payroll. But that was not going to happen anytime soon. This was the hardest thing I would ever have to do.

Better missing them than behind bars, I thought. Can you imagine what their friends would say and do to them? I couldn't put them through that. I felt a tear well in my eye. I would miss Saturday volleyball games, all that gymnastics drama, and all the malaise that goes with parenthood. I knew they wouldn't forgive me for what I was about to do ... and who could blame them? I just hoped they would never find out.

With packed bag in hand, I made my way down the creaky, old stairs and into the kitchen to find that Sam had scrambled eggs and a fresh cup of coffee waiting on me. *God, this is going to be hard. Just keep acting normal.* It was already half past five, and I had a seven-thirty flight to Atlanta to catch, which meant I had to leave for the airport by five forty-five.

I double-checked my inside suit coat pocket to make sure I had what I needed. Everything was securely in place. I left my passport in its normal place under Sam's in the vault behind the mirror in our bedroom. If I were going to disappear, there could be no suspicions left to chance. I sat down with Sam to a breakfast of scrambled eggs, dry whole-wheat toast, black coffee, and my vitamins. Everything was going according to plan.

At precisely 5:40, just like clockwork, my driver knocked on my door. I got up from the table and made my way to the front door. Jim, our company handyman, took care of most of our needs, including driving to the airport.

"Good morning, Jim," I said. "How are you?"

Jim replied, "Freezing. You got room in that bag for me? South Carolina is going to be a bunch warmer than this place. I checked the Internet last night … supposed to be in the low seventies in Beaufort. Taking your clubs?"

"Not this trip, although it crossed my mind more than once. Sam said if she wasn't going, neither were the golf clubs." We both laughed a bit. I handed Jim my travel bag, and he disappeared into the dark.

"I'll be waiting for you in the car," he said.

I turned to Sam and said, "I gotta go. I'll call you later when I get in. Give the kids a kiss for me when they get up."

And away I went, just like every time before. She blinked the front porch light three times, indicating that she and the two kids wished me safe travels.

I slumped back in the rear seat of the car and told Jim, "Let's go."

My ugly adventure had begun.

We got to the airport in plenty of time. Jim dropped me off at curbside check-in. I boarded on time, and the flight was uneventful—those are the good ones. We landed in Atlanta with an on-time arrival at 9:10 a.m. So far, so good!

CHAPTER 2

The Monday prior to my adventure had started, as did all Mondays at ASG, with a morning meeting at our Ann Arbor offices. My coworkers and I all loved Ann Arbor and did not want to leave that youthful liberal haze felt everywhere within the city. It was a beautiful Monday in Michigan, and trust me, you have to appreciate the good days in Michigan when nine of the twelve months are overcast and bitterly cold … and other three months are just cold! The bright December day greeted me with loads of sunshine. Not a single cloud marred the sky. It was one of those days that makes you glad to be alive, even in Michigan.

I had gotten up early, as usual, and headed out the door for my morning run—a near-daily tradition since college. I guess it really started when I was a kid in high school, running every day before school. The early bird catches the worm, or so they say. So, back then, there I was, a kid looking for worms!

My high school was a small one. Kindergarten through twelfth grades, all under one roof … how great was that? I wouldn't have wanted it any other way. I remember my brother telling me about the hundreds of kids in his grade at Proviso East, a school he attended in the Chicago area—no thanks! That had to suck. There were only thirty-five kids in my class, give or take one or two on any given year. For me, it was just right.

Back in the day, if you had any athletic ability—and I do mean any at all—you were pressured to be in sports from early on. My school was a Class D school. We kidded that the D stood for "dull," which it was. Schools did not get any smaller. The coach needed you just to have enough kids to play any of the organized sports. We played track, football, and basketball, and those who had any ability could really shine. I shone brightly.

I trained all year round: summer, spring, fall, and winter. What was the point of going out for the team and sitting on the bench? If I were going to play sports, I wanted to start. And if I were going to start, I wanted to shine. And if I were going to shine, I would need to put in the time. If I were going to put in the time at doing something, I wanted it to count. I worked hard!

I guess that is when my obsessive traits began to show. At first I thought I was doing exercising so much just to please my parents. But I always knew, deep down, that if it was worthwhile and it was something that I really wanted ... I would step on anyone to get it. Not in a bad way, mind you—I was just going to outcompete those who stood in my path. My coach called that determination.

In my small town, you were either in sports and loved by all parents, or you were one of those who smoked and drank and thus were considered to be on the derelict fringe of our closed-minded little town. If you were one of the latter, you obviously were not going to amount to much. Every town has a derelict fringe.

I drifted between both groups with relative ease. I never really fit snugly into one or the other. I had friends in both camps. Hell, in a small town, that's just the way it is. I was well liked by the parents of those kids with whom I played sports. I was always the polite and courteous young man to the parents, shop owners, businesspeople, and teachers, but come Saturday night, my crowd was of the more adventurous, older persuasion.

I recall spending many a summer evening sprawled flat on my back in the middle of some woods, in an open field, or on a lake shore, giggling like a young girl ... then vomiting my guts out until I was in the fetal position. Ah, the good old days. At the end of such fun, I was always dropped off by my partners in crime at my parents' home, hoping that Mom and Dad wouldn't find out that I had a bit of a wild side and was drunk off my ass. I would duck in the door, offer my parents a quick good-night, and scramble up the stairs to my room where I could let my head stop spinning in peace. I did like my flavored vodkas. They must have known—they had to—but they never said a thing. Such deceptions marked the start of my sales career. I was good at hiding things that mattered.

With my later propensity for smoking pot and drinking with my older friends, I always marveled at how lucky I was. Seems as if most everyone got busted for minor-in-possession or driving under the influence but me. I seemed to have an uncanny knack for bowing out the same night the police stumbled on to the gang making their way to one of the parties in the woods, or coming back from the same. I have always been a pretty lucky fellow—no criminal record, and I married up, as they say.

Meeting Sam changed my life. I immediately fell for her wonderfully vibrant personality. Tall and athletic, with long, blonde hair that tumbled about her shoulders in a most gentle fashion, Sam was one of a kind. She is a wonderful wife and mother of our two kids.

I met Sam one evening in Ann Arbor. I was a graduate student, and she was a senior political science major wanting to go on to law school.

I remember the evening as if it were yesterday. It was the annual University of Michigan Spring Hash Bash. Ann Arbor was an ultraliberal spot in the 1970s; possession of pot, or hash, was punished with only a five-dollar fine. No record of the offense was kept. Back then, people would get a ticket as a memento of the times. Pot possession did not ruin careers as it does today.

It was there on the steps of the Diag that I came across a pretty young girl having difficulty lighting her hash pipe. Being the gentleman that I was, and am, I offered to light her morsel of hash. We both giggled, and she thanked me. We talked for hours and smoked for days after that. From that point forward, we were inseparable, getting married one year to the day after we met. We exchanged vows during the next year's annual Hash Bash on the very steps where we met. Flowers and love filled our hearts and minds. Instead of champagne glasses, we raised our bongs and toasted to our triumphant moment.

Sam was wonderful then, and I wasn't sure how that had changed over time ... but it had. Memories from our early relationship still brought a smile to my face.

I graduated from the University of Michigan at the top of my class, earning a master's degree in business administration. My future was nothing but bright, although my past had been nothing but difficult.

I came from rural poverty, raised in a tiny tourist town in northern Michigan not too many miles south of the Mackinaw Bridge. My mother and I had moved north from Chicago when I was ten years old to escape that urban insanity, while my father finished work in the Chicago Fire Department. My folks were good, honest, and hardworking people who thought they had instilled in me all the right values. I guess you never know who you really are until your character gets put to the test. What I have done, and am about to do, would make them both turn in their graves.

Once settled in Michigan, my mother took a job as the dietary manager at the local county nursing home. When my father and brother joined us some years later, "Lefty," as my dad was known by friends, took employment as the maintenance supervisor at the same place. I grew up as nursing-home brat. Little did I know that my experiences as a child of a nursing-home family would play such a significant role in my future career choices and the events that followed.

Growing up in northern Michigan was picture-perfect in the 1970s—no need to lock your doors at night. The only trouble to get into was smoking a bit of pot or drinking a few beers out of sight of the local cops. Back then, the police really did not have a clue about drugs and such things. If you were really unlucky, as a few were, you might end up getting your girlfriend pregnant, which fucked up many a good future plan. That is exactly why many of my fellow high-school pals couldn't wait to leave that small town. I was one of the few lucky ones who made the break and stayed gone! School was easy for me, and I used my aptitude to my advantage.

During the last year of my master's program at the university, two of my fraternity brothers and I formed Abernathy, Smith, and Grayson. I am the Grayson of the firm. My name is Teasdale Allen Grayson, to be proper. Who in their right mind names their child Teasdale? All my friends called me Tag. I defended myself frequently in high school. It made me pretty tough, leaving a few scars on my face as reminders.

The three of us had drawn straws to select how the names would align in the firm's moniker. Longest straw last ... and so it goes. The three of us had our unique specialties. William Abernathy was the accountant. Thomas Smith was our operations guy. My specialty was marketing, sales, and acquisitions. I loved the hunt of a deal. I found nothing more stimulating than seeking, negotiating, and closing a big deal. The bigger the deal, the better for me; I liked playing the game.

Abernathy, Smith, and Grayson, or ASG, started small. In the beginning, we purchased a single nursing home and fired its administrator. We hired a new administrator and changed the business model. Then, sooner than we thought, we were cashing substantial government checks, taking advantage of unregulated therapy loopholes in the Medicare program, and pocketing hundreds of thousands of dollars each and every month. Within a short period of time, we owned ten facilities and were making money hand over fist. The therapy business was our ticket. We then packaged small groups together and sold them to the highest bidder ... old age was paying significant dividends.

I was in seventh heaven buying, selling, and always making a profit for everyone in the deal. I was on top of the world and at the top of my game. Soon we found ourselves buying nursing homes, small hospitals, home health agencies, and hospice companies. We would run them for a while, cutting expenses and taking advantage of the government at every corner while showing ever-increasing profits.

When we had milked the enterprise for all it was worth, it was up to me to find a buyer ... and buyers are everywhere. To make a deal work in our favor, you have to make him or her think the deal is just too good to pass up. Selling what people think they need or want is my expertise. Managing the greed factor—that is what I do!

I have never worked for another firm; ASG was our baby, and I was loyal to it. That is unusual in today's business world. At forty-seven years of age, I was buying and selling nursing homes, hospitals, and other related health-care entities. I make multimillion-dollar deals while sipping on glasses of twenty-five-year-old scotch and smoking fine cigars. This was what I had dreamed of as a kid! I had made our firm millions of dollars. I had made those who have sold to us wealthy as well, but today ... today I was leaving my life and running like a common criminal. What in God's name was I about to do?

At ASG we started every Monday and Friday with a mandatory stand-up meeting to get a handle on events. We all felt it important to keep abreast of what was going on. No one liked surprises. The morning meetings always started at seven o'clock sharp—no excuses. We all abided by that rule; hell, our little group had made the rule in the first place. Our twice-weekly morning meeting was made up of the key officers of the firm. It was just a small handful of decision makers, about eight of us.

Cindy Field, my administrative assistant, always arrived early to set out a variety of breakfast treats on display for us. She was great at her job, which made my job easier than it should have been. She was great to look at as well. Cindy had long, slender legs and was thin as one could be ... almost too thin. But that was not because she worked at it. She was one of those naturally thin people—the kind we all hated, especially those of us who had to watch every morsel of food that got put into our mouths ... such as me! Cindy was worth her weight in gold around the office, though. Seems everyone wanted to recruit Cindy into their offices, but she never left; she was my girl Friday. The dictionary defines *girl Friday* as "an efficient and faithful woman aide or employee"—Cindy was all of that and much more!

When we hired a new person into the firm, Cindy would be assigned to help get that person situated. And while getting that person situated, it was her job to assess whether they had what it took to be an ASG associate. Not everyone was cut out to be an associate of ASG. Those who did pass the Cindy test were exceptional.

Cindy came from a long line of administrative assistants. I was never sure whether she cared if I called her "CF," but she never objected. I never called her that in public; the CF was just between her and me. And of course, I insisted that Cindy refer to me as Tag. And she did, unless she was pissed about something or someone. Then it was Mr. Grayson. I hated it when she came into my office, closed the door behind her, and started a conversation with, "Mr. Grayson, we need to talk." When she said that,

I would do a quick internal analysis of what I had done to warrant "the talk." And off she would go!

Cindy had two sisters, both administrative assistants at prestigious local liberal law firms. Her mother, too, had been a secretary during her working years. Odd how things like that run in families, but they do. I'll never understand why; the last thing I wanted to do was work as my father had … at things he did not like! Maybe she liked what she did. She must have, because she was great!

We were a pretty health-conscious group at ASG. No doughnuts or other sugar-filled garbage were lying around the office to make people fat. We were image conscious to a fault. We just offered the healthy stuff: granola, fruit, yogurt, and lots and lots of coffee. I was hooked on my morning coffee, along with a favorite morning indulgence: my flavored creamers. I couldn't—or I should say, wouldn't—drink my coffee without it, and Cindy knew my favorite: crème brûlée. She made sure I always had some crème brûlée to go in my coffee. Told you she was great!

Being in the old-age business, we were all acutely aware of the effects poor decisions had on the body and mind. So, from the very beginning, our little threesome all vowed to eat right and do right in all things ASG. Part of doing right was to exercise to keep the mind at the peak of fitness. We offered our employees a gym membership at no cost—the least we could do for our collection of brainiacs. We rode herd over them pretty hard, but paid all our employees very well. The other part of doing right was to only hire those who fit the image we wanted to show the world. Why should we settle for less than what we wanted?

We kept the atmosphere professionally casual at the office. Shirts and ties were a must, but jackets were optional; jeans were never allowed at the office. During the summer months, golf shirts and khaki pants were the order of the day. It was not unusual for one of us to disappear to the golf course in the late afternoon to get in a quick round at the club. I am proud to say that I sport a 6 handicap. As you can imagine, the boys of the firm are a pretty competitive bunch.

Our professional attire was rather an odd code for a bunch of liberal types from U of M … M go Blue. While in school, I had always pictured myself working in a crazy, casual environment. You know the kind: bring your dog to work, pitch the Frisbee over the tops of the cubicle … that sort of thing. In fact, when we began the firm, I recall sitting outside a favorite hangout called Pizza Bob's in shorts, a T-shirt and flip-flops.

We envisioned our firm through the bottom of beer bottles swigged from brown paper sacks, munching on sub sandwiches while sitting under a big oak tree at the corner of State and Packard. Pizza Bob's was right around the corner from our shared house, which we referred to as "the parlor." Pizza Bob's subs, all-night pinochle, and a big ole fat joint … ah, the good old days!

I remember the day, exactly one year before graduation, that the three of us sat on the grass, sipping beers and formulating our business plan. We talked about who or what was going to be our main source of cash flow. We all knew it was going to be the state and federal governments, along with insurance companies and the independently wealthy. It made good business sense for us to fit into their more formally structured world. We were pretty certain we would have to make some changes—both personally and professionally—in order to make the kind of money we all had in mind. The time was at hand for us to clean up and grow up. We were ready, or so we thought! Did I mention we might have been smoking at the time?

The federal and state governments along, with insurance companies and the wealthy, all had their business expectations and protocols. If we were going to take advantage of their programs, we would have to be seen as responsible business partners. We might have been liberal-minded, but we were not stupid.

ASG employed some 250 people, mostly clerical and data-entry types. Those early-morning meetings among the key executives sure did make a statement to and an impression on the others, who supported our vision and decisions. Work was something that we loved, and anyone who did not love it as much as we did would not last long as an employee of ASG.

Our morning meeting ritual always started with our key factor report. We had developed our meeting agenda into a simple formula: finance, threats, and opportunities. Everything we talked about in these meetings could be categorized as one of those three simple key factors. These factors were the core topic of every Monday- and Friday-morning meeting. Friday was our expanded meeting, albeit with the same agenda. If we needed a more in-depth report, we would save it for the Friday week-in-review meeting.

Financials are the lifeblood and number-one priority of any company. Our firm was no different, so first up in our meeting was William Abernathy. In the inter sanctum of the morning meeting, we all referred to Abernathy simply as the Master. He was a genius with numbers. He was the master of our money, and we had undying faith in his abilities.

The Master was a tall, slender man with prematurely snow-white hair, gelled and brushed straight back. Not even the gale-force winds of Lake Michigan could move one hair from its place. Clean cut, with no facial hair, he reminded me of Michael Douglas from the movie *Wall Street*. He was the epitome of a smooth-operating, fast-talking finance whiz kid. Suspenders and all ... right off the set of the movie. Come to think of it, he did not have any waist to speak of, so the suspenders represented as much function as they did fashion. White shirt, flashy tie, wing tips, and pinstriped suit: that was his dress. He looked as if he had been put on this earth to talk money, and when he did, what came out of his mouth was pure gold. It was a thing of beauty to behold. We loved our money at ASG, and the federal government seemed to have a never-ending supply!

The three of us were all about the same age, so his snow-white hair was something of a peculiarity. But it looked great on him, and the women swooned over that full head of white hair. And William, the only lifelong bachelor among us, was our main source of vicarious wild living. He would regale us with stories of his weekend flings. He took advantage of anyone female—except those who worked at the office.

So the Master gave us a short sermon on cash-flow issues. It was all going swimmingly, or so we were told. He could make money appear and disappear, all with the click of a mouse. But as he always said, as long as we kept moving forward, he would be able to justify the path we had taken to get here. We needed to keep the acquisition program in high gear, he explained. The Master was always looking for a good deal and always ready to dump that which was not keeping pace with the expected margins.

Now that our forty-third president, George W. Bush, had exited the White House, the Obama administration was about to change the game of health care. We needed to make as many deals as we could while the deal-making was in our favor. The lack of federal oversight from the Bush administration had played into our business strategy as we had adapted to a faster, looser, and often a bit more risky business plan. When this plan paid huge dividends, we had started to draw some unwanted attention from the regulators.

The Democrats were going to try to socialize the free-market system to some extent. How that would affect us was yet to be seen. Even with the downturn in the economy, we had a strong line of credit and lots of cash on hand to continue to explore new opportunities as they came along.

Any nursing home, hospital, or agency that ran within one percentage point on the downside of the operating budget for four consecutive months was considered a threat to ASG operations. That was Thomas Smith's area of expertise: running the bricks, mortar, and people.

Tom Smith was a man of minimum stature at only five feet five inches, but he ruled his domain as Dick Butkus had ruled the middle of the field as a linebacker for the Chicago Bears in the late sixties. Butkus was a Hall of Fame linebacker who crushed all he played against. He was, and still is, my favorite NFL player.

Butkus played with unmatched ferocity. I remember watching Sunday-afternoon football in the late sixties and early seventies with my dad, another Chicago Bears fan. We would bet on how many opponents Butkus would put out of the game from his bone-crushing hits. Butkus was our man. He never let us down; someone always got pulverized when they tried to run across the middle of the field against him. I always took pity on those poor fools who tried! All who went up against Dick Butkus paid a heavy price.

Tom was the firm's Dick Butkus. He knew the health-care business better than anyone I knew, and I knew a lot of people in this business. He could see a train wreck coming before the train ever left the station. Tom knew how to squeeze every last nickel from the buildings we operated. His staff loved him, too. He was fiercely loyal to those who ran the operations.

But if he thought, for just one second, that you were not doing as you were told or thought you had a better way to run the business, you were history. Tom crushed all those who tried running across the middle of *his* field.

Tom did not take any shit from anyone, just like our man Butkus. He grew up in River Rouge, a tough, mostly black Detroit suburb, and found out the hard way that once you start retreating, it is difficult to regain your footing. Tom would rather stand and throw punches than get kicked in the ass with a boot. If he thought you did not have his back, he would find someone who did.

Tom was loyal to his family and friends, too. He valued a small group that he could trust, and I was a member of that group. I guess his social habits came from not having a lot of close friends as a kid. I had known Tom for a lot of years and had watched him and Susan, his wife of twenty-five years, start and raise their family. Tom coached his son's baseball team and spent every Saturday doing whatever the kids wanted to do. He was a family man through and through; I admired that about Tom. Family was a close second for Tom, but his first love was truly ASG.

We had a great, albeit ruthless, business team!

During our morning meetings, Tom would bring in a variety of people to explain different threats that had popped onto the radar screen. This would give his underlings an opportunity to get a bit more familiar with how the firm worked. It was also our chance to see how Tom's group was developing. Tom was always looking for the best talent he could find. Anyone who was able to survive and thrive at the pace we kept was a keeper. Over the years, plenty of people failed to make the cut.

Opportunity was my thing. It was my goal to keep ten business opportunities in the air at any one time—buying, selling, and always looking. Like I said, I lived the hunt of a deal. So, at our meeting, I did my usual song and dance that CF had prepared for me. I really did not even have much to say that week, but it was a mandatory meeting. I briefly explained several opportunities that we were considering and where we were in the deal process. I had refined the process so that we all knew exactly what to expect. I used stages to explain the process.

Stage one was trolling. Trolling was where we would entertain the idea of a purchase. We would do some Internet research. We reviewed state and federal inspections and deficiency reports. That sort of cursory review did not cost much in the way of time or money, and Cindy was great at it. If she uncovered too many problems, we would pass on the project even before it got started.

Stage two was the initiation stage. We would make contact with a potential client and get a feeling for all the reasons a sale was being sought. I had a questionnaire that we had developed over the years so we could get a handle on the scope of the project. A whole host of issues could be lurking, and they all needed to be flushed out. If I had a keen interest in a project, I would usually schedule a visit to kick the proverbial tires and see where the leaks were.

Stage three was our due-diligence process. The finance guys would pore over as many years of financials as they could get their hands on. The operations boys would review all inspections and surveys, along with anything else Tom wanted. Our legal department would review all contracts and documents: workers' comp claims, patient lawsuits, employee lawsuits, union contracts, and so on. This stage was the most critical one. This was the stage that gave us our leverage to make the best deal we could. This is where our strategy to buy low came into play. This was my playground!

Stage four was negotiation. We combined all of the information we had gathered in the previous stages into a negotiations strategy. This is where Cindy shone the brightest. She could boil down all the information into spreadsheets, graphs, PowerPoint presentations, and a variety of slideshows that would put it all into perspective. She and I would fine-tune the presentation until we were happy with the product. Then we would gather our troops and do a mock presentation. Their job was to poke as many holes into our plan as possible; we wanted no surprises at the negotiations table.

Once a deal was struck, it was on to stage five, when the operations team took control of the project. We handed the project off to Tom, and he was now in control of the project until it reached stage six.

The final stage, stage six, was when we started the selling process. Rather than buying a property, we prepared it for sale, doing everything we could to sell at the highest possible price. We were in this game to make money. We had it down to a science … and we made a killing! The whole process took anywhere from six months to a year.

Once the meeting was adjourned, CF and I went into my office to discuss the week's events: travel, meetings, and the like. We always synchronized our calendars. CF knew more about my activities than my wife or I did. She was my keeper, scheduler, and travel agent. She was indispensable to me.

She returned to her office, and shortly thereafter, she called me on the office phone.

"There is a gentleman on the phone who wants to speak with you," she said. I was the sort of businessman who would talk to anyone who called. I never knew when the next deal was going to arrive.

"Did you happen to catch his name?"

"The gentleman's name is Dillianquest … Nathaniel Dillianquest. He said he was calling from Beaufort, South Carolina. Would you like to speak with him?"

"Yes, I would, but give me a moment before you put him through. Get his contact information, just in case we need to get ahold of him later."

Cindy replied, "Will do," and hung up the phone.

I leaned back in my overstuffed chair and stared up at the ceiling for a moment. *Beaufort, South Carolina? How interesting!* I recalled being in Beaufort some years back. A good family friend had purchased a fifty-two-foot Carver Motor Yacht in Annapolis, Maryland, and invited Sam and me to accompany him and his wife for a week's excursion down the intercoastal waterway to Bohicket Marina at John's Island, South Carolina. It was truly one of the best weeks of my life. I was traveling on the OPB program: Other People's Boat. The only way to cruise!

Before beginning my conversation with this Mr. Dillianquest, I loosened my tie, unbuttoned my shirt cuffs, and rolled up my sleeves. I reached into a desk drawer and pulled out a new legal pad of paper and grabbed a pen. I was a bit puzzled by the call. To date, all our business had been confined to the northeastern tier states. We had no holdings south of Virginia, and that was by design. We wanted to keep our business in an area where we could manage it without huge travel expenses. Actually, the real truth was that none of us liked hotels or spending time away from families, although that was starting to change for me. At any rate, up until then, we had tried kept our business geographically close to the vest.

Cindy rang back through and asked, "Are you ready to speak with Mr. Dillianquest?"

"Yes, CF. Please put him through."

"He is yours on line four."

I greeted the man on the other end in my usual upbeat phone voice.

"Good morning, Mr. Dillianquest. How may I help you?" I inquired.

The voice on the other end replied in a slow, southern drawl, "Well, good morning to you, sir. My name is Nate Dillianquest. I am calling from Beaufort, South Carolina. I have been referred to you by a mutual business acquaintance, one Mr. Anthony B. Schultz. He said he had done some business with your firm in the recent past. He recalls your firm as the only reputable firm that he would recommend."

I leaned back in my chair. I recalled Mr. Schultz and our deal. Schultz was a mountain of a man, at least six foot six inches tall. He owned several businesses. We had bought a nursing home from him a few years before, in northern Michigan. It had been a rather odd deal. Schultz had not been in the healthcare business originally and had found out that it could be a difficult one to make money in. We basically took the business off his hands before it bankrupted him. We were honest with him during the negotiations; it could have ended much worse for Mr. Schultz than it did. This business caused many fatalities.

"Yes, I recall Mr. Schultz. If memory serves me correctly, he got in a bit over his head, and we helped him out of a sticky situation," I said, picturing Schultz in my mind. "Mr. Dillianquest, how does a gentleman from South Carolina cross paths with the likes of Mr. Schultz?"

"My family has had the blessing of meeting many people in our long history. Mr. Schultz was one of the many who crossed our paths in a most delightful way." Nate paused for a moment and then added, "We tried our hand at some natural-gas exploration, and he was our drilling partner. He is a wonderful man—one who knows his limitations."

"Yes, that is true," I replied. "Now, how can I help you?"

"Mr. Grayson," began Nate, his southern drawl ever so pronounced, "my family has been proud to be of service to the people of South Carolina for many generations. My great-great-grandfather, Theodore Dillianquest, served as the commanding General in the Second South Carolina Detachment at the site of the Waxhaw Massacre under direction of the great Southern patriot Governor Rutledge in 1780. The site of the massacre is now the town of Beaufort. I am proud to say that my family helped build this town from those humble beginnings."

After short pause, I said, "That is quite an impressive family history, Mr. Dillianquest."

"Please, call me Nate," he said, "and thank you. I just love telling that story."

"As impressive as that story is," I mused, "how does that get you to me?"

"I was just coming to that part, Mr. Grayson."

I quickly interjected, "Okay, here is the deal: if I am to call you Nate, then please call me Tag. My real name is Teasdale, but those I work with call me Tag. So please, Nate, if we are going to transact a bit of business, please call me Tag."

"Will do, sir ... I mean, Tag," Nate politely corrected himself. "Allow me to continue. My family has many holdings in this community, mostly in the area of construction, real estate, boat building, that sort of thing. This one—this ... *complex*, for the lack of a better term, of health-care concerns—was my mother's pet project. She wanted to give something back to the community. She spent her life's work building Dillianquest." Nate paused to gather his thoughts.

"Back in the eighties," Nate continued, "Mother bought an old, closed-down asylum and began to restore it to what it is today. It took her many years and a boatload of money, but she finally opened a fifty-bed subacute facility in that building. What a project that was," Nate added with a laugh. "But as time passed, Mother and her charity were able to add a hospice agency and a sixty-bed nursing home complete with a twenty-five-suite assisted-living community attached. Not too long ago, she was able to build a stand-alone physical-therapy company. She put all this together on a hundred-acre campus," Nate said proudly. "Father was always happy to see Mother do what she loved to do: take care of people. She was a true giver and actually created quite an impressive end result, if you don't mind me saying so."

I heard Nate take a breath before adding, "My father, God rest his soul, helped Mother along the way, providing the muscle and know-how from his construction and real estate development companies. He was a good man."

After a short pause, Nate added, "Now, Tag, we both know how complicated the health-care business can be. I do believe it is time for our family—and by our family, I mean me—to get out of the business before the business takes out my family—and again I mean me—as it almost did with our good friend Mr. Schultz."

"I see," I said after a short pause. I was lost in his slow, southern pattern of speaking. Listening to him was somewhat mesmerizing.

"Tag," he said, "this campus is situated on prime South Carolina acreage overlooking miles of the intercoastal waterway. Mother even had guest quarters built for visiting families. A little later, I added a few boat slips for those who visited their loved ones via the waterway. It makes for a pleasant Sunday afternoon visit if you're a boater. I keep a small boat handy for my personal usage down at the dock." Nate paused for a moment and said, "When you get down here, we can tour the town by water if you like." I did not respond before Nate added, "All the buildings are reminiscent of the antebellum style of architecture, with some modifications to comply with Mother's personal requirements. It is a very beautiful setting, Tag. The drive is lined with magnificent towering magnolia trees that fill the spring air with their beauty."

"Nate," I interjected, "I am sure it is as beautiful as it sounds … but as we both know, beautiful is only skin deep. By that, I mean no disrespect, but as a businessman yourself, you will understand if I tell you that I must do my research. I will have to get back to you." A thought popped out of my mouth: "Are you speaking with any other firms?"

"No, sir. You are my one and only inquiry to date. I have prepared an overview of the project and will send it along to you shortly. If you please, it will arrive in your e-mail inbox just as soon as you provide me with your e-mail address. You will be able to get a bird's-eye view of Dillianquest," Nate said, and then continued, "As you can imagine, it was named after my dearest mother, who currently is a resident at Danby House." Nate's tone turned somber. "And for your information, Danby House was named after a daughter who died at birth. Danby House is the private nursing facility on campus."

"Your mother is in the nursing home?" I asked, caught a bit off guard.

"Of course. Mother would always say that if the care we provide is not good enough for our family, how in God's name can we expect those in our community who need care to give unto us their loved ones to watch over? They would not respect our good name. She would have it no other way." He added, "My father passed away at Danby House some years ago. He was very proud of what Mother had accomplished over the years. It has been just Mother and me for a while now. I am her only son, and frankly, my priorities do not lie in running any part of a health-care operation. I am sure you can appreciate that."

"Nate, I understand and fully appreciate your situation," I said. "Let me take a look at what you have, and I will get back with you early next week. This week, I am a bit pressed for time."

"Tag," he said, "I hope you understand that discretion will be the key to our success. If you know anything about Southern history, you know that the war is not over yet ... selling to a Yankee could be the end of me."

After an awkward silence, he added, "Tag, I am kidding."

To that, I said, "I'm glad to hear you say that! Let me put Cindy back on the phone, and she can give any additional information you need. Let me say that it was a pleasure to speak with you. I will be in touch soon. Good-bye, Nate."

"Good day to you, Tag. I look forward to our continuing conversation."

I pushed the hold button on the phone and told Cindy, who I knew was listening, "CF, can you pick up on line four and give Mr. Dillianquest our e-mail addresses? Include yours and have him send what he has to both of us. Thanks."

I saw line four go blank on the phone, and I knew she was done with Dillianquest. It would only be a minute or two before she popped her head in the office. Just like clockwork, I heard a light knock on the door, and in she walked.

"Well?" she asked after a long pause.

"Well what?" I said, launching the usual game we would play when something of interest would come our way.

"Well," she said, "don't you just love the way the gentle South speaks? I could listen to that slow drawl all day. Did he have anything of interest I need to know about?"

Just then, my computer spoke to me. I had mail!

"Yes, he did," I said. "Why don't you open his mail and see what he is proposing? I have to go to Toledo for a meeting and will be back in a couple of days. Look at what he has sent and see if it fits our profile. And do me one additional favor: run a complete background check on Mr. Dillianquest— criminal, financial, the whole shooting match. I want to know as much about this guy as possible. He is quite the charmer, isn't he?"

Cindy smiled as she walked out of the office.

I grabbed my coat and briefcase and as I walked by her desk said, "If you need me, you know how to get ahold of me."

Out the door I went.

CHAPTER 3

A long week of contract negotiations had finally ended. I was up and out the door for my early-morning run on another beautiful day. Running gave me clarity and helped me gain perspective on whatever was going on in my life.

Sam, as usual, was waiting for me when I finished my run and returned home. As I entered the house, I could smell the aroma of fresh brewed coffee. It was one of those aromas that led you, like a bull with a ring in its nose, right to its source. I love the smell of fresh-brewed coffee in the morning. Nothing better!

A tall glass of orange juice already sat on the table, and four eggs were on the way. I always started the day with a healthy dose of high-quality protein. Alongside the juice was an 800-milligram tablet of ibuprofen, fish oil, and a multivitamin. Getting older was taking its toll on my knees. The damp cold of Michigan and pounding the pavement made my knees ache. The ibuprofen took the edge off.

I always ate before I showered and got ready to go to work; it didn't make sense for to me to brush, floss, get dressed, and then eat. Most of my shirts had stains on the front of them from past eating disasters, but at least I was a pretty fast learner.

The newspaper was always just to the right of my orange juice. Rituals were important!

Sam asked, "How does your day look?"

"Should be a good one," I said as I pulled my chair back and sat down. I took a long swallow of juice before adding, "We are looking into a project in Beaufort, South Carolina. Do you remember when we were in Beaufort, and how quaint it was?"

"Beaufort, South Carolina?" Sam questioned. "Isn't that a bit far south for you guys?"

"It is, but I was thinking it might be a good move for us to expand our reach a bit more south. You know, it is the largest aging demographic in the United States," I said in a matter-of-fact tone. "It appears that a potential client, the Dillianquest family, allowed 'Mother'"—I held my hands up using my fingers, indicating quotation marks—"to diversify some of the family fortune into the health-care biz. Now that the mother is almost out of the picture, Junior Dillianquest"—again with the sarcastic hand motion—"wants to get out of the health-care biz due to lack of experience and desire. I've got Cindy putting together a source comparison to see if it fits the profile. I spoke to a family member earlier this week. I believe his name was Nathaniel. You would have loved listening to his slow, southern drawl. It was right out of the movie *Gone with the Wind.* Do you remember how much we liked Beaufort?"

Sam did not reply. She did not appear to be interested as she reached for the sports section of the newspaper and took another sip of coffee.

I wolfed down the rest of my breakfast and told Sam, "I need to get into the office a bit earlier than usual. I want to review the Dillianquest file before the morning meeting." I grabbed my coffee and headed to the shower. Shortly thereafter, I was out the door and off to the office.

I got to the office earlier than usual; traffic was light at that time of the morning. I zipped into my parking space, swiftly moved toward the office door, passed the front desk, and saw Cindy preparing the conference room for our meeting.

"Morning," I said as I stopped and poked my head in.

The conference room was a great gathering place, and Cindy was adorning it with the usual breakfast treats and coffee. The Room, as it was referred to, was state-of-the-art, fashioned with all the latest gadgets. During meetings, six LCD screens would rise up from the tabletop, so everyone could view whatever presentation was being shown without visual interference—very cool gadgetry.

The Room sat twelve at the table with large, high-back leather chairs. Seating for eight more was available around the perimeter. We spent a lot of time in the Room discussing projects. At the center was a massive black walnut table that was fourteen feet in length. I had had the table made from some trees felled when Sam and I built our northern Michigan retreat. Black walnut trees are one of nature's finest accomplishments. This massive table was my gift to the firm's future success. It was solid and long lasting, much as we envisioned for our firm.

"Did you happen to get a chance to put a file together on the Dillianquest project?" I asked Cindy.

"Good morning, and yes, it is on your desk, in the yellow file folder."

"Super," I responded in a bright voice. "What do you think?"

"It has possibilities."

Cindy and I had our system. She always had input as to what projects we undertook. Yellow files meant that it could go either way. Red files were exactly that—a red flag—and green files were those with high potential. A file never went out of my office until I approved it to leave.

We tried to keep our approach to projects as sterile as possible. We did not like people and their personalities clouding the picture. This one was an exception, though. Nathaniel Dillianquest had gotten my attention, and I wanted to find out more. I hoped that Cindy had done her homework in her usual thorough fashion. This deal could be exactly what I was looking for.

All during the course of our conversation, I hovered over the coffee cart in the conference room, mixing up my morning brew, flavored creamer included. I asked Cindy, "Do you need a hand doing anything?" knowing that her answer would be no.

"No, thanks."

"Okay. If you get done with a few minutes to spare before we get started, stop by the office. I want to pick your brain about this guy."

"Sure thing," she said.

I sauntered down to my office.

As I entered my office, I shed my jacket and placed it over the back of one of the chairs that sat in front of my desk. I placed my briefcase alongside the desk as I walked to my chair and spun it around so I could sit. I picked up the yellow file folder and sat down. I looked at the folder, and across the top, it read "Dillianquest Source Report." I thought for a moment about what Nathaniel had said about his mother. Dillianquest was her philanthropic project, her effort to give back to the community. Now she was one of the patients at the place. Not many owners wished to be a patient in their own nursing home. I stopped and wondered if this was a good idea for us.

Just then I heard a quiet knock on the door, and in walked Cindy. "Did you get a chance to look at the file yet?" she asked.

"No, I have not. I've been thinking about what Mr. Dillianquest said about his mother. Did you know that she is a patient at Dillianquest?"

"No, I did not, but it must say something about the care they provide," she responded.

"You know, that is exactly what I was thinking. Anything in the file I need to be aware of?"

"I found a few oddities that you need to be aware of," she began, "but nothing extraordinary about the property. Mostly has to do with Mr. Dillianquest. It seems Mr. Dillianquest was quite the party animal in his youth: several arrests for alcohol- and drug-related minor stuff, but no convictions. It sure seems like his good name and a little intervention from Daddy's pals saved him from any jail time. But, interestingly, he does have a felony conviction for vehicular manslaughter. Mr. Dillianquest got a bit boozed up one night, killed a pedestrian, and then fled the scene. He received one year of house arrest and was required to serve in the military— four years in the Marines—but he served no jail time for that indiscretion."

"Interesting," I replied. "Everyone has a little secret, and it seems like Nate's little secret is one we can use in our favor. It is becoming clearer why Dillianquest wants to sell his mother's health-care business," I added without taking a breath. "If my memory serves me correctly, once Mother passes, and ownership reverts to Nate, that felony conviction is going to cause a problem for him with the state and feds. CF, please double check on that statute for me."

"Will do," she said, and out the door she went, adding, "two minutes until the meeting. I will see you there." She was gone.

The Friday-morning meeting was about to begin. All the usual suspects had gathered, and the clock struck seven a.m.

The meeting was a blur of cash-flow forecasts and operational details. I was not really into all the details, as I normally was. I found myself mentally drifting, thinking about the Dillianquest project. *One hundred acres of prime South Carolina land overlooking the intercoastal … that has to be some spot. A guy could chop off a hunk of that land, and it would make for a pretty nice retirement place … and no one at this table would have to know.* My mind kept drifting. *Hell, I could arrange this deal so that I could keep most of the land and turn a pretty tidy profit for myself with no one being the wiser.*

When it came to my turn, as usual, Cindy had my agenda spelled out to a T. A trained monkey could do my report. But when I got to the Dillianquest line, I departed from the usual short format.

"And finally," I said, as if to wrap things up, "I had an interesting phone call after the Monday meeting from a gentleman in Beaufort, South Carolina, by the name of Nathaniel Dillianquest. He is beginning his search to find a buyer for a large-acreage campus that his family owns and operates: hospital, hospice, rehab, and a nursing home. His family history dates back to the Civil War days, and they seem to be well connected in the political arena. Cindy put together the preliminary source documents that will be distributed in the next few days."

Just then, Tom interjected, "Why would we be interested in a project in South Carolina?"

After a moment of silence, I looked up from the yellow file open on the table in front of me and said, "That is a good question, Tom. I will let you know more after I look into this a bit more closely." I then added in a whimsical fashion, "Winter in Michigan is not getting easier on these old bones. I was toying with opening a southern ASG command post! Besides, the South is the fastest growing demographic for people over the age of seventy. It might make sense to look into that, don't you think?"

With that last comment, the meeting adjourned. I stood up from my spot at the middle of the table and said, "Tom, will you and Bill hang back for just a second?" They stopped in their tracks, placed the paperwork back on the table, and waited for the room to clear. "Have a seat for a moment," I said. "I just wanted to let you know that I am going to be calling Dillianquest today about his inquiry. I need to find out a bit more, but we might be able to pull off one hell of a deal here."

"How do you figure that?" Tom asked.

"Well, I get the feeling that Nate's mother is not long for this world, and he is going to inherit this complex lock, stock, and barrel. This has been the mother's project," I said, using the air-quote symbols again. "Nate has not taken a keen interest in keeping this complex in the family portfolio. They are into construction, real-estate development, boat building, that sort of thing. Now, our friend Nate has a felony on his record from some years ago for vehicular manslaughter, which makes owning an entity that takes federal and state funds difficult at best."

"You must be kidding?" Bill questioned with a half-assed smirk on his face.

"No, I am not kidding," I said. "He is a felon and wants nothing to do with the health-care business."

"Can't blame him there," Tom said.

"How did he come to find us?" Bill asked.

"Remember that Schultz deal we did up north a few years back?" I asked. Both Bill and Tom shook their heads. "Well, Nate Dillianquest had Tony Schultz drill some natural-gas wells for him. Schultz told Nate about our deal and how we saved his ass."

"No shit!" Tom said in amazement. "That place Schultz sold us is a cash cow. I wish we had a dozen more just like it!"

"I know," I said. "I am thinking that if we can strike a deal, like we did with Schultz, we could strike gold in South Carolina."

"Cool," Tom said. "Let's see where this takes us."

"I agree," Bill said. "Nothing ventured, nothing gained."

"Keep us posted," Tom added.

"Just like always," I said as we walked out of the room.

Back in my office, Cindy was sitting in one of the chairs facing my desk, her legs crossed and hands folded on her lap atop a stack of files.

"Well?" she said in a pensive voice.

"Well, what?" I replied.

"Well?" she said with a pause for effect. "Do I have to clear your calendar so you can head to South Carolina to meet with Mr. Dillianquest?"

"Well," I said with a longer pause, "I don't know yet. I want to speak with Mr. Dillianquest before we go making any arrangements."

Cindy stood, gazing out the window in my office, looking directly over my head. She leaned forward with both hands placed in the middle of my desk, fixed her eyes directly on mine, and said, "This looks like a fun one, doesn't it?"

I, in turn, leaned forward inching closer to her said, "Yes, it does ... see if you can get him on the phone."

Cindy stood straight up and said as she turned to leave, "Will do, but seeing how it's only eight fifteen in the morning, do you mind if I wait to call until ten-ish?"

"No, I do not," I replied. "Just let me know when you have him on the line." And with that, Cindy vanished from my office.

The couple of hours in between the end of the morning meeting and the phone call to Dillianquest flew by. Before I realized it, Cindy was on the intercom.

"Tag, I have Mr. Dillianquest on line three for you ... the time is ten o'clock exactly."

"Thanks," I replied. "Tell him I will be right with him."

"Will do," she replied. I could see the blinking light on line three stop for a few seconds and then resume. I guessed it was my turn.

I picked up the phone and said in a genuine, chipper voice, "Good morning, Nate. How are you?"

Nate replied in that slow, southern drawl, "I am doing just fine, Mr. Grayson, just fine. Thank you for asking."

I interjected before Nate could utter another word and said, "I wanted to thank you for sending along the information on Dillianquest. It was very nicely done and very informative. I appreciate all the work that went into it."

"Yes, sir," Nate said. "We spent a bit of effort on that." After a bit of a pause, he added, "Father used to say if it was worth doing, it was worth doing well. Words I have tried to live by."

"Your father was a wise man, Nate," I said.

"That he was. Now, about Dillianquest: Tag, might your firm be interested?"

"I believe you have piqued our interest. We need to set up a time for me to come down and look for myself at what your mother has so ably put together."

With an obvious smile reflected in his voice, Nate replied, "Splendid, Tag—just splendid. I will make the arrangements and have you picked up at Willow Run airfield on Monday." Without a pause, he added, "Say about 10:00 a.m.?"

"I don't know if I can move that fast, Nate. I have to check my calendar. I am usually not free at the drop of the hat."

"Not to worry, Tag," Nate replied confidently. "Cindy, bless her heart, was able to shift a few appointments from your calendar next week. She is a rather insightful creature. You are free through Wednesday."

"Yes, she is rather special," I said.

At that moment, Cindy poked her head in the office and said, "Jim will take you to Willow Run right after the Monday-morning meeting." She winked and vanished just as quickly.

"Well, Nate," I said, "it looks like you and Cindy have my itinerary all worked out for next week."

"Indeed." Nate drew out the word for effect. "I will have a plane waiting for you. The tail number is NP603. I trust you won't mind flying in a private plane? The pilot's name is Gwen," he added with a hint of a smile in his voice. "She is an excellent pilot with many hours under her belt."

"As a general rule, Nate, I don't frequently fly private planes. I prefer the chaos of our public airports." After a short pause for effect, I added, "For me, there is nothing more refreshing that waiting in long lines and then having complete strangers perform intrusive body and bag searches." I then added with amusement in my voice, "But for you, Nate … for you, I will make an exception."

Nate laughed out loud on the other end of the phone and said, "My dear sir, I will personally pick you up at the airport here in Beaufort upon your arrival. And if you still desire to have that cavity search, I think I can have that arranged as well." He again laughed and said, "Tag, I am looking forward to making your acquaintance. I will see you Monday … good day to you, sir." He hung up the phone.

For a second, I just looked at the phone receiver in my hand. The first words out of my mouth were, "Cindy, please come in here." She was in the office in a matter of seconds. Looking up at her, I said, "That was a rather peculiar phone conversation. How did I go from checking my calendar to flying to Beaufort, South Carolina, in a matter of seconds?"

"Well," she said with a pause.

"Yes?" I drew out the *s* for what seemed like forever.

"Well," she said again, as she sat in the chair that she always occupied when we were discussing such things in my office, "Well, it happened this way. After you left Monday, he—Mr. Dillianquest—called back to make sure that the e-mail got here okay. He also asked what kind of process we go through to qualify projects. So I told him that we look at surveys, financials, debt service, you know that type of stuff. He said he understood and we said our goodbyes."

After a pause, Cindy added, "The next day, Mr. Dillianquest called back and asked about your schedule for Monday, Tuesday, and Wednesday of next week. I gave him the usual song and dance about having appointments and that it would take an act of Congress to rearrange them. He then said something that caught my attention. He said that his family had little to no debt on Dillianquest, and he was looking for a quick sale. He said he would send a private plane for you and return you when you were done. I looked at your calendar, and there was really nothing that couldn't be rearranged, so I went ahead and took the liberty of moving things about so you could go to South Carolina. It seemed like a risk worth taking," she said in a humble tone.

"Thanks," I said.

I must have looked dumbfounded, because Cindy asked, "Are you okay with what I did? If not, I will call Mr. Dillianquest and cancel the trip."

"No," I said, "you did nothing wrong. I was just wondering if I should take my golf clubs." We both laughed as she exited the office.

I leaned back in my chair, my feet on the corner of the desk, and let my mind begin to drift to the days spent motoring down the intercoastal waterway, puffing on a cigars, sipping scotch, and watching the world drift by. Could that become my life again?

CHAPTER 4

Monday came around as it always did: much too quickly. It arrived right on the heels of a better weekend, though. Our son, John, was a standout volleyball player for the Alma College program. Their team took first place for the third straight volleyball competition. We were very proud of John, as he was an excellent student as well. He always made the dean's list without fail. The game was held on a Saturday several hours away from Ann Arbor on the eastern shore of Lake Michigan, in the city of Holland. Sam and I would use this time at the lake trying to repair our relationship.

We used to spend as much time at the lake as possible, regardless of the season. Days spent in and around Lake Michigan were in short supply and always treasured. We had friends who lived in the village of Saugatuck, the "Cape Cod of the Midwest," as it was often called. It was snuggled just inland from Lake Michigan on Kalamazoo Lake. Saugatuck was a short thirty-minute drive from Holland. It was protected from the harsh winds of the lake by sand dunes that rose from the shore to protect this wonderful, quaint village.

We had packed an overnight bag, as we had decided to spend the night at our friends' house after the competition was finished. Mac and Sue were old college friends of ours—really more Sam's friends than mine, but they were good people. They liked to play pinochle, and anyone who liked to play pinochle was okay in my book.

They had a boy too, named Tim, who was the same age as John. The two boys were friendly enough. As soon as we got there, about five thirty or so, Tim and John jumped in the car and headed to downtown Saugatuck. There was much to do and see in this tiny, coastal Lake Michigan village, as long as it was not in the middle of winter. It had everything one needed, including a variety of shops, art galleries, and tourist attractions.

One of John's favorites activities after a hard-fought volleyball tournament was to grab a half pound of Mackinaw fudge and go down by the docks. He loved hanging down by the river and visiting the local marinas, looking at very expensive boats and daydreaming about owning one someday.

John was in love with girls and boats. Which was fine by me, as Saugatuck had earned a rather peculiar reputation as being very gay friendly … not that there is anything wrong with that. In my book, homosexuality is much like religion. Being of the liberal persuasion, I do not care what you believe or who you believe in—I just do not want you trying to recruit me into your group. Being the protective father type, I did not want John or Tim becoming the focus of anyone's recruitment efforts, either.

The boys got back to the house at seven thirty, safe and sound. We played pinochle for hours while the kids played the latest WII video game. I am sure it was some sort of sport simulation—golf, tennis, or bowling. I remember playing Pac- Man when video games made their debut. I can recall playing in a crappy little arcade in the back of the drive-in, when drive-ins had carhops to get your drink and food for you. Boy, society has come a long way in a short time. I'm just not sure just how good that is.

We always ate our Sunday-morning breakfast at our favorite Saugatuck breakfast hut, called Ida Reds. Omelets, fried potatoes, toast, coffee, and the Sunday paper—how great is that? Sunday was my cheat day for eating. We ate very clean all week long, and Sunday was the day I could eat anything I wanted. Sundays in Saugatuck had to include Ida Reds—it just had to!

Once breakfast was done, we said our good-byes to our friends. We loaded ourselves in the Suburban, and it was back to the real world, Bloomfield Hills. It was time to get ready for work and school.

Like I said, the weekend was great, but Monday came around much too quickly. We arrived home about four in the afternoon on Sunday.

On Monday I got to the office a few minutes before the morning meeting got under way. Cindy was in the conference room, readying it for our meeting. As I walked by, I poked my head in and said, "Good morning, Cindy. Everything under control?"

"Yes, sir. Your meeting notes are in the blue file folder. I put them on your chair."

"You are a gem," I said as I kept on walking.

"You are very kind, sir. I hope you won't forget that when you do my review in a couple of weeks."

I smiled and said, "I am sure you will let me know if I forget something."

Behind me, she just smiled—I could tell.

I took off my jacket and placed it on a chair that faced my desk. I placed my briefcase on the floor alongside my desk and picked the blue folder from the seat of my office chair. Folder in hand, I sat down. I opened the folder, and the document inside read as follows:

Dillianquest
Beaufort, South Carolina
Stage 2, Monday through Wednesday:
County: Lancaster County
In Lancaster County, age sixty-five and older increased 27 percent in past ten years
In South Carolina, age sixty-five and older increased 13 percent in past ten years
Mortality rate: 904 per 100,000
Per capita income: Greater than $85,000/year at age sixty-five or older is less than 1 percent
High potential

There was a big smiley face in the upper right-hand corner of the page and the initials "C. F." at the bottom, along with the date. We kept everything for the file, just in case.

Monday meetings were short, mostly addressing who was going where and why. There was never much in the way of detail. I was always the last to speak, and today was no exception.

I started out with the usual, "Good morning, all." And in my best southern accent, I added, "After today's meeting, I am off to Beaufort, South Carolina, to meet with Mr. Nathaniel Dillianquest of the Beaufort Dillianquests." I continued in my slow, mocking drawl, "I shall remain there, in Beaufort, until I can determine if the property Mr. Dillianquest proposes to sell fits within our portfolio."

I was actually sounding more like William F. Buckley Jr. than a southern gentleman, at which point Tom spoke up: "I hope when you return, you have a better-sounding accent."

"Yeah, I need to work on that." As everyone got up to leave the room, I added, "Everyone have a good, productive week, and we will see you back here on Friday, same bat time and same bat channel." For some unknown reason, I was feeling full of myself.

I had an hour or so to kill before we left for the airport, so I decided to look a bit closer at the criminal background report of Mr. Nathaniel Dillianquest.

On the phone, Nate Dillianquest had seemed affable enough. Maybe in his youth, he had been a bit of a delinquent—one of those "delinquent fringe" types that I had grown up with. Who knew? If I would have been arrested for everything that I had done as a youth, they would have thrown away the key, and I would still be in jail. Oftentimes, success in life was being at the right place at the right time ... or should I say, not being at the same place the police were, when everyone else was.

Just then, Cindy lightly knocked on the door and said, "Your plane is going to be thirty minutes ahead of schedule. I have already alerted Jim. You should probably leave shortly."

"Thanks," I said. "I'm ready just as soon as Jim is."

Jim had pulled the car up next to mine in the parking lot. He and Cindy had already taken my travel bag from my car and loaded it into the company Town Car. I was not big on leaving my car at airports. My personal vehicle had been broken into a couple of separate occasions at the Detroit airport. I much preferred to leave my car at the office, where we had security to watch over such things. It offered better peace of mind!

At that moment, Cindy inquired, "Is there anything else?"

"Nope, I think I have everything. Thanks, and I will call you when I get in."

"Have a safe trip, and give our regards to Beaufort," she said as she disappeared back into the office. I ducked into the backseat, where I could spread out and read a bit more about our Mr. Dillianquest.

"Jim," I asked as we left the office parking lot, "I assume that Cindy told you where we are headed?"

"Yes, sir, she did. We should be at Willow Run in about forty minutes or so. Gwen called from the plane and said she had run into some tailwinds and would be on the ground at about nine thirty, instead of ten."

Jim continued, "Cindy also gave her my cell number, so she could let us know about any change in arrival times."

"Great," I said and sat back in my seat. I pulled the morning newspaper out from the pocket in the back of the front seat. I reviewed the headlines. I saw nothing new, just more of the same economic disasters. I put the paper on the seat next to me, face down. Cindy had fixed a small pot of coffee for me for the trip. I sat back, relaxed, and let Jim do the driving.

As I settled into the backseat, I reached for the file that contained Nathaniel Dillianquest's background information.

"This should be interesting," I muttered to myself as I poured a fresh cup of coffee. "Jim," I said, "coffee?"

"No, thanks," he replied. "I've had my quota for the day."

"Very well," I replied and opened the file on Nathaniel Dillianquest.

Nathaniel Dillianquest was born in 1946 to Virginia Bossinette and Beaufort Dillianquest, who had married in 1937. Danby Dillianquest, Nate's baby sister, apparently died at birth in 1956. Nate graduated from Coastal Carolina University in 1971 with an engineering degree. He did have a wild side and had been arrested several times for alcohol and substance abuse during college and shortly thereafter. And then there was that pesky felony vehicular manslaughter charge in 1972: no jail time, just one year of supervision under Daddy's watchful eye and a four-year stint in the Marines.

"Now that is some political sway," I thought out loud. Jim did not respond. He was used to my mumblings from the backseat.

I continued to read only to find out that Nathaniel Dillianquest had four failed marriages, all dissolved for marital infidelity. It appeared that he had been working for the family business ever since his college days. He was the heir apparent to the Dillianquest family fortune, which appeared to exceed one hundred million dollars. A rich, party boy of a womanizer … what was not to like? I closed the file on Nathaniel Dillianquest and watched as the flat farmland whizzed by.

We arrived at the Willow Run Airport just as Gwen was touching down in a clean, shiny plane. It sported a white fuselage with a silver belly and had black striping down the side. The tail number read "NP603" in black, bold letters. This was my ride. We watched the plane as it taxied to the front of the terminal building. The captain turned the plane on a dime and brought it to a halt. The plane's right-side profile was presented. The right-side engine shut down, and then the left side did as well. I heard an odd deflating sound as the engines slowly wound down to a halt.

As soon as the propeller stopped whirling about, the pilot popped open the rear cabin door. The pilot was tall and thin and one of the most strikingly beautiful bronze-skinned women I had ever seen. As she gracefully navigated the plane's stairs and exited the plane, I put her age at about thirty-five. She looked very distinguished in her captain's uniform—very professional. Her hair was pulled back tightly against her scalp in a long, flowing ponytail. In her tight-fitting jacket and form-fitting slacks, she presented very well!

She glanced over at the terminal building and saw Jim and me standing in the lounge area. She straightened her jacket by tugging on the bottom and started toward us. Her hips swayed as if she were walking down the runway at the Miss Universe Pageant. Her ponytail swung from side to side, and her heels clicked the tarmac with every step. She knew we were watching and was well aware of what we saw. She couldn't help but let a little smile creep onto her face … just a bit of a tease.

I looked at Jim, and he smiled. I smiled back and said, "Let's go meet the captain."

"Gladly," Jim responded. We pushed open the large glass doors that separated the tarmac from the terminal's public area.

As we approached each other, the captain extended her hand and said, "Good morning. My name is Gwen Rios. You must be Mr. Grayson?"

"Please, call me Tag." She smiled and shook my hand with a firm, deliberate grip—one that was meant to instill confidence. As our hands disengaged, I turned to Jim, who was standing at my right, and said, "This is Jim Edwards. Jim works with us at ASG."

Gwen extended her hand and said, "It is a pleasure to meet you, Jim."

Jim shook her hand, looked directly into her eyes, and replied, "The pleasure is all mine." You could tell he was smitten with the captain.

"Now, if you will excuse me," Jim said, "I will get the car and pull it around." Jim disappeared through the large glass doors. A few moments later, an automatic gate opened, and onto the tarmac drove the black Lincoln Town Car. It pulled up close to the tail of the plane. Not a second after the car pulled to a stop, the trunk popped open. I walked to the back of the car and leaned in to grab my bag.

As I did, Gwen stopped me by gently placing her hand on my shoulder and said, "Allow me to get that for you, sir." She reached into the trunk and snatched my travel bag out of my hands. She was up the stairs and back into the plane as quickly as you please.

Jim turned and looked at me with a half-assed grin on his face and said, "Looks like you're in good hands here, boss."

"It surely appears that way, doesn't it? I'll let you know about the return trip. See you later."

"Safe travels."

Just as Jim was about to get in the car, Gwen poked her head out the door and said, "Pleased to meet you, Jim."

To that, Jim replied, "It was nice to meet you as well. Fly friendly." He got into the car and started for the gate. As he got closer, the gate began to open, and in a flash, Jim was gone from sight.

It was just me, the captain, and a plane I had never seen before.

I thought to myself, *This will be interesting.*

I took a few moments to walk around the plane and give it my once-over inspection. After completing one circle, I stopped directly in front of the plane and placed both hands on my hips. I decided to watch as the plane was being refueled. I had mostly flown commercial, except for that rare occasion when I had the pleasure of flying on a corporate NetJets junket.

I tried not to fly at all if I could get away with it. It wasn't that I was afraid of flying per se; it just did not seem possible that several tons of steel should be able to lift off from a perfectly good Mother Earth. With the recent landing of that US Airbus Flight 1549 in the middle of New York City on the Hudson River and the crash in Buffalo, I thought my feelings about flying were very well justified!

Gwen noticed me standing in front of the aircraft and inquired, "Is everything all right, Mr. Grayson?"

"Everything is fine," I replied. "But you know, Gwen, I am always amazed that these things fly. Something about that just doesn't seem right. I mean, I understand the aerodynamics and all ... but it still just doesn't seem quite right, does it? Do you think there is enough rubber on these tires?"

Gwen noticed a bit of apprehension in my questioning and said, "You know, I feel the same way. This plane weighs just less than seven thousand pounds dry. Throw in several hundred more pounds of fuel and cargo, and you have four to five tons of heavy metal, highly flammable fuel, and human cargo."

Somehow, I wasn't feeling any better after those comments. But then she added in a matter-of-fact tone, "But in the five thousand or so landings and takeoffs that I have performed, I have never once had a problem—none whatsoever. This is a great aircraft. There is nothing to worry about."

I went over and kicked the front tire on the landing gear before looking back at Gwen. "This plane passes my inspection. Are we ready to go?"

"Yes, sir," she replied. "Let me sign for the fuel, and we can take off. Go ahead and sit in the right seat, if you like, and strap yourself in. Some good company on the way back will be appreciated."

I said under my breath to myself, "Not sure how good the company will be." I looked around for the sick bag.

With those few instructions from Captain Gwen, I shimmied my way to the cabin and wiggled myself into the right seat. I hoped I hadn't hit a switch or moved a lever that would make us crash after takeoff. I heard the cabin door close and lock. A second later, Gwen appeared in the cockpit and swung around into her seat without any effort whatsoever.

She maneuvered her body like a hand slipping into a glove. She leaned over to me and said, "Are you ready to go, Captain?"

"I am," I replied. Gwen was a blur of switch flipping, wheel turning, and gadget gripping. Before I knew it, we were taxiing down the runway.

After a short conversation with someone in a tower somewhere, Captain Gwen throttled up the twin turboprops. We didn't even stop at the beginning of the runway to prepare for takeoff. It was more like rolling through a stop sign. The engines reached full throttle even before the nose of the plane was headed straight down the runway.

"Here we go," she said. "Put your hands on the yoke and follow along."

A few seconds later, it was wheels up, and off we went. Beaufort bound. I could only pray that it was going to be a smooth, uneventful flight. No river landings, please!

Gwen handed me some headphones, and when I got them on, she said, "We should be in Beaufort in about three hours or so." I gave her the thumbs-up as we climbed through the clouds in search of our cruising altitude.

The trip was pleasant. Gwen gave me a few flying lessons as I navigated the plane. We played a game of dodge the clouds to get the feel of how the plane handled. I had a death grip on the yoke, which Gwen quickly corrected.

She leaned over, placed her hand on mine, and said, "Not so firm. Pretend it is the cheek of your daughter or wife. Soft and gentle ... that is all that is needed." As the minutes turned into hours, my body, hands and mind gradually came to grips with just how easy it was to fly this plane. It actually calmed my nerves while we were in the air.

As we prepared to land, I was still in control of the airplane. We encountered a fairly strong crosswind as we approached earth and the only landing strip at what I thought would be the Beaufort Municipal Airport. While flying was fun and somewhat relaxing, all that fun was about to give way to sheer terror as we lined up for our approach.

Gwen insisted that I could land the plane. "You're a natural at this," she said.

"If you value your life, I hope you will retake control of this plane."

"Nonsense," she said. "You are doing great."

"The plane is sliding sideways, and I don't think it was meant to land that way."

"No, they aren't," she said with a laugh. "Here's a tip: as you drift in the wind, keep your eyes fixed on the runway ahead, the same way you would if your car were in a slide on an icy road. Keep your eyes fixed on where you want to go, not where you are pointed."

"Easy for you."

The closer to the ground we got, the more nervous I became. Just before I was about to beg Gwen to take the controls, she said, "Don't take your hands off the yoke. Just let them ride as we come in for our landing, so you can get the feel of how this works, just like on takeoff."

The plane was a bit sideways, and the flaps were in the down position as we approached the runway. And then, somehow, just before the wheels touched down, the plane was in perfect position for a smooth landing. Gwen reversed the engine thrust and slowed our pace very quickly. At that moment, I reached out and touched her forearm and said, "I don't have a clue how you did that or what you just did ... but thanks for a great flight."

"No problem, sir. That was fun, wasn't it?"

We taxied to a small building with several antennae sticking out of it. The older, run-down terminal building desperately needed an update. It was obviously not the Beaufort Municipal Airport. Gwen stopped the plane's engines. Then, as quickly and effortlessly as she had gotten into the cockpit, she disappeared to open the plane's rear cabin door. I crawled from the plane's cabin and emerged into the bright South Carolina sun. It was a wonderful 75 degrees and breezy. I thought I had arrived in heaven.

I stepped down from the ladder, my bags already on the tarmac waiting. I turned to Gwen and said, "Again, great flight. Thanks so much."

I extended my hand. She grabbed it with a firm grip and said, "You are very welcome."

Just as we let go from our handshake, Mr. Nathaniel Dillianquest emerged from the dilapidated building. "Mr. Grayson, I presume?" he inquired in his slow, southern drawl.

"Mr. Dillianquest," I replied. Nathaniel Dillianquest, whom I had recognized immediately from his file, was an unassuming man about six feet tall with grayish hair. He was not overweight but by no means thin. He was one of those men who would be difficult to describe, if one were asked by a police sketch artist to do so.

"Come, Tag," Nate instructed, "let me help you with your bags. How was your flight, my friend? Did Gwen let you drive?"

"As a matter of fact, she did," I said with a note of enthusiasm in my voice. I added with a laugh, "Quite the daredevil, letting me fly that darn thing, but what a great time I had! Of course, I can't speak for Gwen."

"Gwen, my dear," Nate said, "I trust your flight was uneventful."

"Yes, it was. Mr. Grayson here is a natural pilot. He did a great job flying, and we had a very uneventful flight indeed."

"Marvelous, just marvelous," Nate said. He added, "Gwen here is a wonderful pilot, is she not?"

"That she is," I said in an appreciative tone.

Gwen stood at the door of the plane, getting ready to take it to the hangar for the evening. At that point, Nate waved to Gwen, who returned the gesture and said, "Good afternoon, gentlemen. I will see you later."

Nate gestured to his right and said, "Come, I have a car waiting out back. What do you say we get started?"

"I'm game," I replied.

Nate walked over to where I was standing and picked up my travel bag.

"I'll follow your lead," I said as we headed around the building.

CHAPTER 5

A few experiences from my past bring a smile to my face when I get a chance to think about such things. I am not sure if the experiences were actually that great or if my mind has embellished upon them over the years, but either way, when I think about them, I always, without fail, get that smile on my face.

As a kid growing up in a very touristy town in northern Michigan, I was privileged enough to make friends with some wealthy kids who had summer homes on Torch Lake. Torch Lake drew that kind of family to its fresh, Caribbean-blue waters. Bob Wallick was one of those rich kids who ventured north every summer with his mother and siblings and spent the summer on Torch Lake. His dad came up from Detroit on the weekends. Most of the time, if not all the time, the young would grow restless and bored with the slow pace of summer life and would ultimately venture into town; that was how I met Bob.

Bob and I became fast summer friends, and when Bob got to be of driving age, his dad allowed him to take the family runabout out on Torch Lake. This family runabout was no ordinary boat, by the way. No, his dad kept a 1942 Chris Craft, 23 Triple Cockpit in the boathouse down on the lake. It was a thing of beauty. Torch Light, as it was called, was twenty-three feet of solid mahogany spit polished to a mirror finish. Torch Light cut through the water with the weight of a hot knife cutting through warm butter. It sounded as if someone were riding a Harley-Davidson underwater. It was a chick magnet. It was great!

When we cruised past the Dock Side Bar and Grill on Clam River, the outdoor patio would often erupt in applause at the sight of this piece of art. Summers in the 23 Triple Cockpit were very special. Somehow, some way, I told myself, I was going to own such a boat. Never let the dream die; there is always tomorrow.

My other orgasmic daydream was to own a vintage Chevy pickup truck. Not just any old Chevy truck would do. No, it had to be a fully restored Chevy pickup with a three-piece back window. Years ago, back in Ann Arbor, I had the bright idea of buying an old truck. I bought a 1960 Chevy for the bargain price of only five hundred dollars. That was all I could afford at the time. We fondly called her Old Blue. Every time you brushed up against the truck, it left a blue residue on your clothes or skin—hence the name.

I was the only one who could drive Old Blue, although everyone gave it the good old college try. A previous owner had put a Hurst three-speed transmission in it, which I was quite sure was not standard equipment in 1960. The shifter stuck up through the middle of the floorboard and had a white cue ball as the shifter handle. It was awesome.

It took a while to get used to driving Old Blue; it was a Zen-like process. You had to become one with the transmission. It was very loosely configured, and the gears seemed to play hide-and-seek from those Old Blue did not trust or like. It was actually a piece of shit, but I loved that old truck. I often left the keys in it just to see how far a thief would get before he abandoned her. No one ever tried to steal Old Blue.

Like I said, I think my mind had embellished the memories of my youth. But one day, I still told myself, I was going to drive to the lake in my classic truck, pulling my classic wooden boat. Never let the dream die; there is always tomorrow.

As Nate and I turned the corner and began walking, there I stood, face to face with a fully restored, bright red 1948 Ford pickup truck. I stopped in my tracks. I put my bags down and just stared at the truck. It was beautiful.

"Are you okay, Tag?" asked Nate, likely witnessing a look on my face that one might see only during an orgasm.

"Holy smoke, Nate," I blubbered. "This is gorgeous."

"Yes, it is," Nate said as a sheepish grin crept onto his face. "It is one of my favorites."

"One of your favorites would imply that you have more than this."

"You are very astute, Tag. I admit to being a bit of a collector. I actually have twelve cars in my collection, none of which are newer than 1967." You could tell he was very proud of his collection.

"Maybe we can include a tour of your collection while I am here?"

"Nothing would please me more. Would you care to drive while I navigate?" he asked as he tossed the key toward me.

"I would be most happy to." I caught the key, picked up my bag, placed it in back of the truck, and jumped in. I must have looked like a kid whose father had just let him take the car out without supervision for the first time.

As we left the airfield, I asked Nate about the facilities. "The airstrip is rather unpopulated," I noted. "This must not be the Beaufort Municipal Airport."

"Yes, Tag, you are correct, this is not the municipal airport. It is an alternative field—one used by crop dusters, mostly, and a few private plane owners. See that hanger over there?" he continued in his southern drawl. "That is where Gwen keeps her plane. She is a freelance pilot around these parts." He paused for just a couple of seconds then added, "She is very good at what she does ... and not too hard on the eyes, either, is she, Mr. Grayson?" He laughed loudly and then instructed, "Turn right on the other side of the fence. That road will take us into town." Nate was providing ample hand signals to go along with his directions. "Now, Tag, what would you like to do first? We can get you situated at your accommodations. If you are hungry, we can stop and have a bite to eat, or we can drive around a bit, so you can get the lay of the land—you know, get your bearings."

He paused for a moment, laughed again and said with a big smile, "Getting your bearings in this burg sure as hell won't take you long. The choice is yours, my friend. What'll it be?"

"It's been a while since I had breakfast; I could use some fuel to keep the engines running."

"Sure thing," Nate replied. "Just about three miles up this road, we are going to turn left into the Country Club of Beaufort. We can get lunch there."

"That sounds wonderful."

As we drove for a few more minutes, Nate announced points of interest—mostly tobacco-drying barns and fields and fields of what he called "brown cash." Tobacco was still king of the cash crops in some parts of South Carolina.

As we pulled up to the entrance to the Country Club of Beaufort, we were greeted by a young man who was opening my door just as the truck pulled to a stop.

"Good afternoon, sir," the valet said to me. Another valet opened the passenger side door and said, "Good to see you, Mr. Dillianquest. Your table is waiting."

"Thanks, boys," Nate said as he came around the front of the truck.

Nate threw his arm around my shoulders and pointed me up the grand, sloping, canopied walkway.

"Shall we?" he said and guided me toward the spectacular entryway of the Country Club of Beaufort, the name of which was carved in a large arch in the ornate wooden doors. "My father refurbished the club back in the fifties. We have been its custodians ever since. If something needs tending to, we take care of it … our family legacy."

"My family has had their fingers into just about everything that went on in Beaufort since after the war," Nate continued. "And by war, I mean the Civil War." As we got closer to the massive front doors, he leaned in close to my ear and added, "Those, sir, are the trappings I am trying to eliminate from my life."

Just as those words left his lips, the two very large, solid wooden doors opened, and a petite young woman greeted us.

"Good afternoon, Mr. Dillianquest. I have your table ready for you." We walked through a grand entryway full of pictures of those who had graced this hall with their presence: presidents, governors, senators, foreign dignitaries, movie stars, and a host of entertainers.

Nate stopped at one picture and said, "Elvis and me on the fifteenth hole. It was my first and only hole-in-one," he noted with pride, "and witnessed by the King himself. How cool is that?"

We entered a large dining room decorated in the grand southern style. I followed Nate and our young hostess over fine, plush, flowered carpeting to a large bank of floor-to-ceiling windows overlooking the eighteenth green. Ten or so tables had been arranged in the main dining area, the occupants of which all acknowledged Nate in one fashion or another. Nate was amazing. He greeted everyone he saw but never got bogged with personal conversation. He was a natural politician.

A young foursome just finishing a round of golf stood on the green, shaking hands with each other. They looked up, saw Nate as we walked by, and politely waved. Nate returned the gesture.

We kept walking until we came to another set of doors at the far end of the dining room. Another set of massive, hand-carved oak doors protected the room we were about to enter. As we walked through these incredible double doors, we entered into a smaller dining room enclosed with glass on three sides.

The room overlooked the first tee box of the Robert Trent Jones-designed golf course. You could see for miles looking out the windows. It was a magnificent sight. A tree-lined fairway, perfectly manicured, led the eye into a hazy vista of rolling, tree-filled hills. Nothing was out of place. It could have been an oil painting.

The tee box for the number-one hole was situated exactly in the middle of a south-facing wall of windows. Ten feet below and thirty feet in front of our vantage point, a foursome was gathering on the tee box. Standing and gazing through the window looking over the shoulder of the golfer on the tee box made me feel as if I were a baseball umpire, only on the golf course. The room's position overlooking the tee box gave me the sensation of hovering just behind and above the golfer without interfering with his game.

As a group readied themselves to begin play, I walked ever so quietly to the window, so as not to disturb them. Nate walked up beside me, placed his hand on my shoulder, and said, "Father had this room soundproofed, so anyone who was in here wouldn't bother the golfers. The windows have been treated with a nonreflective dark film, so the golfers cannot see inside." He added, "Father loved five things. He and his buddies would sit in this room for hours. They would drink, smoke cigars, play cards, and watch the club's golfers hit and then chase that little white ball all over the place. Tag," he said as he looked at me with a devilish smirk, "I will let you guess the fifth thing that Father loved to do."

Only one table was situated in the middle of the room. It had two place settings and was adorned with a huge bouquet of fresh-cut flowers. The table was situated directly under a very large, intricate chandelier that must have weighed a ton, if not two. It was almost too big for the room.

As I stood looking at the chandelier, Nate said, "That damn thing. The members had it sent from France years ago, sight unseen. This is where it ended up. I think one of the gents must have lost a bet or something."

A young man waited in the room, standing quietly in the corner. As we walked back toward the table, the hostess pulled my chair out for me and gestured for me to sit. The other waitperson in the room did the same for Mr. Dillianquest. The scotch had already been poured, waiting for the thirsty guests.

"I hope you don't mind, Tag—I took the liberty of ordering a couple of twenty-five-year-old single-malt Macallan. Cindy said you were a wee bit partial to scotch whiskey. I believe this will hit the spot."

As I held my glass up to toast, Nate said, "Here's looking at you." We both savored some of the finest scotch spirits man has ever bottled.

We sat and enjoyed a light meal and equally light conversation until Nate began to talk about his family. Nate cleared this throat, took another sip of Scotch, and said, "Tag, families are an interesting lot, are they not?"

"Indeed."

"The Dillianquest family has been in these parts for many, many years. My great-great-grandpappy, as we like to say in the South, Theodore Dillianquest, helped found this place now referred to as Beaufort. He fought in the Waxhaw Massacre during the American Revolution way back in 1780, in Lancaster County.

"Not many people know that atrocity, Tag," Nate continued. "You will notice a small plaque and a monument across the street from the entryway to Dillianquest. Our family and a not-so-memorable governor dedicated that spot of land to those gents who lost their lives in that massacre." He added, "Our family lost a brave soul in that disgrace."

"Was Theodore Dillianquest one of those who lost his life in that massacre?" I inquired, assuming that he had been.

"No, he was not." Nate smiled. "He made it out alive and escaped capture from those bluecoat devils."

Nate continued his history lesson in that southern drawl that I was becoming very fond of. "History tells a story of a British colonel named Banastre Tarleton. The story goes that Tarleton's loyalist troops marched directly past the Second South Carolina Detachment's white flag of surrender and began slaughtering many of those who opposed his advance."

Nate paused to take another sip and then added, "The story has it that Tarleton's troops believed that the colonel had been shot and killed by the American rebels." He paused for effect and added, "Thinking their leader dead, the troops engaged in a vindictive asperity not easily restrained, hacking those who surrendered to pieces with their sabers. The American rebels lost 113 brave souls that day."

I took a sip of Scotch to avoid having to say anything and gazed out the window for a few seconds. Nate added, "In an odd twist to that story, my great-great-grandfather married the daughter of the colonel. Love cannot be denied. My great-great-grandfather began the family fortune in the slave-trading business."

"Well, Nate, your family is not short on interesting history."

To that, he replied, "My good sir, you don't know the half of it. Would you care for another scotch, or would you prefer to get settled?"

"You know, Nate, after a quick tour through town and a peek at Dillianquest, I wouldn't mind getting settled a bit before it gets too late."

"As you wish," he replied. "As you wish."

As we left the country club's front entrance, I saw that Nate's truck awaited our arrival. Both doors stood open, and the engine was running.

As we approached, a young man inquired, "Will there be anything else, Mr. Dillianquest?"

"No, thank you, lad." Nate reached in his pocket and gave the young man a tip for his service. "Tag, do you care to continue to drive?" Nate inquired.

"No, thanks. I think I will let you do the driving. I can't tell you how much I appreciated you allowing me to drive this fine vehicle. This is wonderful treat for me."

We drove down the long, tree-lined drive with overhanging limbs that made me feel as if we were driving through a leaf-lined tunnel.

I had the feeling that there was a more to Nate's story. "Nate," I said in an effort to prod him along, "your family has quite the colorful history."

"Yes, sir, it does. That is partially why I am exploring the Dillianquest sale," he added. I knew there was something more to the situation.

We drove for a few miles in silence. I could tell Nate was thinking about something, and I did not want to disturb his thoughts. Along the way, we came upon a large construction project that was, for all intents and purposes, at a standstill.

"Tag," he said, "this is another reason." He pointed to the abandoned and now quiet construction site.

A large sign on the property read, "Another Quality Dillianquest Construction Project."

"The country's current economic situation," he said with sigh, "has had a devastating effect on the family businesses. I have had to close too many projects and lay too many friends off. And that," he said thoughtfully, "has taken a heavy toll on my heart."

We were coming into Beaufort from the northeast side of town, looking to cross the intercoastal waterway on the Highway 21 Bridge. As we passed through Ladies Island, it struck me just how much water surrounded this area.

"Nate, this is a beautiful area. I would have never guessed that there would be this much water."

"Yes," he said, "as the old saying goes, water, water all around, but not a drop to drink. All these eddies, inlets, and marshes are saltwater. Have you spent much time around saltwater, Tag?"

"No," I replied. "I have been a freshwater kind of guy all my life."

"There is much work associated with saltwater, Tag. At the end of every outing, you have to wash and scrub everything. The ocean is a formidable foe—one you do not want to test."

We snaked our way to the Highway 21 Bridge, which took us right into downtown Beaufort. Beaufort was a spectacular small town with parks and walkways that filled the water's edge.

"Some years ago," I began to explain to Nate, "we docked a fifty-two-foot Carver right there at this very spot, and if I recall correctly, there was a festival of sorts taking place at this park."

"Could very well be, Tag. We surely do like our festivals here in Beaufort. Hell, seems like there is a festival every weekend in the summer."

"We had a wonderful time here," I recalled fondly. "Very nice place, Beaufort is. We were on our way to Bohicket, just south of Charleston," I said in an approving voice. "This town reminds me of Saugatuck, Michigan."

"Bohicket Marina? You don't say. A very good friend of mine, John Gilbert, owns that little piece of paradise."

Beaufort was a typical small southern town with walkways edging the abundant waterways. Seemingly every house had a big, sprawling front porch with ceiling swings floating in the ocean breeze. Long, flowing willow branches brushed their fingers along the shores of the water's edge. Each limb hung low, with Spanish moss clinging on for dear life. Kids filled the parks, while mothers strolled with babies in carriages and dogs ran close by. Beaufort was picture-perfect.

After a short tour of downtown, we took a left onto King Street and headed south on Highway 281. Nate turned to me and said, "Dillianquest is just a couple of miles down this road on the left, exactly one mile south of Beaufort Memorial Hospital—and yes, we built the hospital, too."

"Good to know," I said. "Where do you recommend I stay?"

"We are on our way to your accommodations, Tag—just a couple of minutes from here, near Dillianquest."

"Sounds good," I said.

"Here is the entryway to Dillianquest now."

"Very nice," I said. Nate slowed down, and we crept by the long, elegant driveway.

"Very nice, indeed!" I said again. The property was lined with a white three-rail fence that seemed to go on forever in both directions. At the entryway were two towering stone pillars that supported an enormous black iron gate that was in the open position. Above the entryway, spanning the distance between the two stone pillars was the name "Dillianquest," scrolled in black iron letters that appeared to stand ten feet tall.

Looking past the entryway, the drive was lined with magnificent, large-leafed magnolia trees, each supporting thousands of huge, white blooms. I felt as if I were looking into a dark tunnel randomly spattered with white dots. As we passed the drive, Nate said, "At night, the lane is lined with accent lights for added dramatic effect." He added with just a hint of sarcasm, "If nothing else, Mother is known for her dramatic effect."

We picked up just a hint of speed along the endless white fence. Before we got to the end of the fence, I noticed that Nate turned on his left blinker. As he slowed, he said, "And here is your accommodation, Tag." We pulled into a driveway that must have been two hundred yards long.

We wound our way through dozens of oak trees that seemed to be hundreds of feet tall and just as many years old. Nate turned to me and said, "This was my grandfather's home at one point. We converted it into a guest cottage. I thought you might like it better than the Holiday Inn."

We passed a large koi pond, skirted around several flower beds, and finally came to rest at the front door.

"Nate," I said, "I do not want you to misunderstand what I am about to say, but you did not have to go through all this trouble on my account. The Holiday Inn would have been just fine."

"Nonsense," Nate said forcefully. "No guest of mine stays at the Holiday Inn. Now, let's get your bag, and allow me to show you your quarters."

With that said, I opened my door, went to the back of the truck, and lifted my bag out from the truck's bed. Bag in hand, I followed Nate into the cottage.

As I expected, Nate's grandfather's house was full of antiques from floor to ceiling.

"Wow," I said as I walked through the foyer. "This is beautiful, Nate. Just beautiful."

"Thank you, and please make yourself at home. I think you will find everything you need is here. Just help yourself to whatever, and make yourself comfortable."

Nate walked into the study to an antique buffet that appeared to be watched over by a large white-tailed deer mounted on the wall. A serving tray sat on top of the buffet, and without lifting his head from his duties, Nate said, "If you don't mind, I will pour us a taste of scotch to drain the dust from these here pipes." He deliberately stroked his throat and laughed. Then, turning and addressing me, Nate said, "To your right is the master suite. Please throw your bag on the bed and join me, won't you?"

I returned to where Nate was stationed in the great room. He was standing in front of a row of windows that overlooked the intercoastal waterway.

"It is a scrumptious view," Nate said as he handed me my drink.

"That it is," I replied.

"Okay, here is the twenty-five-cent tour. We can do it without moving from this spot," he said. "Yes, how quaint."

He chose a remote control from the coffee table in front of an overstuffed leather couch. "Press this button," Nate explained, "and from the top of that large console over there, you will see a fifty-inch flat screen. You can watch the news or whatnot." He continued, "Press this button for the surround sound, and these buttons to change the channels." He paused and said, "Oh, hell, you can figure the TV out on your own, I am sure.

"Over there is the kitchen," Nate said. "You are familiar with kitchen operations, are you not?"

"Intimately."

"Good," he said. "You'll find crème brûlée creamer in the fridge, alongside the coffee and other items."

"Crème brûleé?" I said in a rather astonished tone.

"Yes, that Cindy of yours is remarkable," Nate observed.

"Yes," I said. "Yes, she is."

"Towels and everything you will need are in the master bathroom," he added. "There is a steam shower, if you are so inclined." He paused for a second and motioned for me to follow him to a screened-in porch. "If you just want to relax and read a bit more about me or the Dillianquest family, this is a great spot for catching up." He moved his hands in a gentle circular motion. "The view is quite lovely as well.

"Tag, I will leave you to your devices. There is Internet access at the base of this lamp if you have to plug in, or we have wireless here as well. " He paused as he looked at his watch. "It is four thirty now," he said as he took the last sip from his glass. "I'll be back by about seven thirty to pick you up for dinner." He added in an almost embarrassed tone, "That is … assuming that you would like to go to dinner this evening?"

"I just happened to be free this evening," I said with a smile.

"Great," he said. "It was a pleasure today, sir. I am looking forward to getting better acquainted with you." He extended his hand, and after a firm handshake, he headed toward the door.

"The pleasure was mine, Nate. I will see you at seven thirty."

With a wave of his hand, Nate was out the door.

I collapsed on the rattan porch furniture, took out my phone, and dialed the office to check in for the day. Everything was good—everywhere.

CHAPTER 6

At seven thirty sharp, I heard the rumble of a car driving up to the front of the cottage. I was in the master bath, putting on the finishing touches after what had been a very relaxing steam. As I pulled a comb through my hair one final time, I heard three distinct knocks on the door.

"Come on in," I called as I approached the door. I turned the handle on the door, and on the other side was Nate with a small brown paper sack in his hands.

Nate was dressed in light brown khakis and a vertically striped print Tommy Bahamas shirt. His salt-and-pepper hair was a mess as he ran his fingers through it, brushing it back, trying to get it back under control. He wore the obligatory deck shoes without socks. He looked as though he had just walked off a Caribbean cruise ship.

"Brought a bit more Macallan, just in case you happen to run dry," Nate said as he walked past me on his way to the buffet, where such things were stored. I did not say anything, as I was transfixed on the automobile that Nate had parked in front of the cottage.

Standing and staring out the front door, I said, "I must say, you have exquisite taste in cars."

"Why, thank you," he said, smiling. "The keys are in it, if you care to take a quick spin before dinner."

"That is a generous offer," I said. "I think I will pass on the spin, but I sure would love to hear more about the car."

"Absolutely," Nate agreed as he passed by me again this time, headed in the other direction. "Here," he said as he handed me a tumbler of scotch. I was still standing in the doorway, gawking at his car. "This is a delightful vehicle," Nate explained with great pride, "a 1953 Corvette—the original American muscle car, Tag. This car and those like it have a glorious history," he added, drawing every bit of energy out of each word.

"Did you know that the Corvette got its humble beginnings in the back of a delivery garage in Flint, Michigan? Quite near your home, Tag," Nate continued, swelling with pride. "The boys at General Motors only built fifteen automobiles there. Each one of those magnificent fifteen automobiles were crafted by hand by some of the finest, most skilled autoworkers anywhere. Their first year of full production yielded only three hundred ... and you are looking at one of only two hundred and twenty-five that are left in existence today."

Nate casually walked from the front of the car to back of the car and said in that southern drawl, "Back in 1953, you could get this car in any color you liked." Then, after a long pause, he added, "Just as long as it was Polo White."

We laughed at his joke. We both recalled stories from our grandparents when a Ford motorcar, back when Ford began mass-producing cars, was available in any color you liked ... as long as it was black.

"Yep," Nate continued, "Polo White, with red interior and black canvas top, just as she sits in front of you, is all this car came in. This car sold, brand spanking new, right off the showroom floor, for a mere $3,498. I guess in 1953, that was a handsome sum of money for a two-seat car with no trunk space." His grin broadened. "Now you could easily pay a quarter of a million dollars or more for an automobile such as this," he added as he ran his hand over the smooth exterior from back to front.

"Let's take a peek under the hood, shall we?" Nate said as he strolled to the front of the car. With the ease of a skilled mechanic, Nate popped the hood open. On display was the cleanest engine I had ever laid my eyes on. It was painted blue.

"That, Tag, is the Blue Flame: a six-cylinder, one-hundred-five horsepower engine that, in its original form, was not so sporty. Seems like the boys at GM back in the 1950s were reluctant to share their V-8 powertrain technology with anyone. Over time, a few modifications were made to the Blue Flame, but the one you see before you is exactly as it was when it rolled off the production line on August 18, 1953."

"Impressive," I said. "Very impressive."

"Yes, Tag," Nate said thoughtfully. "Jump in, and get the feeling of this machine."

"Certainly," I replied as I crawled into the driver compartment and placed both hands on the oversized steering wheel, fantasizing about what it would be like to speed down the highway with the wind in my hair.

"Automobiles lend themselves nicely to the re-creation of wonderful memories, don't they?" Nate asked fondly. "Everyone has great memories about their first car, their first accident ... or their first piece of ass in the back seat of their first car." Nate laughed and said, "You'll have to excuse my vulgarity, but believe it or not, I lost my virginity in this car. Can you imagine that? Well, it wasn't really in the car, so much as it was on the hood of the car."

Again he laughed out loud. I could not help but join him, as he had a very contagious laugh.

"Excuse me for a moment, Tag, won't you?" he said, still laughing a bit. He leaned forward and opened the glove box. He reached in the dark hole, stopped for a second, looked at me, and asked, "Care for a cigar? They are very good Cuban cigars. Milder than most, these won't make your head spin!" He laughed again as he got out of the car. "Sure you don't want to take her for a spin?"

"Nothing I would like more," I said. "But drinking and driving is not the smartest thing a man can do these days." After a short pause, I added, "Especially in a car like this."

"Correct you are, sir. Correct you are. That is good advice that everyone should adhere to: one should always stop the car if one is going to drink."

Nate and I burst into simultaneous laughter.

"Now, about that cigar?" Nate asked. He quickly pulled from his cigar case two Cuban cigars and a cigar cutter. "Off with the ends. Here you go."

He handed me a cigar. He foraged about in his front pocket and produced a lighter. I focused on the blue flame that shot out of the lighter, which looked and sounded more like a jet engine than a lighter. Nate rolled the cigar in his fingers as the flame ignited the tightly rolled tobacco. Soon, smoke was wafting into the air. Nate placed the cigar gently in between his lips and began to draw smoke into his mouth. He blew the blue cigar smoke back into the air, and the smoke drifted away.

"These are wonderfully horrible things," Nate said with a smile as he handed me his lighter. I performed the cigar lighting ritual just as Nate had. The smoke rolled from my lips and disappeared into the gentle breeze that caressed this wonderfully perfect cottage of a house.

We walked about the car one more time. I was in awe of this car.

"This is the life, eh, Tag?" Nate said as he looked at me. "Fine scotch, fine cars, and fine cigars. Now, what do you say we get us some fine food to top off the evening?"

"That sounds just about perfect," I said. "Where did you have in mind?"

"Follow me, Tag. First things first," Nate said as he walked toward the house. "I need a bit of a refresher on this scotch. How about you?" Nate did not stop and wait for me to answer his question. He walked straight through the door and headed directly for the buffet.

I followed Nate into the house and over to the buffet, where he was already dropping a few ice cubes into his empty tumbler. Nate grabbed a couple of extra cubes in his tongs and held them out over an imaginary glass. I guessed that was my cue to place my glass directly under the tongs, which I did, and Nate let the cubes fall. Quickly, Nate took the scotch snifter in one hand and poured a tall one for himself. He motioned for me to offer up my glass, which I did, and he poured an equally large amount for me.

"You know, Nate, I am not comfortable drinking and driving," I said.

Nate looked at me thoughtfully and replied, "An astute friend of mine once said, and I quote, 'Drinking and driving is not the smartest thing a man could do these days' … and frankly, my dear friend, I couldn't agree more with that sentiment." Nate began walking toward the porch and said, "Now come, sir. Please, follow me."

We left the house through the door on the screened-in porch. We walked down a short cobblestone path and came to a small, single-car garage tucked in a small grove of lilac bushes. Their aroma was wonderful. The blooms were full and colorful.

Nate pulled on the double doors of the garage, and they opened effortlessly. Nate walked into the dark garage and disappeared from sight for just a second. Then, with the flick of a switch, there was light and there was Nate, standing next to a jet-black golf cart in the form of a H2 Hummer.

"Jump in," Nate said. "Are you comfortable if we drink and drive in this?" He laughed out loud. "Dinner is just over that hill. It won't take us but a few minutes in this." He added fondly, "When I was a kid, Grandfather's place was the best place on earth. My grandfather was a man's man, tough as nails. He took me fishing, hunting … It was a great place to grow up." There was an awkward pause. I could feel that Nate was going to add something to his last thought. "He was more of a father to me than my father was," he added. "He was a good man."

We had been driving for a few minutes when I asked, "Is all of this part of Dillianquest?"

"Depends," Nate replied. "Depends if the buyer wants it or not." Nate stopped the golf cart on a small rise just about one hundred yards away from the intercoastal and added, "If I had my druthers, Tag, I would sell the entire hundred acres—all of the buildings, everything, including Grandfather's cottage. Lock, stock and barrel. But that is not my call, now is it?"

"Well, while we are here," I said, "from where to where does the property extend?"

Nate leaned forward, both arms folded over the top of the steering wheel. He looked to his right up the waterway, paused for a moment, and then turned his head downriver. Nate then pointed to his right and politely replied, "From as far as you can see that way …" He changed direction, pointing to his left, and added, "to as far as you can see the other way … and then some." He paused for a long while. "One hundred acres is a pretty fair chunk of land, Tag."

"Indeed," I said as I took in what had just been laid out to me in very non-legally-binding land terms.

"This one-hundred-acre parcel has quite an upside, from a real-estate perspective, that has yet to be tapped. When better times arrive, there is a ton of money to be made right here on this very spot." Nate paused for a minute and then added, "Location, location, location."

He was right.

Nate sat back in his seat, picked up his tumbler from the cupholder, and held it up as if he intended to propose a toast. I reached forward and took mine from the holder closest to me. We clicked our tumblers together. Nate looked at me, smiled, and toasted, "Happy endings to an auspicious beginning."

"Hear, hear," I replied. We both sipped on that fine Scottish nectar. Nate sat back in the driver's seat and took a big draw on his cigar. He savored the flavor and aroma and then blew the smoke away from us, downwind.

We sat on the hill for a few more minutes. The evening was shaping up rather nicely. It was warm, with a gentle breeze blowing directly into our faces. Our view was that of the intercoastal waterway. A few boats navigated the water in front of us, unaware that we were even alive. Across the intercoastal waterway from the Dillianquest property was protected wetlands. Tall grasses gently waved in the breeze, back and forth. Several long-necked birds that looked like large herons or egrets waded in the shallows, hunting food. Then, from my left, emerged a quirky line of pelicans gliding just inches above the water. That was a rare sight for a Michigan boy. Dillianquest was a pretty special place.

Nate lifted his foot from the brake, and we began to creep forward ever so slightly. "Pretty spectacular, is it not?" Nate questioned.

"Yes, it is," I replied. I was almost in a trance. I could have sat there for hours.

"Well," Nate said, "We can't dillydally too long. We have reservations for eight fifteen." We continued on our way.

We wove our way down the hill and ended at what appeared to be a small, unmanned marina. A long dock spanned the fronts of ten slips. Only one boat was moored to the dock.

"Let me guess," I said, "this boat is where we are having dinner?"

I asked. Actually, boat is not an accurate term to describe what I was looking at.

"Yes," Nate said, "The *Kindred Spirit* will be our hostess this evening." The *Kindred Spirit* was a sixty-one-foot Hatteras cruising motor yacht. When we arrived and departed our golf cart, we walked to the boat, which was moored aft, facing the dock. A small set of stairs leading to the aft entryway, where the door was already open for us, splitting the name *Kindred Spirit* in two.

"Welcome aboard," Nate said invitingly. "Watch your step. That first step can be a doozy."

Just as I landed safely on the back deck of the lower level, I heard what sounded like a familiar voice say, "Welcome aboard, gentlemen. I will be with you in just one moment."

Nate looked at me and said, "That is our able-bodied captain." As we entered the main salon through the sliding door I noticed a long set of slender, dark legs sporting a short tight skirt descending the stairs from the upper level.

"How are you this evening, Mr. Dillianquest?" the captain inquired.

"Just fine, Gwen, and yourself?"

"Couldn't be better."

Not letting two seconds pass, Nate asked, "You remember Mr. Grayson, don't you, Gwen?"

"Of course I do. Good evening, Mr. Grayson," Gwen stated in a matter-of-fact tone. "It is good to see you again. Can I get you gentlemen a drink?"

I must have looked rather stunned, as Nate added, "Gwen here is a very valuable asset to our little community. Several business acquaintances here in Beaufort use her services on a regular basis. Isn't that correct, Gwen?"

Gwen was behind the bar, pouring scotch into two crystal tumblers. She emerged with one glass in each hand. The first glass went to me, and the second went to Nate. "Yes," Gwen said to answer the question. "I am kept very busy."

I looked at Gwen. I really should say I stared at Gwen. She was wearing a short, black, skin-tight skirt and white silk blouse with an epaulet on each shoulder. Each epaulet was graced with three black bars. Her blouse was unbuttoned just enough to ignite the imagination about what lay beneath. I could barely make out the beginnings of her voluptuous cleavage. I forced myself not to stare. I don't think I was doing a very good job, though.

Her hair was pulled back, as it had been earlier in the day, tight to her temple, with a long, flowing ponytail hanging over her right shoulder, exposing very large silver hoop earrings. Her fragrance was a cross between that of a fresh melon and lilac.

I thought to myself, *Just what I need—more mind-numbing alcohol.*

"Are you going to join us?" I asked.

"Thanks, but no thanks. Not while working."

Nate interjected, "Looks like it's just you and me, Tag."

"That works, too," I said. "Do we have time for a quick tour?"

"My pleasure, Tag," Nate said. "Allow me to bring you up to date on the *Kindred Spirit.*"

Just then, Gwen said, "If you will excuse me, I will ready the *Kindred Spirit* for departure."

"Splendid, Gwen," Nate replied, and Gwen disappeared to get the *Kindred Spirit* ready to sail.

"Nate, let me to ask you a question," I said.

"Certainly," Nate said inquisitively. "Fire away."

"Okay, here it is. When you are talking to people about the *Kindred Spirit*, how do you refer to her? Do you refer to her as a motor yacht? A ship? A boat?"

Nate took a sip of his scotch and said, "I call a duck a duck, and a goose a goose. I also call boat a boat. Some folks actually become a tad offended if you don't call their boat a motor yacht. For me, it's a boat, plain and simple."

"That makes sense," I said. "Simple. I like that."

Nate walked to the stairway that led down to the lower level. "There are four berths downstairs. The forward cabin is the master suite. There are guest suites, one on either side of the hallway and one in the aft along with the engine room. All are fully equipped, if you know what I mean, and quite lovely." He beamed. "Please feel free to explore as you desire. The main deck," Nate explained, "where we are now, houses the main salon, bar, and sitting room in the aft area."

Nate was gesturing with his free hand the entire time he was explaining the whereabouts of all the different rooms. "We also have a fully stocked galley forward, with all the amenities.

"A most unique feature of this particular Hatteras," he continued, "is the ability to captain the boat from inside, close to the galley." Nate motioned for me to follow. We left the salon area, walked past the bar, and entered the galley. "Just off to the right of the galley," he noted, "is a full set of controls and helm. In case of inclement weather, one is able to maintain full control of this vessel from the comfort"—he walked over to and opened the refrigerator door—"and convenience of the galley." He laughed.

"Father loved to chew on pickled pig's knuckles for some strange reason," Nate added with a grimace and a sour face. "Said it was a delicacy … used to make me very ill, Tag, very ill to watch a man suck on pig's feet."

Nate continued his story as we walked back into the salon. "Father bought this vessel right from the factory in 1969, up in Cape Hatteras, North Carolina. He would often say that it was one of the best days of his life: captaining his boat, family in tow, down the intercoastal and mooring it at its new home. He was a very prideful man, my father." With a note of fondness in his voice, Nate added, "The *Kindred Spirit* has been in the family ever since. This is, without a doubt, my father's most beloved acquisition. Our family spent many an evening toiling away the hours playing Scrabble, Monopoly, or Father's favorite game, seven-card stud poker, right here in this salon.

"Come, Tag," Nate said, "let me refresh your drink, and then we will poke around on the fly bridge."

"Wonderful," I said as I handed Nate my drink glass.

"More of the same?"

"More of the same."

Nate handed me my drink, full to the brim with twenty-five-year-old scotch. He walked past me with a small wave of the hand. I followed Nate up the stairs that led directly onto the bridge.

"This is where Gwen works her magic," Nate said. "Gwen, my dear," he called in a fond voice, "please tell Tag here about your bridge."

"Gladly," Gwen replied. Gwen was at the back of the bridge deck in a very generous seating area with a round teak table that seated six comfortably. In the middle of this beautiful teak table was a very large vase of cut flowers. On the perimeter of the table were place settings for two. At each setting, Gwen was readying a large portion of shrimp cocktail. The appointments throughout the motor yacht were exceptional, as one would imagine.

Gwen sauntered elegantly toward the two of us.

"I will wait for you in the aft and enjoy what is left of this fine cigar," Nate said with an obvious smile in his voice.

"Tag," Gwen began in a sexy, low voice with a slight southern accent, "this vessel is equipped with all the latest navigational equipment." She walked the few steps around the back of the captain's chair and said, "Starting from the starboard side is the JRC satellite communications and global positioning system. Next to the GPS are the Panasonic telephone and intercom systems," she added. "If you get bored, Tag, I won't be offended."

"No, I am very interested." Truth be told, I was more interested in being as close to this stunningly beautiful woman for as long as I could be. I did not want the tour to end. I hoped I wasn't too obvious. I added, "This equipment appears to be very complicated."

"It can be." Without missing a beat, she added, "This bank of screens contains our radar systems. We can reach out 150 miles and get a clear picture of the weather patterns that will affect our travel."

"Impressive," I said. The equipment truly was—and so was she.

"Engine controls, autopilot, rudder indicator," she said as she swept her hand across each piece of equipment. She kept on adding to the list: "Compasses, depth sounders, radar repeater."

"Wow," I said in true amazement.

Then Gwen added, "The *Kindred Spirit* is powered by twin 650-horsepower Detroit Diesel power plants capable of sustaining a 21-knot cruising speed for hours on end. She holds 2,150 gallons of fuel and can usually get anywhere one desires," she said as she finished my tour.

"Very impressive, indeed," I said. "Does it take much to maintain a vessel of this quality?"

"I am certified in diesel-engine repair and can fix any piece of equipment this ship utilizes. We are seaworthy at the drop of a hat."

"Beautiful and mechanically inclined," I said. "That is a very interesting combination of talent."

"Why, thank you, Tag. May I refresh your drink?"

"No … thank you," I said. I felt my face flush.

My expression must have seemed half bewildered and half love struck, something more fitting for a teenager, as I asked, "How did you get to be so accomplished?"

Just then Nate summoned me from the lounge area at the back of the boat, where he sat with his feet propped up, puffing on his cigar. "Tag, come, sit. Let's eat some of this wonderful shrimp. I had it catered from a great little crab shack the locals love, the Ocean Side Shanty.

"Gwen," Nate asked in a commanding voice, "is William on board yet?"

"Yes, I believe he is."

"Great. What do you say we take Mr. Grayson on a tour of our lovely seaside town? Have William tend to the mooring lines, will you?"

"Right away," Gwen replied. She started the engines and then disappeared from the bridge.

"Can I interest you in a glass of ice wine?" Nate inquired.

"Ice wine? I am not familiar with ice wine."

"Ah, ye … ice wine. It is a most delicate treat," Nate said in a tone that was soft and caring. "I only indulge once in a great while, Tag—only on very special occasions and only with very special guests."

Nate reached toward an ornately carved wooden wine stand directly to his right. He removed a snow-white towel that had hidden the slender half bottle from sight. The cork had already been removed and had been gently replaced. Nate grasped the bottle loosely by the neck and carefully removed the bottle as if it were a bottle of nitroglycerin. He gazed at the bottle as it slowly made its way up from its resting place.

After the bottle cleared its holder, Nate gently dried its exterior with the white towel draped across the bottle's neck. He then wrapped the bottle with the towel, allowing just a few inches of the glass neck to protrude.

He looked at me and said, "Ice wine … nectar of the gods."

Two very small, long-stemmed liqueur glasses stood at the foot of the vase full of cut flowers. Nate took both glasses by their stems and set them down in front of him. He stood, and as he did, he grasped the bottle of wine. He poured each glass three quarters full.

I stood, not knowing what else to do. As I did, he offered one of the glasses to me. I took the wine glass, raised it, and said, "To an incredible evening, to an incredible host, and to incredible talent." We touched our glasses together and sipped Nate's ice wine. Nate nodded in approval and winked.

"Tag," Nate said as we stood looking at each other, "this is a 2000 Royal DeMaria chardonnay. Only sixty bottles of this fine ice wine were produced. They call it ice wine because the grapes are picked only after they have been frozen the on the vine. It is extraordinarily labor-intensive to produce. We are lucky this evening to share your toast. I hope we can do a little business, so I can afford to pay for this." He laughed out loud and said, "Sit, please—enjoy the shrimp. Enjoy the wine."

Just then, Gwen reappeared on the bridge and took her rightful place in the captain's chair. We moved away from the dock. It seemed so effortless and carefree. *I could get accustomed to this*, I thought. We ate the shrimp and made small talk for what seemed like an hour. William was in and out, bringing more food and taking away what needed to be taken away. We dined on a fabulous meal of fresh seafood. Nate could not have been a better host.

Just as the boat began to pass the downtown area of Beaufort, Nate said, "Let me pull this canvas back, so we can get the full effect of our beautiful little town. Gwen," Nate said, "would you be so kind?" Just as Nate finished his sentence, the canvas that surrounded the entire aft area began to move. Shortly, the canvas disappeared out of our line of sight.

"Pretty neat trick," I said.

"Yes, Father had lots of bells and whistles installed. He was a man who enjoyed the finer things in life."

"And you, Nate?" I said. "What about you?"

With a lighted Beaufort as a backdrop, Nate paused for a second and said, "How about a cigar and a scotch, Tag?" He stood and stretched for a moment before wandering over to a small bar that had been hidden from sight behind two mahogany doors.

Nate poured two glasses of scotch, reached into a cigar box, cut off the cigar tips, and lit both cigars. He closed the doors to the bar, picked up both cigars, and walked directly over to where I was standing and enjoying the lights of Beaufort.

He then answered my question: "Me? I just grew up that way."

We were both drinking in the cityscape when Nate broke the silence. "How about you, Tag? You've seen my life. Now, what about you?"

"Me? I'm just a working stiff who just happens to have a great job."

Nate laughed. "Come," he said. "Have a seat. Let's talk.

"Your research probably did not disclose the fact that I am the last Dillianquest," Nate said in a matter-of-fact tone. "My family has been in these parts for a couple of hundred years or better. The Dillianquest family fortune was made like many other early family fortunes were: on the backs of others." Nate's tone had turned somber. "Back before the war, the Dillianquests were slave traders. During Prohibition, the Dillianquests were bootleggers, and most recently, my father was a noted gambler and womanizer. Cards and real estate were his vices of choice." Nate added, "Mother was a church person who just looked the other way and turned the other cheek.

"The Dillianquest family fortune," Nate continued softly, "has its secrets and obligations—secrets that are a burden I no longer want to bear and obligations, my friend, that I no longer desire to keep."

Just as Nate finished that sentence, I heard the rumble of the engines. "We will be docking in just a couple of minutes," Gwen announced.

"Come, let's see if we can get in young William's way while he ties up the boat."

"Of course. I am right behind you."

A small whirlwind of activity ensued, mostly done by Nate and William. Nate threw lines to William while he secured the boat to the dock, careful to leave enough slack in the lines to allow for the ebb and flow of the tide. Out came the bumpers, slung low alongside the boat so the *Kindred Spirit* would not rub against the dock. I mostly stood and watched. Nate was a blur of activity.

When the boat was finally secured, Nate looked up at me and said, "You're a natural sailor, aren't you?"

I shook my head in agreement and laughed.

As we stood on the dock, admiring the *Kindred Spirit*, Gwen appeared on the upper aft deck. Nate and I turned and looked up at her, and Nate said, "Splendid job, my dear."

I chimed in and said, "Yes, Gwen, very nice. Thank you for a wonderful cruise." We waved to her as we exited the dock and drove off in the H2 Hummer golf cart.

We drove through the South Carolina evening on our way back to Nate's grandfather's cottage, my home away from home. When we arrived, I exited the Hummer and said to Nate, "Thanks for a very memorable day and evening."

"My pleasure. There is just one more thing."

"What is that?"

Nate looked at me and said, "Follow me." I followed Nate around the side of the house.

We stopped at the garage attached to the house. Nate entered a code into the garage's exterior door. In a couple of seconds, the door began to open.

"What is this?" I asked Nate.

"If you are going to be with us for a few days, I would guess you would appreciate an automobile for your usage. I cannot see you as one who would prefer to hitchhike about town."

Parked in the garage was a 1964 black-on-black GTO with red pinstripes down the entire length of the car, from front to back.

"It's got a 389 under the hood and a four-speed manual floor shifter," Nate said. "Can you handle that?"

"Wow, Nate. I am speechless."

"Just be careful. She has a lot of spunk."

"I will, and thank you so much. That is very generous of you."

"My cell and office numbers are by the phone, on the business card I left for you. Call me if you need anything—anything at all." Nate began to walk toward the car he had parked at the front of the house and said without turning around, "Good night, Tag. We will talk when you are ready."

Nate slipped into the night. I watched as the taillights of his car zigzagged their way out of the driveway. I could hear the throaty sound of his Corvette disappear into the quiet of the night.

What a day!

I called Sam to check in and see how the kids were doing. Everything was fine. I was glad.

CHAPTER 7

I had set my alarm for 5:30 a.m. so I could get a run in before logging on to the computer. It was now seven fifteen. I had been hitting the snooze button for a while with good intentions of getting up and getting going. I wasn't feeling that chipper. It was slow start to the morning.

I finally mustered enough energy to sit myself up on the side of the bed. I sat there for a while with head in hands. Then I stood up, rather shakily, and stretched for a few minutes in an attempt to get the blood flowing. My mouth felt as though I had eaten a small cotton plantation the evening before. Oddly, though, I could smell the faint aroma of fresh-brewed coffee in the morning air. I did not remember making coffee—or anything else, for that matter—before I went to bed. The smell of coffee meant there was some hope for the rest of the day. *I really should quit drinking!*

As I began the short trip from the bedroom to the kitchen, I noticed the flat screen was in full view. On the screen was a blinking cursor that caught my attention. It led my eye to a message: *Please press enter on the remote control to continue.* After a few seconds of searching for the remote control, I found it on the coffee table in front of the couch. I picked up the remote, pointed it at the TV, and pressed enter, just as I had been instructed to do.

As soon as I pressed enter, the screen went blank, and another message popped up. *Good morning, Tag. You will find fresh-brewed coffee in the kitchen, creamer in the fridge, and aspirin on the counter. The morning paper is on the front doorstep. Once you are up and around, please call me. My business card is in the drawer under the phone in the entryway. Take your time. Nate.*

Lo and behold, as I got to the kitchen, I spotted a fresh-brewed pot of coffee already in the coffeemaker. I looked at it for a moment before reaching in the cabinet directly above the coffeemaker and pulling out a cup. I opened the refrigerator door, and just as Nate had said, the crème brûlée was on the shelf, staring me in the face. Alongside the creamer was a small bag from the Beaufort Bakery. I opened it and inside was an assortment of three fresh bagels. Alongside the bag of bagels was a small container of cream cheese. I knew the carbohydrates would help me feel better.

I went to the front door and looked down to find the *Beaufort Gazette*. On my way back to the kitchen, I opened the drawer in the telephone stand to find Nate's business card.

With coffee, newspaper, and bagel in hand, I headed toward the screened-in porch to get a handle on my day. I sat down and looked out the window at the sprawling yard leading to the intercoastal waterway. The sun was making its way up from the horizon. The birds filled the air with all kinds of exotic sounds. A slight breeze whispered through the screens on the porch. I could smell the sea. I closed my eyes and listened. I tried to count the many different birdcalls I heard. It seemed as if there were a thousand different birds out there, all looking for something.

I looked at the headlines in the *Beaufort Gazette*—more of the same bad economic news. I decided I would plug into the Internet and see what has happening back at the office. I had lots of e-mail, but nothing of an urgent nature. As I scrolled down the page, I noticed one from Cindy regarding the Dillianquest property.

Cindy had sent the property description, along with all the information regarding the buildings situated on the Dillianquest property—good information to have, as I was going to inspect the property today.

After a couple of cups of coffee and a few aspirin, I was starting to feel human again. I thought a quick shower was in order, and then I would call Nate to see what was on the agenda for the day. I knew what I wanted to accomplish, but one thing was for sure: Nate had an agenda, too, although I was not exactly sure what his agenda was.

After my shower, I went back out to the porch and dialed Nate's number, as instructed. It rang twice, and then a chipper Nate answered.

"Hello, this is Nate."

"Good morning, Nate," I said, trying to match Nate's up-tempo greeting. "It's Tag Grayson. How are you?"

"Splendid, just splendid. I trust you found everything you needed this morning?"

"Yes, I did. You are a very gracious host."

"I try," Nate said. "I try."

After a short pause, Nate said in a more matter-of-fact tone, "My best guess is that you would like to visit Dillianquest today."

"Yes, that is my plan."

"Good, good. I have alerted both Sally Smithson and Dianna Wingate that you will be stopping by sometime today. I did not tell them a time, just that it would be later this morning or in the afternoon. Sally is the subacute hospital administrator, and Dianna is the nursing-home administrator. I told them you are interested in investing in Dillianquest and that each should give you her full support and anything you require."

"That sounds great, Nate. Cindy has sent me some information that I need to review before my visit, so that will work out just fine. Will you be joining me for my visit?"

"Not unless you want me to. Both Sally and Dianna are excellent at what they do. You will be in good hands. They will honestly answer all your questions."

"I look forward to meeting them."

"Oh, yes, one more thing," Nate added. "The keys are in the GTO. You are also welcome to use the golf cart if you would rather; the choice is yours."

"Thanks."

"Call me if you need anything; you have my number. Have a good day, Tag." With that, Nate hung up the phone.

I decided to use the golf cart to explore the property a bit more on my way to the Dillianquest complex. I wanted to go back to the boat and take a better look anyway. Last evening had almost been like a dream. The evening was so relaxing that I wanted to double check to see if it had really happened.

I walked to the garage over the cobblestone walkway and opened the doors. The jet-black H2 Hummer golf cart was sitting in its resting place, just as it had been the night before. I walked around the side and lifted myself into the driver's seat. I eased out the door and along the tree-lined trail.

I drove until I got to the hilltop where we had stopped the night before. I stopped the golf cart in the exact spot. The view of the intercoastal was just as fantastic at this time of day. The breeze was just as fresh. The sun was a bit brighter and a little harder on my eyes.

As I looked to my right, I could see a few of the antennae of the *Kindred Spirit.* The antennae were difficult to see, as they seemed to blend in with the tree limbs that hung low and swayed with the breeze. I decided to take a leisurely drive to where the *Kindred Spirit* was moored.

The smell of the ocean was unmistakable. I parked the cart and walked down to the dock where the boat was moored. I looked into the water and watched as a variety of aquatic life darted back and forth—in search of breakfast, I presumed.

I left the dock and drove back along the shoreline until I was, I thought, in the back of the Dillianquest complex. It was as beautiful as I had thought it would be. Large trees graced the manicured lawn. Canopied seating areas lined the decked walkway as they wandered through numerous flower beds. A large glass porch spanned the entire length of the building. Plant baskets and slow-moving ceiling fans hung precariously over the patients gathered in small groups at tables.

I watched what I guessed to be staff come and go with a sense of purpose. Some stopped and talked with the patients, while others focused on their duties. I looked at my watch, and it was already 12:45 p.m. The staff must have been serving lunch on the porch. It looked pleasant.

I looked at my watch again in amazement. *How was I able to waste so much time this morning and get so little done?* I drove the cart to the far side of the building, assuming that it must be Danby House. As I approached the front of the building, I saw that I was right. There on the front door, etched in the glass, was the name Danby House. I looked up the drive toward the main entrance and saw on the left a two-story, older building with eight tall columns announcing the front entrance. It had a bit of the flavor of the old mental asylum that Nate's mother had fashioned into a subacute facility.

I continued to look around from the privacy of my hiding place alongside Danby House. I noticed a newer-looking apartment-type building to my right. *That must be the twenty-five-suite assisted living community*, I thought. It sat separate from the nursing home, which was always an ideal arrangement. Those in assisted living did not want to see what was waiting for them just around the next aging corner. On many of our properties where the assisted-living facility was attached to the nursing home, the residents and families of the assisted-living community always attempted to avoid the nursing-home residents. That attitude always reminded me of a modern-day leper's colony. It was pretty sad how intolerant people became.

I decided to begin my tour with the subacute facility, so I drove along the circle drive to the entrance. I parked the golf cart just off the sidewalk, to the right of the entryway doors. A large, well-maintained lawn graced the front, and at least 150 feet of concrete walkway led to another set of large glass doors with the name Dillianquest Subacute Care etched into the glass.

I opened the door and walked into a magnificent foyer that immediately opened into a two-story receiving area. A large chandelier hanging from the ceiling commanded my immediate attention. It hung directly above an enormous, circular wooden antique table with clawed feet that sat on white marble floors. The table was a statement of grandeur all by itself.

The entire receiving area was filled with flowers, potted plants, and small trees. A large aviary to the right filled the entire room with songs from the birds. Several patients sat in front of the large glass cage, watching the birds. Scattered about the walls were pictures of Civil War battles. The receiving area had small, semiprivate seating areas where families could visit with the patients. Offices lined the left side. I stopped and took in all this space had to offer. It was pleasantly decorated with soothing green and pastel colors on the wall that complemented the furniture, the artwork, and the birds.

As I started walking toward the most obvious-looking office, a middle-aged woman appeared from behind the half-closed door. Professionally dressed and well groomed, she walked directly to me and said, "Mr. Grayson, I presume?"

"Yes," I replied.

She extended her hand for me to shake and said, "We have been expecting you. I spoke with Mr. Dillianquest earlier this morning. My name is Sally Smithson. I am the administrator here. How can I be of service to you?" She was very businesslike. I could tell she was being very cautious with me.

"Please, call me Tag. Mr. Grayson sounds more as if you are talking to my father," I said, trying to break the ice a little with some humor. Sally only smiled a little. "Might I inquire as to what Mr. Dillianquest told you about me and my firm?"

"Nothing, other than you and your firm are interested in investing in Dillianquest, and that I should answer any questions that you might ask."

"Great. Are you able to take me on a tour?"

"Absolutely. Can I get you something to drink or a bite to eat before we get started?"

It was already past 1:00 p.m., so I politely declined. "No, thank you. However, I might take you up on that drink when we finish the tour."

"As you wish," she said. She walked away from me and walked over to another office. "Brenda, Mr. Grayson and I are going to take a tour. We will be back shortly. Hold my calls, please." She then turned to me and said, "Please, Tag, follow me." And off we went on our tour.

We completed the tour of the building in about one and a half hours. We went in every room and stuck our heads in every closet. We clambered up to the roof and down to the basement. We went everywhere and saw just about everything. I did not have the heart to tell her that we could skip the closets, roof, and basement maintenance areas. All I was really interested in was making sure that it had a roof and the building wasn't about to fall in on itself.

When we got back to her office, Sally invited me in for that drink. "What can I get you? Iced tea, soda, coffee, water?"

"I'll take an unsweetened iced tea, if it is not too much of an inconvenience."

"Not at all. I have some right here." She reached behind her desk. Incorporated into her credenza was a fully stocked refrigerator. As she poured my drink, she said, "I like to keep refreshments handy for the family members."

"Nice touch," I said just before I took a long drink of the iced tea. It tasted very good. I knew the caffeine wouldn't do me any harm, either.

As I placed the glass on a coaster on Sally's desk, I asked, "What is your biggest challenge here at Dillianquest?"

Without hesitation, she answered, "It has to be our census. With this struggling economy, more and more families are having financial difficulties. Most of our patients are insured or privately funded. When the economy gets this tough, a lot of folks try to take care of their own and keep the money for themselves. When the census drops, we don't hit our numbers, and when we don't hit our numbers, we are forced to adjust. I am sorry to say that we have been losing money for the past several months."

After a short silence, she added, "I put together our financials for the past several years for Mr. Dillianquest. I trust he shared those with you?"

"Yes, he did. As I read them, this facility has been hemorrhaging money for over a year. The losses have been substantial."

"They have. Just about every facility in the state has experienced a census shortfall."

"I realize it is tough all over," I said. I did not want Sally to start thinking that the first thing we were going to do was recommend that she be fired for not doing her job. "How long have you worked at Dillianquest?"

"I am on my seventh year. I am the only administrator this facility has had. We have low-turnover and high-quality employees, and we are aggressively working on our strategic marketing plan. We have a great team of people here." She stood up from behind her desk and handed me a binder titled "Dillianquest Strategic Marketing and Vision Plan."

I stood up, took the binder from her, and said, "I am sure you do have a great team here. Everyone we met on the tour seemed to be focused on their jobs. I saw lots of smiles and happy faces. I am confident you will meet your challenges head-on. Thanks for the tour."

"You are welcome," Sally said with a sigh of relief. She added, "That plan is for the entire complex, including Danby House."

"Thanks again. I look forward to reviewing it."

Sally looked at me and said, "I will call Dianna and let her know you are on your way to see her."

Sally walked me to the door. At the threshold, she shook my hand again and said, "If you need anything, please do not hesitate to contact me." She handed me her business card. "My home phone number is on the back, in case you need something on the weekend or in the evening." Sally was genuinely interested in helping any way she could.

I walked down the walkway to the golf cart. The afternoon sun was warm, and a gentle ocean breeze filled the air. Dillianquest was a very relaxing setting. As I sat in the cart, I looked back at the building again. It was in remarkable condition. The building was at least one hundred years old. It was apparent that Mother Dillianquest had not spared any of Father Dillianquest's money on the renovation.

If we could get this place at fire-sale prices, we could weather the brewing economic storm and actually do the community a service.

I pointed the cart toward Danby House, about four hundred yards away. It was of similar architecture to the subacute facility. Tall pillars announced the entryway. Large trees framed the front of the building, and a straight walkway led directly to the large, glass entryway doors. Danby House appeared to be a substantially newer facility than the one I had just left. I could tell by the materials used in the construction. The columns were not real stone, and the roof did not appear to be real slate. Nonetheless, the facility blended in nicely with its surroundings.

I opened the large entryway doors and entered. I was equally impressed with Danby House's appearance. The receiving room was divided in two by a very large aquarium. To the right were lounge areas for families to visit. Offices again lined the left side of the receiving area. The entire room was carpeted and quiet. It had a more modern feel to it than the subacute building, but it harkened back to a more historic period in Beaufort's past in the same fashion.

I found myself drawn to the aquarium and walked directly toward it. I stopped and watched the fish as they went about their mundane lives, as fish in an aquarium do. The aquarium was huge. I was in awe of its size. It must have been twenty feet long, five feet tall, and at least two or three feet wide. As I stood there admiring the fish and the sheer size of this aquarium, a voice from my left said, "Mr. Grayson, hi. My name is Dianna Wingate."

I turned and was surprised to see a woman who couldn't have been more than twenty-five years of age.

"Hi, Ms. Wingate. It is nice to meet you."

"The pleasure is mine," she said with certainty and extended her hand. She took my hand with a firm grip, looked me directly in the eye, and said, "This aquarium is like a magnet for people. It draws them in as if it has magical powers."

"Yes, it is very impressive—and, I am sure, quite soothing for the patients."

"Yes, our resident council raised the money for it and maintains it as well."

"No kidding?" I said.

"No kidding." There was a short but uncomfortable pause.

"The residents have about fifty different species of fish and aquatic life in there," Dianna pointed out as we walked around the tank. "Some of the favorites are that blue-faced angel fish. Can you see it hiding behind that sunken warship?"

"Yes, yes, I see it."

"The bright blue, white, and black really stand out in the saltwater. It is a beautiful fish," she added. "And here"—she pointed—"we have a fairly rare pair of yashia goby and candy red pistol shrimp." She looked at me to see if I was paying attention—which I was—before explaining, "They are hard to find sometimes, because they blend in so well with the elegance coral that provides a great hiding place for them."

"I can see where the residents could spend hours and hours sitting and watching these creatures … this is just great. And speaking of residents, where is everyone?"

Dianna said without missing a beat, "Most everyone is in the activities salon. Today we have a Civil War historian, Mr. Gimble, showing local artifacts from the Beaufort museum. When he comes, everyone who is able loves to listen to him speak and see what he brings to the show."

"Now, Mr. Grayson, please come into the office for a moment," Dianna instructed. She turned and walked toward the middle office. I followed. She walked around a large desk and stood for a second as I situated myself.

"Please have a seat," she said, still standing. Dianna sat only after I was seated in the chair directly in front of her desk.

Dianna leaned forward, placing both elbows on the clean desk in front of her. She clenched her hands, as if she were praying, and said, "It is my understanding from Mr. Dillianquest that you are interested in a tour of our facility."

"That is correct."

She looked at me for just a moment and then asked, "Is there anything you care to ask before we take the tour? Can I offer you a drink of tea or water?"

"Yes, I do have a question for you. Nate tells me that his mother is in the nursing home. Is that true?"

Dianna's face broke into a very warm smile. "Yes, she is with us, but truth be told, Mrs. Dillianquest has a special circumstance that is provided for her."

"Special circumstance?"

"Yes. When the Dillianquest family built Danby House, they added a private area for Mrs. Dillianquest. Apparently, Alzheimer's disease runs in her family, and Mr. Dillianquest wanted her to have special care when the time came. The family has a private nurse to care for her every need. Tessa is her nurse. When Mrs. Dillianquest moved into her suite here at Danby House, so did Tessa. She has quarters here at the facility attached to Mrs. Dillianquest's suite."

"No kidding?" I said in an astonished voice. "Mr. Dillianquest must have been quite a husband!"

"Mr. Dillianquest has an interesting history in these parts, and so does the rest of the family, for that matter. Mrs. Dillianquest has done a great number of good deeds for this community. She built the hospital, this complex, the Beaufort Civil War Museum ... the list is seemingly endless. She was a strong, good-natured woman. Today, her health is not so good. The disease is winning the battle."

"I am sorry to hear that," I said in my most consoling tone. "If she is awake when we pass her suite, maybe you could introduce me?"

"If she is alert, I would be most happy to." She stood up from her desk and motioned for us to leave. "How about that tour now? Let's start at the assisted living. Follow me." Off we went on another tour ... my lucky day!

One thing could be said about the ladies who ran these two health-care facilities: they did not scrimp on the tour. Just like on my previous tour, we went everywhere, including the employee lounge area, where I met several of the employees. We toured the kitchen, laundry, and outside storage areas. We toured the outside walking trails. We toured the enclosed Alzheimer's walking area and toured each nurse's station.

At about the two-hour mark, Dianna said, "Just one more area. This is Mrs. Dillianquest's suite." She knocked lightly a couple of times, cautiously opened the door, and announced, "Mrs. Dillianquest, it's Dianna Wingate, the administrator. May I come in?"

Dianna did not wait for a response; she just kept opening the door until she could enter the room. I followed behind a few feet.

The spacious, open two-room suite was divided by a large arch. Mrs. Dillianquest's bed was in the back of the room. There was a seating area with couch, chairs, and coffee table in the front room of the suite. That part of the suite was equipped with a small kitchenette that had all the amenities needed to prepare any type or meal Mrs. Dillianquest desired. On the wall hung a large flat-screen TV on a swivel arm. Several antique mirrors and dressers surrounded the bedroom area. The room was feminine, but functional. The decorations showed a personal touch, including photos and mementos.

Mrs. Dillianquest was lying in bed, quiet and peaceful. No one else was in the room; it was just Mrs. Dillianquest, Dianna, and me.

"She is a beautiful lady," I observed.

"Yes, as you can see, the family has filled the room with memories. She was a very beautiful woman, indeed."

I looked at some photos near the door through which we had entered. I saw a picture of a young Nate dressed in his military uniform and two youngsters alongside Mr. and Mrs. Dillianquest. They looked to be a very happy group.

I looked at Dianna and asked, "Are these Nate's kids?"

Dianna glanced at the picture. "I don't know. I don't believe so."

Dianna touched me on the shoulder and said, "Come, let's let her get her rest." She led the way out of the room, and I followed.

"That is a very unique setup."

"Yes, that is why we refer to it as her special circumstance."

"I see."

As the door closed, I caught a glimpse of a person in Mrs. Dillianquest's room. I turned and said to Dianna, "I hadn't noticed anyone else in the room. Had you?"

"That must be Tessa. There is a medication room off to the left. She must not have heard us. Would you care to meet her?"

"No, that's fine." In the same breath, I asked, "Can I ask you a nonrelated question, Dianna?"

"Certainly. How can I help?"

"Can you point me to a good restaurant in the area? I like to experience the local flavor when I can."

"Absolutely," Dianna said, flashing a faint smile, "One of my favorites is the Ocean Side Shanty on Frogmore Inlet."

"Thanks. I think I'll give that a go this evening for dinner. When in Rome ..."

"Yes, when in Beaufort, crab cakes and the catch of the day at the OSS are in order."

"The OSS?" I questioned as we started to walk back toward the office.

"Yes, the OSS—the Ocean Side Shanty. If you want to sound like a local, you have to call it by its local name, the OSS."

"Is the OSS in the phone book? I will need to get the address."

"Yes they are, but … there is really no need—it's as easy as mud pie to get there from here. You are staying at the cottage, correct?"

"Yes."

"Well, turn right out of the driveway onto 281. Turn right onto Highway 21. You will be headed east. After about eight miles, you will turn right onto Frogmore Inlet Road, and that will take you right to the OSS. You can't miss it."

"Sounds easy enough. I'll take some paperwork to keep me company."

Dianna walked me to the door. We shook hands and said our good-byes.

I walked over to the Hummer golf cart, sat in the driver's seat, and looked at a beautiful setting with a huge upside if we could buy it right. As I drove back to the cottage, I started to wonder why Nate wanted to sell. He had not given me any reason so far—just some cryptic references to family secrets and obligations. Much more to his story remained to be told—if Nate intended to tell me at all.

I parked the cart in the garage and walked the cobblestone path to the cottage. I entered through the screened-in porch and made my way over to the buffet. I poured myself a short scotch. If I was going to make it to dinner, I did not want to drink too much. I took a sip and looked around the cottage. It was beautiful. I walked to the overstuffed rattan couch on the porch and looked out over the intercoastal waterway.

A slight breeze remained in the air at six forty-five. I could hear the faint rustle of the limbs of the trees as they scraped across each other's bark. I put my feet up. It was time for a break. The afternoon had gotten so involved that I had forgotten to eat lunch.

CHAPTER 8

I stood in the shower, letting the water massage my head and pour over my shoulders en route to its ultimate destination: the shower drain. I had been in the shower for at least thirty minutes when I heard my phone ring. I thought about letting it go to voice mail, but instead, I jumped out of the shower and grabbed the phone from the bathroom vanity. Phone in hand, I stepped back into the shower.

"Hello, this is Tag."

"Tag, it's Nate. I hope I didn't catch you at an inconvenient time?"

I replied in my naked, soaking-wet state, "No, not at all."

"Good. I just wanted to touch base with you and see how today went."

"Today was a success. Both Sally and Dianna were very accommodating. Dillianquest is everything you said it would be."

"Glad to hear it. Would you care to grab some dinner at the club with me this evening?"

By then I was standing in front of the mirror and vanity, wrapped in a towel. "You know, Nate, I am still recuperating from last night. Tonight I think I am going to grab a bite locally, lay low, and finish my reading. Sally gave me a copy of the marketing plan. I thought I would read that and review the financials."

"Are you sure?"

"Yes, I think so, but thanks for the invite."

"No problem. Have you given any thought to your return flight?"

"Yes, I am thinking that if I could leave at about one in the afternoon tomorrow, that would get me back in time for dinner with my family."

"One it is. I will alert Gwen. If you don't mind, I will have Gwen pick you up at the cottage on her way. That way you won't get lost trying to find the airfield." Nate laughed. "It might be easier that way."

"Nate," I said with a pause, "if things go as I expect they will with my firm, I will be back in town in a couple of weeks. I will need your attorney's contact information, so I can touch base when the time comes for such things."

"I've already sent their contact information to Cindy in anticipation of your needs. I have been using Belanger, Larson, and George for years. If our paths don't cross before you leave, please, don't worry about the cottage. I will have the housekeepers tidy it before your next visit." After a pause, he added, "I am looking forward to doing business with you, my friend. I hope you have safe travels. You know how to get ahold of me if you need anything else."

"See you in a couple of weeks, then, and thanks for everything, Nate. I will let you know if I need anything. So long."

I looked at myself in the mirror with approval. I picked up the blow-dryer from the vanity top and began drying my hair. Shortly thereafter, I was dressed in blue jeans, sneakers, a white golf shirt, and a blue blazer with gold buttons on the sleeves and front. Some looks were just too good to give up.

I went back out to the screened-in porch and grabbed my scotch, which was almost all water by now. I went through the directions in my head and decided to write them down, just in case. I had been known to forget a thing or two in the recent past. Getting home from some backwater inlet was a top priority list for the night. I found a piece of paper and pen and jotted down the directions in reverse: *Take Frogmore Inlet Road to Highway 21 and turn left. Turn left on to Highway 281 and then left into drive.* I folded the directions and placed them in my jacket pocket.

I picked up my watered-down glass of scotch and headed for the kitchen. I dumped the liquid down the drain and placed the glass in the sink next to my morning coffee cup. I hated a messy kitchen, so I took my morning dishes and hid them in the dishwasher. I didn't know how I had gotten to be so compulsive, but compulsive I was. Now that the kitchen was back in a state of order, I thought I could leave and enjoy the evening.

I went back through the foyer and picked up the binder that Sally had presented me. If nothing else, I would have some interesting reading while dining alone. I was now ready to go to dinner.

I headed back through the kitchen and to the garage. I had all but forgotten about the 1964 black-on-black Pontiac GTO awaiting me. When I opened the door to the garage, my heart began to race, as it had in the eighth grade when the girl I liked stopped by my locker and talked with me. My heart was racing just about that fast, and my mouth got just a bit drier.

The GTO was a beautiful automobile with a 389 high-performance engine and Hurst shifter. The coolest thing about it … it was mine to use for the night. I would cruise to the OSS, have dinner, and then cruise back. I was looking forward to it. It sounded like a good plan.

I walked around the entire car, simply admiring it. It sported a shiny, flawless deep coat of jet-black paint. The finish appeared to be ten feet deep, and it was so shiny that it was like looking into a mirror. From headlight to taillight ran the thinnest of red pinstripes, just under the window molding. The tires were oversized just a bit with big, white lettering. The chrome wheels were highly polished. The interior was black and the dashboard red.

I opened the car door and was hit with that new-car smell. I carefully lowered myself into the driver's seat, sat back, and took in the dashboard. A tachometer was attached to the steering column, just off to the left of center. I looked down to see the Hurst shifter Nate had told me about, just to the right of my right knee. I placed both hands on the oversized steering wheel, hands at ten and two. I just stared out over the hood for a few minutes.

In my moments of daydreaming, I wondered what it would have been like growing up as Nate had. It was obvious he had had everything he could have ever wanted. I wondered how much love he had gotten as a kid. Was it enough? Did his parents shower him with stuff in order to compensate for their lack of affection? He didn't appear to have any kids. Now he was the sole heir to the family fortune, with no one to pass the family legacy on to. I wondered what I would do in that circumstance. He could do anything he wanted, anytime he wanted to. *Now that is some kind of freedom.*

After snapping out of my short daydream, I looked down at the ignition. A key stuck out of it. Attached to the single key was a pink rabbit's foot. I reached for the key and prepared myself to start the engine. I turned the key to the right, and in an instant, the silence of the garage was broken by the deep, smooth rumble of the high-performance engine. I stepped on the gas a couple of times just to hear the race of the motor.

This, I thought, *is going to be a blast.*

I backed out of the garage and turned the steering wheel to the right to head up the long, winding driveway. It had been a long time since I had driven a manual transmission, I thought as I sat facing the long driveway, engine idling. I engaged the clutch and shifted through the pattern engraved on the top of the shifter ball in the form of an H. Up to the left was first gear. Straight back was second gear. Up to the right was third gear, and straight back from that position was fourth gear.

It was all coming back to me in a flood of emotion. It was like riding a bike. I sat and remembered what my dad had told me when he was teaching me how to drive years ago. He taught me in an old VW Bug with the shifter on the floor. The GTO rocked in a gentle idle while I thought about my driving lessons and how wonderful they had been. My dad would take me to our cousin's house out in the country when I was about fourteen or so. He took me out in a big, open field and told me, "Everything about driving a stick is slow and easy." I could still hear him telling me that, as if his head were still poked inside the driver's side window. "Once you learn to drive a manual transmission, you will never forget." His voice had echoed in my head for years.

Now, the clutch was pressed against the floorboard. I was ready to propel myself into the Beaufort social life. I let the clutch out, and with an unexpected lurch, the car bolted forward and just as quickly came to an abrupt, halt snapping my head backward and then forward. Then, suddenly, there was quiet. With eyes wide open, I gazed out over the hood of this magnificent muscle car, one hand on the shifter the other hand on the steering wheel, and began to laugh—silently at first, and then out loud, in a big belly laugh. I sheepishly looked around and hoped that no one was spying on me. I reached for the ignition and restarted the car. This time, the start to my evening was flawless. The second time, it turned out, was the charm.

As I turned right out of the driveway and onto Highway 281, I looked at my watch. It was approaching 8:00 p.m., and I was very hungry. A bagel for breakfast and no lunch was not my normal nutritional routine. I was looking forward to the Ocean Side Shanty. I thought about what Dianna had said earlier in the day: crab cakes and the catch of the day were a must at the OSS. I was going to take her up on that suggestion.

I rolled through the edge of Beaufort in the 1964 GTO. Many people waved at the car. I guess they thought it was Nate driving around in one of his many automobiles. Being the friendly kind of guy I am, I returned all the gestures that came my way.

As instructed, I turned right on to Highway 21 and began the eight-mile trip to Frogmore Inlet. Highway 21 took me immediately over the intercoastal waterway. The Highway 21 Bridge was tall—tall enough so that the any type of vessel could make its way underneath without incident. As I crossed the bridge, some type of military vessel passed below. I slowed down to get a better look at the impressive display of military might.

The area around Beaufort was full of military installations. To the south of the bridge was Parris Island, a Marine Corps training facility. To the north was the Marine Corps air station. The air station must have been close to where Gwen kept her plane. Signs provided directions to these facilities at every intersection, and the bridge exits were no exception.

Highway 21 headed due east over and through the protected wetlands that surrounded the entire area. The waterfowl were everywhere, looking for the same thing I was: dinner. The road took some interesting twists and turns and passed over a lot of bridges connecting the island dots, hopping from one small land mass to another. I bet I passed over twenty concrete connector bridges, just feet above the rising and lowering tides. It was a very enjoyable ride, especially in the driver's seat of a 1964 black-on-black Pontiac GTO.

After what seemed like only a two-minute drive I noticed a road sign on the right side of the road that read "Frogmore Inlet Road," with an arrow pointing to the right. Under the arrow, it read "1/2 mile." I started to slow down. The sun had set, and the sky turned crimson red as the sun's last remaining rays danced off the low-hanging, wispy clouds. It was another beautiful sunset. I looked for my headlight switch and pulled it. They did not do much good in illuminating the road in front of me, but they would alert anyone traveling in my direction that I was headed their way.

I turned right onto Frogmore Inlet Road and saw a sign that read "Ocean Side Shanty, Fine Seafood Dining, Ahead 2 Miles." I left the paved Highway 21 road behind and found that Frogmore Inlet Road was all loose gravel. I slowed my pace considerably on the way to the OSS. I did not want to damage the car's paint job by slinging a rock or two. As I drove the length of Frogmore Inlet Road, I notice several signs that read, "High Water—Do Not Drive Through If You Can't See the Road!" It was becoming apparent to me this area was prone to floods, probably due to hurricanes and tropical storms. *No, thanks*, I thought. *You can keep your hurricanes and tropical storms.*

Just as Dianna had said, the road stopped right at the entryway to the Ocean Side Shanty. Looking at the building, I decided it had been appropriately named. I stopped the car in the road and just looked for a second. A big oak tree stood in the middle of the parking lot, which was cratered with rather large, but shallow holes. Patrons appeared able to park anywhere they wanted, as there was no real defined parking area.

The parking lot itself was constructed of oyster shells that had been consumed over the years and thrown on to the parking area. The building itself was old and weathered and was situated on a point of land jutting out into the marsh. Much of the building appeared to be supported by thick wooden posts. The exterior was unpainted and had that really tired look to it. The roof was tin—some old and some new. Scattered about the parking lot and building were pieces of boats in whole and in part. A small, half-buried hull housed a cement statue of an old fisherman, keeping him out of the weather. The large oak tree supported a mass of Spanish moss, which gave it an eerie look in the waning evening light.

Interesting, I thought as I pulled into the parking lot. I was feeling much more confident about driving the manual transmission. There were a dozen or so cars parked at the OSS. Most were parked up against the building, close to the gangplank that led the way to the front door. I parked off to the side, so no one would accidentally ding the car with their door. Most of the cars were vintage automobiles. Half were trucks and other half a mixture of old and older beat-up sedans. Nate's classic GTO stood out like a sore thumb.

I left the sanctuary of the car and walked unhurriedly over the oyster-covered parking lot to the gangplank. As I stepped onto the gangplank, I heard the creak of the wooden planks under my feet. I stopped and looked up at the building and its marshy surroundings and thought about the tales this place must have to tell.

The interior of the Ocean Side Shanty was one-third bar and two-thirds restaurant. I pushed my way through a pair of large, knotty wooden doors. Hundreds of oddly shaped tree knots had all been put together to make one of the most unique doors I had ever seen. As I entered, the first thing I noticed was the long, carved wooden bar to my left, fronted with lots of fixed barstools and several tables scattered about in an incoherent maze.

I watched a waitress taking an order from one of the groups at a table. There was no hostess stand to greet me as I entered, unlike in most restaurants. Folks were scattered equally along the bar and in the restaurant area. The only person who acknowledged my presence was the bartender, who waved at me to come in. He gestured to a seat at the bar and smiled. I liked this place already.

A waist-high partition separated the bar from the restaurant area. On either side of the partition were tables. The partition continued to the ceiling with what appeared to be long rowing oars separating the two areas. Thick fishnets draped lazily between them, completing the room separation. From the fishnets hung plastic fish, lobsters, and crabs clinging for dear life.

I stopped and looked around the entire place. *You won't find one of these in Ann Arbor.* The vaulted ceiling was held together with exposed wooden crossbeams that looked like old masts from sailing ships. The entire ceiling was awash with fishing nets, harpoons, lobster pots, and clamming buckets. The walls supported stuffed fish of all kinds, including the largest sailfish I had ever seen centered directly behind the bar. Around the entire interior of the restaurant were big blue tarpon, yellowfin tuna, and blue and yellow striped dolphin. I saw fish and sea creatures of all sorts and sizes, the likes of which I had never encountered before.

I looked back over at the bar area, and again, the tall, dark-skinned bartender waved at me and motioned for me to come his way. So I did.

As I walked up to the bar, he asked, "First time to the Ocean Side?"

"Is it that obvious?"

"We get that astonished look a lot from our first-timers."

"I have no doubt."

He laughed and asked, "What are you drinking?" After a short pause, he could see I was looking over his stock. He continued, "You look like a scotch man."

"Very astute. Do you have any Macallan?"

"Ten, twelve, and fifteen."

"Give me the fifteen-year-old with just a couple of cubes."

"Grab a seat, and I'll be right back with your drink," he said as he walked toward the opposite end of the bar.

I sat on the barstool and took in the sights and sounds of the Ocean Side Shanty. My eye was drawn to the bar back. It was an eclectic combination of old ship parts, and I was sure every piece had a fabulously interesting story. The main header of the back bar was a huge timber with engraved letters that were fully intact. The name on the beam read "HMS *Bedford.*" Holding the beam up were several carved turtlebacks in the shape of maidens. According to sailor lore, the carved turtlebacks were placed on the bows of ships to watch and guide the early voyaging ships to safe passage. The bar also included lots of etched glass and mirrors. It was quite a piece of history, I was sure.

"The name is Levi," the bartender said as he slid the tumbler of scotch in front of me. "I'll start a tab for you this evening."

"Thanks," I replied as looked around the bar. "What a great bar back that is."

"Yeah, matey," he said in his best pirate dialect. "The HMS *Bedford* was commissioned in 1698. She was one of Her Majesty's mighty warships back then and carried seventy cannons on her decks. They tell me that the beam that bears her name is from the larboard side of the ship."

"Really?" I questioned.

Levi looked at me square in the eye, leaned over the bar, and responded, "Sure, why not?" before laughing out loud. "I didn't catch your name," he said with a big grin on his face.

"Tag."

"Tag," he repeated in a rather quizzical voice. "That's a first for me, and I've been tending bar for twenty-five years!

"Tag," he said again, as if it were going to change. "Tag, huh? Tag. What's that short for?"

"Not short for anything. The name is simply Tag," I said in a matter-of-fact and slightly irritated tone. It really wasn't any of his business anyway what my name was. I felt as though he were being a little too friendly. All I was interested in was a quiet crab cake and catch-of-the-day dinner, just as Dianna had suggested.

Just then, the phone rang, and Levi said, "Excuse me, I have to get that." The phone was under the end of the bar where I was sitting. The conversation was short. I could only hear Levi's side of the conversation.

"Hello?" he said. After a short pause, he answered, "Yes, he did," and finished the conversation with "Okay, see ya later," and hung up the phone.

He looked at me and said, "Short and sweet—that's just how I like my phone conversations ... and my sex ... short and sweet." He laughed out loud, having tickled himself with his wit.

.Without breaking stride, Levi added, "Are you dining with us tonight?"

"Yes. The crab cakes were recommended."

"You can never go wrong with our crab cakes or the catch of the day."

I thought I would test the waters a bit and see what kind of reaction I would get with my next statement. "I am in town on business and had dinner with Nate Dillianquest last evening. He mentioned that the Ocean Side had catered the food. It was very good."

"Ah, yes, you are the out-of-town guest Nate said was coming to dinner. I dropped the food off at the *Kindred Spirit* last evening myself. How did you like the stone crab claws? They looked awesome."

"They were exceptional. Nate is quite the host."

"Yeah, the Dillianquest family has done lots for Beaufort over the many years. Yep, Nate's a character, all right."

Just then Levi motioned to one of the waitstaff to come over to the bar. "Annette," Levi said, "this gentleman's name is Tag. Please prepare Nate's table for him. He will be dining with us this evening."

"Thanks, Levi," I said and then turned to greeted Annette. "Annette, it is nice to meet you."

Levi looked at me and said, "Annette will take you to your seat when you are ready."

"I am ready," I told her.

"Please follow me."

As we started weaving our way through the maze of tables, I looked back at Levi, smiled, and asked, "Is the *Bedford* the real deal?"

Levi smiled back and said, "Sure is."

I did not know whether I could believe him or not, but he knew what I wanted to hear—the true mark of a salesman.

Apparently Nate had a usual table. I followed Annette to the far side of the restaurant. It was at the opposite side of the room from the bar. I found myself in a quiet corner of the restaurant slightly secluded from the other patrons.

Nate's table had a front-row seat to Frogmore Inlet, and the inlet was lit up like an airfield. Huge lights attached to the roof on the outside of the Ocean Side Shanty shone brightly on the inlet's wild creatures and plant life. The tide was out. It was a great view. Annette pulled my chair out for me.

Just as I sat down, Levi appeared to set my drink down in front of me, smiled, and said, "Enjoy." I returned the smile and nodded.

I looked at my watch. It was already after nine. Annette came up to the table with menu in hand and asked, "Would you care to look at a menu?"

"No, I'll have an order of crab cakes and the catch of the day, grilled."

Annette asked, "Do you care to know what the catch of the day is?"

"Nope. I love a tasty surprise."

"As you wish, sir. What type of dressing for your salad?"

"Balsamic, on the side."

"Will do. I'll be back with your bread in just a moment." She disappeared from sight.

Dinner was an incredible array of taste and texture. Levi kept my glass full of scotch, only to be interrupted by a glass of chardonnay when the crab cakes arrived. I was very happy I had taken Dianne's advice. The crab cakes and catch of the day were to die for.

As I pulled back from the table, Levi appeared again with yet another glass of scotch. Before I could say anything, he explained, "This one is from that dark-haired woman at the bar."

I looked up at Levi and said, "Excuse me?"

"This is from that lady at the bar."

With that, I turned and looked toward the bar. Walking straight at me was a tall, slender, dark-skinned woman with jet-black, silky hair swaying side to side as she found her way closer to my table. Her eyes were as black as a moonless night. Her jeans fit snugly against her thighs, as if someone had sprayed them on her curvy hips. The cuffs of the jeans were rolled up, exposing a tattoo of a scorpion on her right ankle. I could hear each step she took in her six-inch stiletto heels. This vision wore a white T-shirt under a tight black leather waistcoat. I thought that someone must be playing a trick on me.

As she got to my table, she took the drink from Levi's hand, looked at me, and asked, "Can I buy you a drink?"

"Not to accept such an offer would be rude, would it not?" I responded and pointed to a chair with a sweeping hand motion. "Would you care to join me?" As the words left my mouth, I couldn't believe what I had just said and done. I felt myself slipping toward uncomfortable feelings and thoughts. I hoped I could control myself. Too much alcohol was not a good thing.

She pulled out a chair and sat down. She brought with her white wine in a long-stemmed wine glass. Red lipstick had printed itself on edge of the glass. The glass was three quarters full; it had just been poured. I did not recall seeing her enter the Ocean Side.

She placed her drink down in front of her. She leaned back in the chair and crossed her legs. She wore a sheepish smile that turned into a devilish grin as she said, "I came to shoot some pool, but there is nobody here. Do you play?"

"I'm not all that good."

"Neither am I. Come on," she said as she got up from the table. "Shoot a game of pool with me." After a short pause, she added, "Please?" She extended her hand to me as I was sat at the table. I took it, and she helped me to my feet.

"I don't see a pool table."

"It's on the other side of the bar." Still holding my hand, she pulled me across the room toward two large glass doors at the end of the bar, away from the front door. As we got closer to the glass doors, she let go of my hand. She opened the doors and in a small room was a pool table that just fit the space: red felt with leather pockets. It was a good-looking pool table.

I said, "Excuse me for a moment. I need to wash my hands. I will be right back."

"Hurry back. I'll rack."

I walked past Levi, who was cleaning up behind the bar, on my way to the restroom. I looked at my watch and was astonished to see that it was just past eleven, and I hadn't called Sam yet. I always tried to call at 10:00 p.m. sharp when I was away traveling. As I went into the bathroom, I plucked my phone from my pocket and called home. As I stood over the urinal, Sam answered the phone.

We had a short conversation after I apologized for calling late. She was glad I was okay. The kids were fine.

I hung up the phone, washed my hands, and headed back toward the poolroom, having thoughts about this girl I had just met that were just plain wrong.

As I entered the room, this gorgeous creature, whose name I still did not know, said, "I got your coat while you were washing up and hung it up over there. Hope you don't mind."

"No, not at all, and thanks. My name is Tag. What's yours?"

"Contessa. I'll flip you for the break." She flipped a silver dollar into the air and let it land on the tabletop. As soon as it hit, she covered it with her hand. "Heads or tails?"

"Your call," I said.

"What a gentleman," she quipped. "Tails," she said as she removed her hand to expose the coin. "Tails it is—my break."

Contessa had already racked the balls when I was in the bathroom and had in her hand a cue stick she had selected from the rack mounted to the wall. I walked over and eyed each cue in the rack as they stood like soldiers at attention, ready to do battle.

Just then I heard Contessa say, "I've got the only really straight one in the house. We can share, if you don't mind."

"Nope, sharing is good. I am sure I can lose at pool just as well with a straight cue as one of these others. Break away," I commanded. I was getting just a bit tipsy from the Scotch.

We played several games of stripes and solids, and I think the match was about even. We had been playing for about an hour or so when Levi poked his head in the room and said, "If you don't mind, I am going to close these doors. Annette wants to vacuum a bit before we close the restaurant side."

"Sure, go ahead." Contessa looked at me and said, "Loser breaks. It's your shot." She smiled, flipped her hair around, and handed me the cue. I lined up the cue ball and took steady aim. With a deep breath, I let a power stroke go that barely hit the cue ball, sending it off to the side rail and completely missing the rack of balls at the end of the table.

Stunned, I looked over at Contessa and she back at me as we both broke out into uproarious laughter until tears formed in our eyes.

After a few minutes, Contessa said, "Nice shot. Did you learn that in college?"

"Nope. That is one of my patented confidence-building shots. Now

I have you right where I want you," I said and laughed, feeling a bit buzzed.

Contessa snapped back, "Sounds like fun."

Contessa was tall—about five feet, ten inches, I guessed—with silky, long, jet-black hair. Her hair glistened in the dull bar light. She swirled it about in a most erotic fashion, brushing it back off her forehead with her full open hand. Her low-cut jeans exposed a firm stomach with just the hint of a tattoo peeking out from the front of her pants. Her snugly fitted T-shirt commanded my attention. I found myself staring lustfully at her. She smelled as she teasingly sauntered back and forth in front of me.

As she bent over the pool table directly in front of me, she stroked our shared cue and struck the white cue ball without success. She looked at me and did not say a word. She just smiled, tossed her hair back, and handed me the cue—but was not eager to let it go. Contessa was tempting me.

Her dark eyes twinkled like diamonds in the low-hanging bar lights. And when she looked at me, she shot lustful thoughts directly into my soul. Her attention was fixed solely on me. I was mesmerized and drawn wholly into her spell. I was no match for her or the scotch.

As she purposefully leaned over the table, my eyes were treated to an unbelievable sensual feast. I stood transfixed, seemingly helpless, staring at this exceptionally beautiful woman … so firm, so finely shaped. I felt like a thirteen-year-old boy who was seeing his first naked woman—one who was willing to do anything he asked. I had been reduced to a quivering mass of useless male flesh, unable to even form a coherent sentence.

The pockets of her jeans bore an embroidered symbol from her heritage, a symbol that meant love … or so she said. The swirl of beads and colors that did not let my eyes look away. It kept my attention fixed upon her gorgeous, firm ass … there was no reason to fight it. I couldn't. She was winning this battle. The stilettos firmed her legs. Her perfectly shaped ass swayed from side to side as gracefully as palm fronds in the cool evening breeze. Watching her walk about the small, confined room kept me in a trance.

As she passed in front of me this time, she ever so slightly brushed against my groin, sending waves of chills to every nerve ending in my body.

She glanced up at me as she handed me the pool cue that we shared. Her scent was intoxicating. I was lost in her. She leaned into me, pressing her breasts into my chest and whispered in my ear with her hot, moist breath dancing off my neck, her warm hand caressing my side. "It's your shot."

I placed my hand in the small of her back and pressed her closer to me. I leaned back against a barstool, legs apart. She came willingly. Her body pressed tightly against mine. I pulled on her hair and held it firm in my hand as I drew her closer and closer to me. Her head tilted back, exposing her neck, long and smooth. I could not resist any longer. I willingly allowed my lips to gently caress the smooth skin of her neck. My tongue just barely touched her skin.

My breath felt deep and hot. I felt her quiver in my arms. I let go of her hair and followed the curves of her back to the firm, tight ass. I pulled up firmly with both hands, and she pressed deeper and deeper into my clutches. My pants were beginning to fill. Every breath I took of her intoxicating scent made be feel as if I were having an out-of-body experience.

She pulled back from our embrace and said, "Give me a ride into town. Come on, let's go." She grabbed my hand, and we started toward the door.

"Wait a second—let me get my coat." She stood by the door as I retrieved my sport coat from the hook. This couldn't be happening, could it?

We emerged from the poolroom, and I noticed that it was one thirty in the morning. *God, what am I doing?* I thought, but I just couldn't help myself. Levi was cleaning up behind the bar when I stopped and asked about the bill.

"Levi, what are the damages?"

"There aren't any. Mr. Dillianquest called earlier to order some food and said that he would take care of your bill. Are you okay to drive?"

Contessa answered as we walked toward the door, my hand in hers. "We are fine. Good night, Levi," she said, raising her arm and waving without looking back.

"Be careful! It's real foggy out there."

We made our way to the car, wrapping our arms around each other for support and comfort. We walked around to the passenger side, and I opened the door. As she got between the car door and me, she turned and looked at me. She grabbed my head with both hands and kissed me, her tongue dancing with mine.

We kissed for a long time, and when it was over, she said, "I've wanted to do that since I first laid eyes on you tonight." My head was light and dizzy and seemed to want to spin off my shoulders.

I walked around to my side of the car, allowing my hand to follow the contour of the car so I would not lose my balance. I opened the driver's-side door and slid into the seat. Contessa had already moved close to where I was sitting. She put her left arm around my neck, pulled my head close to hers, and began kissing me on my neck. I was paralyzed.

She kissed me one more time and said, "Are you okay to drive?"

"If I can keep my hands off you and on the wheel, we should be fine."

"If you feel you need to pull over," she said with an air of understanding, "I will understand." She kissed my neck again and squeezed my thigh with her right hand.

I started the car after getting my driving legs underneath me. We started creeping out of the driveway, passing under the big oak tree. The night had been blotted out; there was no sky. The fog was heavy, thick, and wet. It was very difficult to see. I had to use the windshield wipers to keep my sight somewhat clear. A lone security light marked the entryway to Frogmore Inlet Road. I peered back to my right as we crept down the gravel road. The lights of the Ocean Side Shanty slipped away into the dark, gray night.

We headed back to town. I was feeling like a sixteen-year-old boy with his girl close by his side on the bench seat of his dad's car. My hand rested between her legs, which were spread ever so slightly. Contessa sat as close to me as possible. Her left arm slid around my shoulder, and her right hand stroked my chest, her soft, full lips nibbling on my ear. Driving was difficult. We drove very slowly down the old gravel road as Contessa made it very difficult to concentrate on anything other than what she was doing.

We reached the corner of Frogmore Inlet Road and Highway 21. We came to complete stop.

"We turn left," Contessa said. I pressed down on the gas, and left we went, toward Beaufort. The fog was heaviest in the low-lying valleys, but the fog was a heavy blanket everywhere. I shifted through the gears on our way, and as I reached fourth, I could feel Contessa's hand reach between my legs with a gentle squeeze. My pants were full and tight. She began caressing my thighs, and I could feel her unbuckle my pants. I could not and did not want to stop her. My heart pounded wildly with anticipation.

I heard and felt her as she carefully unzipped my tight pants and unleashed my manhood. She caringly stroked and caressed everything that she held in her hand. I could feel her sensual kiss and the soft touch of her tongue. Soon, all I could see was the top of the back of her head between my legs, my right hand in the middle of her smooth, braless back. The warmth of her mouth consumed me.

My left hand gripped the steering wheel tightly, knuckles white. I could feel the car accelerating as I pushed myself back into the driver's seat. My head was tilted back, and my eyes were closing more with every second that passed.

It felt as if I were about to pass out; my headlights were spinning. Suddenly I heard a loud thud, and the car bounced into the air as if we had run over a speed bump.

Contessa sat straight up in her seat, choking a bit. "What in the hell was that?"

"I don't know. I heard the thud and felt the car bounce, but I did not see anything." I slowed the car down and pulled off the road as best I could. We stopped on the other side of a bridge in a gravel area where fishermen stopped alongside the road.

"I wonder if you hit a deer?"

"A deer?" I said.

"Yeah, a deer. The islands are full of them. They get hit all the time around here, especially at night."

I leaned back in the seat and put myself together. I leaned over and kissed Contessa. "I wonder if Nate has a flashlight in the glove box?" I turned on the overhead light and opened the glove box. No luck.

"I have a small one in my purse," Contessa said.

"Okay, let's see what the damages are." I turned off the car but left the headlights on high, so we could see.

Contessa handed me her small flashlight, and we both got out of the car from the driver's side. The fog seemed even thicker than it had been the entire trip. Still light-headed from our evening, I walked with Contessa around to the front of the car. The right-side high-beam headlight had been broken out; only the low-beam light was working.

A closer inspection revealed some blood on the chrome light casing and on the bumper.

"You may be right," I said. "It looks like we hit something. I wonder if we killed it?"

"Oh, God—I hope you killed whatever you hit, and it's not lying wounded in the road."

"I'm going to walk back and see what we hit. It can't be that far back. Maybe we didn't kill whatever it was, and it is okay. Why don't you stay in the car? I'll be right back."

"No way," Contessa protested. "I'm going with you."

"Fine. Come on, let's go." We put our arms around each other and started walking through the damp fog that swallowed everything in its sight. After we had walked about fifty yards, I looked back, and the taillights of the car were no longer in sight.

"This makes me pretty nervous," I said.

"Me, too."

We took a few more steps and heard a gurgling sound. That noise stopped us in our tracks. Something out there was gasping for air.

I shone the light back and forth across the road, seeing nothing. We stopped again and listened. The gurgling was coming from just over the embankment to our left. I swung the light, searching for whatever was making that frightening noise. We then saw the brush move. I shone the light toward the brush to reveal a shoe.

"Oh, my God!" Contessa shrieked. "I think we hit a person!"

Contessa immediately waded into the brush without hesitation. I stood on the side of the road for what seemed like an eternity, in total disbelief, my eyes fixed on what was happening in the brush.

"Come," Contessa said urgently. "Help me!"

I started into the brush, and as I got closer to the body, I could see Contessa kneeling over him with her head next to his face, trying to listen for breath.

"Is he alive?"

"I don't know. We have to get him up on the road, so we can start CPR," she instructed. We struggled to get the body onto the roadside.

We laid the body of a younger white male on the road. Contessa looked at me and said, "Let me see if he is still breathing."

I watched as she placed two fingers alongside the neck of the unknown body. She then bent over his face again and tried to listen for any signs of breathing. I could tell from the look on her face that there were none. She then felt his wrist.

She looked up at me and said, "I think he's dead."

"Dead? Dead! What in the fuck do you mean, dead? He can't be dead!" I grabbed my head with both hands and bent over. I started walking around in circles, muttering to myself, "Oh, my God, what are we going to do?" I must have said it loudly enough for Contessa to hear.

Contessa came over to me, grabbed me by my shoulders, and said, "Tag, Tag. Get ahold of yourself. Take a deep breath, and try to relax for a second." After a few seconds, she added, "I know this guy." She was looking me straight in the eye. "He's a homeless, lecherous parasite who lives on the island. He's a thief. Him being dead is not a bad thing for the island … no one will miss him." She left me standing in the road and went back to the body that lay near the ditch.

What Contessa had just said to me finally sank in, and as I approached her, I asked, "What are you suggesting?"

"I haven't suggested anything yet," she said, kneeling over the body. "Let me think. You've been drinking, and you killed a man in Nate Dillianquest's car. You're a married man out with me. You could call the police, but that would end your career and your marriage, and you would most likely end up in jail for several years. Drunk drivers who kill people go to jail ... even in the South!"

"We have no choice but to call the police," I said, on the verge of outright panic. "What else can we do?"

"Listen to me, Tag, and listen to me carefully. Here is what we are going to do," Contessa said in a calming, but stern voice. "We are going to carry him to the bridge we just crossed, and we are going to throw him over into the marsh," she said breathlessly. "The crabs and other critters will dispose of his body long before anyone finds him." After a short silence to catch her breath, she added, "Fishing season doesn't open for another couple of months. No one will come down there, and by then, he will have vanished without any trace. Now, let's get moving before someone drives by. Grab his arms, and I'll take the legs." She commanded, "Come on. Hurry!"

With my hands under the dead man's armpits and Contessa lifting him by his feet, we were able to move the his body the fifteen yards from his resting spot alongside the road to the bridge. The bridge had a cement guardrail wide enough for us to hoist the body onto before he took his final plunge.

"Grab a few rocks to weigh the body down," Contessa instructed.

I searched for and found a couple of flat shale rocks and placed them inside the coat he was wearing. Contessa zipped his coat tight and then, without any hesitation, pushed the body over the edge and into the water. We heard the splash ten feet below.

"Come on. Let's get the hell out of here." She took my hand, and we ran back to the car. We both jumped in from the driver's side. I started the car, and away we went.

Breathless and panting, I looked at Contessa. "This can't be the right thing to do. We have to call the police."

After a lengthy pause, she said, "Listen, Tag. It was the only thing we could do. Drive carefully. Don't give the police a reason to stop us. Just be calm, and we will be okay."

After a few moments of silence, I asked, "Contessa, who is ... I mean was ... that guy?"

"I don't know a lot about him, only that he was a drifter—his name is Jason something. He showed up in town a few years ago. He's been in trouble with the police for breaking and entering and shoplifting. I have only spoken with him a few times, and he was very incoherent and strange. He was a very scary fellow."

Contessa moved closer to me, placed her left arm around my shoulder, and whispered in my ear, "It'll be all right."

We made it back to the cottage without incident and were both still pretty intoxicated. I pulled into the garage and turned the car off.

"Do you mind if I come in?"

"No," I said. What else was I supposed to say after what we had just gone through?

As we entered the cottage, Contessa passed me by on her way to the buffet. "Come on, let's have a drink to settle the nerves." She had obviously been there before, as she knew where everything was.

She poured us both a scotch and found some soft music on the stereo. She took me by the hand, pulled me to the sofa, looked straight into my eyes, and said, "Here, take a drink—it will calm your nerves."

I took a large gulp and put my head in my hands as I leaned forward. Staring at the floor, I said, "What in the fuck have we done?"

Contessa playfully pushed me back on the sofa and sat on my lap. She took the drink from my hand, placed it on the coffee table, and began to squirm and grind on my crotch. The room began to spin, and my vision was blurred.

I watched as she began to dance in front of me. I touched her smooth, supple skin. She slipped out of her bloodstained T-shirt and threw it on the floor beside the couch. Her jet-black hair caressed her firm breasts as each bounced with the rhythm of her dance. I forgot what had just happened.

She kicked off her heels and thrust her hips in front of my face, wanting me to unfasten her blue jeans. It was as if I were in a dream. I reached out, unfastened her jeans, and watched as she wiggled her way out of them. I recalled seeing her in thong underwear, and a small snake tattoo led my eyes right to her glory. The rest of the night was a blank!

CHAPTER 9

The next morning, I rolled over in bed. I searched to see if Contessa was there. She wasn't. It was only me. My head was pounding. It felt as if I'd been hit with a three-pound sledgehammer.

I lay in bed with the pillow over my face, thinking about the night before, trying to remember. Had it been real? No way—it couldn't be. I sat up in bed, my head still in a fog, and looked around the room. *Nothing out of place ... it must have been a very bad dream.*

Weak-kneed, I stood up alongside the bed and noticed the clothes I had worn the night before in a pile on the floor at the foot of the bed. I walked over to them, leaned down, and picked up my shirt. There was blood on it. I just stared at it and then dropped it back onto the pile. I could feel my heart miss a beat. *I am so fucked.*

In a panic, I went immediately to the garage. I flung open the door, and the GTO was there. I methodically made my way around the front of the car, scared to death about what I was going to find. The headlight was broken, the paint had been scratched, and blood had splashed the bumper and headlight. I felt my heart pound hard as my knees buckled. I almost collapsed in fear on the floor of the garage. I looked at the damage and noticed clumps of short, coarse brown hair wedged in the headlamp and on the bumper. I felt the blood drain from my face.

Stepping back from the car I saw a note on the windshield in an envelope with my name on the outside. I walked over and plucked it from its resting place. I took the note out from inside, which read, *Tag, call Nate on your way to the airport and let him know that you hit a deer last evening* *on your way home from the Ocean Side. <u>Do not do anything to the car.</u> He will believe you. He has hit a couple deer on that very road. C.*

I walked back into the kitchen. I had not realized the time; it was just past eleven thirty. I stood in the middle of the kitchen, wondering what to do. I saw my phone lying on the counter. I picked it up and dialed 911. I was ready to push send ... but I couldn't. All I could hear in my head were Contessa's words: "If you call the police, you will end your career, you will end your marriage, and you will end up in jail." God, I did not want to go to jail. I was in a horrible situation made much worse when we covered up the crime by throwing the body into the marsh and fleeing the scene. I put the phone back down on the counter, found some aspirin, and poured some juice into a glass. I walked over to the half bath just off the kitchen and heaved my guts out.

At twelve thirty, a blue jeep Cherokee pulled up in front of the house. It was Gwen. She was right on time. She came to the door and knocked.

"Come on in," I said. "I will be right there." When I emerged from the bedroom with my travel bag in hand, I saw Gwen dressed in her captain's outfit, standing on the porch, looking out across the yard with her back toward me.

Without turning to greet me, she said, "Isn't this a beautiful place? It would be tough to give up." She turned and faced me, and before I could process what she had just said, she added, "Are you ready to go?"

"I think so." Gwen reached for my bag, but I stopped her hand. "That's okay—I'll get it."

We left the cottage. I placed my bag in the backseat, and Gwen started down the driveway.

"You are right, Gwen: this is a beautiful place, and it would be very hard to leave," I whimpered in a pathetic voice. As she drove, I peered out the window through bloodshot eyes. It seemed like only a matter of minutes before we were pulling into the airfield.

Gwen parked the car at the gate to the tarmac. I grabbed my bag from the backseat, and we walked together to the plane that was sitting waiting for its passenger and crew.

I looked at Gwen and said, "I have to make a call. I'll only be a second." Gwen disappeared into the plane.

I walked to the rear of the plane and pulled my phone from my pants pocket. I called Nate's number. It rang several times and then went to voice mail.

In as chipper voice as I could muster, I said, "Hey, Nate, it's Tag. I had a bit of a mishap last night. I hit a deer with the car. It's in the garage at the cottage. Just let me know how much it costs to repair. I am so sorry. I feel horrible. I will call you in a couple of days. Gwen and I are about to head back to Ann Arbor. It was great to see Dillianquest, and again, I am very sorry about the car." I ended the call and headed for the plane.

Gwen was in the cockpit, waiting for me. She looked back into the cabin and asked, "Care to fly right seat?"

"Thanks, but if you don't mind, I think I will just stay back here and catch some sleep."

"Sure thing. Alka Seltzer, aspirin, and Dramamine are all in the drawer under the sink. I didn't want to say anything at the house, but you look a bit under the weather. And yes," she added with a pause and noticeable smirk on her face, "barf bags are in the seat pocket to your right ... just in case."

"I look that bad?"

"Yes, that bad."

Gwen wiggled by me and closed the rear cabin door. As she went by me on her way to the cockpit, she said, "We will be under way shortly. I'll try to make it as smooth a flight as possible."

"You are an angel," I said and closed the blinds on the cabin windows. Darkness was going to be my friend.

The flight was uneventful, and we landed at the Willow Run Airport three and a half hours later. I was awakened by the sounds of the propellers reversing as we touched down for a flawless landing. We taxied and came to a stop in front of the terminal. Gwen did not shut down the engines as I had thought she would. I was readying myself to exit the plane.

Gwen unstrapped herself from her seat, made her way to me, and sat directly in front of me with the propellers still whizzing about.

"There is just one more thing, Mr. Grayson," she said, looking directly into my eyes. With a deep sigh, she added very carefully, "The sale of Dillianquest must go forward, Mr. Grayson. And the Dillianquest sale must go forward in the amount of at least fifty million dollars."

A long silence ensued in the plane. Gwen sat back in her seat and glared at me with cold, black eyes. "Do you understand, Mr. Grayson?"

Caught completely off guard, I protested, "I can't make things happen like that."

Gwen leaned forward in her seat and from behind it pulled a large manila envelope. She looked at the envelope and then at me and said, "Fifty million dollars, Mr. Grayson." She opened the envelope in a slow, deliberate fashion and pulled from it a photo of my handwritten note that contained the directions from the Ocean Side Shanty. She handed it to me to review. My heart was about to explode and jump through my chest.

"Your handwritten note, Mr. Grayson, could end up close to where you dumped the body last night." She said those words, "where you dumped the body last night," in a cold, stony, matter-of-fact tone.

She reached back into the envelope and pulled out another photo of the damaged GTO with blood on the bumper and headlight. She handed it to me so I could see the picture. Without any hesitation, she said, "With just a little bit of help, Mr. Grayson, I can all but guarantee that Beaufort's finest could trace the car used in that unfortunate fatal hit-and-run accident back to you."

My head was hanging low. I felt as if I were going to vomit.

Gwen reached back into the envelope and pulled from it several more pictures. She tossed them onto my lap. They were all from the living room of the cottage, when Contessa had danced in front of me. There I was, holding on to her jeans as she progressed through various stages of undress. "What do you think your wife would say if she were to see these?"

The pictures kept coming. The next pictures were from the bedroom of the cottage. It was of Contessa and me, naked in bed. Gwen pulled out several more of Contessa and me sprawled out naked in every conceivable compromising position.

"Those are pretty damning pictures, Mr. Grayson," Gwen observed casually. "I cannot imagine what your wife and partners would think or do if they were to see all these pictures."

The plane propellers swirled in my head. I could feel my heart pounding harder and harder in my chest. I felt as though I were going to pass out.

"And in case you hadn't noticed, Mr. Grayson," Gwen added in a voice that snapped me from my daze, "You are minus one blue blazer. It would be a shame if that somehow found its way to Highway 21, wouldn't it, Mr. Grayson?"

During the long pause that followed, Gwen gathered the pictures from my limp hands. She put them back in the envelope and placed it on my lap. "These are yours to keep, Mr. Grayson. Consider them a friendly reminder of your fifty-million-dollar mission."

Gwen added coldly, "The purchase of Dillianquest, Mr. Grayson, will be good for your business. Here is a tip, Mr. Grayson, that will help you: it is only known by a select few that the Dillianquest family fortune vanished along with many others in the recent Bernard Madoff scam." With an air of sarcasm in her voice, Gwen added, "I have no doubt, Mr. Grayson, that you are aware of Mr. Madoff's Ponzi scheme?"

After a thoughtful pause, she added with a tone of contempt in her voice, "Nathaniel Dillianquest will jump at your fifty-million-dollar offer. And just think," Gwen added, "your firm picks up a choice South Carolina business and prime low-country real estate at a bargain price. You will find that the Dillianquest complex will appraise well in excess of sixty million dollars, even in today's depressed market. Everyone is a winner here, Mr. Grayson. There are no losers … yet."

After a pause that seemed to last a lifetime, she added, "Mr. Grayson, the purchase of Dillianquest is good for you, too. When you make this deal happen, you will get your freedom back to do with it what you will."

With that last remark, Gwen went back into the cockpit and shut down both engines. She moved past me in the main cabin and opened the rear cabin door. With my bag in her hand, she disappeared into the Michigan sunlight. I sat there for just a second. I tried to gather my wits about me as best I could. I got up from my seat, stuffed the envelope into my briefcase, and left the plane.

Waiting planeside, standing next to the car with the trunk opened, was Jim. Gwen greeted Jim warmly, saying, "Jim, it's so nice to see you again."

"The pleasure, again, is all mine."

Gwen handed Jim my bag, and he placed it in the car trunk. I was walking toward the car when Gwen stepped in front of me and extended her hand. I took her hand, and she squeezed just firmly enough to make her point. She looked me in the eye and said, "I am looking forward to your next visit." I nodded.

Jim had the back door open. I slunk into the seat and waited for Jim to get in. Jim sat in the driver's seat, looked into the back, and asked, "Good trip?"

"Crazy." After a lengthy pause, I told Jim, "Let's sit here and watch for a minute."

"Sure thing, boss."

We watched as Gwen took off and headed south. We watched until her plane disappeared from sight, but I knew that being out of sight was not the same as being out of mind.

I am so screwed!

CHAPTER 10

Claudette Stevenson had worked at the law offices of Belanger, Larson, and George for fifty-seven years. Claudette was the first employee hired by the then-single-person law office when it was founded by Michael Abraham Belanger back in 1952. Since that meager beginning, practicing law had become the Belanger family tradition. Michael Belanger II, who was fondly called Junior, had followed in his father's footsteps, going to the same law school and joining the same fraternity, as had his father.

When Michael Belanger Sr. had passed away in 1994, the senior managing partner had become, and remained, Michael Abraham Belanger II. The Belanger family had enjoyed a long and distinguished history with the University of South Carolina School of Law.

Michael Abraham Belanger III, born to Mary Ann and Michael Belanger, was the couple's only child. Abe, as he had been called since birth, was destined to take over the family firm and follow the tradition handed down from father to son. Like it or not, Abe was going into the family's law practice and would follow in the family's very successful footprints. That was the way it was going to be. Abe was directed to that end in every facet of his meticulously prepared childhood.

Abe was known by family, friends, and Junior's co-workers at the firm to be somewhat of a genius, graduating magna cum laude in 2000 from the USC School of Law. Not only did Abe graduate with his jurist doctorate, but he also earned a master's degree in computer science in his spare time while studying law.

Abe was keenly interested in expanding and protecting the family business that his grandfather and father had worked so hard to build. Abe's grandfather and then his father had led the family to great wealth and prestige in South Carolina. Over the years, the Belanger family had cultivated powerful political friends in both state and federal offices.

The early years of the practice had been primarily devoted to real estate, probate, and related financial transactions in and around the Beaufort area. When Junior joined the firm after law school, he expanded the firm's interests into the arena of criminal defense, much to the dismay and protest of the senior Belanger.

After some struggle, Junior excelled in vigorously defending client's interests and began to earn a well-deserved reputation as one of the best defense attorneys in the great state of South Carolina. Junior's courtroom antics and no-holds-barred approach to his clients' defense caused him to be known as something of a junkyard dog willing to do whatever necessary on behalf of his client—the kind of defense attorney one wants in a life-and-death battle. Sometimes the methods were a tad bit unsavory, but the results were always impressive.

The addition to the firm's principals in Larson and George brought an expertise in financial investments; Securities and Exchange Commission filings; intellectual property; and fraud litigation. Soon the law offices of Belanger, Larson, and George enjoyed a reputation in circles of wealth as a one-stop shop for all legal requirements and family necessities. The firm took the womb-to-tomb approach to legal advice and counsel for the richest of South Carolina society. Discretion could be counted upon.

Abe, now a junior partner in the firm, was developing a deepening passion for electronic surveillance. As a child, Abe recalled being exposed to some of the more unsavory aspects of his father's chosen profession. Extortion and death threats were just a few of the unintended consequences of a criminal-defense practice. It was Abe's mission early on to bring the law firm into the twenty-first century to protect the family and firm against such threats.

Over the past couple of years, Abe had installed surveillance equipment in the firm's conference rooms and public areas. No one, including Junior, was aware of the existence of the monitoring equipment. Knowledge of such things would only work against their intention. Abe had devised an ingenious method of capturing clients' actions and conversations, in their own words, and saved them on a hard drive located in a secret office behind a false wall in his basement

Abe's system was brilliant. When someone walked into a monitored area, their motion would trigger the video- and audio-recording devices. The devices were hidden from sight and strategically located to record the entire surveillance area, with no blind spots. After thirty seconds of complete silence or lack of movement, the equipment would stop recording automatically.

This was where the pure genius of Abe's design was apparent. After the recording was complete, the software that Abe had written would search for specific words or aggressive changes in normal voice inflection or pattern. If the system detected aggression, it triggered the recorded activities to be saved to the system's hard drive and displayed its findings on the monitor as a system alert.

If the activity recorded was of a passive nature, the system would save it to a temporary file for thirty days and then delete it from memory. The passive activity could be viewed if necessary, but if the general nature of the interaction did not raise any red flags or system alerts, it would often be deleted without ever being viewed.

Abe named his system PASS, after the Passive-Aggressive Surveillance System software he had written. He believed that his surveillance program had a huge potential as an emerging market for the firm to explore. Abe was using the office as a test site to refine his product before taking it to market, complete with operating-system examples.

Abe was so pleased with how the system was performing that he expanded its use to all offices at the firm, believing that covert surveillance of this nature would save the firm in the long run, protect the privacy of those he worked with, and create the necessary data support to market the system to other security-conscious companies. Abe believed this would be the system that made his father proud of all his hard work and brilliant innovations.

When Abe arrived home from work, he would usually pour a glass of red wine and venture to the basement to secretly review the day's PASS activities. The monitor that sat on the desktop displayed all the necessary information. At a glance, Abe was able to determine how many recorded activities had taken place during the day. But the most important information the system displayed was how many recorded activities had triggered a system alert—a must-watch for the novice voyeur.

It was a bright spot in Abe's day to review all the saved system alerts. He was often amused by the heated arguments that took place behind closed doors. It yielded much in the way of office secrets. All too often, the system would catch the sordid love trysts that took place between his father and any given secretary when Junior was supposed to be attending a late-night client meeting or business dinner.

If Abe thought the action important enough, it would be logged, dated, categorized, and filed in the system's hard drive. Abe had many saved files of his father and several of the women who worked at the firm. Abe saved each system alert on DVD as backup to be used at a later date if necessary. Abe had amassed at least one hundred system alerts saved onto DVD, all stored in a fireproof vault.

It was a well-kept secret in the firm that Junior had a propensity for taking many of the more sensitive conversations out of the office to the shed. The shed was Junior's private woodworking shop at his home. The shed was detached from the house, and no one could hear what was going on or being said. No one could overhear conversations that may compromise a case or endanger the firm. Junior often directed clients to meet him at the shed rather than make an appearance at the office. It was an unwritten rule at the Belanger household that the shed was off-limits to everyone—no exceptions.

The Belanger's estate was situated north of town on fifty acres of beautiful rolling South Carolina hills. The property had several ponds fully stocked with fish, a riding stable, and several working barns. Five thoroughbred quarter horses trotted inside a white fence alongside visitors as they made their way up the gently winding, paved drive to the pillared front entrance to the country mansion.

Mary Ann, Abe's mother, rode and cared for her beloved horses. The long drive was lined on both sides with crepe myrtle trees. The house was meticulously landscaped. A large fountain of a man riding a horse raised on its back haunches greeted guests as they walked toward the front doors.

Junior was a man who enjoyed working on projects around the house and spent many hours out in the shed. Junior was an excellent craftsman, hand carving wooden duck and small-animal decoys out of balsa wood in his spare time. He said it relaxed him and took his mind off work.

On a rare occasion, Junior would take Abe into shed, where they would carve together for hours, oftentimes saying nothing. Abe did not show much of an interest for woodworking, so as time passed, father and son spent less and less time together.

As a young man growing up in the shadow of such a dominant, overbearing personality, Abe recalled many evenings when men showed up at the house and immediately excused themselves to go out back to the shed. Junior always told Abe that he was working on a project for the men. Mother knew the truth, but never said anything; regardless, Abe was not fooled by their flimsy excuses.

Early on, Abe had snuck out to the shed and listened to his father and the other men talk about things children should never hear. Abe had heard bits and pieces of conversation that involved murder and rape and other things that raised the hair on the back of Abe's neck. Abe never told his father or mother about the things he had overheard. Abe was afraid of what might happen to him and his family if anyone found out he knew of the secrets in the shed.

About a year after Abe began surveillance operations at the firm's offices, he decided to expand the surveillance profile to include Junior's workshop at the family's home as a precaution. The workshop was secretly wired for sound and video. If something unexpected happened to dear old Dad, Abe would have the goods on the culprit—in their own words.

Belanger, Larson, and George had been the legal beacon in the Beaufort community for many years. When Abe joined the firm, he began performing many hundreds hours of pro bono work on behalf of the less fortunate. The mainstay of the firm's cash flow was the representation of the wealthy families in the area. The firm kept many family secrets. The pro bono work was well received in Beaufort.

For as long as memory served, Michael Belanger Sr. had been the personal lawyer for the Dillianquest family. When the senior Belanger passed away from cancer, the responsibilities of the Dillianquest family fortune and many other families were handed to Junior to manage. It was the responsibility of the firm to continue advising their clients generation after generation and keeping family secrets … secret.

As the firm's pro bono champion, Abe had taken on many such causes over the few years he had been practicing law with his father's firm. Abe did not possess the cutthroat instincts necessary to keep the firm's criminal-defense practice alive.

Abe was considered by his father to be a bleeding-heart liberal and too soft for his own good. Junior had earned a reputation for taking on the tough cases and winning … at any cost. Junior was sure that Abe would not have what it took to run the firm when it was his turn and was not afraid of telling him how he felt. An ever-widening chasm was opening between father and son.

CHAPTER 11

It was late in the afternoon on Friday when the phone rang at the law offices of Belanger, Larson, and George. Claudette Stevenson was at her desk and on the job. In her usual efficient way, Claudette picked up the phone after two rings and said, "Good afternoon, Belanger, Larson, and George. How may I direct your call?"

"Good afternoon, madam," a very formal voice echoed on the other end of the phone. "May I speak with the principal of the firm, Mr. Belanger, please?"

"Mr. Dillianquest," Claudette said in a motherly tone, "I will ring his office and see if he is available."

"Thanks, darling. I can never sneak by you." Then Nate quickly added in a playful, flirtatious way, "You know, if you ever want to leave that office, I've got a spot for you in mine."

"Yes, sir, Mr. Dillianquest, I appreciate that. Now, I am going to place you on hold for one moment and see if Mr. Belanger is available."

Less than a minute later, Claudette was back on the phone with Nate, explaining, "Mr. Belanger asked if you could hold for a minute, or he will call you back on your mobile—whichever you prefer."

"I'll hold."

"He will be with you in just a few moments. Always a pleasure, Mr. Dillianquest." With that cordial exit, Claudette placed Nate on hold, forcing him to listen to nondescript, symphonic Michael Jackson music.

Nate had made this phone call to Junior from the back of the *Kindred Spirit*, where he had been sipping Scotch for a couple of hours, pondering his future. It was a chilly day for Beaufort. Nate wore a black sweatshirt, heavy white-striped jogging pants, and a plain black baseball cap. He sat and watched the birds feed in the marsh across the intercoastal waterway.

Nate thought of how shitty his life had gotten. Mostly he thought about his mother's health, which was a concern. Her Alzheimer's disease had left a strong physical body but had ravaged her mind, leaving her unaware of her surroundings. Her doctor recently told Nate that she could live like this for five, ten, or even twenty years. She was unable to recognize those she had once cared for deeply and loved with all her heart. It was difficult for Nate to see his mother on a daily basis in this horrible condition. Nate sat on the *Kindred Spirit*, depressed, single, and alone.

A few minutes went by, and then the hold music stopped.

Junior announced his presence. "Nate, what's the good word today, partner?"

"Not much good in the world today. How are you, Junior? It's been a while since I've seen you." After a short pause, Nate added, "Sounds like you have me on speaker."

"I do have you on speaker, Nate. I've been wrapped up in the murder-for-hire case in Greenville. Abe and I have been pouring over some of our client's testimony. I tell ya, people do some pretty stupid shit thinking they can get away with murder."

"That they do."

"Abe is sitting here with me."

"Hi, Nate, it's Abe. How are you?"

"Doing all right and everyone I can," Nate said with a little chuckle.

"What's on your mind, Nate?" Junior asked.

"No offense, Abe, but can you take me off speaker, Junior?"

Junior picked up the phone and placed the receiver by his ear as he leaned back in his overstuffed leather chair. In one quick motion, Junior hoisted his feet and placed them on the edge of his desk.

"Okay, it's just you and me, Nate. What's up?"

"I am in a bit of a quandary, Junior. I need to talk with you privately and off the record."

"Sure thing. If you like, I have an hour or so that I can clear for you right now."

"I appreciate that, but I think we need to take this one to the shed."

"No problem, Nate. I can meet you tomorrow evening." Junior continued without hesitation, saying, "I have an engagement this evening that I would prefer not to break."

After a pause on Nate's end of the phone, Nate said, "Look, Junior." Impatience crept into his tone. "If this evening's engagement is with one of your skirts, I'm asking you as a friend to break the date and meet me at the shed at nine sharp."

"Sounds rather urgent," Junior said questioningly, hoping to get Nate to elaborate.

"It is, or I wouldn't be asking. And one favor, Junior: bring a copy of Mother's last will and testament with you."

"Her will? What do you need with her will?" Junior sounded more forceful now.

"Junior," Nate said tersely, "just bring a copy of the fucking will with you tonight, will you? I'll see you at nine."

With that, Nate tossed his phone on the table to his right. The phone slid on the tabletop and came to rest alongside the .38-caliber pistol lying next to the bottle of scotch. Nate tapped his fingers against the half-empty glass of scotch in his left hand and stared out over the water.

Junior removed the phone from his ear and just stared at it for a few moments. Junior had heard that desperate tone in Nate's voice before, but it had been a long while. He knew that Nate was in trouble again, but did not know exactly what was going on.

As he hung up the phone, Junior mumbled to himself, "Trust-fund babies are a giant pain in the ass."

He pressed the intercom button. Claudette answered, "Yes, sir?"

"Claudette, will you please make a copy of Mrs. Dillianquest's last will and testament and bring it to me?"

"I'll have it for you in just a moment."

"Thanks, and Claudette, one more thing. Please call Mary Ann and let her know that I will be home for dinner tonight at about six thirty."

"Will do."

In a few minutes, there was a polite knock on Junior's door, and Claudette walked in.

"Here is your Dillianquest request, sir." Claudette made her way over to Junior's desk and placed the file on the corner. Claudette then added, "I spoke with Mrs. Belanger and let her know that you would be joining her for dinner tonight at six thirty. Is there anything else?"

"No," Junior said with a smile as he picked up the file. "That should do it. Thanks."

"If there is nothing else, I will see you Monday. Good night."

"Have a good evening. See you tomorrow," he said mindlessly. Claudette closed the door behind her, and the office fell quiet.

Junior got up from his desk and deliberately made his way across his large office. He stood before a wall of law books and ran his finger across their spines. His hand found its way to a cabinet door where he pulled out a new bottle of bourbon and a crystal tumbler. He cracked open the bottle, smiling when he heard that distinctive sound a new bottle of whiskey made when its seal was first broken. He held the bottle to his nose and slowly moved his head from side to side across the bottle's opening, savoring the rich smell of blended whiskey.

Junior poured the crystal tumbler half full and then screwed the top back on the bottle and replaced it in the cabinet. He walked back to his chair and sat down. Junior reclined in his deep plush office chair and said out loud as he held the glass up in the air, as if he were presenting a toast, "Nate … this missed piece of ass is going to cost you dearly, my friend." With that, he tossed back his head and swallowed the contents in the glass, all in one gulp.

Junior put the glass down on the desk with force and stared at it for just a few seconds. He stood up from his chair and stuffed the Dillianquest file into his briefcase. He walked over to the coatrack and then methodically put on his jacket. Junior wondered what Nate was up to as he dressed himself for the ride home.

As he left his office, he turned off the lights and closed the door. Walking down the hall toward the reception area, he noticed that everyone had already gone for the evening. He stopped in the middle of the receiving room and remembered that it was Friday night. Junior stepped out of the office and onto the street. A slight chill nipped at the air.

CHAPTER 12

The gate was already open when Nate arrived just a few minutes before nine in his light tan 1941 Lincoln Continental coupe. Nate turned into the well-lit driveway and drove toward the main house. The evening was dark and cold. Nate extinguished his driving lights, using only the antique car's running lights. Nate tried to make his presence a bit less conspicuous to Mary Ann. Mary Ann was well versed in the goings-on at the shed.

The main house was majestically lit, creating an illusion about the exterior that made it look much larger in the night. As Nate drove closer to the main house, a slightly dimmer set of blue lights defined the driveway to the shed. Nate veered to his left and drove in first gear toward the lights of the shed, which played hide-and-seek with the trees. Nate pulled his car to a stop and there, leaning against the entryway door, was Junior.

Junior was as big a man physically as he was in personality. Junior stood six feet two inches tall and, despite putting on a few extra pounds over the years, was in pretty good physical shape. Junior always said his good physical condition came from chasing women. He kept his hair color dark to hide his age. He was a strikingly good-looking man with green eyes and a bright smile.

Nate opened the car door and greeted Junior. "Thanks for meeting with me tonight, Junior. I really appreciate it."

Before Nate could close the car door, Junior had walked over to where Nate was standing and placed his hand on top of the door, holding it open.

"You know, Nate, of all the cars you own, this one is my favorite. A 1941 Continental Cabriolet—you can't beat that."

Junior began walking around the car, running his hand along the smooth exterior. He continued, "I just love that long hood and those rear-fender skirts." Junior's voice filled with genuine appreciation. "I mean, what's not to love? Solid wood dash and leather seats. You can just picture Lawrence Olivier on his way to the Oscars in this car, can't you, Nate?"

Nate did not respond. He just shut the car door and walked over to the entryway of the shed, turned, and asked Junior, "You got any scotch in there?"

"Sure do, and ice in the ice maker."

"Glad to see you got that thing fixed."

"They couldn't fix the goddamn thing. I had to get a new one. Said there was too much sawdust in the coils, and it ended up burning itself out. Pour me one while you're at it, will ya?"

Junior's woodworking shop was equipped with every machine and tool known to man. Junior had a lounge area in the back with a flat-screen television and four large recliners, so the boys could talk in comfort.

As Nate nosed around the workbench, Junior asked, "Did you bring any of those Cubans with you tonight?"

"As a matter of fact." He reached into his sweatshirt pouch and pulled two cigars out. "Got a cutter around here anywhere?"

"I'm sure we can find something." Junior went over to a drawer, pulled out a utility knife, and handed it to Nate, saying, "Here you go."

Nate cut the tips of the cigars and handed one to Junior. "I thought you gave these things up?"

"I did, but here is how I figure it," Junior said. "We fire these bad boys up and hopefully by the time we finish smoking them, we'll have concluded whatever it is you wanted to talk to me about."

"Sounds like a plan," Nate said as he threw Junior his lighter.

"Come on. Grab that bottle, and I'll put some ice in the bucket, and we'll go in the back, and you can tell me what the fuck is bothering you." Junior put his arm around Nate's shoulder, and they began walking toward the back of the shed. The men stopped, and Junior looked directly into

Nate's eyes and said, "You aren't thinking about suicide again, are you, Nate?"

"Not at the moment," Nate replied with no expression in his voice. "But under the circumstances."

Junior turned toward Nate until they stood toe-to-toe with each other. Junior had both hands on Nate's shoulders. Junior quickly said, "Bullshit, Nate. If you're thinking suicide, I might as well dial up Doc Jones and get him out here right now."

After a short pause, Nate looked at Junior and said, "No, that's not why I came out tonight."

Junior placed his arm back around Nate's shoulder and resumed walking. "That's good, Nate, because I ain't no fucking shrink and don't want to be picking up the pieces of your life."

The two finally got back to the lounge area of the shed. Junior sat in his usual chair and placed his glass on the table that stretched out in front of each of the recliners.

"Have a seat, Nate." Junior pointed to a recliner directly opposite his. "What's on your mind?"

"Did you bring a copy of Mother's will?"

Junior pointed to a manila envelope that lay on the table. "It's right there."

Nate reached over and picked the envelope off the table. He opened the unnamed envelope and slid the papers out that were inside. Nate stared at the front cover of a thick white bifold. The title read, "Last Will and Testament of Savannah Grace Dillianquest."

Nate nervously tapped the folded document against the palm of his left hand. He looked up at Junior and said, "We have been friends for an awful long time, Junior." Nate stared at Junior with a half-drunk smirk on his face and continued, "I hope at the end of this evening, we're still that way."

"Me too, Nate."

"I got a lot of shit running through my head, Junior. I need some help," Nate said as he began pacing around the room.

Junior began feeling a bit uncomfortable. Nate always carried a

.38-caliber pistol with him. Junior believed that Nate was just a wee bit off his rocker that night.

Still sitting in the recliner, Junior replied, "I'm all ears, Nate." But before Nate could say anything, Junior added, "Are you carrying that .38 with you?"

"Nope, left it on the *Spirit*."

"Why don't you have a seat, Nate?"

"No, I don't think so," Nate replied as he continued to pace about the room. "I am a bit wound up. I need to keep moving."

"Suit yourself, Nate. Why don't you just come out and tell me what's on your mind?"

Nate kept on pacing about the room while thumbing through the will, obviously looking for something. Nate folded the pages back on themselves, exposing one page that he was intent upon reading in its entirety.

A few minutes of silence ensued while Nate read the page from the will. When he had finished reading, Nate looked up at Junior without any expression on his face and said in a very matter-of-fact tone, "I need you to change Mother's will."

Junior returned the look he received from Nate and said in an equally level tone, "Nate, you know I can't do that. Your mother gave me explicit instructions that her will was not to be altered in any fashion. As an officer of the court, I have a duty to uphold her wishes. I am sorry—it can't be done." Junior offered his sincerest attempt at consoling Nate.

Nate was still pacing around the room—rather manically at this point. He went to the table, picked up his glass, and took a long drink. Nate placed the glass back on the table and said to Junior as he began pacing again, "I really don't give a flying fuck about your duties, Junior. You owe this to me."

Nate's face reddened, and his voice rose. "If your father hadn't introduced my family to that scumbag Bernie Madoff, none of this bullshit would be happening. Your firm invested everything we had with that thief, and now it's all gone. There is nothing left—not one fucking penny. I've had to sell nine of my goddamn cars, Junior. I am flat fucking broke, and it's your fault!" Nate was all but yelling at Junior at this point.

Junior knew from years of experience that keeping his mouth shut was the best way to defuse a potentially bad situation. Junior thought that his old friend just needed to vent his frustration, and he was not going to get in the way by saying something that may trigger a violent outburst.

In his role as legal counsel, Junior often played the part of psychiatrist to his clients. Anything that was said in the shed stayed in the shed. Junior sat back in his chair and acted relaxed, although he was not, and put on an air of confidence. He remained quiet and just listened.

Nate was still pacing back and forth, puffing occasionally on his cigar and drinking his scotch. Then, all of a sudden, Nate stopped pacing. He walked with calm intent to the recliner and sat down directly opposite Junior. Nate sat on the edge of the chair, leaning forward over the table, his elbows propped on his knees.

Nate looked directly at Junior and said, "Here is what I know." He leaned back in the recliner, cigar in his right hand and glass of scotch in his left, and crossed his legs, his ankle coming to rest on his knee.

Nate looked more relaxed than he had all evening as he said, "Do you remember when we were twenty-three, Junior?" Nate paused for a few seconds, reflecting back on better days. "We both had just graduated from college. You with your law degree and me with my engineering degree, we were destined to take over the family businesses. Man, we had the world by the short hairs, didn't we, Junior?" Nate's tone had mellowed to sentimental.

Nate took a long pull on his cigar and blew the smoke into the air. Nate blew several smoke rings as he leaned back in his chair, poking the cigar through them as they drifted into the motionless air. Nate's face became a bit more serious as he added, "On July 11, 1972, all that changed for me."

Nate began speaking in a very sober voice. "If you recall, Junior, you and I were out partying that night, hitting all the usual bars in Beaufort, just two little rich kids out on the town." Nate stopped talking and paused, looking for a response from Junior, but none came. "You do remember July 11, 1972 … don't you, Junior?" Nate inquired.

Junior remained silent and fixed his eyes on Nate with a look of contempt that was meant to kill.

With a quirky smile, Nate added, "We drank a bit too much and smoked a bit, too, that night, and as I recall the accident, Jason Holt lost control of his bicycle and swerved directly in the path of my car."

Nate's face had lost all expression as he said, "What in the fuck is a thirteen-year-old kid doing out at three in the morning?" He had pictured the accident thousands of times in his head. He had become void of any feeling about the incident.

"I can still hear the sound Jason's body made as he hit the bumper of the car," Nate said. "If memory serves me correctly, Junior, I wanted to stop and help, but you insisted that we leave that poor kid to die in the street. The doctors said he died several hours after the accident. It must have been a horrible way to die, don't you think, Junior?"

Nate was prompting Junior for a response. Junior sat without saying a word. Nate added, "We could have saved that kid's life if we weren't so fucked up."

After a short pause for a puff on the cigar and a pull on his drink, Nate continued. "When it came time to take the fall for the accident, it was me left holding the bag." Nate sounded oddly resigned to what had happened. "No one ever found out that you were in that car with me, Junior." Junior sensed that Nate was proud of the fact that he had kept their secret but was unsure still where Nate was going with his story.

"To this date, nobody knows what part you played in that kid's death." Nate took a long draw on his cigar and blew the smoke into the air. He got up from his chair, walked over to the counter, placed a few ice cubes in his glass, and poured more scotch. Nate turned to Junior and asked, "Need a refill, Junior?"

"I'm good, thanks."

Nate walked back to his chair, resumed his position, and continued, "Yep, your daddy did his level best ... and for me, that meant four years in the Marines, but no jail time!" Nate then added with a smile, "Your old man could really pull some strings. I guess the apple didn't fall far from that tree."

Nate propped up both feet on the edge of the table and continued, "You know, Junior, the ironic thing about me serving in the Marines was they put me into the South American Drug Interdiction Unit. Go figure that one out." Nate said with a slight laugh, "Your old man had quite the sense of humor. Here we kill an innocent boy while high on drugs, and your father somehow got me in the South American Drug Interdiction Unit." Nate, now with a larger smile on his face, looked at Junior and said, "And once again, your law firm saved my sorry ass."

Nate paused for a moment to reflect, took a deep breath, and then continued. "You know, I never did tell you the truth about what happened in Colombia." Nate settled back into his recliner. Junior knew this was going to take a while, but he didn't know where he was going to be taken. Nate continued in a slow, dramatic storyteller's tone, "It was early in the morning in the mountains. The sun was just barely up, shining on the hillsides. There was fog in the valleys. It was really quite a beautiful morning." Nate paused to take a drink of Scotch.

"My unit was on a routine reconnaissance flight. We were in our helicopter, looking for evidence of remote cocaine huts. There was just the three of us, two pilots and me. I was the new guy, so they made me the spotter."

Nate paused again, thinking and reflecting. "We had been flying pretty low, just above the treetops, when I spotted several huts and drying tables. I signaled to the boys, and we circled a couple of times, making sure there were no FARC militia in the area. The last thing we wanted to do was fuck with the local crazy-ass terrorists."

Nate continued with his monologue while Junior listened intently; the latter had never heard this story before. "The huts looked abandoned, so we set the chopper down and decided to investigate." A bit of intrigue could be heard in his voice. "The pilot and copilot had been running surveillance for several years, and they had developed some local distribution connections with the natives."

Nate stopped for a second, took a long pull on his cigar, and then added, "Whenever we happened to find any extra bags of coke, we would take it to the local natives and sell it or arrange to have it smuggled back to the States. The pilots lovingly referred to it as their retirement fund." Nate stopped for another drink of Scotch.

"At the time, Junior, I really didn't give a shit what they did. I was just along for the ride. I didn't give much thought to getting caught up in a drug-trafficking scandal. Besides, the death of that poor Holt kid was eating me up inside."

Nate paused, took a long sip from his drink, and then continued. "I often thought about jumping out of the chopper just to ease that pain," Nate explained in a sad tone. "Anyway, we landed the chopper in a small clearing and started looking around the place for drugs. We were all pretty nervous as we approached one of the huts. As we got close, two people bolted from the hut and started running toward the jungle, screaming something in Spanish." Nate's face was turning white as he recalled the incident. "I panicked," Nate said with an escalating intensity, "and without a thought or blink of an eye, I pulled up my rifle, and I shot and killed both of them. Just like that!" Nate paused as he relived the incident. He seemed to be transported back to the very instant in time when he had pulled the trigger.

Nate continued in a slow, deliberate, and cold tone, "I shot them in the back as they were running away. I didn't know what they were saying, Junior. I had no fucking clue, and at that point, I didn't much care. I just shot them dead before something happened to us." He spoke with finality.

By this time, Nate was leaning forward in his chair, both hands clutched tightly together. His head hung low. Junior had heard several murder confessions in his career, but never one from such a close friend. Junior worked hard at remaining calm and distant from the conversation. He leaned back in his chair and offered nothing to console his close friend. He puffed on his cigar, took a drink from his glass, and waited for Nate to continue. Nate was obviously in pain.

After a long and awkward silence, Nate sat back in his chair and continued, "As we searched the area, I discovered two infants covered in blankets in a box in the corner of one of the huts. As I got closer to the hut, I heard them screaming and crying. Their cries were muffled and faint. I could barely hear their screams, as they were buried in lots of blankets." Nate continued, "I guessed the two that I shot were the infants' parents.

They must have been making a run for it and were going to come back for the kids later."

Despite being clearly saddened by the story he was telling, Nate continued. "They were very cute and so tiny," he said with a smile. "I picked them up and held them both until they quieted," Nate added in a calm, caring voice.

"The first thought that ran through my mind was that of Mother and how she had lost her only daughter." Nate had lost the smile from his face. "As I looked at these newly orphaned children, I thought they would make Mother very happy."

Nate's voice became a bit colder as he continued with his story. "There was a lot of coke wrapped up and scattered all over the fucking place. The huts were empty and ransacked. It was obvious that whoever was there had evacuated in a hurry." His voice became more frantic. "We loaded up twenty kilos or so of coke in the chopper. We dragged the two bodies, one female and one male, into a hut."

Nate paused to take a deep breath and said, "I remember finding several cans of fuel by a generator. We splashed the huts with the fuel. One of the guys wrapped a pole with the shirt from the guy I had shot and soaked it with fuel. We were going to burn the huts and the bodies and destroy the evidence." Nate paused for a moment and continued, "I remember him standing there with the torch in his hand ... and then the other guy turned to me and said, 'Toss the babies into the hut.'"

Nate's pace had become very fast and panicked. "I drew my sidearm and pointed it at the two and said, 'These babies are not going to die today!'" Nate paused, took a deep breath, and then continued, "Then, with a flick of the Bic, the torch was tossed into the hut, and in just a couple of seconds, the whole place went up in flames."

After a lengthy pause, Nate added in a less hurried tone, "We seemed to have struck the mother lode. We had fifty or sixty pounds of prepackaged cocaine and two baby girls." Nate stopped, took a draw off his cigar, and leaned back deep into his recliner.

Nate looked at Junior and said, "I had no idea what to do with those two infants. I just knew I was responsible for them now. No one said anything. It became an unspoken understanding between us: they took the coke, and I took the babies, and if anyone found out ... someone would die."

Junior heard a sense of relief in Nate's voice as he continued, "We diverted to a small village where the local connection lived. We off-loaded the drugs. That's where I met an elderly woman. She was the big mama of those who lived in the village where we landed. I assumed she was the mother of the locals that my Marines had been dealing with. Luckily for me, one of the pilots spoke a little Spanish, so I had him translate for me. I gave the two infants to the woman and told her I would be back for them. It was obvious that she was in control of everything that went on in that little village. The girls were in good hands."

Nate had calmed down considerably now as he said, "I told her I was going to take them to America and take good care of them." Nate paused for a moment. A small smile crept onto his face. "I remember her big smile. I could read in her face that she was happy they would be spared her hard life." Nate seemed to be feeling a bit better as he continued, "I told her that I would send money, and someone would come and get them as soon as possible."

After a deep sigh, Nate continued, "Of course, you know the rest of the story, Junior. It was you who arranged for the babies to be brought to the United States. It was you, Junior, who transferred the money to the government officials in Colombia, and it was you, Junior, who personally saw to it that Gwen and Contessa had all the fake paperwork to remain in the United States." Nate was calm as he said, "The only thing you did not know is that I killed the parents of Gwen and Contessa in cold blood."

After a short pause, Nate added, "Those two baby girls sure did make Mother happy, didn't they?" A big smile appeared on his face for the first time that evening, but it soon faded. He took another long pull on his cigar and another long drink of Scotch while Junior patiently sat in his chair, expressionless, wondering where all this was going to end.

Nate continued with his story, leaning back in his chair. "Now, Junior, let's zoom to the present day, shall we? We all know the economy is in the shitter. No news flash there." Nate leaned forward, placed his glass on the table, and said, "It's only a matter of a month or two before it takes me under, as it has so many other unfortunate fucking schmucks."

Nate took a deep breath, let out a sigh, and said, "The mall project is dead, and I owe everybody millions. The apartment project is dead, and I owe everybody millions. There is nothing on the horizon, Junior, that gives me any hope. I owe millions upon fucking millions to just about everyone."

Nate's slow, calm delivery made Junior nervous as he added, "I have leveraged everything just to stay afloat. And frankly, Junior, me staying afloat is no more likely than me flying to the moon."

Nate stopped, took big draw on his cigar, and edged his way to the front of his chair. As he blew the smoke into the air, he laughed out loud. "And then there is our good friend Bernie Madoff. What a piece of work he is ... fifty billion dollars lost to a fucking Ponzi scheme." Nate picked his glass up from the table and raised it to his lips. But before he took a drink, he said, "Our family's donation was just a mere hundred million dollars, Junior—just a drop in Bernie's fifty-billion-dollar fucking bucket."

Nate took a drink, sat back in his chair, and said, "That fucking Madoff. He sat in our living room, ate and drank with Father and Mother, and reassured them both that everything was right on track ... double-digit returns, guaranteed. Dad ate that shit up!"

Nate wiggled his way back to the front of his chair, elbows on his knees, hands clenched. In a disgusted tone, he said, "And your firm, Junior, handled all the family's investments. Where in the fuck were you guys? Where in the fuck was the SEC when all this crap was happening?"

Nate collapsed back into his chair, clearly exhausted, and said, "The only thing I have left, Junior, is Dillianquest." After a lengthy, soul-searching pause, Nate added, "I am embarrassed to tell you this, Junior, but in the light of things, who really gives a shit, right?" Nate laughed and said, "I have been embezzling hundreds of thousands of dollars from Mother's foundation to make ends meet." Nate sat straight up in his chair, looked directly at Junior, and said, "And I'll be damned if I am going to give half of the only inheritance I have to those two."

Junior was well aware that Nate could cause him, his family, and the firm a great deal of trouble if he told that story to anyone else. After a lengthy pause, Junior interrupted the silence.

"Nate, I know you know that I tried to get your folks to bail on Madoff back in 2000, when the Boston SEC let me read a memo from Markopolus. Your old man wouldn't hear of it, though. You know how stubborn he was. I tried, Nate. I really did try."

"Sure you did," Nate said in a soft voice.

"Nate, what are you asking me to do? You know I love you like a brother, and I'll do anything I can to help, but what exactly would you have me change in your mother's will that makes a difference?"

"Well," Nate said, sitting more upright in his chair, "according to the will, upon Mother's demise, Contessa and Gwen each get 25 percent of Dillianquest, and I am to receive 50 percent. So, here's what needs to be done ... I want you to cut both Gwen and Contessa completely out of the will." Nate became a little more animated in his tone as he delivered the rest of his plan. "Once that is done, you need to open an offshore account for me ... an account that cannot be traced by US authorities."

Nate got up from his chair and started pacing around the room, stopping at one of the workbenches. Nate paused at the workbench and then picked up a half-carved wooden duck. As he studied the duck, Nate said in a steady voice, "I intend to sell Dillianquest in the next month or two. I found a firm by the name of Abernathy, Smith, and Grayson in Ann Arbor, Michigan, that specializes in health-care businesses."

Nate put the duck down and turned and faced Junior whose expression had not changed. Junior had not moved from his chair. He took a long draw from his cigar. Junior, with head tilted back, blew his smoke into the air and watched as it disappeared. He did not make eye contact with Nate.

At this point, Nate was becoming a bit more manic. His pace had quickened considerably as he said, "Those Yankees have no business holdings in the South. I know I can interest them in Dillianquest."

Nate was talking and moving quickly. He took a couple of deep breaths, and in a more slowed and controlled pace, said, "You'll need to get Brad Zeta to fluff up the appraisal a bit, like you did for the mall and apartment projects. You can pressure Zeta to appraise the property at sixty-five million or so. I know those Ann Arbor Yankee boys will gladly pay eighty-five to ninety cents on the dollar for a property like Dillianquest."

Nate, looking a bit less crazed, added, "That's an easy fifty million dollars. Hell, I'll pay Zeta twice his usual fee … no." Nate paused, and then looked directly at Junior as he said, "No, tell Zeta his cut will be one hundred grand." Nate added with a look of satisfaction on his face, "Yes, one hundred thousand dollars should do the trick for Brad."

Junior leaned back in his chair, watching intently as Nate developed his plan out loud.

Junior puffed on his cigar and said, "Slow down, Nate. You won't mind if I ask a few questions? I need to wrap my head around your plan before I can commit to anything. You understand that, don't ya?"

Junior got up from his chair and walked over to the bench where Nate had toyed with the carved duck. Junior picked up the duck and said, "You know, Nate, I wouldn't dream of putting a half-carved duck on the water and expect it to draw in other ducks." Junior was not sure just how stable Nate was at this point.

Nate made his way to his chair, sat down, and replied, "I understand."

Junior had the floor and the complete attention of Nate. Junior began pacing in front of Nate, who sat quietly in his chair. Junior looked as though he were about to deliver closing arguments at one of his trials.

"It's true, Nate: you and I have been through our fair share of shit together. I'll give you that. And yes"—Junior paused to take a puff of his cigar—"we've even bent a few rules along the way to keep a step ahead."

Junior held his drink in his left hand and cigar in his right as he paced slowly and thoughtfully back and forth. Junior suddenly stopped and looked directly at Nate, as if the latter were a member of a jury, and said, "So far, I am with you, my friend," Junior paused for effect and then added, "I really only have two concerns, Nate, that need some attention, and I hope you have given them some thought."

Junior resumed his slow, deliberate pacing. He took another draw on his cigar and said, "My first concerns are the girls and Abe." Junior stopped and again looked directly at Nate. "Did you know that Gwen and Abe are going to be engaged next week?"

Nate, seated in his chair, said, "Yeah, I know. I heard Contessa tell Mother something to that effect last week or so." Nate looked back at Junior and said, "But that really doesn't matter, Junior. Now what is your second concern?"

"Not so fast, Nate," Junior said, deliberately slowing Nate down. "All three of those kids are aware of your Mother's generosity and the content of her will." After a short pause, Junior added, "But for me … for me, Nate"—a smirk appeared on Junior's face—"for me, and I hope you don't take this the wrong way, I don't want my son, as weak and snotty-nosed a piece of shit as that boy is, I don't want him marrying that … that … that fucking half-breed from South America." Junior's voice had become animated.

He paused to take a drink from his glass and then added, "Don't get me wrong, Nate. Gwen is a sweet girl, and I love her to death, and your family has done great things for those kids and all."

Junior stopped and walked over to where Nate was sitting and sat on the edge of the table. He leaned forward, placed both hands on his knees, and looked Nate squarely in the eyes from three feet away. He said, as deliberately as he possibly could to make his point, "But there ain't one drop of southern fucking heritage in that girl's veins." Nate's body relaxed after Junior uttered those words. He was pleased to hear the hatred in Junior's voice.

Junior stood up from his seated position, walked back to his chair at the opposite end of the table, and added, "Cutting them from Mother's will, will certainly send up a red flag."

Nate, about to hook his longtime friend into his scheme, said, "Not to worry, Junior, not to worry. I've got that all figured out."

Junior said, "The other concern I have is your mother. According to Doc Jones, she could live for several more years. That's going to be an issue, don't you think?"

Nate sat back in his recliner and appeared to think for a minute. He did not want to look like just another scheming lowlife of the sort that

Junior was used to dealing with. Carefully, Nate said, "I have given your concerns some forethought, Junior, and here is what we need to do."

Nate stopped for a second, took a puff from his cigar, blew the smoke straight up into the air, and then said, "First, we change the will and have it witnessed and notarized by Claudette. You know that won't be a problem. I am sure she could use an extra fifty grand for her upcoming retirement."

Nate got up from his chair, began pacing in a thoughtful manner, and said, "In a codicil to Mother's will, Gwen will get the plane, and Contessa will get the *Spirit*. I brought both titles with me tonight. They are both free and clear and unencumbered."

Nate reached into his sweatshirt pouch, pulled an envelope from inside, and said, "I've already signed these." Nate tossed the envelope on the table. "You can have them for safekeeping—a little insurance policy for the kids." Nate took a sip of his drink and then said, "The plane and *Spirit* are both worth about a million each." Nate spoke as calmly as if he were planning a summer vacation when he added, "That should get them settled." With an approving grin, Nate continued, "With you taking care of the will, and Claudette as our witness, there's no reason it should be contested. No one will be the wiser, and they won't be able to prove a thing."

Nate, having covered all but one of the objections, added, "As far as Mother's health is concerned ..." He stopped and turned, looking directly at Junior as he said, "It is unfortunate that Mother will pass in the next month or so."

Junior looked at Nate with a puzzled expression on his face and said, "How the hell can you know that?"

Nate was slow and reserved in his response. "I am with her every day, and each day she seems to be getting weaker and weaker."

Nate continued in a sympathetic tone, "Her mind is completely gone now because of Alzheimer's." He paused, hung his head, and said, "Now her body is following and failing just as quickly."

Nate paused and took a big draw from his cigar. As he blew the smoke into the air, he looked directly into Junior's eyes and said, "I just don't see her strong enough to live much longer. I am truly going to miss her when she passes."

Junior looked back at Nate, who had a half-assed smirk on his face. "Nate, what are you telling me?"

Nate looked back at Junior and said calmly, "I think the good Lord will be coming to take Mother soon."

Nate took another draw off his cigar, went over to his chair, and sat down. He reached for his glass of scotch, took a big drink, and said, "And when she passes, Junior, those Yankee boys from Ann Arbor will gladly transfer the funds into your account." With an ever-widening smile, Nate looked at Junior and said, "And if memory serves me correctly, I owe my good friend and trusted counsel six hundred and fifty thousand dollars … give or take a few bucks." Nate paused and said with a smile in his voice, "You would like to get paid, wouldn't you, Junior?"

Nate, speaking as if he were now in compete control, said, "And Junior, here is where I think you will like what I have to say." Nate smiled at Junior and continued, "When you get the transfer from our newfound Yankee friends, you will keep a total of one million dollars. That's an extra three hundred fifty thousand dollars as a bonus for your services." Nate paused and added with a chuckle, "You can call it your own Dillianquest stimulus bailout if you like."

Nate paused to catch any reaction from Junior, but none came. Nate added, "After you take your million and pay off Zeta and Claudette, you will wire the remainder to my offshore account, and just like that … it's done. Everyone's a winner, Junior. Everyone's a winner."

Junior was a bit stunned, trying to gather in all the details of Nate's latest scam: killing off his mother and pocketing all the cash. After a lengthy silence, Junior said, "What about all that other bullshit you laid on me tonight, Nate? What happens with that?"

"It all gets buried with Mother. Any and all evidence of your involvement in anything we talked about tonight gets buried with Mother." After a short pause and a sip of scotch, Nate said, "What we have talked about tonight gets buried with Mother. The story ends right here and right now, Junior. You can trust me on that."

Junior walked over to the counter and took two fresh tumblers from the cabinet. He filled both with ice and then poured scotch over the cubes, listening to the ice crackle as the warm scotch hit the frozen water. Junior picked up both glasses and walked over to where Nate was standing, by one of the workbenches. He handed Nate his glass and nodded without saying a word.

After a moment, Junior raised his glass to Nate and said, "I am in, Nate. But this is the last time we will ever have this conversation. When you get your money, you disappear for good. Now look me in the eye, Nate. You understand? You disappear forever."

Nate looked at Junior, smiled, and said, "Gone for good!"

Junior took a sip of his scotch, paused, and looked at Nate with a bit of contempt. "I'm in, Nate, but my fee is five million dollars. Take it or leave it."

Nate laughed in shock. "Five million. Are you out of your fucking mind?"

Junior smiled at Nate, took a deep breath, and said, "I must be out of my fucking mind if I'm going along with your insane plan. You do realize, old friend, that I will be an accessory to the murder of your mother. For that, the price is five million dollars ... take it or leave it. I really don't care."

Junior reached for a drawer under the workbench. He opened the drawer, reached in, and removed a .22-caliber pistol. Junior held the pistol in his right hand and then placed it on the counter in front of Nate.

Looking Nate directly in the eyes, Junior said in a solemn, matter-of-fact tone, "One way or the other, Nate, you disappear forever. Do we have an understanding? This is the last deal we do."

Nate looked at Junior and with a smile and said, "Fuck 'em all, Junior. You make your end happen, and I'll lead the sheep to the slaughterhouse, and when it's all done, you will never see me again, old friend."

They both raised their glasses in a toast and at the exact same time said, "Fuck 'em all!"

CHAPTER 13

On the Sunday morning after Nate and Junior hatched their plan in the shed, Abe decided to go down to the basement in his house to check on PASS to see if anything of interest had transpired over the past few days. Due to the heavy workload at the office, Abe had not had a chance since Wednesday evening to check the system.

Sundays were good days to make DVDs and delete files from the system. Abe went outside to get the Sunday newspaper, grabbed a fresh cup of coffee, and retired to the basement for a few hours to do his work.

Abe was an average man, slight of build, about five feet seven inches in height, with brown hair and glasses. He was nothing like his father. Abe was quiet and did not relish the spotlight as his father did. Junior had little in common with his son. Abe took after his mother's side of the family. He was the pride of his mother's efforts and the apple of her eye.

To ensure that Abe wouldn't venture far from the home nest, Junior had given his son a few acres of the family's land. Once Abe had started with the firm, he had built himself an average-looking four-bedroom ranch-style house on a corner of the family acreage. It was a much more conservative homestead than that of his parents. It had its own entrance and was out of sight of the main house.

Junior had tried to get close to Abe, but it was difficult for him. Mary Ann wanted her son to be close to her, so that when Abe had grandbabies, grandmother Mary Ann would be close at hand.

It was a slow start to the morning. Abe and Gwen had been out that Saturday night for dinner, drinks, and pool at the OSS. Abe had dropped

Gwen off at her place after two in the morning. As Abe entered the basement's secret office, he immediately was drawn to the system's monitor, flashing the words "SYSTEM ALERT—SHED." Abe had not seen a shed alert in a while. He put down his coffee and laid the newspaper on the floor next to his chair.

He entered his pass code, and on the screen popped up images of Nate Dillianquest and his father entering the shed. The time stamp was 9:03 p.m. Abe reached for his coffee and newspaper, convinced the footage was going to be of a rather boring conversation about financial decisions that nobody cared about—something the system had flagged by mistake. Just to be sure, though, Abe put down his coffee and newspaper and turned the volume up so he could hear exactly what was being said. He sat up in his chair, paying closer attention to body language and the conversation.

Abe watched the men light up their cigars and get a couple of drinks; nothing extraordinary at this point. Then Abe heard the conversation turn to suicide. That really caught Abe's attention. He couldn't believe what he was hearing. He listened to his father ask Nate about whether the latter were considering committing suicide—again.

Abe couldn't believe his ears. Nate Dillianquest was suicidal? Holy shit! As the conversation developed between the two men, Abe sat still, his eyes fixed on the screen. He was mesmerized by the cold, calculated monologue Nate was having with his father, who just sat there and listened.

Abe kept listening and watching, but he couldn't believe what he was seeing and hearing. Nate Dillianquest implicated Abe's father in the death of Jason Holt.

Just as Nate finished his sentence, saying, "Nobody knows what part you played in that kid's death," Abe stopped the video and stood up, his face white with shock. He had an overwhelming urge to run. He bolted from the room and ran upstairs as fast as he could, skipping every other step on his way up. He ran into his master bathroom and stopped in front of the mirror. He leaned over the sink and splashed cold water on his face.

With water streaming from his chin, splashing on the countertop, he looked back into the mirror. Abe just stared at himself in disbelief. He knew at that very moment that his life was about to change. He did not quite understand the dramatic turn it was about to take, but somehow, his life was going to change. It would never go back to being the same again.

He bent over the sink and splashed more water on his face. Abe thought to himself, *My father is a killer … Oh my God, my poor mother.*

He walked shakily into the kitchen and gazed out the window over the sink for a long while. With both hands flat on the counter, he bent over at the waist to try to catch his breath, which had become too fast. He couldn't slow his breathing. He was starting to hyperventilate. He fumbled around in a drawer and found a paper sack to place over his mouth. He got his breathing under control, but he was still shaking uncontrollably.

Abe walked over to the kitchen table and placed his head on his folded arms. Once Abe was able to gain control of his shaking body, he got up from the table and walked to the stairs that led to the basement. He stood at the top of the stairs, eyes glazed over, and glared into the dark basement abyss. He took one step and sat on the stair. It was too painful to proceed. *One step at a time*, he thought. Abe started back down the stairs to the horror that awaited him in the basement.

The door to the office that hid the monitoring system was wide open. He could only stare at the freeze-framed picture he had left behind. He was sickened at what he saw, but was strangely drawn back inside, even if he was afraid to find out more about his father and Nate Dillianquest. After mustering up enough courage, Abe went back into the office.

Abe's finger was poised over the play button. Thinking that the worst had to be over, Abe vowed he would watch the remaining video in its entirety without stopping. His finger touched the play button. It seemed difficult to push the button hard enough to restart the recording.

After an hour, the recording automatically stopped as the two men left the shed. Abe sat silently in the room and lost himself in the black screen. He stared into the darkness in total disbelief.

He couldn't process what he had just seen. He wondered if his father and Nate knew of the recording devices and were playing a trick on him to teach him a lesson. After a moment's thought, he decided the recording was real; his father and Nate were not that smart.

Abe was paralyzed. He was at a complete loss as to what he should do. Should he turn the recording over to the police? There was no real proof of any wrongdoing. And what if he did? It would only expose his father and wreck the lives of his mother and all those who worked at the law offices. Should he do nothing? He had knowledge of a double murder, kidnapping, international drug trafficking, extortion, and embezzlement.

Abe did not know what to do. He sat there, numb.

After a while of just sitting and thinking, Abe decided to play the recording again, and then again and again. Each time, Abe became a bit more detached from what he was seeing and hearing. After the shock wore off, Abe started thinking like the trained lawyer he was. Abe began taking notes, trying to get a better understanding of just what was on the recording.

In the corner of Abe's secret basement office was a flip chart. Abe decided to dissect each event into its component parts. He started with the vehicular homicide of Josh Holt. Abe plotted the events as he knew them on the pages of the flip chart. He had some knowledge of the events from past conversations with his grandfather and father. Abe had reviewed the firm's case file on Nate Dillianquest.

When Abe finished plotting the Josh Holt homicide on the flip chart, he tore the pages from the easel and taped them to the walls of the office.

Abe next focused his attention on the double homicide in Colombia and the kidnapping of the two infants. Abe, standing at the easel, stopped writing for a moment, remembering how he had fallen in love with Gwen.

Gwen was a beautiful woman. Abe had known her since grade school. Back then, Gwen didn't have much to do with the likes of a geek like Abe. But when they both took flying lessons and discovered they shared a deep interest in aviation, that common interest turned into true love.

Gwen was one of the two sisters kidnapped by Nate Dillianquest from the jungles of Colombia and raised by the Dillianquest family. It was very difficult for Abe to outline the events that Nate had so brutally and callously detailed in the recording. Just thinking of how Gwen's parents had died trying to save her and her sister's lives made Abe weak in the knees.

It was even harder to believe that Mr. and Mrs. Dillianquest, close friends of the family whom Abe had cared for deeply, could have known that their son had murdered two people and then kidnapped their children, bringing them home so she could raise them. It was mind-boggling.

A deep sadness overtook Abe as he continued plotting his father's involvement in all of the sordid and horrific events. Abe's father had bribed Colombian officials, assisted in the kidnapping and human smuggling of two infants, and forged federal documents so the two kidnapped infants would never find out their place of birth or the identity of their parents. As Abe wrote of his father's involvement, tears streamed down his cheeks.

This was horrible. He could not believe his eyes or ears. No one could justify actions like these. Abe tore the pages from the easel and taped them next to the others. The list of atrocities was growing. Abe stood there and stared at the pages that outlined the ruin of his family. He had only just begun to realize how bad it was going to be.

Abe next turned his attention to drug trafficking by members of the United States Marine Corps. He wondered who the two pilots were. Nate had been very evasive and vague when he described his partners in crime, never mentioning anyone by name. Abe only knew that they had both been pilots in the Marines. It would be an easy job to connect the two pilots to Nate Dillianquest. If nothing else, the Marines kept good records of their missions. Abe did know one thing for sure, though: Nate Dillianquest had implicated himself in an international drug-smuggling ring.

Abe had been sequestered in his basement office for hours, working to gain some kind of an understanding of what was on the recording. He did not realize that it was already six thirty in the evening when the phone rang. Abe was so focused on what he was doing that the phone rang several more times before he realized what was happening.

Abe walked out of the office and over to where the phone lay on the coffee table next to the couch. Nate just stood there, eyes fixed on the phone, staring at it. Abe noticed on the caller identification that the phone call was coming from his parents' home phone, so he decided to let the phone call go to voice mail. Abe was in no shape to talk to anyone. He needed a few moments to gather his wit about him. He sat on the couch and listened to the message over the speakerphone.

On the other end of the phone, his mother said, "Hi, darling. I trust you and Gwen are still planning on coming to the house for dinner this evening? I'm planning on you kids for seven thirty. Call me back. Love you." The phone went silent. Abe had all but forgotten about the dinner plans for that evening.

Abe took a few deep breaths to slow his heart down. After a few minutes, Abe decided to pick up the phone and call his mother back. Abe stood up beside the couch and called. The phone only rang twice before Abe's mother picked up.

"Hi, darling."

Abe replied in an artificially tired-sounding voice, "Gosh, Mother, I almost forgot. I was just lying down. I thought I might be catching that bug that's going around. But I actually feel fine. And yes, you can count on us. We should be there at seven thirty sharp, just like we planned."

"Perfect, dear, seven thirty is fine. We are looking forward to seeing you and Gwen. Bye-bye, sweetie." She hung up.

Abe collapsed back onto the couch. After a few minutes, Abe thought maybe he should call back and cancel; he did not know if he could face his father after what he had witnessed on the recording.

But then it dawned on Abe that this would be a good test. Abe wanted to see how his father would act around him tonight. If the recording were a hoax, it would be pretty easy for his father to let the cat out of the bag. On the other hand, if dear old Dad was his usual charming, condescending, self-righteous, asshole self, the recording was real. Abe prayed to himself that what he had seen was just a joke in bad taste.

Abe stood in front of the sliding glass doors that led to a back patio from his basement walkout. A pond and horse stable framed his backyard. With wireless phone in hand, he called Gwen's number. Gwen knew it was Abe calling and answered the phone in her lowest, slowest sexy tone.

"The only thing I am wearing is a smile. How soon do you want me over?"

Abe melted on the phone. His voice quivered as he said, "Oh, Lord, darling, you must have forgotten we're having dinner with my folks this evening. Can you be here by seven twenty?"

"Sure. Should I wear something more than my smile?"

CHAPTER 14

At seven twenty sharp, Abe's doorbell rang. Abe was in the master bathroom, still a bit stunned from the events that he had been chronicling downstairs in his secret office. He heard a voice in the house saying, "Pizza delivery."

Abe smiled at himself in the mirror. He felt lucky to have such wonderful women in his life.

"I'll be right out," he called.

Abe emerged from the master suite dressed and ready to go to supper at his parents' house. When Abe turned the corner to enter the kitchen, he saw Gwen leaning up against the refrigerator. She was holding a small pizza box just under her smooth, flat belly. The pizza box and six-inch stilettos were the only things Gwen was wearing ... that is, except her smile.

Gwen was tall, with bronze, smooth skin and a perfect set of soft, full breasts. Her nipples stood erect. She held her legs slightly crossed as she leaned to her right. Her jet-black hair, parted in the middle, fell about her shoulders. Large, silver hoop earrings jutted through her silky hair. She was a vision of beauty.

Abe stopped in his tracks. His eyes ravaged her body, starting at her well-formed calves and moving up to her wonderfully shaped breasts. A smile broke onto his face. In that instant, Abe had completely forgotten all about the atrocities hanging on his basement office walls.

With a sly schoolgirl grin on her face, Gwen removed the pizza box, exposing her pussy. "Shall we dine in tonight?"

Abe gaped for a second, speechless, before they both burst into laughter.

Gwen added, "I know we have to go to your parents' for dinner. I thought I would just tease you a bit. Give me a minute, and let me put some clothes on." Gwen began walking toward Abe, who was frozen.

Gwen strutted like a runway model, moving her fine wares from side to side. Abe was standing in the entryway to the rest of the house when Gwen strolled up to him, placed her open hand on his hardening cock, and said, "Maybe we can leave a bit early this evening and have our dessert here?" She squeezed just a bit and then released her grip on his manhood. She kissed Abe on the cheek, walked into the master suite, and got dressed.

Gwen came out in a matter of minutes wearing a sleeveless and backless short black dress. Abe eyed his soon-to-be wife and thought she would look great in a mechanic's jumpsuit. Gwen was one very sexy woman.

Gwen and Abe arrived at the mansion at seven thirty sharp. Abe rang the doorbell, and then Gwen and Abe opened the front door and announced themselves.

"Hey, it's us!" Abe shouted.

From a distance, they could hear Abe's mother's response: "I'm in the kitchen—come on back."

Junior and Mary Ann Belanger's home was an impressive display of modern art and southern heritage. The entryway was expansive, with a thirty-foot ceiling. A huge crystal chandelier hung from the ceiling, supported by gold chains.

The floors were a white Italian marble with deep multicolored swirls wandering aimlessly, like lazy rivers through light, airy clouds. To the right was the coat closet. Abe took Gwen's shawl and hung it up carefully. They walked through the hall that was to the left of a grand stairway that circled its way to the second floor.

The stairway was also made from Italian marble with a hand-loomed colorful runner that greeted all who entered this grand old home. Each visitor's eye was immediately drawn to the hand-carved wooden railing that wound its way to a second-story balcony overlooking the entryway foyer. Abe's mother took great pride in her home. She had spent years decorating and refurbishing her old southern mansion.

Gwen and Abe found their way into the kitchen. Abe's mother stood over the stove, thickening her gravy. Mary Ann Belanger had draped her voluptuous figure in a full-length sleeveless dress with a very subtle flower print, accessorizing it with two full stands of pearls. She protected her dress with a soft yellow cooking apron. Mary Ann usually wore her hair pulled back, sometimes in a bun and other times, like this evening, in a simple ponytail.

Gwen entered, made her way directly to Mary Ann, kissed her on the cheek, and said, "You look wonderful this evening." Gwen leaned her head back, nose pointing into the air, and said, "My, something smells absolutely delightful. What can I do to help?"

Mary Ann answered, "You are so sweet and kind, dear. Just have a seat and keep me a little company while I send Abe to the shed to retrieve his father." Abe's mother turned to Abe and said, "Would you be a sweetheart and go to the shed and tell your father it is time to get cleaned up for supper?"

Abe walked over to his mother, kissed her on the cheek, and said, "Mother, I would be happy to." He walked to where Gwen was standing, kissed her on the cheek as well, and said, "I will be back momentarily. Don't start without us."

As Abe walked out the kitchen door, he could hear Mary Ann ask Gwen, "So tell me, dear, how are you? Anything exciting going on in the life of Gwen these days?"

Abe smiled and shook his head as he walked down the path toward the shed. Mother had promised she wouldn't say anything to Gwen that might spoil the surprise he had in mind for that evening.

Junior had left the outside lights on in anticipation of Abe coming to get him for supper. The daylight savings time change had not yet occurred, so it was just starting to get dark at seven thirty. As Abe approached the shed, he had to remind himself to act as if nothing were wrong. *Just be your usual self, and don't give anything away. Just be normal ... whatever that is.*

Abe knocked on the door and walked in. Junior was sitting in a chair at one of his workbenches, holding a wooden duck in his left hand.

Abe announced his presence by saying, "Hey, whatcha working on?"

Junior turned in his chair and looked at Abe, head tilted down, eyes peering over his reading glasses.

"Hi, son. I'm putting the finishing touches on the *Aix sponsa*." Junior held his prized carving up to the light to admire.

"*Aix sponsa?*"

"Yep," Junior replied. "The North American wood duck to you commoners." Junior laughed and said, "This is one of the greatest ducks to ever take wing."

Abe walked up to his father's side. "It sure is beautiful. What are you planning on doing with it?"

"This one will probably go in the study or maybe to the office. I haven't gotten that far yet. Mother said you may be catching the bug that's been going around the office."

Abe scanned the shed, looking at the tools his father had hanging from the wall, and replied, "I thought I was. Must have just been a bit tired. Amazing what a nap will do after a tough week."

Abe paused for a second and decided now might be a good time to bait his father, opening the door for his confession. "How did your week end up? Last thing I recall is you and Nate on the phone. How is Mr. Dillianquest, anyway? We sure don't see much of him anymore."

Junior jumped right in without missing a beat. "Nate is a piece of work, is he not? He is truly is one of a kind, and thank God there is only one Nate Dillianquest. I don't think the world could handle another."

Junior was making some fine adjustments to the wooden decoy and was talking without looking at Abe, focusing instead on his work.

Abe then added, opening the door even wider for his father's confession, "How is Nate's mother? Alzheimer's is such a devastating disease."

Junior looked up at the ceiling and away from his decoy. He was clearly thinking of something to say. Abe thought to himself that this could be the moment of truth, when Junior spilled the beans in a moment of father-and-son confidentiality.

Junior put down the decoy and spun around on his stool, looking for Abe. "She has good days and bad. She could outlive us all, but then again, she could be gone tomorrow." Junior paused for a second and then added, "Nobody but the good Lord in heaven really knows, Abe—not even Doc Jones." Junior got up from his stool, walked over to Abe, put his hands on his son's shoulders, and said, "Be thankful that our family doesn't have a history of Alzheimer's disease. Boy, you could just take me out back and shoot me if I were in that condition."

Abe took a deep breath and said, "Is that what Mr. Dillianquest wanted to talk to you about?"

Junior, returning to his stool, said, "That and a few other family details. Nothing earth-shattering—just the usual Dillianquest drama."

"Yeah, if only the walls could talk."

Junior walked back to where he was sitting and pushed the stool closer to the workbench. He placed the carving knives he was using away in their drawer, walked over to Abe, and said, "Thank God they can't." Junior put his arm around Abe's shoulder. "Now let's go get something to eat before your mother tries to prosecute us for gross neglect of a prime rib."

Junior and Abe entered the house through the door in the kitchen. Mary Ann was carrying different dishes to the dining room, where Gwen was setting the table. Junior walked over to his wife, kissed her on the cheek, and said, "Smells scrumptious, doll. I will go change and get cleaned up for supper. I'll be right back."

Mary Ann replied playfully, "Don't dillydally, or we will be forced to start without you."

As Junior was leaving the kitchen to head up the grand stairway to the master suite, he said, "And there will be hell to pay for those who feast without the king." His laugh faded as he disappeared from sight.

"Abe, darling, would you be a sweetheart and carry this into the dining room for me?" Mary Ann handed Abe a whole standing rib roast perched proudly on a huge cutting board. Abe took the platter and vanished into the dining room, leaving the swinging doors to come to a natural halt. Mary Ann followed with a large bowl of mashed potatoes and a bowl of her famous gravy.

Gwen had finished setting the table and was pouring everyone a glass of one of Junior's finest Bordeaux. Earlier, Mary Ann had ventured down into the wine cellar and selected a 1947 Petrus. When Gwen finished pouring the wine, Mary Ann took the bottle and placed it in front of Junior's seat at the head of the table. There was no way he could miss that bottle even if he tried. Abe's mother was making this evening a very special one.

Junior had a very extensive wine collection in the basement wine cellar. The cellar had originally been dug to hide slaves on their northern route out of slavery. Later, as the house went through several renovations, the hideout became a wine cellar. Junior retrofitted it with climate controls and a tasting area, but left the rustic, cobbled-stone look intact. The wines were protected by a large, arched wooden door flanked by gargoyles perched on stone shelves.

When wine came into the cellar, Junior always placed a "drink by" date on each bottle's neck. That was to ensure that each bottle would be enjoyed at its peak flavor. Junior had over five thousand bottles of wine in the cellar, and he enjoyed at least one bottle an evening with his wife during dinner. The best of Junior's treasures were kept under lock and key … and this was one of Junior's best bottles.

Junior made his way into the dining room, where everyone was gathered. He walked directly to where Gwen was sitting, leaned over her shoulder, gave her a kiss on the cheek, and said, "I must have missed you when we came in from the shed. You look lovely this evening, my dear. How are you?" If nothing else, Junior could charm the socks off a goatherd.

"I am well, Mr. Belanger. Thank you for asking," Gwen replied in an equally charming tone.

Junior made his way to the head of the table and pulled his chair out. But before he sat down, he paused and reached for the bottle of Petrus that had been displayed for him to see.

"I see Mary Ann found the keys to the treasure room," Junior said with a big smile on his face. "There must be good reason to celebrate?" As he sat down, he looked directly at Abe and Gwen, who were seated facing each other on opposite sides of the table.

Abe picked up his glass of wine and said, "I would like to propose a toast. A toast to the most charming, elegant, and compassionate person I have ever had the opportunity to fall in love with." Abe paused for just a second and stood to finish the toast, but he decided to walk over to where

Gwen remained seated. Abe got down on one knee and said, "To the woman of my dreams."

Abe then hoisted his wine glass, bowed his head slightly, and continued, "To the woman of my future ... and to the woman who will bear my children one day. I raise this glass and toast the woman who I pray will become my bride." Abe paused for dramatic effect and then continued, "With all my love, Gwen, I raise this toast to you and request your hand in marriage."

Without hesitation, Gwen jumped up and gave the biggest hug and kiss Abe had ever had. Abe, wrapped in Gwen's arms, looked over at his mother and saw that tears were streaming down her cheeks.

Abe glanced over at his father, who held his glass up into the air and said, "To the happy couple."

Once Gwen let go of Abe, everyone held their wine glasses high in the air. Each glass gently touched the other as the family savored the moment before they drank from their glasses.

Abe reached into his pocket and took out a ring box. "I haven't heard the word yes, but I am hoping that you will marry me."

Gwen looked at Mary Ann, who had the biggest smile on her face, and then looked at Junior, who smiled and winked. She looked back at Abe and said, "I would be honored to be your wife, as we are already soul mates."

With that, Abe slipped the diamond engagement ring onto Gwen's finger and said, "It's official: I am madly in love."

The main course was full of conversation dominated by Many Ann and Gwen talking about wedding plans, dates, and announcements. Junior and Abe were both pretty quiet on the subject but really couldn't have gotten a word in edgewise even if they had wanted to. The women at the Belanger household were in full wedding mode. For a short while, Abe had forgotten all about what had taken place just the other evening in the shed.

Gwen and Mary Ann cleared the supper plates with very little help from the men. Junior and his son sat at the table and shared niceties with each other as they waited for the women to rejoin them.

As Gwen and Mary Ann sat back down at the table, Junior picked up the bottle of wine and gestured to Gwen, offering her a refill. Gwen placed her hand over the glass, glanced at Junior, and said, "I wish I could. This wine is fabulous, thank you, but I have an early flight in the morning."

Abe, looking a bit disappointed, said, "You do? I hate to hear that."

Gwen explained, "I have to be in Spartanburg by six to pick up some clients, so they can be in Jacksonville, Florida, for an eight-thirty meeting."

Gwen paused, reached for Abe's hand, and said, "You remember, don't you, sweetie? I told you that just a couple of days ago."

Abe said, "I do remember now. I guess I was distracted by the wedding proposal."

"That's certainly understandable."

Junior looked toward Mary Ann and asked, "How about you, my dear? Would you care for another taste of wine?"

"I would," she said. She turned to Abe and asked, "How about you, dear? Care for a little refresher?"

Abe got up from his chair, walked to where Junior was seated, and said, "Absolutely. I have a feeling it will be a long time in between bottles of Petrus."

Mary Ann asked Junior, "How is Nate doing?" She paused for a moment and added, "Was it Friday night he came to the shed?"

Junior laughed a bit and said, "Abe was asking about Nate earlier. To tell you the truth, I think Nate is having some difficulty handling his mother's health situation." Junior took a sip of wine. "And you are correct, dear. It was Friday evening. Nate stopped by and wanted to do some reminiscing, talk about his mother, and bounce some future plans off me. He had some fine cigars and about drank me out of Scotch. Nothing earth-shattering." Junior laughed again. "Just a couple of old-timers talking about the past."

As Junior finished his last sentence, Abe stood and said, "Supper was outstanding, Mother." Abe pushed his chair back. He needed to leave after witnessing his father's performance. Abe walked over to where his mother was seated, placed one hand on her shoulder, and said into her ear loudly enough for all to hear as he made eye contact with Gwen, "Thanks for helping me tonight. Everything was perfect."

Mary Ann had a big smile on her face as she reached up with one hand, took Abe by the back of the head, and pulled him close. She gave him a big kiss on the cheek and said, "I wish you two the most happiness a couple could have. I hope that you will both be as open and honest with each other as your father and I have been." Abe almost choked but remembered that he must act normal, so he just smiled.

Abe went to the coat closet and gathered Gwen's shawl. He gently wrapped it around her shoulders. Mother and Junior walked them out the front door and onto the landing. Junior gave Gwen a hug and kiss on the cheek. He wrapped his arms around Abe and gave him an awkward hug and a pat on the back. Abe's mother was in tears again but gave both a hug and kiss.

Junior and Mary Ann disappeared back into the house while Abe and Gwen drove the short distance back to Abe's place.

When Abe and Gwen got back to the house, Abe looked at Gwen and said, "You know, I don't recall you telling me you had an early flight."

Gwen laughed and said, "I don't." She kicked off her shoes, walked to the couch in the great room, flung herself on it, and continued, "I love your mother to death, but I just couldn't spend an evening as wonderful as this with your father."

She lay on the couch with her head on the armrest and continued, "We both know he thinks you are marrying beneath your status if you marry me." She sat up on the couch and tapped the cushion next to her in an effort to get Abe to come and sit with her.

"I don't think he thinks that at all," Abe said as he walked over by the couch and stood in front of Gwen. "Yes, he is an asshole, no doubt. But the real question is, are you still willing to marry me?"

Gwen sat with her legs spread apart, facing Abe directly. She answered, "Yes, I will still marry you ... but on one condition." Gwen pulled her dress slowly up her thighs. Gwen was not looking at Abe. Her eyes were trained on her dress as it inched its way up her thighs, revealing the smooth and slender pair of long legs.

Abe's eyes were fixed on what he was about to experience. Gwen stopped just short of fully exposing her pussy and said to Abe, "The condition is that we finish dessert right here and right now."

Abe kneeled in front of Gwen and put both hands on her smooth thighs. He leaned into her and kissed her neck, his breath becoming deeper with each passing second. Her skin was smooth to the touch, and her legs were open for his pleasure. Abe felt the muscles of her legs quiver as he moved his hands toward her hidden delight. Abe's fingers dug into her flesh, and when Gwen shivered, he knew he was sending chills to every nerve ending in her body. Her pussy was wet with anticipation.

Abe's enchanting creature of a fiancée laid herself out in front of Abe, tempting him to do whatever he pleased. Abe smelled sex in the air. His heart pounded, and his mouth was full of her perfect breasts when he looked up at her and said, "You are one dirty girl, and you know, I just love dirty girls."

Abe's tongue danced around Gwen's firm nipples before he kissed his way down to her stomach. Gwen placed one hand on either side of his face and pulled his head from between her legs.

"I am your dirty girl," she agreed. "And you had better never be caught loving any other dirty girls, or I will make it so you never love again."

Abe smiled. Gwen kissed her lover on his lips, long and slow, slipping her tongue deep into his mouth. Gwen placed Abe's head back between her legs. Her head leaned back on the couch. Her grip on Abe's head loosened. Her breath deepened. Her body filled with ecstasy.

CHAPTER 15

Abe couldn't sleep that Sunday night. He couldn't stop thinking about the recording. At 4:00 a.m., he found himself in the basement of his house, looking at the recording of his father and close family friend Nate Dillianquest talking about all kinds of unspeakable activities. Abe picked up where he had left off the evening before, plotting the dirty deeds of two conspirators. Abe was relieved to think that his father had nothing to do with the international drug-smuggling ring Nate was involved with. It was a small consolation in the scope of all the wrongdoing.

As the recording continued, Abe jotted down on the flip chart the connection between Bernie Madoff and the lost Dillianquest fortune. Abe wondered how many other family fortunes had been lost as a result of being introduced to Madoff by his family.

The Madoff scandal was a huge social embarrassment for the Belanger family. While Abe would never consider committing suicide himself, he certainly could empathize with Nate. After losing everything, Abe could understand how a person could contemplate such a thing.

Most disturbing to Abe, however, was the plot regarding the last will and testament of Sarah Grace Dillianquest. Abe was appalled by the willingness his father had shown to be a conspirator in such an unthinkable fraud. Abe had a difficult time believing that his father would have no problem cutting Gwen and Contessa from what was rightfully theirs so he could be paid off.

Abe's disappointment grew with each passing minute the recording droned on, as did his anger. Michael Abraham Belanger II was going to forge the last will and testament of Sarah Grace Dillianquest. Abe's father was willing to desecrate the most sacred of documents and was happy to do it for his own personal gain. Abe thought to himself just what a cold, calculating, and manipulative bastard his father was.

Abe was having a difficult time wrapping his head around so much deceit. Abe stopped and started the recording often, but he continued. His father, the man he had grown up admiring and seeking advice from, was going to knowingly present fraudulently prepared real-estate appraisals in order to swindle a firm out of millions of dollars. He had agreed to launder money for Nate after the fact. And oh, yes—his father was going to stand by and do nothing while Nate Dillianquest set out to murder his own mother. What kind of monsters were these two men?

Abe taped up all the pages outlining all of the crimes and activities that his father and Nate Dillianquest had been involved in on the office walls. The list was as long as it was horrific. It was almost impossible to believe that the two men in Abe's life who meant so much to him could have been involved in such terrible crimes. But in truth, Abe's father and his father's best friend were crooked, corrupt, and as treacherous a pair of criminals as South Carolina had known.

At about seven thirty that morning, Abe decided to take advantage of the seed he had planted yesterday about not feeling well. He would say that he had caught the bug that was going around the office. Everyone would understand. Abe called the office and left word with Claudette that he would not be in today. How could he face his father or Claudette knowing what he knew?

After the phone call, Abe went upstairs to get another cup of coffee. Just as he arrived at the empty coffeepot, Gwen came into the room. She walked over to him, put her arms around his neck, and whispered in his ear, "What happened to you last night?"

After she kissed his cheek, she let go and reached into the cupboard for a coffee cup. As she discovered the coffeepot was empty, she asked with sleepy eyes, "And what happened to all the coffee?"

"I was just about to make another pot. Have a seat, and I'll make us some breakfast and fresh coffee." Abe lovingly walked over to Gwen, kissed her on top of the head, and said, "There is something that I need to tell you."

Gwen rubbed her eyes and said, "That sounds too serious for this early."

"We can wait if you want. It's not going anywhere. Let's have a good breakfast, and then we can talk."

"That sounds more like it, sweetie," Gwen said in a delicate voice. "I'm thinking one of your world-famous omelets."

"One world-famous omelet, coming up," Abe said as he made his way to the refrigerator and took out the ingredients.

As Abe filled up the coffeepot with water, he said, "Last evening was incredible. I hope everything works out like we plan."

After a short silence, Gwen asked, "Why wouldn't it? Everything is perfect."

Abe did not respond; he just went about making the coffee and omelet. Gwen got up from her seat at the kitchen table and retrieved the morning newspaper from the front porch. She returned and opened the paper to the front page. She tucked both legs under her on the seat and said, "God, I hate reading the newspaper or listening to the news on TV. It is just gloom and doom. There is never any good news ... ever."

Abe did not say anything; he just kept cooking.

After a few minutes, Abe looked up from his kitchen duties and said playfully, "If I do the cooking, will you catch the dishes?"

"Sure thing. We could make that a permanent deal if you want." Gwen laughed.

"We will keep it open for negotiations," Abe said as he placed his world-famous omelet in front of Gwen.

She looked up at him with adoring eyes and said, "You are a wonderful man, and I am a very lucky gal." Abe smiled and sat down to his part of the omelet.

When they had finished breakfast, Abe said to Gwen, "Come on, I'll help you with the dishes."

"Thanks, but what about work? Don't you have to get ready for work?"

"Oh, work ... I called in sick today. I'm not going in."

Gwen turned, looked at Abe, and said, "That is so not like you. Is there something wrong?"

"It's that thing I told you we need to talk about, Gwen. It's going to take a while to get through it all."

"Oh, my God. Are *we* okay?"

"I proposed to you last night. Yes, we are beyond okay ... we are *great!*" Abe paused and then added, "But some other stuff has come up that we need to talk about, that's all."

Abe looked at Gwen and added, "This involves Contessa, too. Would you please call her and tell her that we need to talk as soon as possible? See if she can come over right away."

"Abe," Gwen said in a shaky voice, "you are starting to scare me."

"Look, sweetheart, we have a serious situation that we all need to discuss. Now, please, Gwen, call Contessa and see if she can get here right away ... please."

"Okay, but what do I tell her?"

"Tell her the same thing I told you. Tell her whatever you want, but please, get her over here. I don't want to have to go through this but once." Abe put more coffee in his cup. He leaned over to Gwen, kissed the top of her head, and said, "You know I love you. Now, please, call your sister." Abe placed the phone on the table and said, "I'm going to take a shower. When you get done talking with your sister, why don't you come and join me? I'll wash your back." Abe left the room.

Gwen never made it back to the bathroom. Abe finished blow-drying his hair and dressed himself in sweatpants, sneakers, and a long-sleeved T-shirt. He entered the kitchen, thinking that Gwen would be there, but she was not. He looked around the house, but Gwen was nowhere to be found. Abe became a bit panicked and began calling out Gwen's name.

"Gwen? Gwen, where are you?"

Abe stopped and listened and heard a faint reply: "I'm out here."

Abe made his way out the kitchen's sliding glass door to an elevated deck that overlooked the same pond and stables that Abe had been looking at earlier. Abe stepped on the deck and said, "What are you doing out here? I thought you were going to come and take a shower with me."

Gwen looked up at him and said, "Yesterday, life was as perfect as it gets. You proposed to me. I said yes. You gave me a ring. I couldn't have been happier." Gwen took a deep breath, let out a sigh, and continued, "Now, this morning, it seems like everything has changed."

Gwen started crying. Abe sat beside her, pulled her in close, and said, "Nothing between us has changed. I love you, and we are still going to get married." Gwen looked up at Abe and smiled. Abe gently wiped the tears from her eyes.

They sat and held each other for a few moments, and then Abe said, "But some events that affect you and your sister came to my attention yesterday that we need to talk about. Did you get ahold of Contessa?"

Just as Gwen was about to answer Abe's question, the doorbell rang.

"That must be her," Gwen said.

Abe made his way to the front door and opened it to find Contessa dressed in her nursing uniform.

Abe said, "Come on in."

As Contessa stepped into the house, she replied, "Thanks, Abe, but what the heck is going on?" She was noticeably upset.

"Please, come in. Gwen is on the back deck. Would you like a cup of coffee? It's fresh. I just made it."

"I think I need some after the conversation Gwen and I just had," Contessa quickly replied.

"Go out and see your sister. I'll bring your coffee to you. Two sugars, right?" Contessa nodded in the affirmative, walked through the kitchen, and joined her sister on the deck.

Abe poked his head out of the kitchen door and said, "Let's go downstairs, where it is a bit warmer. I'll bring the coffee." The threesome made their way downstairs into a large sitting area with an oversized couch and two reclining chairs arranged around a coffee table. Six people could comfortably sit and talk. Gwen and Contessa sat on the couch while Abe sat across the table in one of the recliners. The sitting area was surrounded by floor-to-ceiling bookshelves, one of which concealed Abe's secret office.

Abe set the tray with coffee craft and cups on the table in front of the girls, poured each a cup, and handed it to them. Then he poured a cup of coffee for himself, sat on the edge of the recliner, looked directly into the eyes of both Gwen and Contessa in turn, and said, "What I am about to tell you is going to be very difficult to listen to." Abe reached for his coffee cup, took a drink, and added, "I am going to tell you an unbelievable story that is going to change our lives forever."

Abe paused as he swallowed hard and said, "It's going to take a while for me to explain, so please"—Abe paused again—"just bear with me." He was clearly nervous.

Both Gwen and Contessa were comfortable on the couch as Abe began his story.

"For the past few years, before you and I"—he looked at Gwen— "became serious, I had been working on a secret surveillance project. A project that I am confident that once patented would allow me to create a legal niche for the law firm. I call it PASS, which stands for Passive-Aggressive Surveillance System." Abe took another sip of coffee and then added, "The system comprises micro cameras and microphones. When deployed, it secretly records the conversations and actions of those who are monitored."

Abe looked at both girls and said, "I won't get too technical, but the system's software can determine by voice inflection or intensity if any aggressive behavior is taking place. Once the system detects aggression, it records the activity and transmits it to a remote hard drive." Abe looked at the girls sitting on the couch, both of whom appeared to be paying close attention. "Are you following me so far?"

Both Gwen and Contessa nodded, and then Contessa said, "But what does your project have to do with us?"

"I'm getting to that," Abe said. "Once the system has identified aggressive behavior or activity"—Abe used his fingers as quotation marks—"the system's operator has the ability to review the exchange, and if warranted, can save a copy for use at a later date." Abe paused and added, "For example, if someone were to threaten the life of an attorney whose office was being monitored, and that attorney came up dead or missing, the system would have good use for law enforcement. At least that is the operating theory.

"Anyway," Abe said after taking a deep breath, "Friday night, Nate Dillianquest met with my father in the shed behind the house." Slowly and deliberately, he said, "Father often uses the shed to have conversations with clients that need to be off the books." Again, Abe used the air quotation marks to highlight specific words. Abe stood up, walked to the back of his chair, leaned on it, and said, "Some time ago, I deployed the system in the shed to protect my father against possible threats. He had no knowledge that I had done so." Abe took a deep breath and continued, "Yesterday morning, when I got down here to the office, I noticed that the system had identified an alert at the shed."

Just then, Gwen said, "What do you mean, down here at the office? There is no office down here."

Abe looked at Gwen and said, "Once I got the system up and running and all the kinks worked out, I was going to tell you everything, Gwen, I swear. I never want to keep anything from you."

As Abe was responding to Gwen's question, he walked over a wall of books to the right of couch where Gwen and Contessa were sitting. Abe stopped, looked back at them, and said, "From this point forward, there is no turning back. Whatever we decide today or in the future has to stay with us ... agreed?"

Abe looked at both Gwen and Contessa, who said in one voice, "Agreed."

Abe removed a book from a shelf and pushed a button on the back bookshelf wall. He then swung a large section of bookshelf open like one giant door that stretched from floor to ceiling. Directly behind the bookshelf was another, more normally sized door. Abe turned the handle on the door and pushed the second door inward. It opened and exposed, for the first time to anyone besides Abe himself, Abe's secret office.

Abe looked back over his shoulder and said, "I originally had it built as a safe room in case of a natural disaster or nuclear blast. But when I started working with PASS, I retrofitted it into an office." Abe turned and faced both Gwen and Contessa. "You two are the only ones who know about this space. I know I can trust you both. Our lives may depend on it."

Abe's secret office was completely self-sufficient. Food and other supplies were neatly arranged on a series of shelves that reached from floor to ceiling on one side, eight feet tall. The room had everything several people would need to survive for at least thirty days. It wasn't a cold-feeling place; it was warmly appointed with rich cherry paneling around the entire room. A desk and two chairs faced a small bank of five monitors. Several keyboards and lot of subtly blinking LCD lights could be seen on a large switching station. Shortwave radio equipment was neatly stacked alongside the desk in a dedicated tower. Two electronic game systems had been wired in as well.

Gwen and Contessa were both obviously dumbfounded. They looked at each other with a mix of surprise and fear in their eyes but said nothing. Exposed and taped to the walls of the office were the large flip-chart pages of notes that Abe had been working on. Abe closed the interior door but left the bookshelf door askew. He did not want them reading anything about what had taken place before he had a chance to explain what they were about to see and hear.

Abe made his way back to the coffee table. He picked up the carafe and poured himself more coffee. With cup in hand, he walked over to his chair, sat down, and said, "Here is where the story becomes a little more difficult to believe."

Abe sat on the edge of his chair and continued, "The Dillianquests have always told the story that both of you were the miraculous adopted children from Colombia. The story has it that the Dillianquests never wanted to change your last name from Rios, just in case any of your long-lost relatives wanted to find you, so that they could do so, if they had a mind to."

Abe paused for a minute and continued, "Because it was the Dillianquests and the Belangers, no one ever doubted the veracity of their story. Hell, one of the most respected law firms in the South handled all the paperwork. No one would ever question the legitimacy of your presence in the United States. And believe you me, everyone thought the Dillianquests were wonderful to have raised two orphaned infants as their own." Abe paused as he took a sip of his coffee. "Nobody in their right mind would ever question the intentions of the Dillianquests, now would they?"

Gwen and Contessa gave Abe their full attention. In a sober tone, Abe said, "Friday night, Nate told my father, in explicit detail, just how the two of you came to reside with the Dillianquests." Abe got up from his chair, walked over, and sat down on the edge of the coffee table in front of both Gwen and Contessa. Abe reached out, held one hand from each sister, and said, "What I am about to tell you is just horrible. It will forever alter our lives." Abe paused thoughtfully and said, "It could ruin the lives of people we love and care about."

Gwen looked at Contessa and then back at Abe and said, "Jesus, Abe, what are you talking about?"

Abe, still holding the hands of both girls, looked at each in turn and said, "On Friday night, Nate told my father that when he was in the Marines, he was assigned to a South American Drug Interdiction Unit." Abe took a deep breath and said, "Nate claims that he was on a routine mission when he and two helicopter pilots landed in a jungle opening in Colombia and began searching some abandoned huts for cocaine."

Abe's heart was to about to jump through his chest as he continued, "According to Nate, two unidentified people ran from one of the huts. Nate said he shot them both dead as they ran toward the jungle. He said he shot them in the back and without provocation." Abe squeezed their hands a bit harder as he continued, "The two people he shot … were your mother and father."

Gwen looked at Contessa without expression. Contessa's shoulders sank, and a tear welled up in her eye. The single tear made its way down her cheek and fell onto her hand, which Abe still clasped tightly.

Abe stopped and reached across the table for some Kleenex. He placed the box in between Contessa and Gwen. He knew the Kleenex would be used. As Abe sat back from the table, he said, "The three Marines burned the bodies to hide any evidence."

Contessa said with a cracked voice, "You can't be telling us the truth."

Abe replied, "It's all on the recording, in Nate's own words."

Gwen said as she held back the tears, "Oh, my God. This can't be true." Gwen and Contessa began to cry, and then Gwen said through her tears, "We need to see the recording, Abe. I need to hear it for myself."

Abe got up, walked back to his chair, and said, "I know this is very difficult. At first I couldn't bring myself to consider it." Abe's voice was shaky. "My family is deeply involved in this, too. All of us are going to be affected." His tone turned even more somber as he pointed toward the secret office. "What is on that recording will change forever the lives of a great many people we love and call our friends and family. We, the three of us, must stick together."

Contessa cleared her throat and said, "We need to see the recording, Abe."

Abe sat in his chair and said, "There is a lot on that recording, Contessa, and it is all very disturbing." Abe took a deep breath before adding, "There is one more thing I need to tell you before you view the recording for yourself."

Contessa looked over at Gwen and then back at Abe and said, "What's that?"

Abe sat forward in his chair, took a deep breath, and said, "I believe Nate is planning on killing your mother."

Contessa gasped. Gwen immediately moved close to Contessa and put both arms around her, pulling her tight. Contessa was shaking and crying uncontrollably.

Gwen looked up at Abe and said, "Are you out of you mind? What is going on? What are you doing?"

Abe stood up, walked to the other side of Contessa, placed his arms around both Gwen and Contessa, and said, "I fear for our lives. Nate has already admitted to killing three people and is plotting along with my father to kill your mother." Abe was quiet for a minute as he held the shaking girls and then added, "We have got to deal with this in some form or fashion. I don't want *us* to be next!" Abe laid his head on the tight mass of huddled, sobbing flesh.

After a few more minutes of crying, Contessa looked up at Gwen and said, "We have to see this with our own eyes." She turned and looked at Abe, who was sitting by her side. "Abe, please—show us the recording you've been talking about."

Abe got up from his seated position next to Contessa and said, "I will ... but you have to promise me that what you are about to witness can't leave this room. Not yet, anyway."

Contessa and Gwen looked at each other and said in one voice, "We promise."

Abe walked over to the office doorway and pushed the inner door open. "Come in and have a seat." Abe paused for a second and then said, "I love you both with all my heart, and right now, my heart is breaking." He wiped the tears from his eyes. "I have spent hours down here, listening and watching, hoping that it was all a cruel hoax." Abe blew his nose into a Kleenex and continued, "But I have come to the conclusion that this is not a hoax. What you are about to see is real ... and very difficult to watch."

Abe motioned to Gwen. "Gwen, you sit here, and Contessa, you here." Abe pointed at one of the keyboards and said, "Press this button to start the recording and this one to pause it. I am going to let you watch the recording by yourselves." Abe placed his hand on Gwen's shoulder and said, "When you're done, or if you need anything, I'll be just outside the door."

Abe leaned over and kissed both Contessa and Gwen on the top of their heads.

"You are not alone," he told them. "Don't forget that. We are in this together, and I love you both very much." Abe backed out of the office and just before he closed the door behind him, he said, "Whatever we do ... we will do together."

CHAPTER 16

I walked by the ASG conference room on the to my office to prepare our Monday-morning meeting. I neglected to say anything to Cindy, who was already in the room, preparing. I was reading from my phone, and oblivious to the goings on around me.

The text message read, "Call me ASAP 843-867-5309 – C." I knew it was Contessa. I was simultaneously excited and scared to return her call.

Cindy followed me into my office and asked, "Well, are you okay? You seem very distracted."

"Sorry about that. I was just reading a text about Dillianquest."

"Anything good?"

I set the phone down on the desk and said, "Not really. Just need to get prepared to begin negotiations."

Cindy picked up the now-green folder labeled "Dillianquest Project" at the top and handed it to me, saying, "Tom has all the operating statements, Bill has three years of financials, and Legal has everything they need, except a current real-estate appraisal."

I looked at Cindy from behind my desk and said, "Great job, Cindy." As I picked up the file I said, "I need to touch base with Dillianquest's attorney."

I paused as I tried to think of the attorney's name. Cindy interjected, "Mr. Dillianquest's attorney is Mr. Michael Belanger. His phone number is right here."

"Thanks, I don't know what I would do without you," I said in an appreciative voice.

Cindy was halfway out of the office when she turned and said, "I know," with a smile. "Don't be late for your meeting. It starts in one minute." Cindy disappeared, and I grabbed a few files that I needed, including the Dillianquest project, as it was now called.

The Monday-morning meeting started right on schedule. Bill gave a positive future-looking financial review. Tom's operations were running about as smoothly as one could expect.

Everyone had known that the Obama administration was going to make everything health-care more difficult. Finding $787 billion in stimulus was going to hurt. It was going to come in part from Medicare and Medicaid reimbursement cuts—our bread and butter.

When it got to my turn, I apologized, saying, "I know we are not supposed to get real deep on Mondays, but I want to move forward with the Dillianquest project." I paused, looked at Bill, and said, "Bill, are we okay with the financials?"

"Nothing major now—a couple of minor issues with the foundation, but I think Legal can write some language into the purchase contract to indemnify us from any future problems. Tom will have his work cut out for his team to get staffing and spending under control. But you have a go from my end as long as the final price is right."

I glanced over at Tom and said, "Mr. Bricks and Mortar, what say you?"

"After reviewing their staffing patterns and the operating and marketing budgets, I'm thinking we could very well have another Schultz project on our hands. I see a profitable upside to Dillianquest if you don't strap us to too high of a fixed cost at purchase."

I smiled at Tom and said, "I'll do my best. I get the distinct feeling that Mr. Dillianquest is a motivated seller."

I then turned to Ed, who was in the meeting to represent the legal department, and said, "What is the good word from Legal, Ed?"

"It looks pretty good from our perspective. There is limited exposure from the liability side—two small workers' comp claims, but no patient or employee litigation. It seems pretty clean. The only thing we need from you at this point is a current real-estate appraisal."

"Super. I have to speak with Mr. Belanger today anyway, and I will get that for you just as soon as possible."

With that, I stood up and said, "Thanks, guys. Seems like we have concluded stage three. We can now move the Dillianquest project to stage four. I will keep you posted regarding negotiations. Everyone have a good day and better week."

We all left the conference room and I went back to my office. As I sat in my chair, I studied the message on the screen. I had been distracted by the events in Beaufort. Sam and I had not gotten along well over the weekend after I returned from my trip. The accidental killing of an innocent man, the affair with Contessa, and the threat from Gwen had my guts in a knot. I told Sam the faltering economy and an impending Medicare audit were causing a lot of stress for me at work. I was not at all sure she bought what I was selling.

As I was blankly staring at the text message on my phone screen, Bill tapped on the office door.

"Hey, Bill, come on in. What's on your mind?"

Bill turned, closed the door quietly, and walked to the chair directly in front of my desk. He sat and looked at me for a moment as he propped one foot against the top of my desk and pushed the chair he was sitting back on two legs.

My heart skipped a few beats. I thought maybe Bill suspected something was not quite right with the Dillianquest project.

But Bill's face grew a little smile as he said, "I've been thinking about the Dillianquest deal, Tag. This could be a really good deal for the firm." Bill, still leaning back in his chair, pursed his lips while he nodded his head up and down. "This could be a *very* good deal for the firm. I'm not sure what one hundred acres of intercoastal waterway frontage is worth these days, but it must be worth a small fortune, don't you think, Tag?"

I felt much more comfortable now that the conversation had begun pleasantly. "There is a shitload of potential here, Bill. The place is fantastic. Old Man Dillianquest spared no expense putting those buildings together." I leaned forward, put both elbows on his desk, and added, "The ground that Dillianquest sits on is pretty fabulous."

Bill looked me straight in the eyes and said, "Yeah, you're right. I looked at the promotional package that Nate Dillianquest put together. It is rather impressive."

"Nate is giving us the exclusive on this. No other firms are in the bidding."

Bill, still leaning back on the two legs of his chair, said, "Doesn't that strike you as odd? Good, competitive bids get the price up."

I glanced out the window behind my desk for a second and then looked back at Bill. "Well, Nate said a couple of interesting things while we were together."

"What's that?"

"He said he wasn't interested in selling to any of his southern cohorts. He was only interested in selling to Yankees like us. Probably wants to save face in the state health-care association. He also said that his family businesses were in the tank. We drove by a couple of the construction sites, and they were all at a dead stop. Then I did a little checking of my own. Just out of curiosity, I was looking at a list of Bernie Madoff victims posted on the CNN website, and lo and behold, there was the Dillianquest name. It looks like Bernie took them for about a hundred million."

Bill grimaced. "Ouch. A hundred million, huh? That would make you want to kill somebody."

"Sure would. One person's bad fortune is another person's opportunity." I leaned back in my chair and said, "There are a lot of dynamics at play here. I don't want to fuck Nate to death on this deal, but if he walks away with a case of the sore ass after negotiations … I won't feel too bad." Bill and I both laughed.

"What are the northern limits in your mind?" Bill asked.

"I'm thinking anywhere between eighty and eighty-five percent of appraised value, top end."

As Bill stood up he said. "Good luck. Let me know how it goes."

"I'll keep you posted."

As Bill left the office, I stood up from my desk and closed the office door. I picked up the phone from atop the desk and reread the text message over and over again. I sat back down in my chair, turned, and faced the window. I put my feet on the credenza, leaned back, and called Contessa. My heart pounded wildly. There was no moisture left in my mouth.

The phone rang only once before Contessa answered it.

"Hell-o, good-looking. How was your weekend?" Contessa spoke in a low, very sexy voice. Her words were slow, and she spoke with that now-familiar southern drawl. She knew how bad my weekend had been.

"It was actually the worst weekend of my life. That's how my weekend was."

"Darling, don't get your panties all twisted in a knot," Contessa said with a smile in her voice. "The only way anyone finds out about anything … is if you tell them."

Contessa paused long enough to let that thought sink in for a moment and then added, "Listen, sweetie. You are way too smart a man to let that fine little ass of yours wind up in places it doesn't belong. We both know stripes make you look fat." Contessa laughed at her own joke.

Contessa heard me take a deep breath on the other end then added, "Tag, my dear, everything is going to be just fine. Don't you worry about a thing."

"Look, Contessa, how can you say everything is going to be fine?"

"Tag," Contessa said smoothly, "just listen to me, and everything will be just fine." She paused for a second and then continued assertively, "I need you to do something for me." Contessa paused, listening, and then added, "Actually, sweetie, I need you to do a couple of things for *us*." Contessa emphasized the word "us" as she finished her thought.

I felt myself breathing heavily when I said, "And those things for *us* would be?"

Contessa said with a sigh, "I need you to call Nate Dillianquest today at 3:00 p.m. sharp. Can you do that for me … please?"

I addressed her request in a questioning tone. "And what am I supposed to call Nate about?"

"Call him and tell him that you want to come back down to Beaufort on Thursday to meet with him and Belanger about the sale of Dillianquest." Contessa was silent for a few seconds before she added, "I need him to excuse himself from Mother's room to talk to you in private. He reads the Bible to Mother every day at 3:00 p.m."

I paced back and forth in my office, the phone glued to my ear. "Okay, I'll call Nate at three today, but Thursday is too soon," I objected. "I have other obligations. I can't cancel them."

Contessa was silent on the phone as I attempted to regain some semblance of control of my life when she said, "Tag, sweetheart." Paying no attention to my objections, she continued, "Clear your calendar from Wednesday through Friday. Call Belanger and Dillianquest today and set up a meeting for Thursday late afternoon. Tell Nate that you would like to take another evening cruise on the *Kindred Spirit*—you know, drink a scotch or two and work out the details of the sale. That should put him in a good mood." Contessa sounded upbeat. After a pause, she said, "Tag, I hope you are getting this. Our future, sweetie, depends on it."

I was still pacing manically in my office and said, "I've got it."

Contessa said with a sigh of relief, "Wonderful, darling, because there are a couple more things you need to do."

"Of course there are," I said, resigned to the fact that I was not in control of anything at this point.

"Nate will offer to have Gwen pick you up at the Willow Run Airport. Accept his offer, but insist that your company pay for the expenses. You know, to keep things aboveboard and all."

Contessa paused for a few seconds, forcing me to respond by saying, "All right. Then what?"

Contessa, now in full control, added in a cheery voice, "Nate will offer you the cottage and a car, just like last time."

"Okay."

"Accept the cottage, but tell Nate you are going to rent a car at the airport. You know, just in case you hit another deer."

"Is that all *we* need to do?"

"Tag, dear, I sense a bit of sarcasm in your voice. It is not very becoming."

Attempting to hold back my anger, I said, "Look, I'm willing to do as you ask, but this could ruin my family, career, and *me* ... forever!"

"You know, darling, I get wet just thinking about our night together." Contessa, speaking as if she had had him in the palm of her hand, added, "I can't wait to see you." After a deep sigh, she added, "Don't get distracted by all this other stuff."

I felt my face getting flushed as I said, "I can't stop thinking about that night at the cottage." My voice was shaky. "I can't wait to see you again." I knew that he had lost all control.

I knew I was too far down a bad road to protest too much about how I was being manipulated when I said in a more sober voice, "How did Gwen get pictures of us together, and how did she know about the bridge?"

"Tag," Contessa said. "Tag, darling." She changed the subject, completely asserting her control. "That night we spent together means a great deal to me." Contessa sounded very vulnerable when she added, "I hope you believe me when I tell you this … but I've never been a part of this kind of thing, ever. I don't know what came over me. I am not the kind of woman who does this sort of thing."

I could feel I was being played even harder when Contessa added, "I am very drawn to you, Tag. And I think we both know that an evening like the one we shared … an evening as hot as that was … would have never taken place if you were truly happy at home. It is obvious to me that your wife is not taking care of your needs."

Contessa added, "Tag, sweetie, after that night together … I think you know I can take care of *all* your needs." Contessa's breath was heavy on the phone.

I heard Contessa take a long, deep breath on the other end of the phone, but I didn't say anything. She paused, and as she was exhaling, said, "Tag, you know nothing is ever exactly as it appears."

Contessa, sounding contrite, continued, "I will be in the plane when Gwen picks you up on Wednesday. I will explain everything then. I will answer every question you have." After a long pause, Contessa added, "I'll see you then, my sweet. Be strong. Don't forget to call Nate." The phone went silent.

In the basement office of Abe Belanger, back in Beaufort, South Carolina, Contessa ended the call and laid the phone on the desk. She leaned back in her chair, and with a confident smile, she looked at both Gwen and Abe.

"It's almost done," she told them.

Back in his Ann Arbor office, Tag paced frantically back and forth behind his closed office door, muttering to himself, "Oh God, what the fuck have I done?" over and over and over again.

CHAPTER 17

Nate Dillianquest showed up at Danby House at his usual time, 2:30 p.m. As was his custom, Nate poked his head in the office of the administrator and said, "Hi, Dianna. How are things going? Do you mind if I come in?"

Dianna had been expecting Nate, as this was his normal routine. "Please, please, come in and have a seat. I poured a glass of tea for you," she said in a most accommodating way. She lifted the glass of tea from the tray and handed it to her guest. Dianna added, "Finally looks we are going to get some decent weather. They can keep their cold up north." She smiled.

Nate came into Dianna's office, holding in his hand a small chocolate shake from the local malt shop. "Do you have a couple of napkins? I don't want to leave rings on your desk."

Sitting behind her desk, Dianna said, "Sure do," and reached in one of the drawers in her credenza. Dianna retrieved several napkins that had "Danby House" stamped into them. She placed the napkins on her desk in front of Nate.

Nate sat the malt down and said, "Mother's really been enjoying her malts lately. There's sure not much else in her life anymore. Alzheimer's is a dreadful disease." Nate sat back in his chair, and a smile emerged on his face when he said, "I remember as a kid, Father would load Mother and me in the car, and he would take us into town on Saturday nights. He would take us to Rye's ice-cream parlor and treat us to anything we wanted." Nate looked directly at Dianna. "Mother and I really enjoyed our malts.

She always got the same thing: a double-thick, double-chocolate malt. I remember she would have them make it so thick, you couldn't even suck the malt through the straw."

Nate smiled and added thoughtfully, "Funny what you remember from your childhood. I can see Mother swirling that straw around in the malt, using it like a spoon. Then she would suck the malt out of the straw from the bottom—and then lick the straw clean." Nate laughed, tilted his head a bit to one side, and added, "Come to think of it, that's exactly how I drink my malt."

Nate paused, still reflecting back on his youth, and said, "Father worked so much back then that Saturday night was our night at the malt shop. It was always just the three of us. Saturday night was our night." After a short pause, Nate looked at Dianna and said fondly, "You know, Dianna, I miss those days. I'd give anything to relive my youth again. Those were wonderful years."

Nate paused again, this time a bit longer, and asked a rhetorical question of Dianna: "I wonder if Alzheimer's lets Mother remember just how much she loved to go downtown with Father and me for a double-thick, double-chocolate malt?"

Dianna looked into Nate's eyes and said in a very kind voice, "Nate, I am sure your mother remembers those days with great fondness."

To break the ensuing awkward silence, Nate said, "Thanks for the tea." Nate held up his glass as if he were offering up a toast, took a long sip, and added, "I see the dogwoods are starting to bloom in the woods. Spring will happen quickly once she gets going."

Dianna replied, "I have had enough of winter. I am looking forward to spring."

"I think we are all looking for a change, Dianna," Nate said as he stood up from his seated position.

Dianna was ready with the usual operations report that she and Nate discussed every day. Standing in front of her desk, Nate said, "Listen, I think we will skip the reports today, if you don't mind?" He picked up the malt and walked toward the door. He stopped, turned back, looked at Dianna, and asked, "Is Doc Jones in the house?"

"Yes, he is. He is making rounds with Priscilla, the Director of Nurses."

Nate was still standing in the doorway of Dianna's office when he said, "Great, I need to speak with him. I'm a bit concerned about Mother's health. She hasn't been very communicative of late." Nate waved good-bye with his free hand and said as he left the office, "I'll talk with you later. I'll be down at Mother's if you need me."

Dianna simply said, "See ya later."

Nate disappeared down the hallway and headed toward his mother's suite. Nate knew every resident by first name. Nate walking the halls of Danby House was like the president of the United States making his way to the podium at the State of the Union address. He stopped to talk to and touch everyone he came in contact with. He made everyone he talked to feel important.

When Nate arrived at his mother's room, Contessa had just finished freshening her up. Contessa had just helped her from the bathroom into her wheelchair and was fussing over her hair and straightening her dress. She had Nate's mother looking very spring-like in her flowered dress and white shawl. She had even put some fresh flowers into Sarah's hair.

Sometimes Nate would take his mother for a stroll around the facility and visit with the other residents. Other times, he would just sit with her in the lounge area in her suite while she and Nate visited. As Nate walked in, he addressed Contessa in his usual manner.

"Hey, Tessa. How is Mother today?"

"She is a bit slow today. I don't think she is feeling all that well."

"Does she recognize you?"

"No," Contessa said with a sigh. "Everybody is new to her today." Contessa acted as if she knew nothing about what Nate had planned for their mother.

"I'm sorry to hear that," Nate said with a note of sadness in his voice.

Nate kissed Sarah on the cheek and said, "Hi, Mother. I brought you your favorite: double-thick, double-chocolate malt." Contessa handed Nate a spoon. Nate took off the lid, scooped a little bit of malt onto the spoon, and wet Sarah's lips with the sweet concoction. She licked her lips, and a big smile came across her face.

Nate walked around behind the wheelchair and said, "Come on, Mother. Let's move into the sitting area, and you can enjoy your malt." Nate began pushing her into the other room, away from the bedroom and dressing area.

Contessa looked at Nate and said, "Go ahead, Nate. I'm going to tidy up in here and get ready for her three o'clock meds."

Nate turned and looked back over his shoulder at Contessa as he pushed Sarah into the next room. "Anything I can do to help?"

"No, just keep doing what you're doing. Mother loves her malts."

Nate and Sarah sat in the lounge area of her suite while Contessa cleaned up the bathroom, straightening towels and drying the water that had splashed onto the floor. She looked at her watch, and it was 3:02 pm. She stopped what she was doing and began to question if Tag had bailed on their plan. Then, just as she finished that thought, she heard Nate's phone ring. Contessa stood motionless, listening as Nate answered his phone.

"This is Nate. How can I help you?" was his standard greeting. In a few short seconds, she heard Nate say in a cheery voice, "Tag, good to hear from you. How are things?" There was a silence on Nate's end of the phone, and then Contessa heard Nate say, "Thursday? Yes, Thursday afternoon should be just fine." After a momentary pause, Nate said, "Tag, can you hold on for just one second?" Nate put his hand over the phone's microphone and said in a loud voice, "Tessa, I am going to take this call outside. Can you watch Mother until I return?"

Contessa walked back into the room. "Sure, Nate."

Nate replied in a whisper, pointing to the hallway beyond Mother's room. "These walls have ears." Nate laughed as he left the room.

Contessa ducked back into the med room and got a small screw-top specimen jar. She quickly made her way over to where Nate had placed the malt cup, making sure that Nate was not coming back into the room. Contessa picked up the malt and poured a small amount of malt into her specimen jar. As she walked back to the med room, she made sure the lid was secure. Contessa opened the refrigerator and placed the specimen jar out of sight behind rows and rows of Ensure that lined one complete shelf of the refrigerator.

Once she had secured her sample, Contessa went back over to where her mother was seated and spilled the rest of the malt on the floor, throwing the malt cup to make it look like an accident. Contessa got up, and went into the bathroom to get some towels. She waited until she could hear Nate coming back down the hall before she started to clean up the mess. Contessa could hear him talking to someone.

As they got closer, she recognized the second voice as that of Dr. Jones, Sarah's personal doctor and the medical director of the facility.

The door opened, and the first through was Dr. Jones, who greeted Contessa by saying, "Hi, Contessa. How's our patient today?"

"She's been a little bit combative today."

When Nate came in the room, he asked, "What happened to the malt?"

Contessa, kneeling on the floor with towels in hand, said, "When I was giving her three o'clock meds, she knocked the malt out of my hand and onto the floor. She caught me by surprise." As she was cleaning up the mess, she added, "I'll get her another one from dietary."

A noticeable agitation revealed itself in Nate's voice when he said, "Tessa, you know how much Mother likes her malts from the ice-cream parlor. I'll go get her another one."

Contessa was a bit agitated as well when she said, "Nate, she'll be fine. Missing one day of her malt won't kill her, now will it?"

Nate sighed. "You're right. I just hate to see her slipping away right before our very eyes." Nate sat down on the couch beside Sarah and said, "What's going on with Mother, Doc?" as he reached out and took her hand.

Dr. Jones looked at Contessa. "Do you have her chart?"

"I'll get it for you. It's in the med room." Contessa retrieved the chart and handed it to Dr. Jones. "Here it is. We just got her blood work back today that you ordered."

Dr. Jones replied, "Great, thanks."

He took the chart and sat next to Nate on the couch.

"Let's see what we've got here, Nate." After a minute or so of reviewing Sarah's chart, the doctor said, "We did some liver- and kidney-function tests, and the results are not good. Her liver and kidneys are shutting down at an accelerated rate."

Nate sat back in his chair. He looked at his mother sitting in her wheelchair, sleeping. He looked at Contessa, who was seated in a chair directly across from both men, and then he looked at Dr. Jones, "What exactly are you saying?"

Dr. Jones took a deep breath and thought to himself, *God, I hate these conversations,* and then he looked at Nate and said, "Sarah is in her nineties. She has done many wonderful things for the people of Beaufort, and you should take pride in that. Her body is not filtering her blood. She will become more and more confused and disoriented." Dr. Jones reached over, placed his hand on Nate's leg, looked over at Contessa, and said, "I think you both should prepare yourselves for the worst. If her body keeps deteriorating at this pace, I don't think she will be with us more than two months." There was a short pause as Dr. Jones took a deep breath and then added, "And I'm being very optimistic."

Dr. Jones stood and walked over to Contessa. As he hugged her, he said, "I'm very sorry. She is a wonderful woman. No one should have to die like this." Dr. Jones turned to Nate and said, "I'm sorry, old friend. Contessa and I will keep her comfortable. If you need anything to help you sleep, just let me know."

The doctor made his way to the door, stopped, looked back, and said, "If you two need anything—anything at all—let me know."

Contessa and Nate said at the same time, "Thanks, Doc."

Nate stood and said to Contessa, "I guess I knew it was coming. It's just hard to hear it said out loud."

Contessa did not say anything. She was full of rage inside. She walked over to Sarah and kissed her on the cheek. She looked at Nate and said, "I'm going to take Mother outside for some fresh air. Do you want to come?"

"I don't think so. I've got things that I need to tend to. Thanks, though. You two enjoy." Nate kissed Sarah on the cheek and Contessa on the forehead and left.

Contessa took her purse into the bathroom. She tried to wipe the kiss from her forehead as she stared into the mirror.

From her purse, she took out her phone and called Gwen.

"Can you come to Mother's? We need to get this sample to the lab in Charleston as soon as possible. See you when you get here—be careful." She walked back out into the room, where Sarah was sleeping in her wheelchair.

Contessa knew not to say anything in front of the cameras and microphones that Abe had planted in her mother's room. Contessa bent over and whispered into Sarah's ear, "I won't let him get away with this, Mother. He is going to pay dearly for all he has done."

CHAPTER 18

N P603 touched down at 3:15 p.m. Gwen was right on schedule. Jim and I waited and watched from the black Lincoln Town Car parked near the tarmac as the pilot skillfully guided her aircraft to the front of the Willow Run Airport terminal building.

Jim had been babbling about how lucky I was to sit alongside such a wildly attractive woman as Gwen for hours on the flight to South Carolina. It was easy to tell how smitten he was with her. Most of the conversation went in one ear and out the other. I was too absorbed in my own thoughts to even care about what Jim was talking about. This day was going to be a day like no other.

As the aircraft came to a stop, Jim and I walked through the large glass doors of the terminal building and onto the tarmac. Jim carried my garment bag, and I clutched my briefcase.

The propellers came to a slow halt. The cabin door popped open, and the stairs unfolded. Gwen emerged like a Monarch butterfly from her cocoon. Standing erect in the doorway of her plane, the beautiful Gwen made her way down the ladder to the tarmac.

As she walked toward us, we could only think of her stunning beauty. Gwen wore a black pantsuit that fit every curve of her body like a glove over a hand. The flowing stovepipe pants covered her shoes, allowing only the shiny tips of her toes and heels to be seen as the cuffs of her pants bounced playfully with her walk. Her jacket, fitted tight to her waist, had black silk vertical stripes that reflected the bright sun. Her jacket just barely covered her full breasts. She was wearing a white shell top. Her silky, jet-black hair was pulled back tight into a ponytail, revealing long, silver fish-scale earrings that glistened in the afternoon sun. She had our complete attention.

As she approached, she reached her hand out toward mine and said, "Mr. Grayson, it is so good to see you again." She shook my hand with a firm, tight grasp. She then looked at Jim and smiled. As she grasped Jim's hand, she said, "And Jim, what a pleasure it is to see you again. You look well."

Jim beamed as brightly as the sun as he shook her hand and said, "Gwen, you look absolutely radiant. I love your suit. You could give some tips to Mrs. Clinton on how to wear a pantsuit."

Jim was still holding on to Gwen's hand as she said, "I think you are a dangerous one." We all laughed for a second then Gwen said, "Mr. Grayson, I am going to top off the tanks. If you would like, climb aboard, we will get under way in a just a few minutes."

I glanced at Jim and reached for my garment bag.

"I'll get that bag for you," Gwen said. She reached and took the bag from Jim's hand. "Jim, it was nice to see you again."

Jim nodded at Gwen, looked at me, and said, "Let me know about your return."

I stopped at the top step of the plane and looked back at Jim. "Will do," I said and then disappeared into the plane.

Contessa sat in the passenger's cabin in one of the seats facing the rear of the plane. She had already poured a glass of scotch and had it in her hand as I made my way into the plane. I sat down in the seat that faced Contessa and placed my briefcase on the seat on the other side of the aisle.

I took a deep breath and said, "Hi," in a rather pathetic tone.

Contessa smiled at me with her perfect smile, handed me the glass of scotch, and said, "Tag, my dear, you are going to have to do better. You don't sound very glad to see me." Contessa immediately got up from her seat and flung herself directly onto my lap.

She held my face with both hands and gave me a big kiss, pressing her hands on my cheeks. After a long, sensual kiss, she pulled back, looked me right in the eyes, and said, "I've missed you, and mister, there are no funky moods allowed on this aircraft." Contessa was bright and cheery and full of herself.

She wore a light-blue denim sundress with burgundy cowgirl boots. Her long, silky black hair, parted in the middle, fell gently down about her shoulders. She smelled just as she had when we were fully entangled at Nate's cottage. I closed my eyes and inhaled deeply. Her scent whisked me back into that sexual embrace.

Contessa regained her position directly across from me.

"I've thought about you a lot, too." My eyes quickly darted out the plane's window to see if Jim had been watching. It would be difficult to explain if Jim had seen our embrace. I was relieved to see the back of the car leaving the parking lot. I looked back at Contessa and said, "I ... I mean we ... have to be careful. I don't want anyone to have reason to be suspicious."

She reached over, caressed my cheek, and said, "You are right. We need to be discreet. I just couldn't help myself." She reached over to the bar, poured herself a glass of white wine, and said, "It must be five o'clock somewhere."

Gwen was making final arrangements on the tarmac, signing paperwork for the fuel. As she entered the aircraft, she closed the cabin door behind her. Gwen made her way to the cockpit, and as she maneuvered by, she said, "We should be wheels up in less than five minutes." Gwen entered the cockpit without effort, preparing for takeoff. In what seemed like seconds, Gwen had both engines humming. The plane started toward the runway.

Contessa placed her hand on my knee, winked, and said, "This is my favorite part of flying. I just love to feel the sheer acceleration at takeoff."

Just a few seconds later, Gwen had both throttles at full speed as the plane set me back in my seat from the force of the engines. I looked at Contessa, who gazed out of the window as the plane accelerated. Gwen was all business up front as the plane roared down the runway. Gwen pulled back on the yoke, and NP603 left the ground. As the plane's nose lifted toward the sky, I let myself sink deep into the seat. Gwen was headed for the clouds; we were on our way.

After Gwen trimmed the plane's propellers and reached cruising altitude, Contessa sat up on the edge of her seat and looked at me with a great big smile. "I'll bet you're wondering what all the hubbub is about." She shrugged slightly and continued, "When we talked on the phone Monday, I told you I would fill you in on the rest of the story."

I looked at Contessa without showing any expression, took a drink of scotch, and said, "Yes, you did."

Contessa reached over her head and knocked on the wall of the cockpit. From around the cockpit wall, Gwen's head appeared. Contessa reached up, placed her hand on the side of Gwen's face, fondly stroked her cheek, and said, "Gwen and I are sisters."

I felt my face go from blank to dumbfounded. "You're putting me on. Goddamn, I should have known. There is a slight resemblance."

Gwen smiled, winked, and said in a sarcastic voice, "I'm glad to see that nothing gets by you." She laughed.

I looked at both Gwen and Contessa and said in self-defense, "I try not to assume anything in my line of work."

Contessa playfully slapped Gwen's cheek in mock anger and said, "Be nice to my sweetie. He has been through a lot this past week."

Gwen, still looking back at me, said in a very apologetic tone, "Sorry, Tag. I have forgotten how much stress you've been under."

And with that, Gwen disappeared back into the cockpit.

Contessa then added, "Actually, it's been pretty stressful for all of us."

Contessa propped her boots up on either side of my seat and put her hands in the middle of her spread legs, forcing her dress down in between her legs—but not before I caught a glimpse of her pure white panties.

Contessa saw my eyes dart directly between her legs. She leaned back in her seat, took a sip of wine, and said, "It's a pretty complicated story, sweetie, so I won't delve too deeply into all the gory details." Contessa paused and sighed. "I will try to help you understand how fate has put us together."

Contessa took another sip of wine. As she lowered her glass from her lips, she gazed into it for a few seconds and then looked at me. I was watching her every move.

"Fate is a funny thing, my dear." Contessa paused for a moment, swirled her wine high on the sides of her glass, and watched as the wine crept back to its resting place. "One never knows exactly how one will handle fate when one comes face-to-face with it."

Again Contessa paused and lifted the glass to her lips. The wine seemed to take forever to reach her imperceptibly open mouth. Contessa removed the glass from her lips and said, "Fate is upon us, Tag." She had the slightest of smiles beginning on her lips when she added, "Our future depends on how we handle what is headed our way."

I searched for some feeling or emotion that I could understand, but there just wasn't any. I did not feel the sense of impending doom I had anticipated standing in the Willow Run terminal building. I did not feel any sense of shame for what I did or was doing—the shame I had felt throughout the long, agonizing weekend had disappeared. The only emotion that I could identify at that moment was an odd sense of excitement, an exhilarating and overwhelming sense of adventure.

As I looked out the window at the passing clouds, I fantasized about what it would be like to leave all I had done and created behind. I asked myself an unthinkable question: *What will it be like to leave Sam, the kids, and work behind, and just vanish into thin air?* I just didn't have an answer.

As my mind drifted with the passing clouds, Contessa squeezed my leg and said, "A penny for your thoughts."

I looked at Contessa and said, "My thoughts aren't worth a penny. Why don't you continue with what you were saying?"

Contessa took a breath and said, "When Nate was younger, he spent time in Colombia." Contessa wore a serious expression. "The Dillianquest family saved us from the poverty that is rampant in that part of the world. Mother took us in and treated us like family. We are so grateful to her. She had lost a daughter at birth, and we became the daughters she never had."

Contessa took a deep breath, let out a big sigh, and then continued. "Mother put me through nursing school, and Gwen through aviation flight school." Contessa paused for a moment to gather her thoughts. "It was like she was getting us ready to stand on our own two feet. I think she knew Nate would not take care of us after she was gone. Mother is a very special and intuitive woman."

Contessa took a sip of wine and said, "Nate has always been a little resentful of Gwen's and my close relationship with Mother. Sometimes he makes us feel as if we're outsiders or servants, as if we are here to take care of Mother's needs and drive his boat and fly his plane for him." A sudden sadness came over Contessa as she added, "After Father passed, Nate tried his best to run the family's businesses, but he really did not have Father's business sense. He was doomed to fail."

In a slightly harsher tone, Contessa added, "He's a trust-fund baby. Mother and Father didn't make him work for much of anything, so he doesn't know how to run a business. And then, with the economy, everything went to hell for Nate." Contessa shook her head in sympathy for Nate. "Gwen and I were never really involved with the family businesses. All of that was left for Nate." Contessa said with just a slight smirk, "He's even sold several of his antique cars to make ends meet." Her smirk widened as she said, "I know that breaks that little shit's heart."

Contessa refilled both her glass of wine and my scotch. I was getting a bit more comfortable as I drank and listened to Contessa talk. She was beautiful to look at. I couldn't help myself. I kept undressing her in his mind as she continued her story. I wasn't paying that close attention; I was too busy reliving my moments of ecstasy in her arms, and I couldn't wait to return.

Contessa caught my attention when she said, "I knew he lost everything in the Madoff scam." She paused and said, "After that, it all started to make sense." Contessa lifted her glass to her lips, but before she took a drink, she said, "Then it finally dawned on me that Nate was going to sell Dillianquest." Contessa took a drink of wine.

Her intensity began to show again. The pace of her speech quickened. "All those conversations with Dianna about needing an appraisal and putting together a video." Contessa took a deep breath. "Nate said it was for the bank, so he could refinance. What a load of crap that was." She paused for a second. "It's the video he sent to you, isn't it?"

I sat more erect and said, "Yea, we did get a video from Nate about Dillianquest."

"I knew it. Well ..." Contessa took a few deep breaths and slowed her pace back to normal. "Once I figured out just how bad off Nate's finances were, I pressed Barb for some information."

"Barb? Who's Barb?"

"Ah, yes, you don't know Barb, do you? Barb Hayden is the treasurer and secretary of the Dillianquest Foundation. She is also the facility bookkeeper." Contessa said with a half-assed grin, "For some reason, Barb confides in me. She told me that Nate had been screwing her for the past year or so. She was scared to death that her hubby would find out." Contessa laughed. "She also told me that she and Nate had been skimming thousands and thousands of dollars from the foundation."

Contessa took a sip of wine and said with that same smirk on her face, "God, what a mess she was, crying and carrying on like there was no tomorrow. Leave it to Nate to exploit a weak spot. Then, one day, a few weeks ago, Nate was standing outside, near Mother's window, talking on his cell. I don't think he knew the window was open. I heard him talking to you or someone in your office, making arrangements to come down and look at Dillianquest. Then, when you showed up in the building the same week, looking at 'investing'"—Contessa used air quotes—"I knew something was up."

She sat on the edge of her seat, looked directly into my eyes, and said, "I was very pleasantly surprised to see such an interesting and handsome man looking to invest in our little facility." Contessa leaned forward, gave me a kiss on the cheek, and then sat back in her chair. "When I heard that Dianna recommended the Ocean Side, I just had to go and see what I could find out from you."

I sipped on my Scotch, but did not say a word; I just kept on listening.

"When I called Levi at the OSS, he said you had just arrived. I had Gwen and her boyfriend drop me off outside and sent them away. I felt confident that I could get you to take me home." Contessa looked sad when she added, "Don't hate me for this, Tag, but Gwen and I just wanted a little insurance to make sure Nate's deal went through. If anyone could fuck this deal up, it would be Nate."

Contessa fidgeted in her seat and then added, "We had no intention of ruining your life in the process." Contessa took a long pause and looked sad when she added, "You see, Tag, Dillianquest can only be sold upon Mother's death. Her health is getting worse by the day. When Dillianquest is sold, according to Mother's wishes, Gwen and I stand to inherit 25 percent each, and Nate gets 50 percent."

Contessa sat back in her seat and took a long, slow sip of her wine. She looked at me with those big dark eyes and said in a somber voice, "Two things happened that night at the OSS that were out of my control." Contessa leaned forward and held my hand. "The man that was killed that night, Jason Holt, was an accident, and I am sorry about that. But I wasn't about to let a transient piece of shit like him get in the way." Contessa squeezed my hand harder and added, "The other thing was that, sometime during the evening, I fell for you. It started out as an act, but somehow, I let my feelings get in the way."

I squeezed her hand. "I guess that is where fate entered the picture?"

"Yep, fate has a sneaky way of changing everything." She sat back and smiled.

I smiled back at her and said, "So what does fate have in mind for us now?"

"Well, sweetie, I want to propose something to you that I have been thinking about a lot." Contessa looked a bit nervous as she sipped her wine. "You don't have to commit to anything or say anything. Just think about it—that's all I'm asking." Contessa sat back in her seat and added, "You do what's right for you."

I nodded in agreement but remained silent. I leaned back in my seat and took a long, slow sip of scotch.

After Contessa built up her courage, she said, "You need to strike a deal with Nate when you are out on the *Kindred Spirit*." Contessa was slow and deliberate in her speech. "Nate will have his attorney, Michael Belanger, with him. You haven't met him yet; he's a lawyer. Don't bend over in front of him," she said with a smile.

Contessa looked deep into my eyes. "Don't ask me how I know this, but I know that Nate will agree to fifty or so million dollars." Contessa paused. "Which is a good deal for all of us, your company included."

Contessa looked out the plane's window. A tear rolled down her cheek when she added, "When Mother passes, God rest her soul, your company takes possession of Dillianquest." Emotion rose in her voice. "And the money from the sale of Dillianquest will be deposited with Belanger for distribution at the reading of Mother's will."

She continued in her slow and deliberate fashion, "Then, as soon as possible, you catch an early-morning flight to Atlanta with a connection to Myrtle Beach, just as if you were flying to Beaufort to take possession of Dillianquest."

Contessa paused for a second. "Here is where you control your fate, Tag." She looked directly into my eyes. "Upon arrival in Atlanta, you will go to baggage claim, where there will be a driver waiting for you." Contessa took a sip of her wine. "Look for a man holding a placard with your name on it." She paused. "This is the important part. He will hand you a key to a locker. Go to the locker and get the package that will be there for you."

Contessa sat up on the edge of her seat and said, "Once you have the package in your possession and you have read what will be in the envelope ..." Contessa paused and looked deep into my eyes and heart. "You will then have to make your decision."

Contessa stopped and reached for my hand. "At that point, you can either continue to Beaufort or go with the driver." Contessa squeezed my hand and then released it, saying, "If you decide to go with the driver, he will take you to a private airfield, where Gwen and I will be waiting for you." She sat back in her seat. "If you decide to join us, we are going to fly to South America in this plane and start our lives new. We will be able to live well on our inheritance. Gwen and I want to find our true family."

Contessa had become noticeably happier when she talked about finding her family. She added, "But if you decide you do not want to go with me and start a new life, just tell the driver that you are continuing on to Beaufort. Go back through security and continue your life." She looked at me and said circumspectly, "Your fate is in Atlanta. Think about what is right for you. I know what is right for me, and I am doing it."

I sat back in my seat and stared out the window. As I did, Gwen looked around the corner of the cockpit and said, "We're about twenty minutes from touchdown. You kids will want to make sure you're buckled in."

I couldn't believe that we were about to land at the Beaufort Municipal Airport. Contessa leaned forward, touched my hands, and said, "I know it's a lot to think about, but first things first. Get the deal done. Then you can think about your future."

The plane touched down and taxied to the terminal. I looked at Contessa and said, "I don't even know your last name."

"Rios. Contessa Maria Rios."

"Well, Contessa Maria Rios, when will I see you?"

"Gwen and I have a few things to take care of this evening, and I don't know how long it will take us."

Just then, the plane stopped outside the terminal building at the regional airport. Gwen made her way to the rear cabin door, swung it open, and let down the ladder. In an instant, Gwen was standing outside the door.

Contessa took my hand and said, "Get the rental car and go to the cottage. I am going to fly back to the hangar with Gwen and help her put the plane to bed." Contessa squeezed my hand. "Gwen and I have a few things we need to take care of, but if I can get done in time, I will stop by the cottage this evening ... but I can't promise."

I squeezed Contessa's hand back and said, "I'd like that." I kissed her on the lips and exited the aircraft.

On the tarmac, Gwen was waiting.

"Welcome to Beaufort."

"Thank you, Gwen Rios, for an interesting flight." I picked up his travel bag from the tarmac and disappeared into the terminal building.

Before the door closed behind me, Gwen was back in the cockpit of NP603, and she and Contessa were readying the aircraft for the short hop north to put the airplane to bed for the night.

I got in the rental car and watched the King Air 90 bank hard to the right and disappear beyond the trees.

I sat for a while after the plane was out of sight. I looked at my watch. It was seven forty-five.

CHAPTER 19

Gwen and Contessa got to Abe's house about nine thirty after housing the plane in its hangar. Gwen rang the doorbell and let herself and Contessa in, yelling to Abe, "Hey, sweetheart, it's me and Tessa."

From the basement stairs, they could hear Abe say, "I'm in the office. Come on down." Gwen and Contessa made their way down to the office, where Abe was looking at the monitors, his fingers clicking the keys of the keyboard.

Gwen walked over to Abe, placed her hands on his shoulders, kissed him on the cheek, and said, "What are you working on?"

Abe turned in his chair, pulled Gwen onto his lap, and asked, "How was your flight?"

Gwen put her arms around Abe's neck and replied, "You'll have to ask Tessa. She did all the talking."

Abe rotated in his chair and found Contessa leaning up against the entryway door.

"How is our friend Tag holding up?" he asked.

Contessa smiled at Abe, walked over to the chair beside him, and said, "I think he'll do just fine."

Abe looked at Gwen and asked, "Has Nate asked you to pilot the *Kindred Spirit* for their outing tomorrow?"

"No, he hasn't."

"Okay, that must mean that Nate is planning on piloting the *Spirit* by himself. Sounds to me like he doesn't want you two to know what is going on." Abe looked over at Contessa and said, "I know that Mother's will has already been amended, and the property appraisal is done. I guess the only thing they need to do is settle on a price."

With a bit of distress in her voice, Contessa asked, "How will we know what happened?"

Abe looked at Contessa. "Well, you've got Tag eating out of your hand, and if that somehow fails, I've got the *Spirit* wired for sound and video. As a matter of fact, we'll have front-row seats to the whole thing." Abe added with a big smile, "I've got it set so the video and audio will stream right here into the office in real time."

Gwen looked at Contessa and then back at Abe and said, "Do you mean we can sit here while they are on the boat making the deal and watch the whole thing go down?"

"That's the plan."

Gwen gave Abe a big hug and said, "You are a genius."

Contessa looked at the monitor in front of Abe. "What else are you working on?"

Abe turned full circle in his chair. Gwen got up from his lap and stood behind Abe with both hands on his shoulders. All three were looking at the wall of monitors when Abe said, "I got to thinking about your suspicions, Tessa, that Nate was poisoning Sarah. So I went back as far as I could with PASS in her suite at Dillianquest. Oh, and that reminds me." Abe reached over and grabbed the Fed-Ex package lying on the desktop. He handed it to Contessa. "This came for you today. It's from the lab in Charleston".

As Contessa tore the package open and began reading the lab results, Abe continued, "Anyway, I went back and started reviewing your mother's condition each time Nate gave Mother her a malt." Abe pointed to the middle monitor. "Watch. The results are frightening. I've edited the recordings, and you can see how quickly Sarah's health deteriorated after Nate started feeding her those laced malts."

Just as Abe finished his sentence, Contessa tossed the papers on the desk in front of Gwen and Abe and said, "I knew it. That fucker has been poisoning Mother with ethylene glycol."

Stunned by Contessa's announcement, Gwen looked at Abe. "Ethylene glycol? What's that?"

"Ethylene glycol is commonly known as antifreeze."

Gwen's face went white as she said in astonishment, "Nate has been feeding Mother antifreeze in her malts?"

"Yes, the miserable piece of shit has been poisoning her with antifreeze."

Abe had pulled up WebMD on one of the other screens. "Listen to this," he said. Abe began reading from the screen. "It says that ingesting even a small amount of ethylene glycol is highly dangerous and causes loss of memory, confusion, disorientation, and progressive lethargy. The alcohol interrupts the neurotransmitters and ultimately causes death." Abe again pointed to the middle monitor and said, "Oh, my God. We're watching your mother being murdered by Nate."

Abe ran the edited recording again, and the three watched the screen showing Nate coming into Sarah's room, feeding her the malt, and then leaving, taking the malt container with him each time. Sarah's condition was rapidly deteriorating before their very eyes.

Gwen reached up and touched the monitor. "God, Mother. I am so sorry." Tears streamed down the women's faces.

Abe placed his hand on Gwen's hand, which was on the screen, and looked to his left at Contessa as he said, "There is no doubt that Nate is killing your mother." He moved Gwen's hand away from the monitor. "The question is, what are we going to do with this information?" Abe paused and then rose from his chair. "Come on. Let's get out of here and go sit in the library. We need to get away from these screens."

The three made their way outside the office and sat in the library. Everyone was speechless. Finally, Abe stood and walked over to the bar.

"Does anyone care for a drink? I know I could use one."

Contessa said, "Yes, please. I think I need a shot of bourbon."

Gwen said, "Make it a stiff one for me."

"Bourbon it is," Abe said as he took a bottle from the bar and set it on the coffee table, along with three shot glasses.

Abe poured three shots of bourbon and handed one to each. He held his glass high into the air and said in toasting fashion, "Revenge, my dears, is a dish best served ... unannounced."

The three touched glasses, and the bourbon disappeared—time and time and time again.

CHAPTER 20

I did not sleep well that Wednesday night. I kept hoping that Contessa would make an appearance, tossing and turning with one eye open, but she never did. Finally, at about seven fifteen, I decided to get out of bed and make a pot of coffee. It looked to be a beautiful day in Beaufort. The sun was just beginning to shine, and the birds sounded as if they had gotten an early start to the morning.

As I made my way from the master bedroom toward the kitchen, I noticed the TV was in its upright position, and the cursor was blinking at the beginning of a message that read, *Please press enter on the remote control to continue.* I was familiar with that message. I picked up the remote control, pointed it at the TV, and pressed enter.

Just as quickly as I pressed enter, the screen went black, and another message popped up: *Good morning, Tag. I trust you arrived without incident. I left a copy of the real-estate appraisal for your review in the drawer in the foyer under the phone, where you found my business cards last trip. Mr. Michael Belanger II and I will meet you at the Kindred Spirit at three this afternoon. The golf cart is in the garage. I trust you can find your way to the Spirit. If, in the meantime, you should require anything, please call my cell. More cards can be found in the drawer under the appraisal. I am looking forward to seeing you again, Tag. Best regards, Nate.*

I just smiled and started flipping through the channels. I settled on CNN to get caught up on all the latest economic disasters that had been taking place since yesterday. After a quick review of the headlines, I went into the kitchen and fixed a pot of coffee. I then went back into the bedroom and put on my jogging clothes. A short run would be just what the doctor ordered to get the day started on the right foot.

I exited the screened-in porch and headed down the pathway to the intercoastal. When I arrived, the marsh across the waterway was brimming with all kinds of birds searching out a seafood breakfast.

I headed upriver in the direction of Dillianquest. The sky was blue, and the sun was rising but still low on the horizon. The cool morning breeze was crisp and redolent with the distinctive aroma of the sea.

I began running under the huge oak trees with their heavy limbs hanging low along the shore of the intercoastal waterway. Jogging allowed my mind to wander. As I ran, I began thinking about the bridge and how an innocent man was killed. The memory of the noise of the body hitting the car made my skin crawl. I recalled how we had thrown the body over the bridge and into the cold, dark waters below. I could still hear the splash of the body as it hit its watery grave. As my mind wandered back to that night, I felt the rush of a panic attack.

Those thoughts stopped me cold in my tracks. I found myself looking directly up toward Danby House. I was doubled over, trying to catch my breath, my head up and eyes fixed on the building in front of me. I put both hands on my knees, trying to calm myself and regain some composure.

As I breathed heavily, my mind left that ugly night of the killing, and I began to wonder whether Contessa was working with Sarah this early in the morning. *There's only one way to find out.* I jogged toward the stately buildings, leaving those horrible thoughts behind at the waterway.

Contessa was already at Sarah's side when I appeared at the bedroom window. My sudden appearance at the window startled her, but her surprise quickly turned into a big, inviting smile.

Contessa motioned with her right hand for me to go around the building to the side entrance to Sarah's suite. I quickly disappeared from sight. Contessa hurried to the back door and unlocked it. As she opened the door, there I stood.

Contessa pulled me into the back room by the lapels of my running shirt. She threw both arms around my neck, and we kissed passionately. Contessa released her arms and said, "What are you doing here?"

With a bead of sweat running down from my forehead I said, "I missed you last night. I did not know if you would be here this morning, so I thought I would stop by and take a chance."

Contessa looked over at Sarah and said, "She took a turn last evening. Her breathing is becoming labored, so one of the girls called me. I've been at her side since one thirty this morning."

I took Contessa's hand and said, "I'm sorry."

"Dr. Jones left a short while ago. He got her comfortable. He doesn't think she will be with us much longer."

I walked over to Sarah's bedside and looked at her. "I lost both my parents in an automobile accident. I remember that I wished I could have had more time with them to tell them how much I loved them. When someone is taken in an instant, the hole that leaves in your soul never seems to get filled." I looked up at Contessa from the bedside and said, "Embrace the fact that you have been able to comfort her for as long as you have. You know God will be waiting with open arms to greet you both in heaven when He decides that it is your time."

Contessa looked at me with a tear in her eye and said, "I know this is part of life's cycle, and that all life ends." Contessa walked to where I was standing next to Sarah's bed.

After a loving glance, she leaned over, took Sarah's hand, and continued, "God accepts all His children with open arms. Mother has been one of God's very special children." Contessa looked up at me. "Being able to spend as much time with Mother as I have been, has allowed me to give back what she has given to us in her time of need." Contessa paused for a moment, still holding Sarah's hand. "This woman gave love unconditionally. She raised Gwen and me like her own daughters. She gave us a future that we would have never known in the jungles of Colombia, and for that, I will be forever grateful."

Contessa tucked Sarah's hand back under the sheets and caressed her forehead with her open palm. She fixed the sheet so that it lay gently under Sarah's chin, so she would stay comfortable. "I will stay and do what I can until her soul is resting comfortably in hands of our Lord." She took my hand and pulled me into the sitting room of Sarah's suite, where we sat on the couch. Contessa was quiet for a moment and then said, "Let me get you a cup of coffee. I have some crème brûlée."

I smiled, sat back on the couch, and said, "That sounds wonderful. You will be joining me, won't you?" I asked as Contessa disappeared into the medication room.

A few seconds later, Contessa reappeared with two cups of coffee. She placed one in front of me, held the other in both hands, and then sat down in the chair that faced the couch directly in front of me. "Are you still meeting with Junior and Nate this afternoon?"

I must have looked a bit puzzled hearing the name "Junior" for the first time. Noticing my confusion, Contessa explained, "Michael Belanger is also known as Junior. His father's name was Michael also. To avoid any confusion, I guess they started calling Michael the second 'Junior.'" Contessa took a sip of coffee, sat back in her chair, and added, "When Junior had his son, he also named him Michael Abraham Belanger, so they call him Abe to eliminate any additional confusion."

Contessa smiled. "You know, man's vanity is a funny thing. Men have tried desperately for hundreds of years to leave a legacy long after their own demise." A tiny smile grew on her face. "Man has named his male children after himself for generations." Contessa paused, crossed her legs, and took another sip of her coffee. "Don't you find it rather odd that you never hear of a mother naming her daughter after herself?"

I thought for a moment while I took a sip of coffee. "I have never thought about it … but you are correct. It's only the male of the species who tries to leave his namesake intact by naming the male child after himself."

Contessa said with a full smile on her face, "I'm just thankful that the namesake, in many cases, ends up being so very different from the one he was named after."

I nodded in agreement. Contessa reached into her smock pocket, pulled out a piece of paper, and handed it to me. "When you get back to the cottage after your meeting, call me at this number."

We both started walking toward the back door. When we got to the closed door, Contessa said, "We'll talk more tonight after your meeting.

You and I have to remain very discreet, though. We cannot afford to let anyone find out about us. You can't trust either one of these guys."

Contessa wrapped her arms around me neck and kissed me hard. She held my face in both her hands, looked deep into my eyes, and said, "I know this will sound bad, but giving Nate the very best deal you can helps us all. If you decide to leave with me, Nate getting a better deal means that we will have more money to start our new lives together."

I looked at Contessa but did not say a word. I kissed her on the forehead, began to jog, and then stopped and looked back at her. "I don't know what I am going to do about your invitation. But I want you to have as much as you can to start your new life."

I turned and jogged back toward the waterway, quickly disappearing from sight.

CHAPTER 21

The phone rang only twice at two thirty in the law office before Claudette answered the phone in her usual fashion.

"Good afternoon, Belanger, Larson, and George. How may I direct your call?"

Nate uncharacteristically got right to the point. "Hey, Claudette. It's Nate. Is Junior available?"

"Yes, he is. He has been expecting your call. One moment, and I'll connect you."

In a matter of seconds, Junior answered the phone in a rather upbeat fashion.

"Nate, are you on your way to pick me up?"

"Yes, as a matter of fact, I am about ten minutes from your office. I just wanted to remind you to bring a copy of Mother's will with you, just in case Mr. Grayson needs to see it to settle any frayed nerves."

Junior leaned back in his office chair, holding a copy of the will in his hand, and said, "I have it in my hand as we speak. Don't worry, Nate. We will get his deal done today. You had better be thinking just where in the world you want to go." Junior laughed. "Drive by my office window and toot your horn, and I'll meet you on Wilson Street."

"I'll be there in a few minutes," Nate said, and then the phone went silent.

Shortly before three, I left the screened-in porch of the cottage and made my way down the path to the garage. I opened the garage door, and inside sat the H2 Hummer golf cart, ready to roll. I sat behind the wheel of the golf cart with a big smile; it was a blast to drive. *How cool would it be to live on a piece of property like this after the company takes over Dillianquest?* My daydream was quickly ended when the phone rang.

"Hi, this is Tag."

"Tag, it's Bill. How are things going with the Dillianquest deal?"

"I'm just headed down to meet with Nate and his attorney. What's up, Bill?"

Bill said in a rather cold-sounding voice, "We just received official notice from the feds that we are under investigation for Medicare fraud. Not sure what all this bullshit is about, but you need to know this is going to cost us a boatload to defend."

I pulled the golf cart out of the garage and began driving toward the *Kindred Spirit.* "I am not following. I was under the impression it was a standard Medicare audit, not a fraud investigation. What in the hell is that all about?"

Bill paused for a moment. "Listen, Tag, I'm not sure we should go forward with this acquisition unless we can steal the goddamn thing. We will need all our reserves for legal counsel. After looking at that bloated appraisal and seeing what underdeveloped property on the intercoastal was selling for ... unless you can buy it for sixty cents on the dollar, we'll need to walk away from this thing."

Bill caught me totally off guard. I had to pause for a moment, knowing that not buying was not an option. As the blood drained from my face, I said, "Bill, the market is going to turn in the next year to eighteen months, and holding that much property will give us an opportunity to dump it fast and make some quick cash. I don't think we should bail just yet ... let me see what I can do. Plus ... if we each took a few acres off the top for ourselves, this place has retirement written all over it."

I was just about to reach the *Kindred Spirit.* I was still out of hearing range of both Junior and Nate, who were standing on the dock, when I told Bill, "Look, I'll beat these boys like a rented mule. I'll call you when I am finished with negotiations. And thanks for the added incentive." A bit shaken, I proceeded to the dock.

As I arrived, Nate waved. I returned the wave and said, "Nate, good to see you again. How's the car? God, I feel horrible about leaving you that way."

Nate laughed and extended his hand. "Not a problem. The car is as good as new. We'll just bury the repair costs in the sale price of Dillianquest." We laughed.

"Done deal," I agreed.

Nate put his arm around my shoulder as we headed for the *Kindred Spirit*. Junior was standing on the dock at the stern of the boat, waiting for the two of us to arrive. As we got close to Junior's position, Nate announced, "Tag, I would like you to meet Michael Belanger. Michael is the son of the founder of Belanger, Larson, and George and is the principal partner in the firm. His daddy and he have been taking care of the Dillianquest family forever." Junior reached out his hand for me to shake.

"Tag," Junior said, shaking my hand. "Please, call me Junior. Most everyone does around these parts. It's a pleasure to make your acquaintance. Nate has told me quite a lot about you. He even said you've had a run-in with a local nuisance."

At that moment, my heart stopped. I flashed back to throwing the body over the bridge. I swallowed hard and then repeated, "Local nuisance?"

Junior laughed and said, "Yes, Nate here said you bagged a deer with one of his expensive hunting vehicles."

I laughed, and with relief, said, "Yes, yes, I did. And it scared the hell out of me. It appeared from nowhere. I only heard the thump."

Junior, still laughing a bit, said, "They have become our number-one public enemy around these parts. They are everywhere. You have got to be careful driving around here, especially when the fog rolls in."

Nate butted in and said, "Gentlemen, why don't you two take this conversation upstairs? I'll get the boat ready for castoff."

As Nate began to untie the lines, he said, "Junior, you know where the scotch and ice are. Would you mind doing the honors?"

"No, not at all, Nate," Junior said without hesitation. "Come on, Tag. Give me hand topside." As we entered the boat, Junior said without looking at me, "Tag is an interesting name."

"Well, my real name is Teasdale Allen Grayson. You can imagine. It was a little tough in school, having a name like Teasdale."

"Indeed," Junior said with a laugh.

"After many an ass whipping came the name Tag."

Junior laughed again and said, "Good move, Tag."

"A lifesaver."

Junior obviously knew his way around the *Kindred Spirit*. When Junior and I got to the bridge, Junior went directly to the bar and took out three tumblers from the cabinet. He then reached down and pulled out a bottle of twenty-five-year-old Macallan.

Junior looked at me. "Macallan okay with you?"

I smiled broadly. "That's my drink."

Junior put four ice cubes in each glass and filled them to within a half inch from the top. He picked up one for himself and one for me and walked to where I was standing, watching Nate finish his chores. "If this is your drink, you are in good company." Junior held his glass in the air to toast. I offered up my glass in return, and we took a healthy drink of scotch.

Nate appeared on the bridge and said, "I see you two have started without me. I hope this is not how the entire evening is going to go."

Nate laughed out loud, took his drink from the bar, and walked toward us. Junior said, "Good scotch waits for no man, so hurry your ass up!"

"I'll drink to that." Nate walked to the back of the bridge of the *Spirit*. As he looked over at Dillianquest, Nate said, "Tag, different futures lay ahead for both of us." Nate paused for a moment. "Dillianquest has brought us together to make that happen." Nate stopped and took a long sip of his drink. "But before we get bogged down in the seriousness of the moment, here is what I have planned." Nate walked back over to the lounge area where Junior and I were sitting, sat, and said, "I've got us a mess of cold crab with crackers and whatnot for our trip. I though we would take a slow ride upriver and discuss how we can make this Dillianquest deal work for all of us." Nate leaned forward in his seat, looked at Junior, and said, "Any objections, Counselor?"

"None from me."

Then Nate turned his attention to me. "Any objections from you, sir?"

I put my hand to my chin and then said, "Did you get Club crackers?"

"I did, sir."

I said with a smile, "Then, Captain, I have no objections. Just want to know what I can do to help."

Nate smiled back and said, "Did you bring your checkbook?"

✳   ✳   ✳

Gwen, Contessa, and Abe were gathered around the monitors, watching the events on the *Kindred Spirit* unfold. Abe had prepared food and drink so they could watch the entire negotiations take place. They looked as if they were getting ready to watch the Super Bowl.

On the office counter, Abe had several bottles of white wine, an array of cheeses and crackers, and an assortment of smoked fish. Gwen looked at Contessa and said, "It makes me want to vomit watching Nate act like there is nothing wrong. I'd like to reach through this monitor and rip his balls off."

Contessa got up from her seat, walked over to Gwen, put her arm around her sister's shoulder, and said, "I know. I have to see him every day, and knowing that he is trying to take everything away from us that Mother wanted us to have is enough for me to want to kill him, too. He makes me sick."

As Gwen and Contessa hugged, Abe said, "He will get his just desserts. Now, can I get y'all a glass of wine?"

✳   ✳   ✳

Nate sat in the captain's chair, started the engines, and said to Junior, "Would you mind casting off those last two bow lines, so we can get under way?"

Junior got up from his seat and walked toward the stairs that led to the lower level.

"You got it, Captain," Junior said and disappeared from sight.

Nate looked over at me and asked, "If you would be so kind as to freshen up our drinks while we are waiting for Junior to give us the good word, that would be just about perfect."

I echoed, "You got it, Captain."

Just as I drowned the ice cubes in scotch, Junior hollered from the lower deck, "We are good to go."

Nate replied, "Thanks, there, mate." He turned to me and said, "How are those drinks coming?"

"They're good to go." I handed Nate his drink.

Just then, Junior reappeared on the bridge and was met with a fresh tumbler of scotch, to which he said, "Tag, your timing is impeccable."

Junior and I stood behind Nate, who was perched in the captain's chair as the *Spirit* crept forward from its berth.

Nate said, "These tides can make coming and going from the docks a bit tricky. We are right at the top of the tide, so this departure will be easy. There really isn't any current to speak of now."

I looked out the back of the boat at the pillars on the dock and said to Nate, "Wow, there is no current. You know, as a kid from Michigan, I never would have given that much thought."

"Knowing the tides around here can save your life."

After about thirty minutes of cruising and pointless conversation, Nate pulled into a small body of water and slowed the engines. Nate looked at Junior and me, we were now seated in the open area at the back of the bridge, and said, "I think we'll anchor here awhile and have a bite to eat."

I asked, "Is there anything you need us to do?"

"No, y'all are good. We are equipped with an electric anchor winch. One flick of this switch, and away she goes." After a few short seconds, it was easy to tell that the anchor had taken hold, as the bow of the boat turned and faced the ebbing current.

Nate got up from his captain's chair and walked back to the lounge area where Junior and I were sitting. He stood in front of us and reached for both of our glasses, and said, "Refresher?"

Both Junior and I handed our glasses willingly to Nate, and said, "Thanks, Captain."

Nate made his way back to the bar and refreshed each drink with ice cubes and more scotch. As Nate was standing at the bar, he reached down and pulled a cigar box from a lower cabinet. Nate cut the tips of three Cuban cigars, placed all three in his shirt pocket, picked up the drinks, and headed back to the lounge area.

Upon his arrival, I stood up and reached for both Junior's and my glass and set them down on the table. While Nate took a seat, he reached into his shirt pocket and pulled out the three Cuban cigars.

He held one in his right hand, passed it under his nose, took a deep breath, and said, "Gentlemen, here is what I am thinking. We fire up these marvelous little coffin nails, and we get a deal before we are finished with them. What do you say to that?"

I reached toward Nate and said, "Let's fire 'em up. We have a lot of work to do. But the real question is, is there enough scotch on board to strike a deal?"

Nate laughed. "Schultz said you were a willing participant. I like that." Nate looked over at the bar, "There's more than a case in the cabinet, and if that's not enough, I'll call Levi at the OSS and have some delivered. How's that?"

"That," I said, "is comforting. So nice to know you have all your bases covered."

Nate passed out the cigars, and we shared the lighter. Once the cigars were lit, I pulled from my jacket pocket a tape recorder and placed it on the table.

I looked at Junior and said, "I'd like to record this session, so we have no misunderstandings. Once we reach a sales price that we all agree to, I will turn off the recording. Are there any problems with that?"

Junior looked over at Nate and then at me. As he reached into his pocket, Junior said, "Obviously, you won't mind if I record it, either. I do hate misunderstandings as well."

I looked at Junior, laughed, and said, "This little device has saved my ass a ton of problems on more than one occasion."

Junior returned me gaze and said, "I never leave home without it."

218 | *Stephen Michael Marek*

Junior and I punched the record buttons on our recorders and placed them on the table.

I opened the discussion. "Allow me to state for the record that I have full authority to set and agree to a price of purchase for the Dillianquest property on behalf of Abernathy, Smith, and Grayson. The presence of Mr. Michael Belanger, from the firm of Belanger, Larson and George, counsel for the seller, will act as witness to any agreed-upon transaction and will present the buyer with appropriate buy/sell agreements upon conclusion of these negotiations." I reached for my glass and took a sip of scotch before taking a big puff on the cigar.

I put my glass down on the table and continued, "Okay, now that the obligatory disclaimers are out of the way, let's get to the meat of the topic." I looked at Nate. "You contacted my firm, Nate. I agreed to come down and look, which I did. What are you looking to get from the sale of Dillianquest?"

Nate was sitting deep in his chair with legs crossed. He held his cigar in his left hand and the tumbler of Scotch in his right. He said, "I picked your firm for three very specific reasons, Tag. The first reason is that you are not from the South." Nate took a drink from his glass. "I know all these so-called operators down here, and they are all pretty much the same. Dillianquest's reputation wouldn't last long in their hands. It would be cut, slashed, and trashed, and before you knew it, I would be known as that son of a bitch who sold it to make a few bucks."

Nate took a long draw off his cigar and blew the smoke up into the canopy that covered the lounge area. Nate smiled and said, "The second reason, Mr. Grayson is the reputation of your firm's operations. I have personally called most of your facilities and have spoken with staff. The staffs at those facilities, Mr. Grayson, speak very highly of Mr. Thomas Smith and his operations team. I think I heard the terms 'tough,' 'fair,' and 'dependable' most often to describe ASG's operations team."

Nate got up from his chair and walked to the open area at the back of the lounge. He looked back across the marsh and said as he turned, "The third and deciding reason was our mutual friend, Mr. Anthony Schultz."

Nate took another pull on his cigar, blew the smoke out into the ocean air, and said, "Mr. Schultz told me on more than one occasion that you, Mr. Grayson, drove a hard but fair bargain." Nate walked back toward the lounge area. "Mr. Schultz has high praise for you, and I do value his opinion. In his time of greatest vulnerability, you gave him a fair deal."

Nate sat down in his seat and said, "You asked me what I was looking for, and I'll be as straight with you as I can."

Nate took deep breath. "It's hard to say this, but my family's fortune, over one hundred million dollars, was lost in the Madoff scandal. The entire fortune—everything we had—was lost. So I am forced into selling the only thing that is not leveraged, and that is Dillianquest. If I don't sell Dillianquest, I stand to lose everything. If I sell Dillianquest, I can pay off my debts and hold my head up in this community. That's where your reputation for honest, fair play comes into the picture, Mr. Grayson."

I was leaning back in my chair with legs crossed. My eyes had not veered from their intended target. I took a long pull on my cigar and a drink of scotch.

Nate looked directly at me and said, "You asked me what I wanted to get from Dillianquest. Well, Tag, I'd like to see 90 percent of the appraised value for the Dillianquest property and associated businesses."

Nate sat back in his chair and took a sip from his glass. He watched as I processed his first offer.

I reached in my jacket pocket, removed a copy of the appraisal, opened it, and looked it over, trying to stall for a little time to think.

I closed the document and said, "Nate, my firm has reviewed the appraisal, and a couple of issues jumped out at us."

I edged my way to the front of my seat. "First, the appraised value is overstated. The comparables cited in the report are old sales of property, made when the real-estate market was at its highest. We realize that not much has sold while the market tumbles downward, but we have to be realistic here. The second part of that equation is that the deal has to be good for both parties, not just one side."

I stood up from my seat and walked to the back of the boat. "You're in business, Nate. We both know that paying 90 percent of an overstated and rather inflated value on this deal is only a good deal for one of us." I turned and looked at Nate. "My partners would be my partners no more if I came home with that deal. I am sure you can appreciate that."

Nate got up, walked to where I was standing, and said, "Well then, what can you sell your partners back in Ann Arbor?"

I leaned against the back railing of the boat. Looking out over the water, and without looking at Nate, I said, "How much do you owe, Nate? What would it take to get you even?"

Junior stood up at that point and said, "Tag, I think we are off course just a bit with that question."

Nate interjected, "No, that's okay, Junior. I'll answer his question." Nate took a sip of his scotch. "I'm in the hole about twenty-two million, give or take a few hundred thousand dollars." Nate leaned next to me, "You know, if it weren't for that fucking Madoff, we wouldn't be having this conversation. My mother and father put a lot of their life's blood, sweat, and tears into Dillianquest. I can't, and won't, just give it away."

I puffed on my cigar and turned and faced inward, leaning back against the railing, and said, "We don't expect you to give it away, but we do expect this to be a bit painful for you. Let me think for a minute." I walked to the captain's chair and played with the steering wheel for a few moments before turning in the chair and facing both men. "Nate, consider 50 percent of the appraised value. Taking into account what you owe, and the overstated price of Dillianquest, that leaves you about ten million dollars to put in your pocket."

Just then, Junior got up from his seat. "Nate, if you don't mind, what do you say we get to a bottom line that we can all live with? Because fifty cents on the dollar is a waste of all our time."

Nate looked back over at Junior. "Please, be my guest."

Junior, still puffing on his cigar, took it from his mouth with his right hand, held it up in front of his face, and said, "If we are going to get a deal before these things are smoked up, we had better get to the bottom line." Junior took a puff on his cigar, blew a smoke ring in my direction, and said, "We need 75 percent to make this thing work." Junior took a sip of his scotch and said, "Give me your glass, and I'll refresh these while you think on that number."

Junior took my glass, walked over to the bar, and set both glasses down on the counter. As he reached for some fresh ice, Junior said, "In round figures, Tag, 75 percent of the appraised value is roughly equal to forty-eight million dollars. That's twenty-five points below appraised value, which is one hell of a deal, considering where the real-estate values are around here."

Junior poured the scotch into the glasses, turned, and handed me mine, saying, "Tag, 25 percent is a pretty good goddamn discount for oceanfront. We aren't Detroit or Miami. Property is still worth a good bit in Beaufort." Junior was clearly feeling pretty good about his argument. He took a sip of Scotch and added, "And that Dillianquest property is a damn fine piece of property, Mr. Grayson."

I walked to the back of the boat, right past Junior and Nate. I looked out over the railing and said, "Dillianquest is a fine piece of property, no doubt, and it comes with a couple of very nice businesses attached—and that is, after all, my primary focus."

My mind, just for an instant, flashed to those pictures of and Contessa and me. My heart pounded, and my breathing quickened. A bead of sweat appeared on my brow. I took several deep breaths making it appear as if I were drinking in the crisp ocean air in an attempt to regain my composure.

I looked at my cigar and said, "Okay, here's the real deal, gentlemen. With the state of health care headed God only knows where, my firm shouldn't even be talking about buying Dillianquest. Shit, who knows what Obama and his crew are going to do? So, to get this deal done—and frankly, Nate, you need this much more than we do—we are both going to have to stretch a bit. Hell, as a matter of fact, I was on the phone with my office just before I got here today, and we talked about closing this deal down. Now, having said that, my firm is willing to offer 62.5 percent. That's just over forty million dollars. And believe me when I tell you, that is as good as it gets from us. You still walk away with eighteen million. Still not too bad!"

Junior looked at Nate and said, "Tag, will you excuse us for a moment?"

"Certainly. Take all the time you need."

Junior and Nate excused themselves and went down to the lower level. I stayed in the back of the lounge, looking out over the marsh and the wildlife.

This deal had too much riding on it. All I could do was wait and hope Nate would bite, because if he didn't, all hell would break loose.

More birds gathered around the boat, each looking for a free meal. A light breeze stirred the air, and I was feeling more than a bit nervous, knowing that I had gone further than the firm was willing to go. I sipped my scotch and smoked on my cigar. I knew there was nothing to do at this point, except wait.

A few minutes passed, but it seemed more like an hour before Junior and Nate reappeared on the bridge.

Nate walked over to where I was and said, "How is your cigar holding up?"

"Mine's done. How's yours?"

Nate looked closely at his cigar and said, "Mine's finished, too" before throwing it overboard.

I watched as the cigar hit the water and then looked at Nate, who said, "We finished those bad boys just in time to seal the deal. Don't ya just love it when a plan comes together!"

I looked at Nate with a big smile, and threw the cigar overboard as well, and said, "It's a done deal at 62.5 percent?"

Nate smiled and took my hand. "Yes, my friend, 62.5 is the magic number. You have got yourself a deal. We just need to work out a few details."

"Any deal breakers?"

"Nope, just a few minor timing issue."

Junior walked over to us and said, "Can I buy two gents a drink?" He patted us both on the back and said, "It's a good deal when everyone is happy. Come on, belly up to the bar. Nate, would you like to do the honors?"

Nate walked to the bar and took three new tumblers from the cabinet. "It would be my pleasure. I recommend the twenty-five-year-old Macallan."

*　　*　　*

Contessa looked over at Gwen and Abe and said, "Nothing can happen until Mother passes. With this deal, Nate is going to kill Mother soon to get his hands on the money."

Abe looked back at Contessa and said, "According to the newly amended will they just forged, total control of Dillianquest reverts to Nate upon the demise of your mother."

As tears rolled down her cheeks, Contessa said, "That fucker has to pay for his sins."

Abe got up from his chair and put his arms around Contessa. "He will, sweetie. He will."

*　　*　　*

We held our glasses high in the air, and Nate offered a toast: "Here is to Mother and Father, who leave this world a better place. Here is to Abernathy, Smith, and Grayson, who will soon be the caretakers of the Dillianquest legacy. And here is to me, who will take the money and run."

We all laughed out loud and touched glasses. Then we each took a long drink from the refreshed tumblers of scotch.

Nate said with a sense of accomplishment, "Let's hoist anchor and head home."

Nate returned to the bridge and said to Junior, "Why don't you and Tag work out the details while I head us back to the dock?"

"Come, Tag, let's go sit in the lounge and let Captain Ahab here take us back to port." Junior put his arm on my shoulder and guided me to the open air of the far aft lounge. As we reached the seating area, Junior said, "Have a seat, and let me go over some of those details Nate was referring to."

"You have my undivided attention. I'm all yours."

Junior sat down opposite me. "Not really much in the way of logistics." Junior took a sip of his drink and then placed it on the table between us. Junior, now sitting back in his chair with legs crossed, said, "Here's is how we see the transaction taking place. According to Sarah Dillianquest's will,

Nate acquires full rights of ownership of the Dillianquest property upon her demise. Sarah, as you know, is not doing well and is expected to pass at any time."

Junior sat forward in his seat. "Nate's folks were saints. This is very difficult for Nate. I have a copy of the will for you if your care to review it." Junior leaned forward and handed me a copy of the will. I accepted it and placed it on the table in front of me, unopened.

Junior got up from his seat and made his way to the railing overlooking the wake of the forward-moving boat. With both hands gripping the railing, Junior said, "I am happy to see a firm with your integrity continuing Dillianquest's good work, Tag." Junior paused while I stood and walked to where he was standing at the rear of the boat, watching the water swirl as the *Spirit* glided upriver.

"We will do our very best to live up to what Mrs. Dillianquest has created and what the Beaufort community expects from us."

Junior turned and looked me squarely in the eyes and said, "For our community's sake, I hope that you do. An awful lot of good, hardworking people depend on the services and jobs that Dillianquest provides. We do not want to see that tarnished. Beaufort is very proud to have such a fine facility in our midst."

Junior walked back over to the table and picked up his drink before returning to where I was standing. He continued, "Nate has requested that, when Mrs. Dillianquest passes, ASG wire the agreed-upon funds into my firm's account." Junior paused. "What is your time frame for acquiring those funds?"

"I can have the money within the week."

Junior nodded in approval. "Nate is requesting that you place a twenty-four-hour hold on the funds to make sure everything is in order."

I was now facing Junior, leaning against the back railing on my right elbow. Junior cocked his head to the left a bit and continued, "We can have all the paperwork and the closing complete prior to that same twenty-four-hour period." Junior stopped for a moment and said, "If any of this does not meet with your approval, just stop me, and we can discuss it."

"So far, so good."

Junior took another sip of his drink and squared himself with Tag, leaning on his left elbow, before continuing. "After the funds have been released and you are in possession of a free and unencumbered title to Dillianquest, you can take possession at your convenience."

Junior took another sip of his drink and began tapping his wedding ring against his glass. He added, "Nate will do as you wish regarding the transfer of records, meeting with staff, or anything else you would like as a practice of acquisition."

Junior stood upright, faced me, and presented his hand for me to shake. I gladly grasped Junior's hand, and then Junior added, "If you are in agreement, and I think you are, stop by my office tomorrow morning before you head back to Ann Arbor. I will have the terms of this agreement drawn up and ready for your signature."

I nodded in agreement and left Junior standing at the back railing of the boat.

I walked up to where Nate was sitting in the captain's chair, patted him on the back, and said, "I am sorry to hear about your mother's deteriorating health." I sat beside Nate in a separate chair and added, "I lost both my folks. I know it is not an easy time. But please rest assured that we take very seriously the legacy your family leaves behind." I paused for a moment. "We will do everything in our power to keep the trust the community of Beaufort has placed in Dillianquest intact."

"Thanks, Tag. That means a lot to me." Nate picked up his glass and held it high in the air. "I wouldn't be selling if I weren't 100 percent sure that your firm would be an excellent addition to the Beaufort business community." Nate took a drink from his glass. "Besides, I don't know jack shit about the health-care industry. Well," Nate added with a smirk, "that's not exactly true. I know enough about the health-care industry to know that I should be nowhere near it trying to make a living at it."

Nate got up from the captain's chair, looked at me, and said, "Ever pilot a motor-yacht like this before?"

"No sir. Can't say as I have."

Nate walked behind me, guided me into the captain's chair, and said, "It's a slice of pie. Go ahead and take the helm. It drives just like a car."

Nate pointed upriver, "All you have to do is stay between the buoys—green on your right and red on your left."

Nate turned and started to walk toward the back of the boat, where Junior was standing, and then stopped, turned, and said to Tag, "And this time, my good friend, if you hit something … I *will* send you a bill."

CHAPTER 22

After mooring the boat, I headed back toward the cottage in the H2 Hummer. I pulled the cart under a tree that overlooked the intercoastal. It was a beautiful view. I retrieved my phone from my pocket. I needed to make three phone calls.

I sat back and watched as the waning sunlight fell on the marsh, creating a golden-brown hue on all that stood before it. All the usual suspects were gathered in the ebbing tide, looking for a free seafood meal. A gentle breeze ruffled the bud-clad branches of the mighty oaks; spring was getting under way.

I sat in the seat of the Hummer, holding my phone. I couldn't help but think that I had done a good thing this evening, including saving my own ass. Soon, ASG would be the proud owners of Dillianquest and all the property that it sat on. We was sitting on a gold mine, and I knew it.

I dialed Bill's cell in hopes of catching him before he got home. The phone rang a couple of times before Bill answered.

"Tag, what's the good news, buddy?"

I replied with a noticeable smile in my voice, "Thirty-seven-and-a-half-point discount off the appraised value."

"All and all, I think we can live with that. Good job!"

"Thanks. I'm sitting under some huge oak trees, watching the native wildlife grab a bite to eat in Nate's H2 Hummer golf cart." I laughed. "Tough duty."

In a kinder voice, I added, "Bill, you are going to like this place. Like I said, it has retirement written all over it."

"I can't wait to see it. Any bumps in the contract?"

"Just one. We can't take possession until Nate's mother passes. Good news and bad news there."

"What's that?"

I took a deep breath, reached into the cupholder, took a drink of scotch, and replied, "She is not doing well and is expected to pass at any moment."

Bill replied in a rather odd tone, "Is that the good news or the bad news?"

Staring out across the water, I waited a moment before I replied, "Both, actually. The guy has lost everything, and now he has to sell the family legacy to make ends meet. Can't help but feel a little sorry of him."

"Fuck him, Tag. He'll be walking away with forty-plus million. That eases a lot of pain. And correct me if I'm wrong, but that is the major reason we don't get personal with the projects."

Snapping out of my sympathetic daze I said, "You are absolutely correct. I told them we would have the money by the middle of next week … any problem with that?"

"None that I can see. We will need to get this done before the feds start poking around."

"Great. I'll drop by Belanger's office in the morning and have the signed contract faxed to you to get this rolling. I'll be headed back to the office late morning. If you're in, I'll see you then."

"Good job, Tag. I feel another Schultz return on investment here. Fly friendly. See ya." The phone went silent.

I then dialed Sam. After several rings, the answering machine picked up. "You have reached the Graysons. When you hear the beep, do your thing."

I waited for the beep. "Hey, thought I would try to see if you guys were home. Things went well here. We got the deal done. I'm going to have to grab a bite with Nate and his attorney to iron out all the fine print—probably won't get a chance to call at the usual time. Be home tomorrow. Love you guys."

I sank in his seat a bit, closed my eyes, and grasped the phone tightly. I shook his head in disgust.

My mind immediately started to drift back toward the night I had spent with Contessa at the cottage.

Both hands gripped the steering wheel as I leaned forward and rested my head on my forearms. My heart began to beat harder and harder. Palms became damp with sweat. I closed my eyes and thought back to the first time I had caught sight of Contessa at the OSS. As we flirted and played pool, I had decided she had a body to kill for ... and I had. That evening had haunted my mind ever since it had happened. I could smell Contessa's hair as it draped across my face when she straddled me, pinning my arms above my head on the couch. It had been so long since my passions had been aroused to those heights.

I sat up in the cart seat and began pressing in Contessa's phone number. After entering the first digit, I stopped. I slumped back in the seat. How could I be doing such an awful thing to the kids? What had they done to deserve such a betrayal?

I closed his eyes and pictured Contessa in all of her naked willingness. I am weak; I couldn't help myself.

My life had turned out just as I had planned. I married my college sweetheart. Together, we had a great family. I helped start and run a successful business. But there was a huge vacuum in my life. There was no sexual excitement. All that passion and lust had left some time ago. I wanted the shivers that ran up and down my spine to return. I needed those uneasy feelings in the pit of my stomach. I wanted my body to heave each time I reached orgasm. I wanted, no needed, to lie naked next to the firm, tight body of a younger woman—one who craved me as much as I did her.

I stared blankly out over the waterway. I brought myself to finish calling Contessa's number. I waited with eyes closed. The phone rang only once before Contessa's voice spilled quietly out of the phone.

"Hey, sweetie. Are you all finished?"

I could feel my heart about to jump through the phone when I replied with a crack in my voice, "Just got off the boat. Can you meet me at the cottage?"

Contessa answered in a low, sexy voice, "I'm already here waiting for you," and hung up the phone. I collapsed back into my seat as a huge smile grew on my face.

I slid his phone back into his pocket, leaned forward, snatched the glass from the cupholder, and took a gulp of scotch. My mouth was dry as I headed back toward the cottage—full speed ahead! My heart was pounding as anticipation saturated my every nerve.

I parked the Hummer in the garage and walked toward the cottage. Contessa was standing in the doorway of the screened-in porch. She was wearing a short black dress with a slit up the right side and black calf-high leather boots. Her hair was pulled to one side and draped gracefully over one shoulder, stopping just above her full breast. Her large, silver hoop earrings showed through her silky hair. She smiled and with red lipstick said, "How was your meeting? You look pleased with yourself."

I had no way of knowing that she, Gwen, and Abe had watched the entire negotiation from the comfort of Abe's basement office.

As I stopped directly in front of Contessa, I said, "It was very productive … does it show?"

"Indeed it does," she said as she stretched her arms out to embrace him. "Did you get the full amount?"

I stopped and looked directly into Contessa's eyes and said, "Not the full amount but close; we settled just north of forty million."

Contessa, still standing with arms open and inviting said playfully, "Forty is not fifty, but it's better than a sharp stick in the eye."

I was relieved at Contessa's remark. I walked into her open arms, and we kissed while standing in the entryway. Contessa's tongue playfully darted in and out of my mouth. Contessa pulled her head back slightly and then whispered in my ear, "Are you coming in?"

I pulled back and said, "No. Here's what I want to do."

Contessa looked surprised. "And, what's that?"

"Let's get a bag of burgers and go someplace where we can be alone and sit by the ocean."

Contessa laughed. "Are you kidding?"

"No, I am not." I paused for a moment. "Do you recall the last time you and I were in this cottage together?" I shook my head and then added,

"Your sister handed me a bunch of photos of you and me." I placed my hands on Contessa's hips and moved her out of the way. I walked into the cabin and said, "I'm pretty confused at this point, Contessa, but there is one thing I know for sure: I sure don't want more pictures of you and I screwing like a couple of rabbits handed to me on the plane again tomorrow ... although, I do want to screw like a couple of rabbits!"

I walked into the house and took two bottles of wine from the wine cooler. I then went into the kitchen and rummaged around a few drawers before I found a corkscrew. Contessa could hear my rummaging from where she was standing next to the television consul.

As I left the kitchen on my way to the master bedroom, I said, "Why don't you grab two wine glasses from the cupboard, and a roll of paper towels, while I get a couple of blankets from the closet?"

Contessa smiled and saluted as she said, "Aye, aye, captain." In just a few minutes, the two of us had put together what we needed to go the beach in the chill of a spring evening.

As we drove from the cottage, I placed my hand on her thigh, and said, "You look absolutely beautiful this evening. I am glad we're together. "

Contessa said with a snort, "I didn't think you noticed."

"Contessa, I hope you can appreciate the position I'm in." Contessa moved closer to me, put her left arm around my shoulder, and tenderly kissed me on the cheek as I drove. "Just a couple of weeks ago, I was doing what I do and had no troubles." I paused as I turned out of the driveway and onto the highway, headed toward town. "I am incredibly attracted to you, Contessa. When I touch your skin or smell your hair, I want to stay as close to you as I can." I squeezed her thigh tightly and then added, "I feel like my head is going to explode."

We pulled into a fast-food restaurant drive-through and ordered too much food, paid, and turned back onto the highway toward Beaufort. I quickly glanced from the road to Contessa and back again and said, "Since I have met you, I've killed a man and covered up any evidence of the crime. I've begun cheating on my wife, and I'm being blackmailed by you and Gwen into this Dillianquest deal." I shook his head back and forth. "What's even more fucked up is that I don't seem to care." I looked directly into Contessa's eyes. "And I'm seriously considering throwing my entire life and career away to be with you." I hesitated for a moment and said, "Jesus Christ, how crazy is that?"

Contessa leaned into and started kissing my neck. Her hand slowly reached in between my legs sending chills up my spine.

Contessa could feel my swelling when she whispered in my ear, "Are you really thinking about leaving with me?"

I swallowed hard and eased my legs open so Contessa could feel everything. "At this very moment, I would do anything for you."

Contessa released her tender grip from my manhood and said, "It does my heart good to hear you say that." Contessa looked out the front windshield and said, "Turn east on Highway 21. Let's go to Hunting Park. That will be fun, and private."

As we drove east, I said, "Ya know, Junior gave me a copy of the will. It read as though Nate is going to be the sole beneficiary of the Dillianquest sale." I took a deep breath. "I read that you will get the *Kindred Spirit*, and Gwen will get the plane." I paused for a moment. "I thought you said that you and Gwen were going to each get 25 percent from the sale of Dillianquest? Nate is going to get over forty million dollars when it's all said and done."

We drove for a few minutes without saying anything. Then I said, "I don't recall reading that in the will. I hate to say it, but Nate might be going to screw you and Gwen out of millions of dollars." I patted Contessa's thigh and said, "Money makes people do some horrible things ... even to the ones they love."

"I know it doesn't say that in the will, but that is Mother's wish." Contessa took a breath. "Nate has always done what he said he would. And he said he would give us what Mother wanted us to have when the time came. I don't think we will get screwed out of anything, sugar."

We entered the park after driving the last couple of miles in silence. We were both enjoying the closeness of each other. Contessa snuggled my right arm as we pulled into the park. I rolled my window down. We could hear the thunder of the waves crashing on the beach. We could smell the scents of the ocean.

A lighthouse beacon flashed as it lit the way for those sailors at sea. We found a quiet area and parked in a dark and remote area, away from all the intruding lights. The headlights of the car illuminated the endless water that was the Atlantic Ocean. It was pitch black outside. I reached over and guided Contessa's mouth to mine. We kissed deeply.

We pulled ourselves apart after kissing passionately, gathered up the wine, burgers, and blankets, and started toward the beach. But before they got to the ocean, Contessa squeezed my hand and stopped me in my tracks. "You know, Tag …" Contessa took a deep breath and after the dramatic pause, continued, "knowing what I know about Nate"—again she paused, as if in thought—"Gwen and I will probably receive more than we deserve when Mother passes."

"I hope you are right."

"I think I am. Let's not talk about that anymore, okay?"

Contessa and I walked down the beach a short distance and found a perfect place. We spread out the blanket on the beach and opened a bottle of wine and poured ourselves a glass. Contessa sat next to me, took her glass, held it high in the air, and said, "Yes, a toast."

I held my glass up in the ocean air and said, "To the fate that awaits us in Atlanta." We touched wine glasses and drank.

CHAPTER 23

G wen sat at her mother's bedside, holding her hand, making sure she was comfortable. Sarah had been resting well the past few days, but that evening, her breathing was a bit more labored. Contessa had already called Dr. Jones and Nate to explain the change in Sarah's condition before Gwen had arrived. Contessa feared that Nate's handiwork was finally taking its fatal toll.

Contessa had been in and out of the med room, making sure Sarah had everything she needed and wanted for nothing. Contessa was devoted to caring for the person who had given her so much to live for in life. It was now Contessa's turn to return the favor and give all that she could during Sarah's last days on earth. Contessa's mother had been a fighter, and she was not giving up easily, but she was no match for the poison Nate had been feeding her. It was excruciatingly difficult for both Gwen and Contessa to watch, knowing that Nate had been methodically poisoning their mother.

Gwen looked up at Contessa and said, "Have you heard much from Tag since the meeting last Thursday?"

Contessa looked at Gwen with an ever-widening smile and said, "I got a text from him on Sunday or Monday. I can't remember which. The poor guy is as confused as a bat flying in the sunlight."

"I'll bet," said Gwen with a laugh. "Can you imagine?"

Contessa laughed with Gwen and said, "No." Contessa paused, slapped Gwen's wrists, and said, "We are some very naughty girls." Both girls began to laugh out loud.

Just as they did, Nate walked through the door and said, "You two seem to be in good spirits. Do you want to share?"

Startled by the intrusion, Contessa said, with just a little laugh left in her voice, "If you don't laugh … you will end up crying."

Nate looked at Contessa as he drew closer to Sarah's bedside. "Is she doing any better?"

Contessa, barely able to control her disgust, said, "No, not really. Dr. Jones should be here any minute."

Nate took hold of his mother's hand. "Is she comfortable?" "Yes, she is. Doc has her on morphine to ease any pain she may be experiencing."

As Contessa finished her sentence, Dr. Jones knocked and then entered Sarah Dillianquest's room. "How's the patient?"

"Her breathing is shallower now. Her heart rate has decreased."

"Thanks." Dr. Jones walked over to the side of the bed where Nate had been standing and said, "Nate, I understand you have been spending quite a little time at your mother's side."

"I have. I want to be with her when she passes."

Dr. Jones placed his stethoscope on Sarah's chest and listened intently. He then moved the device, listened again, and repeated the procedure several more times.

He wrapped the stethoscope around his neck and took Sarah's wrist in his hand to feel for her pulse.

He shook his head and said to Gwen, Contessa, and Nate, "Let's talk in the other room."

Dr. Jones walked into the sitting area. He stood facing the wall for a few seconds before turning to the group. "Her lungs are beginning to fill with fluids. She has a weakened pulse."

Dr. Jones reached out and took both Contessa and Gwen's hands, looking at Nate. "I don't think she has much more time. A month, a week, or a day … it is too hard to tell. I want to be optimistic, but when we are called by the Lord, we all must go to Him."

Dr. Jones walked back over to where Sarah lay in her bed and said, "Not much else I can do for you, dear." He placed his open palm on Sarah's forehead and said, "Your race is almost over. Your reward is waiting for you on the other side of the finish line." Dr. Jones leaned forward and kissed her on the forehead.

Dr. Jones turned, walked back to the seating area, and said, "Contessa, do you have everything you need to make her comfortable?"

Contessa looked at Dr. Jones with a tear in her eye and said, "Yes, sir, I do."

He turned and looked at Gwen. "Are you going to be all right, Gwen? I can give you something to help you sleep."

Gwen walked over to Dr. Jones, gave him a big hug, and said, "You've been good to all of us, Doc, especially Mother. I can't tell you how much your compassion means to us."

Dr. Jones smiled. "Thank you. She and all of you have been a pleasure to know and care for." Dr. Jones walked over to Nate and said, "If you need anything, Nate—something to help you sleep or just someone to talk to—call me."

Dr. Jones had treated Nate for severe depression when he returned from military service in South America. Post-traumatic stress disorder was a serious mental illness. Dr. Jones knew that Nate could again easily slip back into that darkness after losing his mother.

Nate extended his hand in friendship to the good doctor, and as they warmly grasped each other's hands, Nate placed his arm around the other man's shoulder and guided him to Sarah's bedside.

"Doc, I am going to stay with Mother again tonight." Nate looked down upon his mother, whose eyes were closed. She was resting peacefully. Nate looked back up at Dr. Jones and said, "I really think Contessa needs a break. She has been an angel." Nate positioned himself between the doctor and the seating room, where Gwen and Contessa were seated, and said, "I'd like for you to give Mother something that will allow her to rest peacefully through the night."

Dr. Jones looked down at his patient and then placed his right hand on Nate's left shoulder. "She is resting well now. I will leave an order with the nurse to give her something that will help relax her at midnight. She will rest easy, without pain, tonight."

Nate looked at the doctor with welling eyes and said, "You've been a good family friend, Doc. Mother always thought you were sent to us from above."

Nate and Dr. Jones shook hands and shared a warm embrace. Dr. Jones patted Nate on the shoulder as he walked toward the sitting room. Dr. Jones stopped in front of Contessa and Gwen and looked at each with great compassion.

"You and Gwen need to get some rest," he told them. "Sarah is resting well. I'll stop by in the morning. Good night, and get some rest." Dr. Jones pushed open the door and disappeared into the hallway.

Nate turned and walked toward Contessa and Gwen, who were still seated on the couch in the sitting area. He walked toward the girls. When he reached the sitting room, he sat in one of the chairs that faced the two sobbing girls.

"Why don't you two go home and get some rest?"

Nate sat forward on the edge of his chair. "I'll stay with Mother. She will be fine tonight. If y'all want, the cottage is open." Nate sat back in his chair and said, "This is terribly hard on all of us. If something happens, you will be the first I call. Now why don't you two go and try to get some rest? You both look exhausted."

Gwen and Contessa both rose from their seated position at the same time and walked to Sarah's bedside. Gwen stood on the right side of the bed, while Contessa stood on the left. Each girl held her mother's hand and looked at Sarah with big tears streaming down her cheeks. They both knew in their hearts that this might be the last chance they got to say good-bye. Their hatred for Nate was growing in their hearts as they held on to their mother's hands.

Gwen leaned over, kissed Sarah on the forehead, and then leaned closer and whispered in her ear, "I love you. God is waiting for you." She again kissed Sarah on the forehead and caressed her cheek.

Contessa brushed back Sarah's hair with a soft and gentle touch. She fixed the blankets around Sarah's shoulders and placed Sarah's hand under the sheet, careful not to disrupt the IV that supplied the fluids to keep her hydrated. Contessa leaned forward and kissed Sarah on the forehead. Her cheeks were warm to the touch.

Lightly hugging Sarah, Contessa placed her mouth next to her mother's ear and said, "Everything will be all right, Mother. We will take care of things here. You have done God's work. It's okay to go home."

Contessa caressed Sarah's cheek one more time as she turned to leave the room.

Nate, standing at the foot of Sarah's bed, said, "If anything happens, I'll give you a call." Nate walked to the corner of the room, pulled a chair to his mother's bedside, and said, "I think I will read her favorite psalms tonight."

Contessa said, "I'm sure that will comfort her." Nate placed the chair close to Sarah's head and looked at both Contessa and Gwen.

"Go ahead," he said. "We'll be fine. Go get some rest. I'll call if something happens."

Nate sat down in the chair, took a deep breath, and let out an audible sigh. He reached into the nightstand drawer directly in front of him and took from it the Bible.

Contessa and Gwen walked toward the door and stopped. They turned and watched as Nate opened the Bible and began to read.

He reached for Sarah's hand and held it tight. They heard Nate begin reading, "The Lord is my shepherd, I shall not want. He makes me lay down in green pastures ..."

Contessa looked at Gwen, and both girls made the sign of the cross on their chests, bowed their heads, and held hands tightly.

Nate continued in a quiet, controlled, and slow voice: "He leads me beside quiet waters. He restores my soul; He guides me in the path of righteousness for His name's sake. Even though I walk through the valley of the shadow of death I fear no evil, for You are with me; Your rod and Your staff, they comfort me. You prepare a table before me in the presence of my enemies; You have anointed my head with oil; my cup overflows. Surely goodness and loving kindness will follow me all the days of my life, and I will dwell in the house of the Lord forever."

Gwen and Contessa said in unison, "Amen." Nate turned in his seat. "Oh, I thought you two had already left."

Gwen blew a kiss toward Sarah and said, "We're leaving now, Nate. You have my number. We will be at Abe's. Call if you need us." Nate waved good-bye with his free hand and returned his attention to Sarah. Both Contessa and Gwen turned and left the room.

CHAPTER 24

Nate sat at Sarah's side quietly for a few minutes and then read the same Bible passage again. After Nate finished the verse, he stood up and walked back and forth in front of Sarah's bed, pacing, his head down and his hands tightly clenched. He paced back and forth, repeating the same sentence over and over in a quiet voice.

"Forgive me, Lord, for what I am about to do. Forgive me, Lord, for what I am about to do. Forgive me, Lord, for what I am about to do."

Nate sat back down at Sarah's bedside and read the same psalm from the Bible again. At the end of the verse, he stood up and resumed his pacing, reciting the same request for forgiveness over and over and over again.

This ritual continued. After each reading, Nate would get up and walk back and forth in front of his ailing mother's bed. With each pass, Nate would look at Sarah and say again, "Forgive me, Lord, for what I am about to do."

At midnight, one of the nursing staff knocked on the door. Nate was just finishing reading the psalm when he turned, faced the door, and said, "Please come in."

Jan, the staff RN, walked in the room. "Hi, Mr. Dillianquest. I have something for your mother that will help her sleep through the night."

"She seems to be a bit fidgety. I hope this will relax her."

Jan walked by Nate and stopped at the IV pole. She took the cap off the syringe and injected the contents directly into the IV.

"The doctor ordered morphine," she explained. "This will help relax her. She will sleep comfortably through the rest of the night." Jan extracted the needle from the IV line and placed the needle in the container hanging on the wall in the med room. As Jan left the room, she turned to Nate and said, "Do you need anything, Mr. Dillianquest? Can I get you a blanket or pillow?"

"No, thank you. I have everything I need."

Nate turned back and gazed at Sarah. He watched as the morphine took an immediate effect. He could see Sarah's face relax as the drug pulsed through her veins.

He smiled and said, "Rest, my angel. It won't be long now." Nate reached out, touched her cheek, and said again, "It won't be long now. All this misery will be behind you."

Nate read from the Bible and paced for several more hours. At four o'clock in the morning, Nate put the Bible on his mother's chest and folded both her hands across the Bible's cover. He looked at Mother with a sense of duty and brushed her hair back. Nate got up from where he was seated and walked over to his jacket, which hung behind the med-room door. Nate reached into one of the inside pockets. As he did, he looked toward the door. Nate stopped and listened but did not hear anything.

From his jacket pocket, Nate pulled a large-gauge syringe filled with a lethal dose of the ethylene-glycol concoction.

Nate turned, walked toward the hallway door, and opened it unnoticed. Nate looked down the hall to his right and then his left. Nate saw Jan sitting at the nurse's station, working on the computer. There was no one else in sight. Nate cautiously closed the door. He did not want to arouse anyone's attention.

Nate held the syringe in his hand, warming its contents. Nate eased toward Sarah and stood at the foot of her bed, watching her sleep.

As his eyes drifted toward the IV stand, he said in a very quiet voice, "Please, God, forgive me for what I am about to do." He watched the IV for a moment as it dripped saline solution into his mother's veins, gripping the syringe in his hand tighter and tighter. Nate turned and crept toward the IV, keeping his eyes fixed upon his mother.

As Nate approached the IV, he reached out and grabbed the fluid bag in his left hand. As he held it, he heard a knocking on the door. As he turned and looked toward the sound, he let go of the bag.

Nancy, a nursing assistant, came in quickly and whispered, "Hi, Mr. Dillianquest. How is your mother doing?"

Nate was startled by the intrusion. He cleared his throat, gathered himself, and then replied, "She seems to be doing okay for the time being."

Nancy felt Sarah's forehead and then looked at Nate and said, "I'll check back just before I go home at six thirty. If you need anything, please, just let us know."

"Thanks."

Nancy left the room just as quickly as she had entered.

Nate sat in his chair alongside his mother and took a deep breath. He closed his eyes for a moment and said in a quiet voice, almost mumbling, "God, forgive me for what I am about to do."

Nate sat forward in his chair, touched Sarah's cheek, and said, "Your time here on earth has come to an end. You can go freely on to heaven and be with your beloved husband. I will take care of what you have started. May God bless your soul."

Nate stood up abruptly and plunged the syringe into the IV, emptying the bluish-green contents into the line that fed directly into his mother's veins.

Nate was mesmerized by his own actions. It was as if he saw himself working in slow motion. As he pushed on the syringe plunger, it only took a few seconds for the contents to transfer from the syringe into the IV line.

When Nate was finished emptying the contents of the syringe, he walked over to his jacket and returned the syringe to his pocket. Nate turned and walked to the foot of the bed, where his dying mother lay.

Nate genuflected, made the sign of the holy cross, and said again, "God forgive me for my sin." Nate stood, walked to his mother's side, and collapsed back into his chair. Nate was overcome with exhaustion. He watched as his fatal cocktail made its way to his mother's body.

As the poison disappeared from the IV line into his mother's body,

Nate held tightly onto Sarah's hand. Her body quivered slightly for a few moments and then went limp. Nate took the Bible from his Mother's chest and placed it alongside her now dead body. He placed his hand inside his mother's hand and laid his head down, resting it on their intertwined fingers. Soon Nate fell asleep from exhaustion.

At six fifteen, there was a light knock on the door, no answer came from inside. Nancy opened the door to Sarah Dillianquest's room and saw Nate sitting in a chair, leaning forward, with his head on the side of his mother's bed, sleeping. Nancy quietly walked to the opposite side of the bed from Nate lay and held Sarah's wrist in her hand. Nancy could feel no pulse. Nancy quickly turned and headed for the nurse's station to alert Jan.

A few moments after Nancy left the room, Jan entered and walked swiftly to the side of Mrs. Dillianquest. She placed her hand on Nate's mother's forehead. It was cool to the touch. It was clear that Mrs. Dillianquest passed away a few hours earlier, in her sleep. Jan walked to where Nate was sitting and touched him on his shoulder.

He lifted his head and looked at Jan. Jan looked at him and said, "I'm so very sorry, Mr. Dillianquest. It appears that your mother passed away quietly and peacefully during the night."

Nate's head sank down, but he did not say a word. Nate bent over at the waist and held his head in his hands.

Jan placed her hand on his shoulder and said, "I will call Dr. Jones and Contessa." She squeezed his shoulder. "Stay with Sarah for as long as you like. I'll be right back."

Nate sat up in his chair, looked at Jan, and said, "Thanks, but I'll call Contessa, if you don't mind?" Nate took a deep breath. "If you would call Dr. Jones, I would appreciate it." After a moment, Nate said, "Who will call the funeral home?"

Jan, who was almost at the door to the hallway, stopped, turned back to Nate, and said, "I will let them know."

"Thanks again."

Jan turned, pushed open the door, and left the room.

Nate sat up in his chair, held Sarah's hand, and said, "I'm so very sorry, Mother. I'm so very sorry."

Nate got up from his chair and wiped the sleep from his eyes. He pushed the chair that he had been sleeping in back into the corner of his mother's bedroom. He walked into the med room looking for his phone. He reached into the pocket of his jacket, which hung on the back of the med-room door, and started feeling around for the phone. As Nate reached for the phone, he felt the outline of the syringe at his fingertips.

Nate stopped looking for his phone for a moment. He held the needle in his hand, but did not remove it from its hiding place. Nate let the needle fall from his fingers back into the deep recesses of his pocket.

Nate found his phone and sat on the couch. It was already seven ten in the morning. He called Gwen.

Gwen's phone rang twice before she answered. "This is Gwen."

Nate replied in a somber voice, "Hey, it's Nate."

"Is everything all right?"

"No. Mother passed last night in her sleep."

Gwen started to cry and said something that Nate could not understand.

A moment passed in silence before Contessa came on the line. "Mother passed last night?"

"Yes."

"What time?"

"Jan said she must have passed somewhere between four and five. I fell asleep in the chair, and when Jan came in, she had already passed."

Contessa, already resigned to the fact that Nate had killed Sarah, said, "We'll get ready and be over shortly." The phone went silent in Nate's ear.

Sarah's room became busy with staff from the nursing home trying to get things ready for the funeral director. Nate was insistent that nobody touch Sarah's body until Gwen and Contessa arrived.

Nate excused himself and went outside using the back door to his mother's suite. Nate walked away from the building and took a seat under a large oak tree that shaded Sarah's room from the afternoon heat. He had placed a large, beautiful bench there, where he and his mother would sit and talk for hours. Nate sat on the bench for a short while before taking the phone from his pocket to call Tag's office.

Cindy and I were discussing the purchase agreement and the transfer of funds when my private line rang. I leaned back, picked up the phone from the credenza, and said, "Good morning, this is Tag."

"Morning, Tag. I wanted to let you know that Mother passed last night."

"I am sorry to hear that, Nate."

"Thanks." After a short pause, Nate added, "I am ready to move quickly, Tag."

"I see. Give me a second. I am going to place you on hold. I'll be right back with you."

"Fine."

I looked at Cindy and said, "Do you know if we are ready with the Dillianquest funds?"

Cindy held up her finger as if to tell me to wait for a second, got up, and went to her desk. She returned with the Dillianquest folder. She pored over a couple of pages and then said, "Everything seems to be in order. We can transfer the funds today, but they won't be released until Friday, at 5:00 p.m."

I nodded in agreement, took Nate off hold, and said, "Sorry about that, Nate. You caught me off guard a bit this morning."

"Is there anything wrong?"

"No, no, we're good. I guess I didn't expect your mother to pass so quickly. I am sorry for your loss."

"We were preparing for it, but it's always a shock. We will miss her greatly."

I spun around in his chair and said, "Nate, are you okay to continue? Do you need a little time?"

"No, please, I'm fine."

"Okay, here's what going to happen. We will transfer the funds into Junior's firm's escrow account. He can make the funds available to you after five o'clock on Friday evening. So far, so good, Nate?"

"Yes. So far, so good."

"Great. I will plan a trip to Beaufort on Monday to take possession of the property. If you can be there to break the news to Dianna and Sally on Monday afternoon with me, that would be great." I stopped to take a breath. "I will work with them to schedule employee meetings, and we are off to the races."

"Thanks, Tag. If you need anything, call me. See you Monday." Nate ended the call and headed back into Sarah 's room.

When Nate walked into his mother's suite, he noticed Gwen and Contessa standing in the sitting area, talking with Dr. Jones. Nate walked up to the three and hugged Gwen and then Contessa.

"She passed while I was sleeping," he told them. "I tried to stay awake, but I guess I was just too exhausted."

Dr. Jones placed his hand on Nate's shoulder and said, "There was nothing you could have done to keep her alive. When the good Lord calls, it's our duty to go."

Nate did not respond to the doctor's comments. He just looked at Contessa and Gwen and said, "She is in a much better place. Nothing can hurt her now."

CHAPTER 25

Junior's phone beeped and vibrated on his desk late Friday afternoon. He did not pay much attention to the incoming text message, as he was reviewing the paperwork necessary to open secret offshore investment accounts in both his and Nate's names.

Junior thought he would be damned if he was going to pay exorbitantly high income taxes on his earnings. He was hell-bent on finding a safe tax shelter. Junior had several clients that had used offshore accounts, but he had never personally set up an offshore tax shelter.

He was pleased when a client pointed him in the direction of what appeared to be an easy to set up and very discreet tax shelter in the United Bank of Switzerland. He sat at his desk in front of his oversized flat-screen monitor, entering passwords and account numbers on his computer. He was almost finished.

When Junior concluded his activities on the computer, he picked up his phone and pressed the text-message button. The message was from Nate: "Meet me at the cottage at nine. We'll transfer the funds from there. Drink to celebrate. Bring titles."

Junior put the phone down on this desk and smiled. He could picture in his mind his five million dollars flowing from one account and into the other. Junior got up from his chair and walked to his private bar. He stood back and opened the cabinet bar doors as if he were the king of the world. He couldn't help but smile a very big smile. This was his biggest payday ever!

Junior reached for a bottle of Johnny Walker Blue Label from his personal stock of scotch. He plucked a couple of ice cubes from the ice maker, held them a few inches above his glass, and let them fall into the crystal tumbler. The cubes bounced like two roulette balls on a roulette wheel, finally coming to rest at the bottom of the glass. Junior unscrewed the cap to the bottle of scotch and poured his favorite drink over the ice cubes, listening to them crack as the warm liquid swallowed them whole.

Junior walked back over to his desk and retrieved a cigar from his upper right hand desk drawer. He cut the tip off, put the cigar in his mouth, and leaned back in his chair, still smiling about his five-million-dollar payday. As Junior put his feet up on his desk, there was a knock on the door.

"Come on in."

Claudette entered the room and said, "You look pretty comfortable. Do you need anything before I leave for the weekend?"

"No, I'm good."

Claudette stood directly in front of Junior's desk, looking straight at him. "How is the retirement plan coming?"

"This weekend will be good for your account."

Claudette smiled and then turned and started to walk out of Junior's office. Before she left, she said, "After all that's gone wrong in the stock market, I could use a little bump in the account. See you Monday." Claudette shut the office door on her way out.

CHAPTER 26

N ate was just entering the funeral home when he heard his text alarm go off on his cell phone. He stopped on the stairs leading into the building and looked at his phone's screen. It read, "1 text message." Nate quickly looked at his phone and saw that the text message was from Junior: "Meet at the cottage—8:30. We'll transfer funds from there. Drink to celebrate."

Nate put his cell phone back in his pocket and smiled as he walked into the funeral home.

As eight o'clock approached, the crowds that gathered to show their respect grew larger and larger at the Beaufort Funeral Home. Sarah Grace Dillianquest had been enormously popular. Many considered her to be the matriarch of this tightly bound community. Nate stayed at his mother's side, greeting everyone who came by to pay their respects. The room was filled with hundreds of flower arrangements. Memorial pictures of Sarah chronicled her good works, from a picture of her standing in front of the day-care center she had helped organize and finance to one of the groundbreaking ceremony at Danby House. Tears were in abundance.

Nate handed the outpouring of love graciously. He expressed his appreciation to everyone who stopped by to share condolences.

Then, at 8:10 p.m. sharp, Nate had a sudden emotional breakdown. Nate knelt down at the side of his mother's casket and began to weep. Several mourners standing close to Nate offered their handkerchiefs, and he graciously accepted one. Nate stood, placed his hand over the folded hands of his deceased mother, bowed his head, and said a short prayer.

When Nate lifted his head, he announced in a soft voice, "Please excuse me. I need to get some fresh air." Nate made his way out of the funeral home.

Nate walked across the street to his 1941 Lincoln Continental Coupe, placed both hands on the top of the car, and leaned forward. He glanced as his watch. It was eight twenty. He opened his car door and sat down in the driver's seat. As if he were moving in slow motion, Nate started his car, stared out the front windshield for a few seconds, and then pulled away from the curb. Soon he was out of sight from the funeral home and on his way to meet Junior at the cottage.

Night was beginning to settle in on the coastal town of Beaufort as Nate turned left onto the winding drive that led to the cottage. Nate had turned his headlights on just a few miles earlier. As he approached the cottage, he looked at his watch: eight thirty, right on the button.

Nate pulled up directly in front of the garage doors and turned the car off. Opening the car door, he placed both feet on the ground while still sitting in the car. He saw no sign of Junior.

Nate mumbled to himself, "You would think for five million dollars, the fucker could be on time for a change."

Nate stood up and stretched before closing the car door. He walked toward the front door of the cottage, breathing in deeply, enjoying the ocean air. He was pleased with himself. Nate placed the key in the door lock and turned it, opening the large front door. He pushed it open and entered. As he shut the door behind him, he turned to his right and flicked the light switch on. As he took his first step forward into the foyer, he noticed a shadowy figure out of the corner of his eye. Startled, Nate instinctively stood erect and faced the intruder.

Before Nate could utter a word, the masked intruder struck Nate in the side of the head, knocking him to the ground, unconscious.

The intruder searched Nate and found a loaded .38 revolver strapped to his ankle. He removed the gun from its holster and placed it in his coat pocket.

Nate was dragged by his shoulders into the living room, where two seats had been arranged in front of the fully displayed television. The intruder placed Nate in an upright, seated position facing the flat screen and bound his legs to the chair using plastic zip ties, careful not to cut off Nate's circulation. The intruder reached his glove-clad hand into his pocket and placed the pistol on the console.

From his back pocket, the intruder removed two kitchen towels and wrapped Nate's wrists firmly. Nate's hands were tied behind his back with more zip ties, with care not to leave any ligature marks on his wrists. Nate was bound hand and foot; he wasn't going anywhere. His head dangled forward. He remained unconscious.

The intruder looked as his watch, and it was eight fifty. Nate's head began to move a bit, and then a little more, until Nate regained consciousness.

The masked man sat in the straight-backed kitchen chair directly in front, facing Nate. Nate shook his head from side to side. His vision was a bit blurry, but once conscious, he shouted, "Who are you? What do you want?"

The intruder remained silent and held his index finger up to his covered lips, signaling Nate to remain quiet.

Nate glared at the masked man and said, "Fuck you, you piece of shit. Let me go, you coward." The masked man calmly got up from his chair and walked away from Nate and into the kitchen as Nate was yelling, "Let me loose—please! I will give you what you want!"

The intruder walked back into the living room, where Nate was bound. He had a white cloth in his right hand. He sat down in front of Nate and again held up his right index finger in front of his hidden lips, signaling Nate to be quiet.

Nate replied, "You bastard, do you know who I am? Let me loose. We can work something out!"

The masked man shook his head from side to side. He walked behind Nate and placed a chloroform-soaked cloth over the captive man's mouth and nose. In just a few seconds, Nate Dillianquest was quiet again.

Abe removed his mask and yelled, "Contessa, are you ready?"

Contessa came in from the screened-in porch. "Yeah. Is Nate okay?"

"He'll be fine. Now go take your position in the kitchen. Father should be here any minute."

Contessa went into kitchen and sat at the table. Abe fashioned a gag around Nate's mouth and then loosened it to let it fall around his neck. Nate's head bobbed forward.

Abe watched and saw car headlights making their way down the drive, getting closer and closer to the cottage. Abe situated himself behind the front door, lying in wait.

The car pulled up, and Junior turned off his engine. Abe heard the car door close.

His heart was pounding wildly. His right hand held a cloth soaked in chloroform.

Junior knocked on the door, pushed it open, and yelled, "Hey, Nate. It's me."

As he entered the foyer, he noticed Contessa sitting at the kitchen table.

"Contessa, what are you doing here?"

"I am waiting for you."

Just as Contessa finished her thought, Abe grabbed his father with his right hand, covering his nose and mouth, and held on to his shoulders with his left arm. Junior fought back, trying to grab the person who was on his back. They spun in a circle twice as Junior tried to fend off his unseen attacker.

In just a few short seconds, though, Junior's knees buckled, and he succumbed to the chloroform. Together, father and son collapsed on to the floor.

"Holy shit," Abe said, as his heart nearly popped through his chest. He rolled off his father's back and stood. He looked down at his unconscious father and then at Contessa. "Help me get him in the chair."

Together, Abe and Contessa dragged Junior to the living room. Abe moved the chair in front of Nate to Nate's side. They hoisted Junior into the chair and bound his legs and hands, just as they had Nate's. Contessa went back into the kitchen and made sure the door was closed. As she returned into the living room, she closed the doors that separated the rooms.

Abe searched his father's jacket and removed the titles. Abe turned and tossed the titles to the boat and the plane on the console that housed the television. He continued to search through his father's pockets and found a .22-caliber pistol. Abe pulled the gun from his pocket and stared at it in disbelief.

Contessa saw the gun and with wide eyes said, "Wow, Nate brought his .38, and your father brought a gun, too. I wonder what they had in mind tonight."

Abe looked over at Contessa, who was standing by the television, and said, "This just keeps getting weirder and weirder. I wonder who was planning on shooting whom?"

Abe retrieved his briefcase and brought it back to the television console. He removed a DVD case and a small prescription vial and placed them both on the table next to the briefcase. Abe returned to his briefcase and removed the laptop. Abe opened the laptop and logged on to the Internet. The screen was facing the two unconscious men.

Abe entered the address to the Swiss bank where Junior and Nate had opened accounts. The bank's online banking page opened, and Abe entered the password and account information. Abe reduced the size of the window on his screen.

In a separate window, Abe accessed his father's firm's escrow account at the main offices of the Beaufort State Bank. Abe logged in on the main page and then into the escrow account. The escrow account balance read $40,625,000. Abe clicked on the X in the upper right corner of his computer screen, and the window disappeared from sight.

Abe closed the briefcase and set it on the floor next to the table. He then opened the doors to the television cabinet and placed the DVD into the player. He turned on the television and set up the system so the cursor was blinking on the screen under the first letter of the sentence that read, *To continue, press enter.*

Abe retrieved another chair from the kitchen and placed it facing his father and Nate. Abe kept his back toward the television screen.

Abe looked over at Contessa and said, "I'll take it from here."

"What happens if ..."

"There won't be any ifs. Go ahead. I'll be done here as soon as I can."

Abe and Contessa hugged, and as she left through the screened porch, she said, "Good luck."

Abe waved. "See you both in a few." Contessa walked into the darkness of the night.

Abe took a deep breath, sighed, and sat in the chair facing the two men. He reached over to the prescription bottle and took out a capsule of smelling salts. Abe stood up, broke the capsule in two, and waved it under the noses of both men. Junior and Nate's heads started to roll from side to side. Both men shook their heads, trying to shake loose the cobwebs that they felt. Their vision was a bit blurry. Both men began to struggle to free themselves.

Nate looked up at Abe, still struggling, and said, "Abe! Thank God! Let me loose."

Junior sat still, looking at Abe, and said, "Son, what is going on? Cut me loose immediately."

Nate was becoming more and more agitated, squirming around. He began yelling at Abe. "Did you knock me out when I came in? You little shit! Let me loose right now!"

"Nate, please don't exert yourself."

"Cut me loose, you son of a bitch, and do it right now. When I get out of this, I'll kill you with my bare hands."

Abe got up from his seat, walked over behind Nate, and pulled up the gag lying around his neck.

Abe returned to his seat in front of the two men and said, "Nate, you two are a dangerous couple of men." Abe leaned forward in his chair, looked directly at Nate, and said, "I would have preferred not gagging you, Mr. Dillianquest, but quite frankly, I think you are out of your freaking mind."

Junior looked at Abe and said, "You are right, son. He is out of his mind. Now cut me loose, so we can resolve this before anything bad happens."

Abe laughed and said, "Before anything bad happens, Father? Surely you jest?" Abe reached over and picked up the remote control lying next to the television on the table. Abe looked back at his father, laughed, and repeated, "Before anything bad happens." Abe looked at both men and said, "It's already too late for that. You two have gone over the flipping edge."

Abe clicked enter on the remote control, and the screen went blank momentarily before showing Nate and Junior talking in the shed.

Abe said, "I won't bore you with all the details—just the stuff I think a jury might find interesting. I have put together a little highlights tape … or, in your case, a lowlights tape. Sorry we don't have popcorn. You'll just have to watch."

Nate and Junior sat stunned as they watched the television where Junior's voice was heard.

"Come on. Grab that bottle, and I'll put some ice in the bucket, and we'll go in the back, and you can tell me what the fuck is bothering you. You aren't thinking about suicide again, are you, Nate?"

"Not at the moment … but under the circumstances …"

"Bullshit, Nate. If you're thinking suicide, I might as well dial up Doc Jones and get him out here right now."

Abe paused the recording, looked directly at his father, and said, "I devised a surveillance system some time ago. I deployed it at the office and in your shed in an effort to protect you from harm. I thought I was doing the right thing. I never expected to find these types of unintended consequences. Oh and Mr. Dillianquest, just so you know, I installed the system in Mrs. Dillianquest's room at Danby House just to keep an eye on things."

"Gentlemen, there is so much horrible stuff on this recording," Abe said very a matter of fact tone, "when I first watched it, I was in shock. How could you both live with yourselves? So as you watch, you'll notice that I've done some nifty editing to keep your interest piqued!" Abe pressed play.

On the television was Nate talking:

"I need you to change Mother's will."

"Nate, you know I can't do that. Your mother gave me explicit instructions that her will was not to be altered in any fashion. As an officer of the court, I have a duty to uphold her wishes. I am sorry—it can't be done."

"I really don't give a flying fuck about your duties, Junior. You owe this to me. I am flat fucking broke, and it's your fault. You do remember July 11, 1972, don't you, Junior? We drank a bit too much and smoked a bit, too, that night, and as I recall the accident, Jason Holt lost control of his bicycle and swerved directly in the path of my car … What in the fuck is a thirteen-year-old kid doing out at three in the morning?"

Abe paused the recording and said, "Father, you were involved in a homicide, and you never came forward. You let Nate take the entire rap, so you wouldn't lose your license to practice law. Very nice, indeed!"

Abe hit play again. Both men looked up at the television in silence and heard Nate's voice.

"Whenever we happened to find any extra bags of coke, we would take it to the local natives and sell it or arrange to have it smuggled back to the States. The pilots lovingly referred to it as their retirement fund. At the time, Junior, I really didn't give a shit what they did. I was just along for the ride. I didn't give much thought to getting caught up in a drug-trafficking scandal. Besides, the death of that poor Holt kid was eating me up inside. I often thought about jumping out of the chopper just to ease that pain. Anyway, we landed the chopper in a small clearing and started looking around the place for drugs. We were all pretty nervous as we approached one of the huts. As we got close, two people bolted from the hut and started running toward the jungle, screaming something in Spanish. I panicked, and without a thought or a blink of my eye, I pulled up my rifle, and I shot and killed both of them. Just like that! I shot them in the back as they were running away. … We dragged the two bodies, one female and one male, and put them in a hut. We splashed the huts with the fuel. One of the guys wrapped a pole with the shirt from the guy I had shot and soaked it with fuel. We were going to burn the huts and the bodies and destroy the evidence."

Abe paused the recording while looking at both Junior and Nate and said, " I think a jury would find this next passage of particular interest" and he hit the play button.

Again, all could here Nate's voice, "We seemed to have struck the mother lode. We had fifty or sixty pounds of prepackaged cocaine and two baby girls."

After an obvious edit, Nate's recorded voice continued saying, "It was you who arranged for the babies to be brought to the United States. It was you, Junior, who transferred the money to the government officials in Colombia, and it was you, Junior, who personally saw to it that Gwen and Contessa had all the fake paperwork to remain in the United States. The only thing you did not know is how I killed the parents of Gwen and Contessa in cold blood."

Abe stopped the recording and said, "You murdered Gwen's and Contessa' parents in cold blood and burned their bodies. The death toll is now three, Nate. You should have jumped out of the chopper when you had a chance. You're a coward."

Abe looked as his bound father and said, "And you're no better than him." He looked back the television monitor and pressed play.

Nate's voice was again heard:

"I have been embezzling hundreds of thousands of dollars from Mother's foundation to make ends meet. And I'll be damned if I am going to give half of the only inheritance I have to those two. I want you to cut both Gwen and Contessa completely out of the will. Once that is done, you need to open an offshore account for me ... an account that cannot be traced by US authorities. I intend to sell Dillianquest in the next month or two."

Abe stopped the recording. He looked at Nate, who was starring straight at Abe, trying to intimidate him. Abe, glaring back said, "You killed their parents. You took them away from any family they had in Colombia, and now you want to cheat them out of everything your mother wanted them to have. What kind of monster are you?"

Abe returned his attention to the television. They all could hear Nate on the recording:

"You'll need to get Brad Zeta to fluff up the appraisal a bit, like you did for the mall and apartment projects. You can pressure Zeta to appraise the property at sixty-five million or so. I know those Ann Arbor Yankee boys will gladly pay eighty-five to ninety cents on the dollar for a property like Dillianquest. That's an easy fifty million dollars. Hell, I'll pay Zeta twice his usual fee ... No, tell Zeta his cut will be one hundred grand. Yes, one hundred thousand dollars should do the trick for Brad."

"So far, I am with you, my friend. I really only have two concerns,

Nate, that need some attention, and I hope you have given them some thought. My first concerns are the girls and Abe, Nate. Did you know that Gwen and Abe are going to be engaged next week?"

"Yeah, I know. I heard Contessa tell Mother something to that effect last week or so. But that really doesn't matter, Junior. Now what is your second concern?"

"Not so fast, Nate. All three of those kids are aware of your mother's generosity and the content of her will, but for me … for me, Nate—and I hope you don't take this the wrong way—I don't want my son, as weak and snotty-nosed a piece of shit as that boy is, I don't want him marrying that, that, that fucking half-breed from South America. Don't get me wrong, Nate, Gwen is a sweet girl, and I love her to death. And your family has done great things for those kids and all. But there ain't one drop of southern fucking heritage in that girl's veins. Cutting them from Mother's will, will certainly send up a red flag."

"Not to worry, Junior, not to worry. I've got that all figured out."

While the recording kept running, Abe looked over at this father in disgust. Junior had tears streaming down his cheeks.

Abe looked at his father with rage in his eyes and said, "You really disappoint me, Father."

"I never meant to hurt you, son."

"Don't bother."

Junior hung his head. Again, they listened to Nate's voice:

"First, we change the will and have it witnessed and notarized by Claudette. You know that won't be a problem. I am sure she could use an extra fifty grand for her upcoming retirement. In a codicil to Mother's will, Gwen will get the plane, and Contessa will get the *Spirit*. I brought both titles with me tonight. They are both free and clear and unencumbered. I've already signed them. You can have them for safekeeping—a little insurance policy for the kids. The plane and *Spirit* are worth about a million each. That should get them settled. With you taking care of the will, Junior, and Claudette as our witness, there's no reason it should be contested. No one will be the wiser. As far as Mother's health is concerned, it is unfortunate that Mother will pass in the next month or so. Her mind is completely gone, and now, because of Alzheimer's, her body is following and failing just as quickly. I just don't see her strong enough to live much longer. I am truly going to miss her when she passes."

Abe stopped the recording, looked at his father, and said, "A snot-nosed piece of shit. Is that what you really think of me ... Daddy?"

Abe again pointed the remote control at the television and pressed the play button. He looked back at the television screen in time to see his father speaking.

"I'm in, Nate, but my fee is five million dollars. Take it or leave it."

"Five million! Are you out of your fucking mind?"

"I must be out of my fucking mind if I'm going along with your insane plan. You do realize, old friend, that I will be an accessory to the murder of your mother. For that, the price is five million dollars ... take it or leave it. I really don't care. One way or the other, Nate, you disappear forever. Do we have an understanding? This is the last deal we do"

"Fuck 'em all, Junior. You make your end happen, and I'll lead the sheep to the slaughterhouse, and when it's all done, you will never see me again. Fuck 'em all."

Abe stopped the recording and said, "If I didn't see and hear with my own eyes and ears, I would have never ever believed it. You two are a piece of work. However, there is one more piece of video that you both need to see. This takes place in Mrs. Dillianquest's room."

Abe pressed play, and the recording showed Nate placing a straw in Mother's mouth. As the two men watched, Abe reached into his briefcase and pulled out an envelope.

Abe stood up from his seat, unfolded the paper, and paraded it in front of the faces of both men to see and said, "Nate, this is a lab report." Abe pointed to the letterhead as he walked in front of the men. "I had the malts that you have been feeding your mother analyzed at Chemco Laboratory. The samples I sent were found to contain ethylene glycol." Abe looked directly at Nate, got very close to his face, and said, "That's automobile antifreeze, Nate. But of course you already knew that, didn't you?"

Abe walked to his father and said, "Your good friend here administered small enough doses over a few weeks that he managed to effectively and slowly poison his own mother, and you are a conspirator in her murder." Abe looked at the television screen and then at Nate and said, "You are truly a worthless piece of human excrement."

Abe pointed to the television.

All three men's eyes locked onto the television screen and watched as Nate walked toward the hallway and opened the door. They watched as Nate looked down the hall to his right and then his left. Abe, close to the television screen, pointed to Nate holding the syringe in his hand. They watched in silence as Nate walked toward Sarah and stood at the foot of her bed. They heard Nate say, "Please, God, forgive me for what I am about to do." Nate stood staring at the IV, still holding the syringe in his hand. Nate turned and crept toward the IV, keeping his eyes on his mother. Then there was a knock on the door; a nurse's aide came and went quickly.

They watched quietly as Nate sat in the chair next to his mother and closed his eyes, saying, "Father, forgive me for what I am about to do." Nate sat forward in his chair and touched Sarah's cheek, and they heard him say, "Your time here on earth has come to an end. You can go freely into heaven and be with your beloved husband. I will take care of what you have started. May God bless your soul."

Junior's eyes were riveted on the television screen. Nate's head was hanging low. Abe sat in his chair, facing the two men, watching their reaction. Junior watched as Nate stood up abruptly, plunged the syringe into the IV line, and emptied the bluish-green contents into the line that fed directly into Sarah's veins. Junior had a look of disbelief on his face as he watched Nate walk out of the picture frame.

Junior looked over at Nate, whose head was hanging low in shame, and said in a loud, disgusted voice, "What in the hell have you done, Nate? You murdered your own mother so you could get your hands on the money!"

Abe looked at his father, "You have little room to be disgusted Father. You are far from innocent!"

Abe pointed to the television screen to watch Nate return into the frame and walk to the foot of his mother's bed. All three men watched as Nate genuflected and made the sign of the holy cross. They heard Nate say in a shallow voice, "God forgive me for my sin." They watched as Nate held tightly onto his mother's hand, and then all watched her body go limp.

Abe turned off the television, walked behind Nate, and untied his gag. Total silence fell upon the room.

Abe looked at Nate and said, "God will never forgive you for what you have done. I think you've convinced yourself that you have been doing the right things for all these years. But the simple fact of the matter is you have the blood of four people on your hands, and three of those lives have yet to be atoned for. God, Nate, you murdered your own mother and the parents of your adopted sisters. You should rot in hell!"

Nate had a strangely serene look about him when he peered deep into Abe's eyes and said, "All those I have touched, I have commanded to a better place. I have lifted two children from their squalor. They are in a better place now because of me. I have taken an infirm elder and eliminated her pain. Mother is in a better place now because of me. You, Mr. Belanger, you cannot take those good deeds from me. Nor can anyone else."

Abe stood up from his chair, looked directly at Junior, and said, "Nate is a sick man. But what say you, Father? In this, your moment of unbridled pride, what possible defense could you utter that would make a difference?"

Abe walked to the laptop computer next to the television. Junior did not say anything. Abe then asked, "And what about my mother and your wife? Did you take her or me into account as you entered into your deals with the devil?"

Abe powered up his computer. He pulled his chair close to the machine and said calmly, "Money, it is said, is the root of all evil, and greed has its consequence. Money changes everything, they say."

Abe opened the computer's closed windows, and up popped the websites to the Beaufort State Bank and the United Bank of Switzerland. He turned in his chair, facing the two men, and said, "Your office, Father—your office has been under my surveillance for quite some time. Now, gentlemen, this is what is going to happen next. And I want you both to pay very close attention."

Abe turned back to the keyboard and entered several codes and passwords. He turned back to the two men and said, "You two are going to love this, because when I press the enter key" —Abe poised his index finger above the keyboard—"All but $687,500 is going to be transferred from the firm's escrow account directly into your accounts at the United Bank of Switzerland, just as you guys had planned. $5 million goes into Father's account, and about $35.6 million, give or take a few bucks, will be deposited into Nate's account."

Abe looked at both men. "Are you ready? Because here we go." Abe dropped his finger on the enter button, and the screen went black and then popped back up. Abe pointed to the laptop's screen and said, "Look at the balance at the Beaufort account, and now look at the balances in the United Bank of Switzerland accounts … pretty neat stuff."

Junior looked at his son and asked, "What are you doing?"

Abe glared at his father and said in a very sarcastic tone, "We're only halfway done here, Daddy. Just wait." Abe turned back to the keyboard and entered in more codes on the laptop.

A different website emerged on the laptop's screen. Abe turned in his chair and said, "And here is the second half of the show. When I press the enter button again, the funds from your accounts will be transferred a least a dozen times to different accounts all around the world. And here is the genius of it all: the federal government will only be able to trace the money from the Dillianquest sale to the both of you."

Nate was squirming wildly in his chair. "You piece of shit! When I find you, I'll kill you!"

Abe walked to where Nate was frantically trying to untie himself. He stopped in front of him and looked at Nate for what seemed to be an eternity with the dead eyes of a Great White shark. Abe cocked his arm back and struck Nate in the face with his fist so hard that it knocked him to the floor.

Abe stood over a bloody-lipped Nate and said, "Please, Mr. Dillianquest, there is really no need to be hostile here." Abe helped Nate back to his seated and upright position, walked calmly into the kitchen, returned with a paper towel, and cleaned the blood from Nate's lip, saying, "I trust you will remain quiet, Mr. Dillianquest."

Nate did not say a word. He glared at Abe with utter contempt.

Abe pulled his chair in front of Junior's position and sat down. Abe looked deep into his father's eyes and said, "Who would have ever thought, eh, Daddy?"

Junior looked at Abe and said in a pleading voice, "Come on, son. We can figure this out. Just let me go. I can handle Nate."

Abe glanced over at Nate and then back at Junior. "Boys, I have copies of the full-length version of what you saw here tonight. If anything happens to Gwen, Contessa, or me even by accident, that information will be released to the authorities. You, gentlemen ... you will spend the rest of your lives behind bars." Abe looked at Junior and said, "And Daddy ... that means you will die there, and how awful would that be?"

Abe got up from his seated position and began to pack the laptop in the briefcase. While he was putting things away, he said, "I've put two million dollars aside for Mother." Abe paused for a moment and then added, "I'll be willing to bet that Mother knows nothing about what you and Nate have been up to. She would be devastated to see that recording." Abe turned to Junior and said, "I would also be willing to bet that Mother doesn't know a thing about all those women you've been screwing."

Abe stopped what he was doing, walked back to his seat, sat down in front of his father, and said, "You need to come clean with Mother about your affairs." Abe paused for a second. "If she wants to stay with you, that's her business. But if she wants a divorce, I've got two million helpers standing by for her." Abe stood back up and said, "By the way, Gwen and I got married yesterday. If anyone asks, we took off on an extended honeymoon."

Abe was again at his briefcase. "I'll call Mother when we get situated. That should give you time to chat. You will pass that good word along won't you, Daddy? I mean, about Gwen and me? I know she will be very disappointed about not being there when we got married. Just tell her that something came up at the last minute." Junior did not say a word; he just nodded in agreement.

Abe had everything back in order at the cottage. The two men remained bound and silent while Abe packed his belongings, and then Junior asked, "What are you going to do with us?"

Abe stood at the television console. He reached for one of the pistols that lay on the console next to his briefcase. He turned, looked at his father, held up the gun, and replied, "I am going to take your .22-caliber pistol with me." He placed the pistol in his briefcase and then reached for the other pistol.

Abe held Nate's .38-caliber pistol up, wiped it clean with a cloth, and emptied all of the bullets from the Nate's gun into his gloved hand. "I am going to leave this gun here. I'm going to put the bullets in this plastic bag and place them at the trunk of the big oak that is just outside the front porch door. You can decide how you want to proceed."

Abe picked up the boat and plane titles and placed them in his case next to the pistol. "We'll be needing these."

Abe walked over to his father and said, "It's hard to love a man like you. I've never been able to live up to your expectations, but you are my father, and as difficult as it is, I do love you in a bizarre, dysfunctional way. I am not going to turn either of you in to the authorities, unless you or Nate force my hand."

Abe walked over to where Nate was bound. Looking him straight in the eye, he said, "Mr. Dillianquest, sir, you do not deserve to live. There is no room in this world for someone as deluded as you. No one would blame you if you decided to take your own life."

Abe walked over to where his father was seated. "Please don't say anything. You've already made this way too difficult."

Abe went to the console and retrieved the knife he had placed there earlier in the evening. He then turned, walked to the back of his father's chair, and cut one zip tie from his left hand.

He returned the knife to the console, looked at his father, and said, "You should be able to untie yourself pretty quickly." Abe was walking toward the front door when he said, "I'm sure you'll figure something out with Mr. Dillianquest."

Abe turned and walked out of the room.

Junior heard the slam of the front door close.

There was silence in the room.

CHAPTER 27

I t is 4:45 a.m. on an early spring morning. The alarm clock buzzes. It is twenty-three degrees outside. I haven't slept a wink. I have been up all night, haunted with the thought of leaving my wife of twenty years and my two children. I am repulsed with myself, but oddly excited at what I am about to do.

I slowly slink out of bed and walk toward the bathroom, the hardwood floors creaking with every step. It sounds as if a percussionist is following me around. We live in a one-hundred-year-old house in an upscale neighborhood in Bloomfield Hills, Michigan. I stop and look back at my wife. She doesn't know that when I leave for this very ordinary business trip, as I have done hundreds of times before, it will be the last time we say our good-byes ... forever!

Being the scum of the earth does not come easily for me, but then again, neither does becoming some inmate's love interest at Jackson State Prison. Thinking of what I have done and what we have become makes me physically ill, but I have left myself no other option: I must leave to protect my family from the humiliation they will all have to endure even if my wife and I divorce. How deluded have I become? Am I leaving to protect my family or me?

As I stand looking at the pathetic reflection of myself in the mirror, I cannot believe what has taken place in my life. With my head hanging low and my hands gripping the sides of the sink, I puke until my guts feel as if someone is pulling them through my mouth with a pair of pliers ... my body heaves in agony.

Just then, Samantha, my wife, places her hand between my shoulders and asks, "Are you okay? Maybe you should go back to bed and call this trip off for a few days ... sounds like you're catching the flu."

I reply in my weakened state, "Go back to bed—I'll be okay. You know I can't call off this trip. Today we take possession of Dillianquest—I have to go. I will wake you before I leave. Now go back to bed; it's too early to be up."

Barely able to look at my disgusting reflection in the mirror, I wonder how this could be happening to me. I have always tried to do what was right, not ever intentionally hurting anyone—or so I made myself believe. Always trying to do the right thing ... how cliché. I close my eyes and contemplate my past, my head still hanging low with shame.

I am not one for wallowing in past mistakes. For someone in my position, hindsight can bring on paralysis, so I start to think about what lies ahead: an unthinkable adventure that will take me to ... where? I am not so sure. But the one thing I am certain about is that my destination will offer warmer weather, firmer bodies, and a ton of cash.

If I stay and end up facing *my* own music, it will certainly mean that I will be sharing a cell with heaven knows who. I envision a mountain of a man with an appetite for boys like me. I hate to think about what kind of terror he and his buddies would rain down on my body. Many people, mostly women and a few gays that I met along the way, have said that I have a very attractive build and great ass. It's that great ass I did not want to share with any of the boys in lockup!

Still leaning on the sink with the occasional dry heave, I think about the evening when all this shit started. I was sitting alone at the Ocean Side Shanty, a small bar and grill off the beaten trail in Beaufort, South Carolina. It had been recommended as a great place to eat. It was located on a dark gravel road on some backwater inlet.

I recall the distinct smell of the evening breeze gently wafting the unique scents of the sea across my face. You could taste the salt in the air. That is something that a kid from Michigan would never forget. The night was pitch-black in the swampy lowland. A single light on the road, barely visible in the dense ocean fog, marked the entrance to the bar. Only a handful of patrons sat inside. I recall sliding onto a stool at the bar and ordering a scotch from a bartender named Levi.

The night started off innocently enough, but somehow I ended up shooting pool with a thirtysomething, drop-dead gorgeous woman who called herself Contessa. She had seemed to appear from thin air. I don't even remember how we got started, but it reminded me of one of those letters I had read in *Playboy* as a young boy, the kind that always began with, "I never thought this could happen to me." To be honest, I never thought my story could have happened to me, either, but it did. It was about to change my life forever—and not for the better!

Contessa was tall, with the silkiest, longest, most flowing jet-black hair I had ever seen. It glistened in the dull bar light. She swirled it about in a most erotic fashion, brushing it back off her forehead with her full open hand. Her hair would tumble back to the same position as before. Her tight, low-cut jeans exposed a firm stomach with just the hint of a tattoo peeking out from the front of her pants. Her snugly fitted T-shirt commanded my attention. Lust was everywhere in my thoughts. She seemed genuinely glad to be there at that moment!

This amazingly beautiful woman was clearly a wonderful blend of exotic South American and Spanish heritage, judging from her richly bronzed, sensually supple skin. She smelled exquisite as she invitingly sauntered back and forth in front of me, taking her turn playing pool. Bent over the pool table, she stroked our shared cue and struck at the white cue ball without success. She did not say a word; she just smiled and tossed her hair back and handed me the cue without acting particularly eager to let it go. Contessa was tempting me.

Her eyes were dark as West Virginia coal and twinkled like diamonds in the low-hanging bar lights. She shot lustful thoughts directly into my soul. She was stunning, amazing—and her attention was fixed solely on me. How could that be? It did not matter, as I was mesmerized and drawn wholly into her spell. I was no match for this creature.

As she purposefully leaned over the table, my eyes were treated to an unbelievable sensual feast. I was transfixed, seemingly helpless, staring at this exceptionally beautiful woman ... so firm, so finely shaped. Dare

I fantasize what having sex with her on the pool table would be like? How incredible! I felt like a thirteen-year-old boy seeing his first naked woman ... one who was willing to do anything he asked. I had been reduced to a quivering mass of useless male flesh, unable to even form a coherent sentence.

The back pockets of her jeans bore an embroidered symbol from her heritage, a symbol that meant love ... or so she said. The symbol, a swirl of beads and colors, would not release my gaze. It kept my attention fixed upon her gorgeous, firm ass ... there was no reason to fight it. I couldn't. She was winning this battle. The stilettos firmed her legs. Her perfectly shaped ass swayed from side to side as gracefully as palm fronds in the cool evening breeze. Watching her walk about the place kept me in a trance.

As she passed in front of me, she would ever so slightly brush against my groin, sending waves of chills to every nerve ending in my body. She glanced up at me as she handed me the pool cue we shared. Her scent was intoxicating. I was lost in her. She leaned into me, pressing her breasts into my chest, and whispered in my ear with her hot, moist breath dancing off my neck, her warm hand caressing my side. "It's your shot, big boy."

Suddenly, the memory of Contessa released its spell on me as Sam came into the bathroom with coffee in hand, bringing me crashing back to reality. I took the cup of coffee and placed it on the sink, kissed her on the forehead, and turned on the shower.

"I thought you went back to bed," I told her.

"I tried to, but I couldn't get back to sleep. I had this heavy feeling in my chest ... you know, something does not feel right. I'll go check in on the kids just to make sure everything is okay."

"Good idea," I said. "I'll be down in just a few minutes."

Standing in the shower with the warm water caressing my body, I wondered if she knew. I quickly reviewed the past months in my head. Had I done something, said something, or left something around that would make her suspicious? I didn't think so. I thought I had been acting like myself, whatever that meant.

Sam was an incredibly insightful person. She would dream with such clarity, and the odd thing was that many of those dreams would come to pass—maybe not right away, but most would come to be reality in some shape or form. I have always downplayed her dreams as coincidental, but this time, she was onto something that she just could not fully grasp. She did not know that her intuition was correct. Something heavy was about to happen to her that she did not see coming … and it was all my fault.

My trip to Beaufort was supposed to be a short one—only a couple of days to wrap up the deal. I jokingly told Sam, "March in South Carolina is going to be so much nicer than any part of March in Michigan. I should take my golf clubs with me and extend my stay."

She replied in a firm, fun voice, "I don't think so, bucko." So I packed accordingly: a couple of suits, a few ties, and some casual clothing, but no golf clubs. I might be scum, but I was not stupid.

Once packed and ready, I entered the kids' rooms for one last look. *Better missing them than behind bars,* I thought. Can you imagine what their friends would say and do to them? I couldn't put them through that. I felt a tear well in my eye. I would miss Saturday volleyball games, all that gymnastics drama, and all the malaise that goes with parenthood. I knew they wouldn't forgive me for what I was about to do … and who could blame them? I just hoped they would never find out.

With packed bag in hand, I made my way down the creaky, old stairs and into the kitchen to find that Sam had scrambled eggs and a fresh cup of coffee waiting on me. *God, this is going to be hard. Just keep acting normal.* It was already half past five, and I had a seven-thirty flight to Atlanta to catch, which meant I had to leave for the airport by five forty-five.

I double-checked my inside suit coat pocket to make sure I had what I needed. Everything was securely in place. I left my passport in its normal place under Sam's in the vault behind the mirror in our bedroom. If I were going to disappear, there could be no suspicions left to chance. I sat down with Sam to a breakfast of scrambled eggs, dry whole-wheat toast, black coffee, and my vitamins. Everything was going according to plan.

At precisely 5:40, just like clockwork, my driver knocked on my door. I got up from the table and made my way to the front door. Jim, our company handyman, took care of most of our needs, including driving to the airport.

"Good morning, Jim," I said. "How are you?"

Jim replied, "Freezing. You got room in that bag for me? South Carolina is going to be a bunch warmer than this place. I checked the Internet last night ... supposed to be in the low seventies in Beaufort. Taking your clubs?"

"Not this trip, although it crossed my mind more than once. Sam said if she wasn't going, neither were the golf clubs." We both laughed a bit. I handed Jim my travel bag, and he disappeared into the dark.

"I'll be waiting for you in the car," he said.

I turned to Sam and said, "I gotta go. I'll call you later when I get in. Give the kids a kiss for me when they get up."

And away I went, just like every time before. She blinked the front porch light three times, indicating that she and the two kids wished me safe travels.

I slumped back in the rear seat of the car and told Jim, "Let's go."

My ugly adventure had begun.

We got to the airport in plenty of time. Jim dropped me off at curbside check-in. I boarded on time, and the flight was uneventful—those are the good ones. We landed in Atlanta with an on-time arrival at 9:10 a.m. So far, so good!

As the plane stopped at the gate, passengers filled the aisle preparing to exit the aircraft. I was seated in sixteen C, an aisle seat. No reason to jump up and stand in the aisle. I waited my turn to get my carry-on down from the overhead. We managed our way to the front of the cabin where we all heard the obligatory, "Thanks for your patronage," from the captain and flight attendants.

Herded like cattle, we finally made it into the terminal. My heart was beginning to pound. After all the time and energy I had poured into thinking about what I would do when this time came, I was still torn between the woman I had committed my life to and the beautiful obsession that had dominated my thoughts of late.

I felt oddly numb, but totally excited. The closer I got to the tram that would take me to baggage claim, the more alive I felt ... the more my thoughts drifted to making love on the beach ... the more aroused I became. I was looking forward to seeing Contessa again. She was waiting for me just a few miles from where I was.

I rode the escalator down to the tram area, staring off into space. I shuffled toward a crowd of people and waited for the next tram to arrive. When it did, we were all loaded onto it like cattle off to market. I did not notice anyone or anything in my surroundings. I was lost in my obsession. The next thing I felt was the tram coming to a halt.

The doors opened, and in a mad rush, I was whisked toward another escalator, which took us to the ground level of the airport. I kept following the baggage-claim signs. It seemed as if I had been walking for miles when I noticed a tall gentleman standing at the entryway to the baggage carousels. He held a sign that simply said, "Tag."

The sign stopped me in my tracks. My mind raced with thoughts of Contessa lying on top of me, naked and happy. Then, for some unknown reason, I flashed back to Contessa and me sitting in the plane. The noise of air rushing by the fuselage filled my head as I heard her say, "Your fate is in Atlanta. Think about what is right for you." I stared at the man holding the sign. I couldn't move.

After a few seconds of seeming unconsciousness, I noticed that man standing directly in front of me, asking, "Are you Tag Grayson?" I must have looked half crazed, because he then asked, "Are you okay, sir?"

I gathered my composure and said, "Yes to both your questions."

He reached into his pocket and said, "My instructions are to give you this key. It is the key to that locker there—number A-201." He handed the key to me and said, "Sir, there is an envelope in the backseat of my car for you as well. Here, sir, allow me to take your bag."

The driver took the bag from my hand. In a weak, dazed voice, I said, "Thank you."

"I'll wait for you right here."

I held the key in my hand and walked to the locker. I stood and stared at the locker for a few moments. I swallowed hard, took a deep breath, placed the key into the lock, and turned it to the right until I could hear the lock open. With my right hand, I lifted the latch and pulled on the lever, and the door opened. Inside was a large duffel bag with a note attached to the handle. The note merely read, "Open me first."

I took the envelope from the locker and opened it. The note read, "Do not open this duffel bag until you have read the letter that awaits you in the car."

I placed the note back in the envelope. I took the duffel from the locker and closed the door. I turned, faced the driver, and walked toward him.

"Is everything okay?"

I looked at him with a puzzled look on my face and said, "You know, I just don't know."

"The car is parked this way." He led, and I followed him through the baggage-claim area outside to a long, black limousine.

When we reached the limo, the driver opened the back door and pointed to a large manila envelope lying on the seat and said, "That envelope is for you, sir."

I fell into the backseat, propped my foot up against the car door to hold it open, and placed the duffel on the floor in front of my seat.

The driver looked down at me as I sat in the car and asked, "Shall I put your bags in the trunk, sir?"

I laid the envelope across my lap and said, "No, no, please, just set it down on the curb."

The driver looked at me and said, "Very well, sir. I will wait for you at the front of the car."

"That will be fine. Thanks."

I fixed my eyes on the envelope for few seconds and then lifted the envelope to my nose. I could smell the intoxicating aroma of Contessa. I deeply inhaled her scent, closed my eyes, and enjoyed. I kept my eyes closed for a few more seconds and thought to myself how crazy all this was. It was like a nightmare that I was somehow addicted to. I opened my eyes and looked at the envelope one more time. I took a deep breath and opened it.

Inside the envelope were a letter and a newspaper. I retrieved the letter, and it read,

My dearest Teasdale (I just love that name),

I know by now you have already made the right decision. How could you not? You are a good person, and I wish you well.

Knowing that your heart is in the right place, I must confess to you a few things that you need to know. First, I really do care for you. Please don't forget that! The time that we spent together, I know I will never forget. I hope you believe that I never meant to hurt you in any way.

Second, the only crime that you are guilty of is that of the heart. I pray that your wife will forgive you if you decide to tell her what happened to you. You are a good man, Mr. Teasdale Allen Grayson!

Third, the person that you thought you hit and killed on the side of the road is not dead. The real Jason Holt was killed in an automobile accident on July 11, 1972, and was actually killed by Nate Dillianquest. I am very sorry for having put you through hell. If you look at the picture that is taped to the back of this letter, you will see the man that you thought you hit, and he is not dead. Look closely at the picture, and you will see that he is holding up a copy of this past Sunday's *Beaufort Gazette*. He is also wearing your blue blazer. You did not kill anyone. The man on the bridge and in the picture was Gwen's boyfriend. I feel so horrible, and I'm so very sorry to have caused you so much pain.

Fourth, the headline on the newspaper that you have before you announced that Nathaniel Dillianquest committed suicide at his cottage late Friday night. I guess all that had happened to him recently was just too much for him to bear. The story has it that Nate was found by Junior Belanger with a single, fatal, self-inflicted gunshot wound to the head. You can read the article for yourself.

And lastly, my sweet, the duffel bag you have with you contains five hundred thousand dollars. Please accept this as a token of my appreciation and a small payment for your torment. Do with it what you will. Your fate is in Atlanta. Who knows when our paths may cross again? Be safe.

Love, kisses, and a splash!
C.

I looked down at the duffel situated between my feet. I leaned forward and lifted the bag to the seat beside me. I unzipped the bag and opened it, exposing its contents. On the inside were stacks of neatly bundled, crisp one-hundred-dollar bills. I fell back into the seat, took a deep breath, and stared off into the blue Georgia sky.

I had my freedom back.

Fate was definitely a tricky thing.

CHAPTER 28

The *Kindred Spirit* had been at sea for five straight days, only stopping to refuel. In the evening, Contessa, Gwen, and Abe found refuge in small-town harbors or protected inlets as they made their way south. In the midafternoon hours on the sixth day, Gwen entered Hawks Cay Marina at Duck Key in the Florida Keys.

Gwen had been monitoring the police- and marine-band radios. The threesome worried that their vanishing act from Beaufort would raise suspicions with authorities. Abe had faith in his father's ability to divert attention away from an investigation in order to protect his own interests.

Feeling confident that no one was looking for them, they decided to take a break for a couple of days and relax. Gwen got on the radio to the harbormaster, announcing their arrival. Gwen picked up the handset to the radio and said, "Harbormaster, harbormaster, this is the *Kindred Spirit*. We are entering your waters. Please direct us to location for transient dockage, over."

A few seconds later, the radio squawked, "*Kindred Spirit*, this is the harbormaster, over."

Gwen returned the hail. "Go ahead, harbormaster, over."

"Upon entry in to the Hawks Cay Marina on your starboard side, you will see piers A as in apple and B as in boy. Your transient slip number is B-07. I repeat, B as in boy, zero seven, over."

"B as in boy, zero seven. Roger that, harbormaster, over."

"Welcome aboard," the harbormaster said. "Happy hour starts in thirty minutes, poolside. Stop by once you get strapped in!"

Everyone was gathered on the bridge. The *Spirit* barely made a ripple in the still waters of the protected harbor as it glided toward its evening resting spot. After they docked and got the *Spirit* squared away for the evening, the threesome made their way to Hawks Cay Resort with only small bags in tow.

Abe checked them in under an assumed name and paid in advance with cash. They rented the Commanders Stateroom, a stately two-bedroom luxury suite, for two evenings. The balcony door was open when they entered, and the gentle ocean breeze greeted them when the entryway door was opened by the bellhop.

The view was spectacular, overlooking the white sand beaches that graced the ocean's floor, which seemed to meander for miles. Each made their way to king-sized staterooms with luxurious private baths.

From the living-room phone, Abe ordered three bottles of chardonnay, a cheese-and-crackers tray, and a basket of assorted fruit from room service. They had decided to skip the happy hour they had been invited to by the harbormaster.

As Abe hung up the phone, he turned to Gwen and said, "What do you say we share a shower?"

"My thought exactly." Abe gave Gwen a quick peck on the lips and said, "I'll go get it going. Don't be long."

Gwen smiled.

Contessa was standing on the balcony, listening to the gentle wash of the afternoon waves dancing with the white sand beach. Contessa's hair swayed gently as Gwen walked up behind her sister, placed her arms around her waist, and embraced her.

Gwen whispered in her ear, "It's easy to second-guess our past. But what is really important is that we find meaning in our future."

Contessa turned and looked into her sister's eyes, smiled, and said, "Together?"

"Yes, together."

Contessa hugged Gwen tightly and said, "I'm going to take a bath … have you seen the size of those tubs?" Both girls laughed and disappeared into their rooms.

The next morning, coffee arrived at seven thirty, compliments of the resort. Contessa, Gwen, and Abe sat on the balcony, enjoying the morning sun and warm breeze. Abe had a pad of paper on the table.

"What are you writing, Abe?" asked Contessa.

"I'm making a list of provisions for the next leg of the trip. If you need anything, let me know, so we can get it before we shove off."

Gwen, who was sitting next to Abe, said, "We will head southwest from here and set a course for Cancun, Mexico. It's a two-day sail."

The three enjoyed their breakfast. As they sat back and watched the gulls glide just inches above the surf, Abe said, "Let's rent a car and go to Marathon Key today. We can get our provisions and visit a couple of museums. We can relax before we leave. What do ya say?"

Gwen looked at Contessa and said, "We're in."

With that, the three retired to their rooms and got ready to face the day.

The day was filled with fun. When they arrived back at the resort, Abe suggested that they take the provisions to the boat and make it ready for their travels. They unloaded the car into the dock carts that were available in the harbor parking lot.

Each was pushing a cart down the dock to the slip where the boat was moored. Abe led the way. As they approached the boat, Contessa noticed a large tarp draped over the back of the boat and said, "Abe, what's that on the back of the boat?"

"Come on, let me show you."

Abe stopped with his full cart directly in back of the boat. Contessa and Gwen did likewise. Abe walked over to dock box B-07, opened it, and removed a silver bucket that contained a bottle of iced champagne and three glasses. Abe took the foil and wire cage off the bottle and wiggled the cork until it popped from its location. Bubbles spilled from the bottle, and everyone laughed.

Contessa asked, "What's the occasion?"

Abe did not say a word as he poured the glasses full. He handed each girl a glass and then stepped onto the swim platform on the stern of the boat.

Abe placed his right hand on the tarp that covered the back hull of the boat, held his glass high in the air, and said, "I toast to you, Gwen, and to you, Contessa, my family now for life. From where we have come to where we shall go, all that can be said is that we are not yet free, but ..."

Abe flung the tarp aside, and across the hull of the boat, giant letters read,

"ALMOST"